THE HOME COMING

A.R. O'BRIEN

Dorrance Publishing Co
585 Alpha Drive
Suite 103
Pittsburgh, PA 15238
Visit our website at *www.dorrancebookstore.com*

ISBN: 978-1-6853-7430-3
eISBN: 978-1-6853-7574-4

THE
HOME COMING

DEDICATION

To Dan, the first man who taught me that I was worthy of love. Thank you for finding room in your heart, and in your family for a lost child like me. To all those of you who've stood in support of me all these years whether it be friendship or support, thank you. To all my boys who have taught me how to love, believe in myself and never lose faith in my craft, I made it to the end so thank you. To Steven, my love, who has taught me that matters of the heart are meant to be cherished and enjoyed in each new moment, I truly couldn't have done this without you. To all those who read my handwritten books for all the years as I grew up and have offered support and encouragement in return, you gave me the courage to keep writing. Last but not least, to all those who read the first third of this book in the beginning many years ago and encouraged me to keep working on it, I finally finished the book! I couldn't have done it without every one of you! Thank you!

PROLOGUE

"What's the matter with you, Brooke?" Isaiah asked, glaring down at her with his hands clenched in tight fists at his side. "You know Father wanted all of this done before sundown."

Brooke fought back the tears that threatened behind her lids. She had been up and working since five o'clock that morning for just that reason. She wasn't afraid her father would actually beat her. He hadn't done that since she was fourteen. It was just that he was always so disappointed in everything that she did. He would put his hands on his hips and glare down at her while he yelled that she was such an epic failure.

She rested wearily against the broom handle for just a moment and met Isaiah's cold blue eyes. "I know, which is why I have been working so hard to get it done." She knew she sounded a bit angry but couldn't help it.

Isaiah stared hard at her, anger making his eyes close to narrow slits. "You obviously haven't been doing enough since it isn't done yet," he challenged coldly.

Brooke's temper flared. "What about you? Don't forget that Father gave us both this job to do and I have already swept and scrubbed out ten of these units, while you did who knows what." Her blue eyes flashed before she got herself in check again.

She knew it was coming and still she flinched when Isaiah's fist slapped hard against her face. "You bitch. You have no right to challenge me. I'm your priesthood head when Father isn't here."

Brooke swallowed her comeback. He would take it out on her after all, and in the end, she would still do the work, only to have him take credit with her father. With a tired sigh she turned back to the broom and swept it hard against the concrete floor. It was much easier to scrub and mop it once she had swept it really good first.

"Well, I have the lantern out here, so I might still be able to finish the last two tonight."

Isaiah stared hard at her. "You had *better* get it done," he threatened in a hard voice. He watched her hard at work for a long while and then said in a gentler tone. "I'm sorry I hit you, sis, but you really need to figure out your place or you will never be able to get married and take care of a husband and his children the way you're meant to."

Brooke didn't even look his way, only kept sweeping. After a long silent pause, he folded his arms across his chest. "I would help you, but cleaning is a woman's job as you well know."

She thought of a few choice things she could say to that nonsense but held her tongue. No sense saying it out loud since he would only get angry and hit her again. Determinedly she put her shoulder into the broom and pushed vigorously against the pile of dirt and bran dust.

After watching her for another long minute, she heard the rustle of his dirty jeans as he turned and left. With a sigh her shoulders slumped and tears of relief fell to the dusty floor.

She was still working on the final unit when she heard someone behind her again. It was fully dark now and the small lantern cast eerie shadows across the circular space like little fires everywhere. She tensed and turned, expecting to see her father standing there behind her.

Instead, her mother stood wringing her hands. "Here you are. I was worried when you didn't come in for dinner."

Brooke smiled gently. "I am almost done now."

Her mother bobbed her head up and down and then looked nervously behind herself into the darkness as if looking for someone there. Slowly she reached into her pocket and pulled out a sandwich. "I know it's not much, but it's all I could fit." She pulled an apple from the other side and handed both to Brooke with trembling fingers.

Brooke rushed forward and took them both from her mother. "Thank you! I am starving." She stepped back and asked quietly, "You aren't going to get in trouble for this, are you?"

Her mother shook her head. "No one saw me take them." She didn't bother telling her daughter how her father had laughed coldly and said that if she couldn't be bothered to make it to the dinner table, she didn't deserve to eat. Brooke would already know the routine. She cleared her throat and in a hopeful voice said, "Why don't you just tell him you want to come back to work in the house with me? Things would be so much easier for you there, you know. Your sisters don't have to work near as long or deal with the men the way you do."

Brooke smiled sadly at her broken mother. "And then I could just openly wait hand and foot on all the men like they did in the eighteenth century, huh?" She softened her tone as her mother seemed to shrink a few inches there in front of her. "I know, I know, it's just that I can't bow down to their misogynistic attitudes, Mother."

Rebecca Reynolds wrung her hands together as she watched her daughter inhale the sandwich and apple. Finally, getting the courage to tell Brooke what she had actually come here to say, she swallowed. "I also wanted to tell you that there was a good priesthood man that came to ask your father for your hand."

Brooke stopped with the last of the apple halfway to her mouth. Her stomach suddenly hurt and with regret she lifted her arm to throw the apple core smoothly out the door and into the darkness beyond. She met her mother's gray eyes and said, "He knows that is the last thing I want. I work extra hard every day just to avoid that happening."

Rebecca met her eyes and then looked down at the floor. "You know your father, dear. I don't think it will matter this time. This man offered him quite a lot to have you as his wife."

The silence stretched between them, but Brooke held her anger in check. It wouldn't do anyone any good for her to strike out at her helpless mother. She nodded abruptly and put the broom back to work. "Thanks for telling me, and thank you for the dinner."

She looked behind her as her mother disappeared into the darkness. Angry beyond words that her father thought he could just give her away to some man of his choosing. She gulped back frustrated tears as the wheels turned wildly in her mind.

Resolve set in, she would find a way out of this. She had to. She would not be confined to living her life the way her mother had. That determination settled her stomach and she smiled. She was only sixteen, but that wouldn't matter to *him*. As she scrubbed viciously at the silver corrugated steel walls, she vowed to do whatever it took to get free.

CHAPTER 1

Heavy tears ran down her cheeks in rivulets, leaving dark splotches on her blue denim button-down shirt. Taking a sobbing breath, Brooke Reynolds gripped the tan faded leather steering wheel in both hands as she slowed the ancient white economy car off the road and onto the shoulder.

She could barely see anything through the river of tears that she couldn't seem to stop and she didn't want to cause an accident on the old highway. While there was usually very little traffic in this one-horse farming community in Idaho, today would be the one time it would be busy and causing an accident was the last thing she needed.

Swiping her hands down her cheeks in a pointless effort to staunch the flow, she reached blindly for the roll of toilet paper that she knew was somewhere on the passenger side floorboard. She supposed she should be grateful for that much. After all, it was due to her father's rules that it was there. He'd told her countless times to always carry a roll of it in their vehicles.

After groping around blindly for a minute, a hiccup shook her shoulders before her fingers finally brushed over the smooth rounded edge of the roll and she grabbed for it. She yanked off several squares and dabbed furiously at her eyes and cheeks. Then she took a deep gulping breath.

She had to pull it together. She had no other choice. No one was coming to help her. No one could save her. After spending her entire life working on her father's farm, he had finally disowned her. It was real this time. He had been threatening her with that weapon for years now, and though she had almost hoped he would do it; she had still been surprised when he'd followed through this time. Somewhere deep down inside, she had always hoped, maybe even believed that he loved her at least a little. He was her father after all. Wasn't there some almighty law or rule somewhere that said a parent should love their child?

Her tears slowed as a white-hot blaze of anger slowly began to unravel inside her and a bitter smile curved her lips. *Screw him!* Brooke thought to herself.

He didn't deserve her admiration. She had spent the majority of her life trying to be perfect and do whatever he asked of her, trying desperately to earn his love. It was all for naught in the end as it seemed that the harder she tried to impress him, the less he cared.

He had told her constantly to be more righteous like her older sisters or better yet sweeter and more docile like her younger ones.

She snorted in a very unladylike way. All he had ever truly wanted from her was her total submission to his egotistical, narcissistic, belief that he could rule her.

She had tried. She really had. Had spent a lifetime trying to quiet her own inner spirit and do as he'd commanded her. But in the end, her spirit always revealed itself. When her spunk finally won out, he would give her that cold stare of disappointment, his pale blue eyes icy and disapproving as if to say, I knew you were just a bad girl and that you could never really be better.

Brooke shrugged off the painful memories. She even tried a little smile. There was definitely a good side to her predicament here. After all, she had her freedom at last! And while it was true that she had no clue what she was supposed to do with said freedom, she was still thrilled about that much.

Fear surged through her and had her stomach in knots. What was she supposed to do now? She was a farmer's daughter raised in seclusion on a small spread in the middle of nowhere Idaho. She had no skills, no education, and not much money to speak of. She had been taught to read and write, though most of her education came from the stacks of books she'd picked up from thrift stores her mother had taken her to. She would buy whatever books she could find that seemed even a little bit interesting, spending the majority of the small pittance she had been allowed to have on such occasions on books.

Most of the books weren't approved of by her parents since they weren't approved scriptures in their religion, but she didn't care. She would hide them, often draping a shirt or long skirt over the top of her armful of books to hide them from view of her siblings and parents. She was always a nervous wreck until they got home and she'd managed to sneak them into the overcrowded single-wide trailer home they lived in and hide them somewhere safe.

She smiled at her thoughts. One more thing she could be happy about—she never again had to hide a book she was reading. Better yet, she could even buy any book her heart desired. A weary frown creased her brow, if she could afford them, that is.

First, she had to get a job somewhere. She wasn't exactly sure what she could actually do, but a decent job was definitely the first thing on her to do list.

She was from a large family and had been born somewhere in the middle of twelve siblings, so it felt a little strange to be alone now. Through her short life there had rarely been quiet moments. Growing up, she would have given almost anything to have a quiet space with some privacy and yet now the silence felt overwhelming.

There hadn't been much opportunity in the three-bedroom single-wide trailer for privacy with her parents and twelve siblings all bunked together. She was lucky if she got to use the bathroom without someone banging impatiently on the door or worse, unlocking it and walking in on her just to make her hurry faster.

Here now the empty silence felt dark, hopeless even. She wiped a loose strand of her red hair back and tried unsuccessfully to tuck it back into the tight french braid on her head. She rolled the window halfway down and hoped for the cool refreshing country air to calm her nerves. Her mind was in a panicked frenzy. How had she gotten here? She took three calming breaths in through her nose and back out through her mouth and reminded herself that this was what she had wanted all along. She felt determination again as it swelled inside her gut and worked its way up to her heart.

It didn't matter how she had gotten here. She was here and she was going to make the best of it. She smiled through her tear-streaked eyes as she placed one hand on her flat stomach and held it there for a calming moment. Then she wiped her eyes once more and pulled back onto the road.

She had $227 dollars and a quarter tank of fuel to go with the fifteen-year-old economy car she had bought for $500 dollars from a nice neighbor woman a year ago. Her father had been angry when she drove it home. He'd told her they couldn't afford the upkeep on another vehicle so she had promised to do extra chores each day to help cover it.

Besides the car, she had only a few changes of clothing to her name, and those she had thrown into a bag and tossed it in the car before she left. She was broke and alone at nineteen and had nowhere to go.

Still, she had to survive and that meant finding work. Her total array of skills was doing farmwork, cooking for family, and cleaning up behind a bunch of men that were pigs. Not much of a resume to have when she was trying to start out on her own.

She sighed loudly and squared her shoulders. Hadn't she read somewhere that those fast-food restaurants would hire just about anyone? She would have to make it work. She didn't have much choice in the matter.

There was no way she was going back to the hellhole she had just left. She had way too much on the line for that and honestly, she just didn't have it in her anymore.

Even if she could get herself to grovel and beg her father's forgiveness, she doubted he would let her come back. She glanced in the rearview mirror almost expecting to see the lights of her childhood home winking back at her. All she saw was darkness.

Out here in the valley, the farms were sparse and often miles apart. It would take almost an hour to drive into the nearest town.

Glancing down Brooke noticed she was speeding and let off the accelerator a little. She stifled a yawn and reached for the lukewarm cola she had grabbed at the soda machine outside the one small local store a few miles from the farm. She forced a couple of swallows down and then slid the can back into the drink holder. She felt warm soda slosh across her hand and bit her lip to hold back the curse.

She realized she had dropped the toilet paper roll in the back again and it was too far to reach while driving. She groaned and wiped the back of her hand against the black knit ankle length skirt she wore. She slowed down and then rolled to a stop at the four-way intersection. Debating silently which way to go, she chewed on her bottom lip.

If she turned right, she would head up the north highway toward the panhandle of Idaho. Left would take her toward the main interstate and from there she could decide whether to head east toward Wyoming, north into Montana, or south toward Utah. She sat undecided for a couple of minutes before finally signaling left and turning onto the highway that eventually connected with a main interstate.

She fought another yawn back and wondered where she could stop and catch a couple hours of sleep. It wasn't too cold tonight and she needed to save her money for fuel so she would have to sleep in her car until she got a job. She glanced around the road. She wanted to stop somewhere that she wouldn't be bothered or bother anyone else. She couldn't see much through the darkness but was pretty familiar with this area. She slowed again and watched for breaks in the fencing that often signaled a pullout or canal road that she could turn onto and park unnoticed for a while to sleep.

Seeing the sloping side of a deep canal ahead she edged onto the shoulder and squinted against the dark, watching for that telling opening in the barbed wire fence that she could pull her car through. Finally, seeing a familiar dark spot, she eased her car off the road and onto the two tire tracks that paralleled the canal. She pulled in just far enough that she wouldn't be visible to passing cars and shut the engine off.

After a quick dry brush of her teeth, she spit toothpaste on the dusty ground and then slid back inside her car and tilted the seat all the way back. With a little sigh of determination, she leaned her head back against the headrest and forced her mind to quiet. Exhaustion won out over the uncomfortable position and within minutes she slept.

CHAPTER 2

Brooke jerked up into a sitting position, feeling groggy at the sound of fingers rapping against the glass of her car window. She looked around frantically, trying to identify what had woken her.

A tall dark-haired man with a slight spray of gray near his temples stood just outside her window. She gulped back a startled scream and one hand flew to her mouth to muffle whatever sound she made even as she reached for the door with her other, to roll down her window. It felt like she had sand in her eyes and the gritty feeling made them water so she swiped impatiently at them.

She stared up for a long moment as recognition dawned. She recognized the man standing just outside her car, though she imagined he had no idea who she was. She had seen him around the valley her whole life, though they had never been introduced or actually spoken. He was one of the longstanding neighbors who her father hadn't much liked. He had come to their farm on a few occasions to talk to her father about things the farming community shared.

Since she hadn't known him personally, she only knew what her father had said about him, which wasn't good. She stared up at him for a minute before trying a smile and saying, "Hello, sir, did you need something?"

Ivan Burton stared curiously down at the young girl who was parked in his field. He had come over to check his alfalfa at first light. He had seen the car there when he'd first drove past but hadn't stopped to take a closer look. When it was still parked on the canal road at the edge of his field when he came back through, however, he'd pulled his truck over next to the older model car. It wasn't uncommon for kids to park out here and make out, but they usually didn't stay out here overnight, and while he wasn't sure how long the car had been there, he also hadn't experienced many teens waking up at the crack of dawn to drive out to the field and make out.

He slid dark sunglasses onto the bridge of his nose as he stepped out of the truck and glanced up at the sun just peeking out over the horizon. It looked like it was going to be a cooker today.

At first glance the car looked empty. It looked vaguely familiar, though he couldn't quite place it. He shrugged to himself. Maybe it had been a breakdown or something similar.

His gaze slid automatically to the tires checking instinctively for a flat. The tires looked good on this side. He walked casually around the car and saw that the other tires were fine as well. With an indifferent shrug, he turned to leave. He'd be back this way later so he would just check then to see if the car was still there. Anyone could have broken down out here and pulled the car off the road so it wouldn't be a hazard to oncoming traffic. No reason to cause any trouble about it until he knew more. He slid the dark glasses closer to his face and turned to leave. If she hadn't stirred just then, he would have completely missed the petite girl curled under the over-sized brown jacket.

Ivan couldn't say why but something struck him deep at the sight. His eyebrows drew together in concern. She was petite with bright red curls sticking every which way. He couldn't tell how tall she was, but she looked pale with fatigue. The light sprinkle of freckles that ran over her nose stood out against her pale skin.

He lifted a hand to knock against the window and then let it fall back to his side again. He really didn't want wake her. He stood there indecisively for a long moment. There was something sad about her that even in the depth of sleep showed on her expressive face. He couldn't shake his natural curiosity and his overwhelming instinct to protect.

He hesitated for a long moment standing there watching her stomach rise and fall slowly. There were many of the old farmers in the valley that didn't like people poking around in their business, though most were friendly. He hated to cause problems for any of the old-timers, but his protective instincts wouldn't let him walk away.

He made up his mind with a sigh and raised his hand to tap a tanned knuckle gently against the driver side window.

She didn't budge and he found himself once again considering walking away. Instead, he lifted his hand to knock a little louder this time.

She jumped and sat up her eyes flying open. Then she began jerking this way and that, looking frantically around. He was wishing that he had just left her alone to rest when her terrified blue eyes finely settled on his.

She seemed to calm a little then, but her swollen eyes teared up and Ivan swore silently to himself. He should never have woken her up. Her lips trembled into a vague smile that didn't quite reach those deep blue eyes and he watched as she fumbled to roll down the window. He smiled kindly as she finally found the right button and rolled it down.

Later he would wonder whether it was how directly she had held his gaze even being obviously upset or the wobbly smile she attempted with a tear-streaked face that demanded his attention.

Once she got the window rolled down, he got a better look at her face and the light dusting of freckles across her nose. He also got a better look at her sapphire blue eyes and realized that she wasn't wearing any makeup. Strange for a girl her age, wasn't it? She looked to be around seventeen and in his limited experience teenage girls were usually pretty picky about that.

He saw the long-sleeved denim shirt she wore as the jacket slid down and something tickled at his awareness, but he couldn't quite put a finger on it. She was starting to act nervous again and her cautious smile began slipping at the edges and he realized that he had been staring. He cleared his throat and smiled as he reached a hand toward her in invitation, "Ivan Burton, ma'am. Good morning."

She reached toward his hand without hesitation and then quickly realized she couldn't reach. Before Ivan could think to step forward, she opened the door and slid quickly out. She was taller than he'd expected. Maybe five feet six inches or somewhere close to that. His cool hand closed over her smaller one as he saw the ankle-length skirt. That feeling that had been teasing at the back of his mind suddenly surged forward as recognition stirred.

He didn't know her personally but knew where she was from now. She grabbed on to his hand and pumped it vigorously. With a quick grin he realized she was also much stronger than his first impression of her. "Brooke Reynolds, sir. It's nice to meet you."

Ivan didn't have any daughters and honestly wasn't sure if having one would have changed how he felt anyway. She was obviously one of the Reynolds kids. Her family's farm was only a few miles away, and he couldn't imagine why she would have spent the night here. His eyebrow raised in question. Why was she out here alone in the early morning? He met her light eyes and smiled gently. "Is everything okay?"

Brooke's smile faltered but only momentarily as she forced it firmly back in place. "Yessir, I'm all good, sir. Just catching a quick nap before I get back on the road." Her eyes widened and she added, "I'm so sorry, sir, was I parked in your way here?"

Ivan smiled again and shook his head. "Not at all. I saw your car here and I wanted to make sure you weren't broke down out here all alone." The corner of his mouth twitched as he said, "I don't get a lot of people out napping in my field."

Brooke looked worried again and turned toward her car. "I'm sorry, sir, I will hurry and get out of your way now, sir."

Ivan grimaced slightly. "It's no problem as long as you're okay and call me Ivan; you're making me feel old." His tone was grumpy, but the smile that followed took the sting out of it.

Brooke just stared at him for a long moment and then turned. "I'll get outta your hair, then. I'm just passing through." She turned to open the car door and leaned down to slide quickly inside. She reached for the door trying to pull it shut, but it didn't move. With a look of concern, she glanced up to see that Ivan had a hand on it holding it from closing. A bit surprised, she leaned out and looked up at him questioningly.

He smiled and held a hand up saying, "Now hold on just a darn minute there, miss. Don't you live just a few miles up the road?" When she didn't respond right away, he said calmly, "The Reynolds stretch is up that way and I'm sure I've seen your car around these parts before."

He saw the sad vulnerable look that came and went in a split second before she pasted on a determined smile and said quietly, "Not anymore."

Ivan's gut clenched at the wounded look she was trying to hide. He didn't have any daughters but something about this girl was really getting to him. His protective nature was shouting at him that this girl needed something or someone, though he couldn't be sure why.

He thought of his Anne back at the house and a quick sharp pang of guilt came but then passed just as quickly. Realizing Brooke had no intention to say any more, he sighed, and pulled his dark glasses off his nose and up onto his head so she could see his eyes directly and asked quietly, "Do you have somewhere to go?"

All of the locals knew that the Reynolds family were tightly engaged with a strange dark religious cult. While he didn't know the full story with Brooke, he wasn't about to let her leave until he knew she was safe and okay.

Brooke breathed deeply and fought the panic that was threatening to well over into hysteria. Why wouldn't the man just leave her alone? She had to get out of here and figure out what her next step was. While she could admit it was nice to talk to someone who seemed to care a little about a fellow human being, she also felt the overwhelming need to get her life figured out.

She tried to smile again, knowing it came off more as a grimace than a smile, and shrugged. She looked into his warm dark eyes and the panic she felt calmed a little. "That is exactly what I have to figure out, sir. Now, if it's okay with you, I will just be on my way." She waited patiently for him to remove his hand from the car door, but he didn't budge. Impatience swelled, but she choked it back and swallowed it.

Ivan knew he couldn't simply let her go off on her own without him first knowing she would be safe, but he couldn't for the life of him think of how to say anything without coming off sounding like a chauvinistic prick. Finally, he relaxed his stance and gently asked, "Have you at least had any breakfast?" With a little luck it would buy him some time with her.

Brooke shook her head, "No I haven't, but I will be perfectly fine to go get some myself, sir."

Ivan only grinned in triumph. "Well, there you have it, then. I'm just headed back to the house myself for some grub. I'm sure my wife Anne has got some breakfast going by now and we would love to have your company." Another pang of guilt surged at Ivan as he mentioned his wife's name, but he brushed it off. Anne would understand why he had brought her home.

Brooke shivered at the thought of trying to eat and talk to strangers but then her stomach groaned. She tried not to grimace and covered it with a smile. "That is absolutely not necessary."

He wasn't even fazed by that remark. He released her car door and turned saying gleefully over his shoulder. "It's settled, then. Just follow my truck and I'll lead the way back to the house." He didn't even see her mouth gaping wide and then closing again. With a cheerful grin, he slid into his truck and turned the key, starting the diesel engine with a roar. He motioned for her to follow him with his hand as he backed onto the gravel road and then pulled onto the shoulder, waiting for her to follow him.

Brooke shivered again. As if she didn't know where his home was!

Everyone who had ever lived in these parts and three towns over knew where the Burton home was. Most people even envied them. A little thrill went through her at the thought of finally seeing the inside of that beautiful home she had driven by countless times over the years.

The father, Ivan Burton had inherited a couple hundred acres from his grandfather and he and his family had run the farm since. If the stories were true, he had gone to Utah for school and had met the love of his life, Anne, there. Since they had both loved the beautiful valley in northern Utah they had stayed there working after finishing college.

They had one toddler son and another on the way when Ivan's grandfather had gotten sick. The young couple had then packed up and moved back to the valley, at Ivan's insistence, to help his grandfather run the small farm.

Though Ivan had gotten his MBA and had a great paying job, it had been important to him to help his sick grandfather out. Farming was in his blood, so it felt natural to work the fields. Since his young wife, Anne, had just finished her residency at a university hospital as well, she had a difficult time letting go of a brilliant job offer, but in the end, she had chosen to follow Ivan home.

Having made many business contacts in the few years at his job, Ivan had soon talked his grandfather into farming by contract. That had been a prosperous choice and they had done so well that within two years they had purchased another three-hundred-acre piece that was handily adjacent to their land.

When Old Man Burton passed away the following year, he'd already transferred all his property along with the water rights to Ivan. This meant that Ivan wasn't required to pay all the inheritance taxes that were usually associated and often made it nearly impossible for the next generation to continue farming.

Ivan was shocked when the will was read as he had fully expected the farm to go to his older brother Don. Don had worked on Wall Street in New York and had for the past ten years, been trying hard to make a fortune buying and selling stock. According to his will, their grandfather had entrusted a good-size chunk of money to his grandson to purchase stock for him. As that stock had since soared and was worth a small fortune, he left the stock to his eldest grandson and the farm parcels, as well as the old farmhouse to his younger grandson who had been more than happy to drop everything and help him out until the end.

Since then, Ivan had taken the farm and opportunity and worked hard to grow it into one of the largest farms in the valley. Ivan always researched the crops he grew and planted according to what he predicted would be a little short that year. Most of the time, it had worked well for him.

He planted mostly potatoes one year only to turn around and grow more barley and grain the next. Many of the local farmers thought that he was a little crazy but couldn't help admiring the insight and courage it took to farm that way. As the farm grew, so did their family.

That small cramped farmhouse became a large country estate as Ivan and Anne picked a beautiful ten-acre piece up the road and built what seemed like a mansion to most of the locals. Western white pines lined the driveway and the wide spread of grass was spotted with weeping willows. The entire landscape with flowering bushes and plants sloped out to the whitewashed wooden fence that surrounded the property on three sides. Off to one side of the house was a half-acre garden spot that was complete with a huge white greenhouse. On the other side, stood a large eight-door beautiful brick shop/garage that was originally built for repairs on farm and personal vehicles.

The house itself was a towering 6,500 square foot blend of mortared rock and wood siding with a large sweeping porch on the front held up by the huge natural pine pillars and pine log railing on either side. The half-round stairs sloped down, made of stamped concrete with natural rock adorning the front of the treads. It was a breathtakingly magnificent view from the front.

The Burtons had a reputation in the valley of being fair and kind. It was a common joke that farmers struggling would say, "Just sell a piece to the Burton family and you'll be okay." They had a reputation of always looking to buy more land, and often paid more than the going rate for it just to tempt farmers to sell to them.

What was once a small farm that lined a mile-long chunk of gravel road was now thousands of acres spread across the valley; rumor had it that in recent years, the spread was even expanding into the next county over. Burton land could often be identified by a field lined with several tractors, swathers, combines, etc., running up and down the field together in an organized line. The Burtons were, at the very least, every local farmer's idea of successful farming.

Brooke was in awe now that she was actually going to see more of said farm.

CHAPTER 3

Brooke felt awkward and out of place as she drove her old car up the long tree-lined driveway. She watched Ivan park on one side of the roundabout in front of the house and pulled in to park next to him. She stared in awe up at the gorgeous home that looked even bigger up this close. She was actually considering driving off in her car before Ivan had a chance to come over to her. She put her hand on the key ready to restart the engine, but then her curiosity won out. With a regretful little sigh, she pulled the keys and tucked them inside her skirt pocket before climbing out to meet Ivan at the concrete steps.

Ivan didn't miss the nervous jangling of her keys in her hand inside her pocket as he met her. "Here we are now." He motioned with his hand for her to precede him up the rounded staircase and toward the massive intricately carved oak front door. He put a hand on her shoulder at the door and she tensed beneath his touch. That bothered him a little and his eyebrows came together in deep thought. He eased his hand away from her shoulder and opened the door, holding it wide enough for her to walk through.

Brooke was trying and failing to be nonchalant about the whole thing, but she couldn't help herself as she stared around at everything inside the door. Off to one side was a beautiful hand-carved wooden bench. Next to it was a beautifully carved wood box shelf designed to be both pleasing to look at and to fulfill the purpose of shoe rack just inside the house.

She watched in silence as Ivan removed his boots and slid them into one of the many empty spots before casually motioning for her to follow. Brooke gulped nervously, and then fumbled at her black, heavily worn, thrift-store-special tennis shoes. Her skirt got tangled around her ankles, tripping her. She caught her balance and leaned against the bench before quickly removing the other shoe.

Ivan was patiently standing there watching her and it made her extremely nervous. She dropped one of her shoes before it made it onto the rack and she hurriedly snatched it back up to put it with its mate.

Glancing up she saw that the top two levels of the shelf were covered with beautiful frames of different shapes and sizes, full of pictures that told a happy tale of a family life.

One picture was of five boys of various ages, all grinning mischievously into the camera and she couldn't help the smile that curved her lips. The eldest had two fingers up behind the younger one's head and one of the younger boys had one arm looped around the shoulders of another. All of them looked happy and full of life.

Another picture was a black and white setting with Ivan and a slim beautiful brunette woman. Brooke didn't think she had ever seen her before. She squinted up at it as Ivan's voice answered the unspoken question.

"That one is my Anne."

She smiled quickly and turned back to him. "You have a beautiful family, sir."

Ivan nodded in agreement, then jokingly said, "The best. Good fortune has always smiled on me in this life."

Brooke couldn't help but smile back and nod in agreement. She liked his light-hearted teasing and wondered what it would have been like to grow up with him as a father. Pain surged through her heart even as she eyed a long entry table also hand carved in natural cherry wood, but she gulped and pushed it away. Focused instead on the many framed photos that covered the sleek table.

In the front was a picture with Ivan and all five boys standing with a golden wheat field in the background. Next to it was what appeared to be a family photo with Ivan, the woman, and five handsome young boys. She glanced up at him through her dark lashes and couldn't hold back her curiosity. "How many children do you have?"

She hadn't seen any pictures of girls, with the exception of one framed picture with the eldest boy and a young girl holding hands. But the way the girl was clinging to him made her think it was a girlfriend. She turned to him waiting for his response.

He gave her a lopsided grin. "Anne and I have five sons together. We tried for a girl, but it seems we were meant to raise a house full of boys. After five strapping sons, we decided it was all we could handle." He shrugged, watching her face closely. She seemed to be dragging her feet taking in every detail of the foyer as they went.

He watched as her eyes widened in awe as the chandelier that hung from the raised ceiling caught her gaze. It was a mixed-modern, yet warm style with black steel vines making their way cheerfully around carved cherry wood. Small LED bulbs fixed throughout gave it an old enchanted feel while also looking quite modern.

Brooke blushed as she realized he had caught her staring. She clenched her hands tightly together in front of her and moved to follow him. It was a wide and long rectangular room, and she thought she could see what appeared to be a kitchen straight ahead.

More photos caught her eye and she turned to see a huge wood-framed portrait of a very handsome man. He looked to be a little older than the other pictures she'd seen, and so she assumed this was a more recent photo of Ivan's son. He had dark brown hair and brilliant green eyes; his full lips curved into a very natural smile. He was very handsome and looked comfortable and relaxed. With a smile she thought how he looked much like a younger Ivan with the exception of those brilliant green eyes.

She took another step forward again and then came to a dead stop, looking up at the next large portrait. He was standing next to an old Ford Mustang in the photo. His blue denim sleeves were rolled up to his elbows and he had a mischievous grin that made her wonder what he was thinking. He had one hand on the hood of the car and his long muscular jean-clad thighs stretched out in front of him as he leaned casually against the sky-blue tint of the sports car. Unlike the more relaxed pose of his brother, he looked almost tense.

The car itself was spectacular, but it was his face that got her attention. He had dark eyes, that looked nearly black in the photo. His long sleek nose angled almost perfectly down to his chiseled pointed upper lip. He would have looked beautiful if not for the fierce rugged look of a couple days scruff on his cheekbones and chin. Well, that and the intense hardened jawline gave away his pensive nature.

She opened her mouth to speak and realized her throat had gone dry. Suddenly feeling embarrassed, she jumped back as though burned in her haste to catch up. Unfortunately, Ivan had stopped just in front of her and she ran headlong into him nearly toppling them both over.

Ivan had been waiting patiently while she perused the photos. He had seen her face when she'd first caught a glimpse of the photo of Cole. Anne had framed that one because she said it reminded her the most of how Cole really was and it was true that it summed up his character. Cole always seemed to have a strong impression with the ladies, though it seemed he thought of them very little.

Ivan was lost in thought when she suddenly jerked around and proceeded to run directly into him. He reached out a steadying hand, automatically trying to keep her from falling, but her flailing arms swooshed back and forth as she tried to maintain her balance. One elbow caught him in the ribs and a low grunt left his lips before he could stop it.

He took one look at her horrified face and suddenly he was grinning. Then he saw her face begin to turn a particularly bright red and he broke into full laughter.

Brooke stared at him, stupefied, and blushing in embarrassment. As soon as she was stable again, she began backing away, her hands in the air. "I'm so sorry, sir, I didn't see you there." Then as if realizing how insane that sounded, she turned an even darker shade of red and stammered. "What I mean is…." She searched for words that weren't forthcoming and then finally rushed out. "I'm so very sorry. I really need to watch where I am going." She felt him shaking and suspiciously her gaze moved up to his face which was … laughing? His shoulders shook and he panted for a minute trying to catch his breath. His laughter was contagious and she felt a rueful smile take over her face as her embarrassment finally faded.

When he finally calmed, he smiled. With a twinkle in his eyes, he said, "I'll have to remember not to ever startle you. You are quite the quick little thing."

Rustling sounded behind him and a pleasant feminine voice called out, "Ivan? Is that you?" Anne appeared in the doorway of the kitchen. She was wearing a light-yellow button-down with small pink flowers and jeans that fit her shapely curves to perfection. She had a brilliant smile on her face, which was fixed on Ivan. She was walking quickly toward them but suddenly stopped as she saw Brooke there behind him. Her surprised gaze moved from Brooke and then back to Ivan before cautiously resting on Brooke again.

Her bright smiling green eyes turned distant as she looked first at Brooke's face and then curiously all the way down her body.

Brooke suddenly felt self-conscious and began wringing her hands together. For the first time since she had been awakened by Ivan out in that field, she thought about what she looked like and realized she must be quite the mess. Her quick glance down confirmed that her skirt and blouse were indeed wrinkled and quite baggy. She blushed as she realized her long curls were most likely all over the place. She tried to smooth back the front, but it was useless as those rebellious curls flew right back into her face.

Unable to stop herself, she threw an accusing glare at Ivan. After all he hadn't even once indicated that she was a mess and she had been so engrossed in everything going on she hadn't had a moment's thought about it.

Ivan just met her glare with a steady gaze and a half smile. Then he extended one arm and pulled Anne over to his side. She allowed him to pull her reluctantly under his arm. He squeezed her arm gently and smiled down at her as he said, "Honey, this is Brooke Reynolds." Then he smiled at Brooke and said gently, "Brooke, this is Anne, my wife." It didn't escape his notice that Anne didn't extend her hand in welcome. He only hoped the young girl wouldn't be affected by it.

Brooke smiled shakily at the woman by Ivan's side. She started to hold out a hand but hesitated when it wasn't reciprocated. Instead, she nodded quickly and murmured, "Nice to meet you, ma'am." Anne only nodded slightly, then tilted her head back to look up at her husband of thirty years as if waiting for him to explain. He only smiled and then gripped her shoulders to gently turn her toward the kitchen. "Brooke and I were just coming in to get some breakfast," he said casually, as though it was the most common thing in the world for him to show up in their home with a random stranger in tow.

To her credit, Anne was only marginally stiff as she ushered them into the bright yellow, white, and stainless-steel kitchen. On the black marble counter Brooke saw huge platters of hash browns, eggs, pancakes, and bacon laid out waiting to be eaten. Brooke's stomach grumbled and she self-consciously put her hand there for a moment.

Anne was the only one that noticed that trembling touch.

CHAPTER 4

Though Brooke had sat up to a table for meals her whole life, she had never experienced anything quite like what was happening now.

Moments after they'd come into the kitchen, she was nearly knocked over by two young boys as they came tearing into the room. They had obviously been arguing about something important that only young boys could understand. The younger boy was trying to grab hold of his brother who was sticking out his tongue and staying just out of reach.

Brooke smiled as she watched them. The boys didn't even notice her there until Anne spoke in a no-nonsense tone, "You boys settle down, you know the rules at the breakfast table." Both boys stopped midfight and turned to look at the adults standing there by the bar. They looked back at each other and murmured something quietly between themselves before turning back in unison to grab clean plates off the large stack on the bar next to the food. Anne clicked her tongue at them and threw an apologetic look at Brooke and said, "Boys, this is Brooke, she is going to be eating breakfast with us. You boys know what good manners are."

She smiled down at them for a long moment and then said with obvious pride, "This here is Dominic, but we call him Dom." She let go of the boy's shoulder she was squeezing and turned. "And this young rascal—" She walked over to the youngest boy and ran a hand through his dark curls. "—this is our baby, Ryker Dane."

Both Anne and Ivan smiled as Ryker groaned with displeasure, "Mom!" He dragged the word out dramatically as only the young can do. "Why do you always have to call me your baby?" he complained. He turned and gave Anne a scowl to accentuate his displeasure and for the first time caught full sight of Brooke. He stopped talking and stared unabashedly. Then he set his plate down and stepped tentatively closer.

Brooke smiled and for the first time since he had first seen her this morning, Ivan thought it was actually authentic.

Ryker stepped forward again getting braver from the smile. He was looking up at her when suddenly he blurted, "You're really pretty. How'd you get all that red hair, huh?"

Brooke ran her hands self-consciously over her hair, trying to push back the loose curls. They bounced right back as soon as she let go. "I was born with lots of red hair. The longer it is the messier it gets."

She held out her hand in a friendly gesture. "It's nice to meet you, Ryker." The young boy looked at her hand uncertainly for a minute before finally reaching forward and giving it a gutsy shake. He stood there looking up at her for just a minute, then smiled back. Wide eyed and with a conspirator's whisper, he asked, "Can I touch it?"

Anne and Ivan, who had been watching the exchange, looked at each other then in curiosity, wondering what he had asked her. When Brooke bent down to his level and leaned her head forward, they both grinned as Ryker grabbed hold of a particularly long red curl and pulled then released it. He laughed in pleasure as it bounced right back up. His parents exchanged smiles as he solemnly said, "I like it. And I like you. Do you want to sit by me?" He turned back to the food before she even answered.

Brooke smiled and straightened to turn to Dominic. He looked to be maybe two years older than Ryker and she guessed he was maybe nine or ten. He had blond hair and brown curious eyes but was obviously too stubborn to act as carefree as his younger brother. His chin went up a tiny notch as he met her gaze head-on. He was old enough to realize something was just a little different about her compared to other people. He waited for her to make the first move.

Brooke was accustomed to people staring at her, so it didn't faze her in the least. She smiled warmly and stepped forward, holding out a hand to him. "Hello, Dominic. It's lovely to meet you." She curtsied playfully as she smiled. He didn't say anything but gave her hand a quick squeeze and then quickly released it. She was unperturbed by his attitude.

While most adults made her feel uncomfortable and inadequate, she loved kids. She'd been raised in a huge family after all and had more cousins than she could count, which meant babies and kids were everywhere.

Since Dom still watched her uncertainly, she pointed to his eyes. "So, I can see that you got your dad's eyes, but where in the world did you manage to get all that blond hair?" Brooke asked.

Dominic's shoulders rose and his chest puffed out in pride making him quite literally grow an inch. He rubbed his hand through his hair and grinned. "No one seems to know," he said with obvious pride. "I'm the only one in my family that doesn't have brown hair. I guess I'm just meant to be a blondie."

Brooke nodded and smiled. "Well, I like it," she said with a determined nod.

When Dominic turned back to the food, she stood still, suddenly feeling awkward again. Her skin prickled and the hair on the back of her neck stood up. She tensed, feeling as though eyes were burning a hole in her back. She swallowed the giant lump in her dry throat and turned before she could lose her nerve. Ivan had moved over to lean against the large, white, farm style sink and was talking quietly to Anne who nodded, then glanced across at her.

She tried to force a smile, but it froze on her lips as she saw the tall figure standing in the doorway. He leaned casually against the doorjamb and her mind flashed back to the photo she had seen earlier of him leaning against that sexy blue car. Her knees wobbled slightly and she was suddenly afraid she would make a giant fool of herself by face-planting or something worse in front of him.

His black hair was longer than in the photo and it curled slightly at the nape of his neck. His arms were lean and tan. Brooke watched entranced as the lean muscle rippled when he lifted them to fold them casually across his chest. He was clean shaven today and she almost wished he had the tiny hint of whiskers from the photo. Her gazed moved up to his eyes and she blushed as she realized he had been watching her with curiosity, and something else that she couldn't quite place. She felt her skin heat even as she willed herself not to blush.

He knew she had been staring at him and that relaxed smug look on his face pissed her off. She shrugged and threw a cold smile at him. "Hello." She bit out the word as though it was distasteful, which only made his small smile widen in response. Her eyes narrowed dangerously, though she bit her tongue and forced a polite smile. She had seen guys like him who thought they owned the world and the women in it and they always made fun of her and her kind.

Cole grinned easily at her icy smile. He stepped into the room with a small shrug as he stepped toward her. "Well, well, what have we here?" he asked no one in particular.

He tipped his favorite ball cap in mock solute at the pretty if somewhat feisty little redhead. She was obviously from that cult he had heard people talk about. He scratched his brow as he racked his brain for a minute trying to remember the name … Reynolds, that was it. Everyone around the valley talked about them. They were weird. They had some kind of religious bullshit cult they believed in where all the women dressed as if they were from the late 1800s for some reason that no one outside it seemed to understand. They were strange by any definition in his book.

His mom hadn't raised him to be an asshole, however, so he held up his hands to show they were dirty from working outside and said, "I'd shake your hand, but they are filthy." He gave her a heart-stopping grin and then turned abruptly to wash his hands in the sink. He had several layers of grease on them as he'd spent the morning working on his latest pet project, a pretty little '69 Chevy Corvette he had picked up from an old farmer in the next county over. He nodded at his parents as Ivan moved out of his way. "Mom, Dad."

His mother smiled and squeezed his shoulder. "Good morning, Cole."

His father looked at him and then at the redhead a long moment before turning his gaze back. "Morning, son. How is it going with Betty?" He turned back to Brooke as he mentioned the car and watched her face, which was still intently watching Cole's back. He grinned to himself and then turned his attention to his son.

Cole shrugged. "I got the new alternator in and she's cranking good now but still doesn't start, so I gotta figure out why." He dried his hands on a dark towel that Brooke now suspected was there just for him and his black hands.

Relief flashed across Brooke's face as his attention was turned away from her. Ivan felt only slightly guilty as he turned back to her and brought it right back. "Brooke, this is my son Cole, Cole, Brooke Reynolds."

He finished drying his now clean hands and turned to give her a quick wink. He rehung the dark towel before strolling casually over to her and holding out a firm hand. "Nice to meet you, Brooke."

Brooke nodded as she gave his hand a quick shake. She smiled and ignored the surge of heat as their hands touched, saying politely, "It's nice to meet you too, sir."

Cole laughed outright at that. It was low and throaty and made her insides quiver and turn to jelly. It also raised her hackles and she took a deep breath to calm her temper as her eyes flashed at him. Why did he keep laughing at her? She hated being mocked!

She had been mocked her whole life. Both by all the people who didn't know them and judged her and her family for the way they lived, and then also by her family themselves. They were constantly mocking her for not being as good as they were. Suddenly, she wanted to cry and for just a moment her face fell before she quickly covered it with a polite smile. She blinked hard a couple of times to hold back the tears.

Cole's gut clenched at the quick look of pain. He watched as she recovered quickly and then raised her chin. He smiled down at her and for the first time it was real. "I wasn't mocking you, Brooke. I'm sorry for laughing. I just don't think I have ever had anyone call me sir. It made me feel old and I couldn't be much older than you, so it struck me funny," he explained quietly. "I meant no offense."

Brooke gave him a curt nod as yet another boy walked into the kitchen. Anne introduced him as Zack and while she shook his hand, Ivan announced that since everyone was present, they might as well eat up.

Brooke stared as the rest of the family grabbed plates and noisily loaded stacks of food on them. At some point someone set a plate in her hands and she looked up to see Ivan smiling at her. Someone else grabbed her shoulders and shoved gently and she found herself in the food line being pushed forward. She turned to see Cole behind her and stiffened. He grinned down at her. "You'd better hurry and load up if you want anything to eat," he joked. "You'd be surprised at how fast it goes." Her stomach growled and she started snatching food herself.

From that point on the meal was absolute chaos. Everyone was talking over the top of each other. She stared dumbfounded at the scene that unfolded in front of her. She found herself wondering how she had gotten here in the Burton house eating breakfast as they all talked and ate. She pinched her leg under the table as she momentarily wondered if she was dreaming. She looked around the table and tried to keep up with what appeared to be five separate conversations. She lost track of every one of them and finally she couldn't hold back her laughter. Her belly shook and her eyes teared up as laughter shook her entire body. She tried to stop, but the harder she tried to stop the harder she laughed. The table went still, then completely silent as everyone stared at her in curiosity. That only made the moment seem more insane and she laughed even harder, holding her stomach in a helpless grip. The panic she felt at the faces all staring at her turned to mush and came out as another long laugh.

And then somehow miraculously she felt calm. Her fear was gone and she breathed easily even as the entire Burton family stared at her as though she had three heads. She smiled around the table at them as she realized that for the first time in a long while she didn't care.

She felt free for the first time in her life and a surge of joy crept up through the tears and the laughter. Then a smile of pure joy filled her face and shone from her brilliant blue eyes. Her complexion seemed to light up with the joy of the moment and she was absolutely breathtakingly beautiful to everyone at the table.

She looked around the table at each of the new faces and then smiled and shook her head. "You guys are all so amazing. You may not realize how rare it is for a family to all feel so comfortable together. Thank you for letting me be a part of this moment. I will remember it for the rest of my life," she vowed seriously as she wiped the last of the tears from her cheeks.

Something clicked inside her heart, and peace enveloped her as she smiled. No matter where she ended up going or what she had to do to get it, she vowed that one day this was exactly what she would have. A happy family that loved each other and felt free to be themselves no matter what. She would be forever grateful for this moment for it had shown her a beautiful example of exactly what she wanted to create. She knew it would be hard work, but it was well worth the effort to her. She smiled again and took a healthy sized bite of pancake as the Burtons smiled at her obvious joy.

CHAPTER 5

After plates were cleaned of food, the kitchen emptied as quickly as it had filled up. Cole excused himself, telling Ivan that he had several pivots he had to go check on today. Anne reminded him to take water and not stay in the sun too long as mothers do. He bent to give her a kiss on the cheek and with a quick wink in Brooke's direction was gone.

When Ivan asked Zack and Dominic to head out and wash down the tractor by the shop, they mumbled complaints under their breath. When those complaints appeared to land on deaf ears, Dom turned to grin at Zack and ran off yelling over his shoulder, "Bet you can't beat me there!"

That, of course goaded Zack into running after him. Brooke heard footsteps all the way down the entry room and until the door slammed behind them, which had her smiling and Anne frowning after them.

Ryker turned to sweetly ask his mother if he could play video games but Anne only smiled knowingly in amusement at him. "You know that you have to get your chores done first, Ryker. But I'll tell you what, if you go weed out in the garden until noon, then you can play after lunch." Ryker's bottom lip jutted out for a moment in rebellion, but when his mother didn't even appear to notice his puckered bottom lip, he turned and gave Brooke a friendly little wave and dragged his feet reluctantly out as well. A moment later, she heard the door close quietly behind him.

After watching him leave, Brooke turned and dutifully started clearing dishes off the table. Anne immediately stepped in. "Oh, you don't need to do that, Brooke. You're our guest."

Brooke shook her head. "It's no problem, Mrs. Burton, I really don't mind. After all I did sort of crash your family breakfast anyway. If it's okay with you, I'll just clean up quick and then I'll be on my way." She smiled questioningly at Anne and then glanced at Ivan. Taking matters into her own hands, she quickly turned and hauled a stack of dirty dishes to put beside the sink.

Behind her back Anne looked at Ivan, one eyebrow raised in obvious question. He still hadn't told her why they had a strange young girl in their kitchen and she was beginning to feel impatient. She was a little curious about the girl and wanted to know more about her family's lifestyle choices but was unwilling to be rude about it by asking.

Ivan shrugged at her as though he didn't know what to say. Anne smiled and rolled her eyes as she turned to clear the remainder of food from the table. She would have to grill him about it later. For now, she needed to finish up here and get over to her clinic.

Brooke had just turned on the faucet and began looking around for a sink plug when Ivan walked over next to her and opened the dishwasher. She glanced down curiously and then her eyes widened in surprise. "Is that a dishwasher?"

Ivan who had just began loading dirty dishes in grinned at her and nodded.

Brooke handed him a stack of plates she had just rinsed and he smiled as he took them. "Thank you." He loaded the rest of the bottom rack and then looked up to meet her blue gaze as he slid it inside and reached for the top rack. "By the way, Brooke, I have been meaning to ask you what your plans are from here."

Brooke hesitated for a moment, taken by surprise. She covered it well by grabbing and rinsing a couple of glasses. "I don't know for sure yet, sir. I guess I need to go look somewhere for a job." She felt her cheeks warm in embarrassment as she admitted, "I don't have much money so I need to get a job right away."

Ivan groaned as she handed him the last of the dirty glasses. She looked up at him in surprise and he grinned. "Stop with the *sirs* already. I already told you it makes me feel old and it's rude to make people feel old, you know. Even if it's true." He winked at her and she laughed.

She rinsed the sink and agreed. "All right, I'll try, sir, but I can't make any promises."

Anne was smiling now as well so Ivan let his shoulders droop down and gave both of them a distinctly disapproving frown. That made both women laugh in unison and Ivan made a grumpy show of giving up on them before he turned serious again.

He cast a quick guilty look over his shoulder at Anne. He knew that they should have had a long conversation together about what he was about to do, but it didn't seem to matter. He was going to do it anyway, consequences be damned.

He waited until Brooke turned away from the sink to ask. "What kind of job are you looking for?" He could see Anne's raised eyebrow in his peripheral vision but didn't acknowledge it. Instead, holding Brooke's uncertain gaze with his own.

Brooke felt a little embarrassed and completely put on the spot. Feeling somewhat ashamed as she met his brown eyes, she shrugged. She cast a quick glance behind her at Anne who had one eyebrow raised as she looked hard at her husband.

Brooke cleared her throat self-consciously as Ivan appeared to be waiting for a better answer and stammered, "I'm not actually sure yet. I mean, I don't have a lot of skills, but I think I've heard my father say that those fast-food places will hire just about anyone." She grimaced at her own muffled murmuring tone. In a louder voice she said, "I'm not afraid of hard work, but I figured I would start there."

Brooke, felt more than heard Anne move closer to where they were standing and she resisted the urge to turn and look.

Ivan gave her a curt nod. "Yeah, I guess that could be a place to start. What about a place to stay? Have you thought about that?"

Brooke did blush at that, but she nodded quickly. "I have." She started feeling panicky, so she took a deep breath and then let it go slowly. "I don't have much money, but I do have my car and I figured I will just have to make do with what little I have until I save money and can get a decent place."

Feeling completely out of her element now, she rushed on. "I really do appreciate the breakfast Mr. and Mrs. Burton, but I think it's time for me to get going." She turned to flash a quick smile at them both before turning toward the door. She paused after a step and said quickly, "Thanks again!" Then she lifted her skirt and rushed forward.

Ivan's strong hand on her shoulder stopped her dead in her tracks and she turned back to look up at him. Her eyes were wide with curiosity as she met his gaze and tried not to shrug off his hand in fear.

He gave her a kind smile. "Not so fast there, Brooke. I feel like I have been trying to stop you from running away since I first found you this morning," he muttered under his breath as he released her shoulders.

Brooke smiled then. She *had* been trying to run away since she had first seen him. It wasn't that she didn't like him or anything. She just had a lot to figure out and she didn't want to be a bother to anyone. She had noticed however that he always found some way to get what he wanted from her, so she waited patiently for whatever he wanted to say before she left. Unable to help herself she mumbled, "I'm sorry," and then because she couldn't resist, she added, "sir."

Ivan chuckled. "I guess that one serves me right."

Brooke nodded but a wide smile curved her lips as she agreed. "It sure does. And honestly, I don't know why you keep trying to stop me from leaving. While I appreciate you feeding me this morning, I really have a lot to do today and I am perfectly capable of taking care of myself." She couldn't help the tiny surge of defiance that slipped into her tone.

Ivan looked chagrined at her words. Then he nodded politely and met her eyes. "I understand how you feel." Then because he didn't have anything to lose, he decided to lay his cards out on the table. It would either work for her or it wouldn't. He sighed loudly and asked, "What if I can offer you another solution?"

Brooke stared dumbly up at him and then glanced at Anne. Eyes wide she turned to Ivan and shrugged. "I don't know what you mean, sir."

He chuckled. "I'm sure you are familiar with farmwork?" He plunged into the deep end. "I am always looking for more farmhands around here. I would be willing to pay you a fair wage and you could start right away."

Now both Anne and Brooke stared incredulously at him.

Ivan continued unperturbed. "You could work on the farm and have your meals here with us." When Brooke still stared at him, he suggested gently, "We have several unused rooms here in the house, so you could have your pick."

Brooke shook her head stubbornly. "While I appreciate the offer, I am not going to put myself right in the middle of your family, Mr. Burton." She looked back and forth between them and offered, "Besides that fact, I have a lot of stuff to work through right now. I just left home late last night and I still don't even know what that means yet for me. I also wouldn't want anything to come back on you." She paused. "Honestly, I don't know what kind of trouble my father might cause if he found out I'm still here in the valley." She shook her head again. "I can't do that to you or your family." She looked at Anne then. "Thank you, but I just couldn't."

Ivan's chin went up a notch and a look of determination settled over those warm brown eyes. He wasn't about to be dissuaded. Anne took one look at that stubborn glint in his eye that she knew all too well and knew the battle was lost.

He raised a hand. "Everyone goes through a struggle from time to time, Brooke." He looked at Anne for a heartbeat, and though she met his gaze and shook her head, he plowed on. "I believe that maybe the most important thing for humanity to do is to show up and help each other when we are struggling." He smiled at her dubious expression. "This is not just some lame form of charity,

Brooke. I happen to need help right now and I think you would be a good fit. I truly believe we can create a win-win if you get my drift." He held up one hand, then looked at both hands in the air and grinned unabashedly. "I need more hands and I'm pretty sure you are more than qualified to help. You need a job and a safe place to stay while you figure things out and I just happen to have those things available." He raised the other hand to emphasize that it was a win-win.

Brooke was shaking her head again as she muttered, "You really don't know my father. He basically told me to get out of dodge."

Ivan felt red hot anger surge at the thought of someone treating their daughter so terribly that she was actually afraid to let anyone help her. Though John Reynolds had a reputation around these parts for being a cold heartless businessman, this was the first time that Ivan found himself actually believing that rumor. Who else could kick this pretty young girl out on the street?

Anne put a soothing hand on his shoulder sensing that he was angry. She cast a warm smile at Brooke as she said, "I don't think many people around here know your family all that well, Brooke." She shrugged. "We've all heard the rumors about your family and their farm, but we never really know what is true." She met blue eyes with her green ones and asked gently, "Did your father really abuse you all?"

Brooke looked away but gave her head a quick shake. "Not anymore." She stopped, searching for the words to explain. "He did beat us whenever we did things that were bad and I guess sometimes when he was angry, but he always said it was what God asked of him." A look passed between the couple, but she didn't see it. "There was a point when I got older that the physical beatings stopped." She shrugged as though it was the most normal thing in the world. "He hasn't taken a belt to me since I was fourteen."

Both Anne and Ivan had their eyebrows up at her comment and she sighed. "I know what it sounds like, but it really wasn't all that terrible. I have a lot of siblings and it usually only happened when I let him down."

Anne looked at her for a long moment. "How old are you, Brooke?" she asked quietly. "I would have guessed you were seventeen now," she admitted with a smile.

Brooke sighed. "Nope, I'm nineteen, ma'am."

Ivan smiled at Anne's sour look at being called *ma'am*. "Well, not to seem insensitive but that just makes the whole situation perfect. You are old enough to come work for me of your own free will and choice," he said the last cheerfully.

He fully intended on having his way with this even as Brooke shook her head again and opened her mouth to argue. "Don't mistake this for something it's not." He gave her a toothy grin. "I fully intend to work you long hard days and get my money's worth. Farming isn't easy, as you well know. It's hard, hands on, and dirty work." He paused, then plunged ahead again, watching her face as he used the last ammunition he could think of. "Unless hard work is a problem for you? Is that it, Brooke?"

Her mouth opened, then snapped closed again. He saw the spark of indignity flash across her fair face as she finally said, "It's not the hard work I'm worried about, sir. I happen to love farming." She smiled. "It's in my blood, you know. My hesitation here is that you have already been so kind to me and I don't want to take advantage you or anyone."

Ivan grinned, knowing he was about to win the hand. He glanced at Anne as he said, "Well, I guess it's settled, then. You can start work tomorrow after you've had a chance to settle in." He held out his hand, but she didn't take it. He let it drop to his side and said quietly, "I will show you around and let you see which rooms we have and you can take your pick from the lot of them."

Brooke adamantly shook her head. "If you do really have a job for me, sir, I will accept it."

He cocked a grin her direction and she held up a hand. "However, I am not going to move in to your family's private space. I will live out of my car for now and if it's okay I will park it on your property until I can save enough to get my own place." When he didn't respond, she added, "If that bothers you, I will find another place to park it." She let her hand fall limply to her side and waited for him to respond.

She could see the wheels turning in his mind as though he was trying to work through the problem in front of him and she watched, curious how he was going to work it out. He tapped one finger on his chin as he thought. When his eyes lit suddenly, she swallowed and he nodded. "That's it! We have the old homestead up the street that's empty right now. You'll stay there. You can look after the place for us in return. I will warn you that it's a bit old and will definitely need some love, but I have no doubt that we can fix that right away."

Brooke finally nodded, quickly wiping a tear of gratitude off one cheek. "Okay, but I will pay you the first couple of weeks rent upfront and then you will deduct rent from my check going forward." It was a statement, not a question and even Anne appeared to be impressed by it. Seeing the stubborn tilt of her jaw and that glint in her eye, he nodded.

Brooke smiled. "Also, if you ever want the space back, then all you have to do is let me know and I will find somewhere else to stay, no problem."

Ivan held out a hand. "Deal," he said as he shook hers firmly.

He winked at Anne and leaned down to kiss her lightly on the lips. He stepped away as he promised to take Brooke over to the house so she could get settled right in.

The two of them were in the foyer putting on their shoes when Anne came walking in holding a set of keys. "You might need these," she said a little smugly and dropped them into his outstretched palm. She turned to walk away but then turned back. "Oh, by the way, Ivan, I know I normally take Fridays off from the clinic, but John called earlier and said there are a few things that I need to handle, so I will be going in for a while today."

Ivan nodded and leaned down to steal a last quick kiss from his wife before releasing her and opening the door.

As soon as she slid into her car and shut the door, Brooke burst into tears. She looked through hazy eyes at the blue sky and said a prayer of thanks to whomever might be out there after all. She couldn't stop a little sob of relief; she was actually going to be okay. Even better than that, she had her freedom and she was going to be okay. She smiled out at the beautiful day and let the worry slide away for now.

CHAPTER 6

Brooke could hardly contain her excitement when she saw the old farmhouse. It definitely needed a good cleaning as well as most of the rooms being desperately in need of a fresh coat of paint, but it had the potential of being home. Once she started working and getting a regular paycheck, she would be able to do more but for now a deep clean would have to do.

Though sparsely furnished, it was a charming red brick house with an open floor plan. There were two decent-sized bedrooms on the main floor, which was nice, as well as a huge bathroom across the hall from the master bedroom with an old shiny white and silver clawfoot tub.

Brooke imagined taking long baths to work out sore muscles after a long day of hard work and smiled. There was only a half bath inside the master bedroom but that suited her just fine. After all, it was only her and she didn't plan on having any guests or roommates. Her heart soared at the thought of having all this space to herself. She had never had one room to herself let alone a whole house and it felt surreal.

It took nearly an hour for Ivan to walk her through. He apologized over and over about how the hot water ran out too quickly and how the old stove only had two working burners. She'd tried not to shove him out the door when he had eventually talked himself into having some handyman come out to fix it all.

She quickly assured him that wasn't necessary and that she had it all under control. He had given her a skeptical look but had finally agreed. She hadn't quite pushed him out but not far from it as she had, backed him slowly toward the front door.

She loved the beautiful old house on sight and couldn't wait to get started with making it her own. Whomever had lived there last had left quite a mess and Ivan had apologized profusely, offering to have someone come clean for her. Then he topped that by once again trying to talk her into moving into the Burton house with his family.

She nearly choked at that suggestion but then let him know she was perfectly capable of handling whatever needed done to make it livable. She had reassured him that a water heater that only lasted twenty minutes was completely fine as she had never taken a shower that long in her life. They hadn't even made it downstairs by the time she had talked him right out onto the front porch and said goodbye.

She did, however, go straight down the carpeted stairs after she closed the door behind him. She was excited to see what was down there. She was only a little disappointed. Brooke couldn't see herself using the small box shower in the corner of the unfinished room. Or the toilet next to it with a wraparound curtain for privacy but it made her happy to know that she could if she wanted or needed to. The washer and dryer were also down here and that area had actually been finished with white painted walls and a beige-tile floor. She sighed happily; it would all do very well for her.

When she finished exploring the basement, she rushed outside to look at the backyard. Excitement flushed her cheeks a warm pink as she imagined all she could do with the large space.

The only thing that dampened her joy was the fact that when she had tried to give him the full $227 dollars, which was all the money she had to her name right now he had refused to take it. She had tried insisting that a deal was a deal, but he wouldn't fold. He told her that the house was in worse condition than he'd remembered and that if she insisted on paying rent the first month, then he would have to insist on having a professional cleaner come and go through the house. If she wanted to clean it up herself, then that would mean she got the first month rent free.

The fact that she was both excited to get started coupled with the idea of having a stranger come in to clean just when she was trying to get comfortable in the space were the reasons she had finally agreed with him. Before he left, he mentioned casually that rent would be one fifty and she balked. She didn't have a lot of experience in real estate but she would have bet anything she had that the property was worth at least seven hundred. She had looked in the wanted ads and seen some of the rental prices even here in the valley. She scoffed at his casual tone and countered with six hundred. He wouldn't agree with that, she knew, but it gave her enough wiggle room to work him down to the four hundred, which was as low as she was willing to go. It took some talking, but he had finally agreed and they shook on it. She had ignored his comment that she was going to give him gray hair and had instead focused on getting him gone.

Once she was finished looking around, she dug a notepad and a pen out of her car and went to work making a list of all she would need right away. Not having to spend what little money she had on rent meant that she could make a trip to the local general store and pick up a few things she could use.

Though he had suggested she come for breakfast again tomorrow to discuss what she would be doing for work she had turned him down. She agreed instead to meet with him after breakfast to discuss it. She wasn't going to turn their life upside down in payment for his kindness. She would need to pick up a few groceries while she was at the store. Just a few things to last until she got paid.

In the end they had agreed to meet at the shop at eight tomorrow morning. She glanced down at her watch. That meant she had the rest of today to get things handled with the house. After today there was no telling just how busy she would be or how much free time, if any, she would have. She took a deep breath and hurried inside to the bathroom. She had been holding it all morning and felt as though her bladder was going to burst.

When Brooke was done with that, she walked back onto the porch for a moment and rolled up her long heavy sleeves, loving the feel of the sun directly on her bare arms. They were white as the day she was born, but that didn't matter, she thought with a smile. That would all change soon.

She started by hauling all the trash outside. She found one cupboard full of half empty cleaners and supplies and went to town on the kitchen. As she went from cabinet to cabinet scrubbing each out before moving on, she emptied the contents onto the gray Formica countertop. She found a half-used roll of garbage bags and a scrub brush and gloves. A couple of cabinets even had a few unopened cans of corn and a box of crackers. She was hot and slick with sweat as the heat of the day kicked in. She walked through the house opening windows to try and let a breeze inside.

Not for the first time in her life, she wished for lighter clothing. Growing up she had been required to wear clothing that not only covered her body from neck to wrist and neck to ankles but also to wear a heavy thick cotton full body underwear that added an extra layer of heat and was somehow supposed to help protect her virginity. She laughed now at the irony of that falsehood. Beside the fact that she felt roasted alive, being fully clothed in ninety-degree weather, it was also extremely restrictive on full movement. And though she had removed the underwear before she had left home the heavy duty button-down and thick knit skirt she wore still felt sticky and hot here in the scorching heat.

That could end now she realized and smiled happily as she reached down and pulled up one side of the loose long skirt she wore. She worked it up into a high knot and then she tied the other side up too. It wasn't a pretty sight, she knew, but she did feel the slight movement of air against her skin and decided it was worth it. She closed her eyes for a minute as she enjoyed the sensation and then she unbuttoned the three bottom buttons of her blouse. With a defiant little huff and feeling a little sinful, she tied the two ends together tightly just below her white cotton bra. Hot air brushed her abdomen and she shivered in delight. Even though the air was hot, the movement felt good.

Brooke slid a hand across her midriff and frowned. She had always been a little self-conscious of her stomach. She had seen pictures of girls in bathing suits on the covers of magazines after all. They all seemed to have these beautiful slightly curvy but flat stomachs. Hers didn't look at all that smooth. Whenever she had dared to look closely in the mirror at her body, she was disappointed. Her stomach looked ridged and only curved slightly, though it did taper on the sides and she did have a curvy waistline. Where theirs looked soft and smooth, hers was hard and ridged. She dropped her hand to her side and shrugged. "It is what it is," she said in a matter-of-fact tone and went back to work.

She desperately needed a shower but had promised herself she would reward herself only when she was done with the cleaning. With that happy thought in mind, she grabbed the last of the full garbage bags to haul out to the garbage can by the road. She hefted it up on her shoulder and made her way outside just as the loud roar of what sounded like a dirt bike pierced the air. She stepped onto the porch and saw a single bike and rider heading up the road toward her. She shaded her eyes against the bright sun but still couldn't make out enough detail to identify the rider. Her stomach lurched nervously, her brothers all had bikes and she didn't want to see any of them yet. She hurried to the can and hefted the full bag inside and then walked quickly back to the front steps.

She climbed them and placed one hand on the doorknob. When she heard the spit of gravel and the engine shut off behind her, she forced a smile and turned. Her breath caught in her throat. She watched as he pulled a helmet off his head and then shook it to ruffle his dark hair. She fought the urge to run and instead let her hand drop to her side as she stepped to the edge of the porch.

She gave a little wave as he turned to look at her. "Hello," she said, trying to sound friendly.

He eyed her tied up skirt and blouse with a narrowed gaze and Brooke wondered if he was judging her because she was being immoral or because she just didn't look good. She tried not to let the thought hurt and instead forced a smile. He swung one long leg off his bike and she watched as the thick muscles of his thigh rippled. She looked away and then forced herself to meet his gaze as he stepped forward.

He nodded a hello. He had seen her by the road lifting a bag of garbage almost as big as she was into the big blue garbage bin. She had lifted it with ease, which had surprised him as she seemed so petite. He thought he had seen her turn and look at him on the road for a second but could have been mistaken since she had turned a moment later and walked quickly back to the house. He rode up and turned off the motor and kicked out the kickstand. He pulled of the black helmet he wore and set it on the seat of the bike, running his hand through his messy hair as he turned toward the house.

She was standing on the porch now staring down at him with that unnerving blue-eyed gaze. He forced a grin. He stepped closer and sucked air into his lungs through his teeth. Damn she was hot. He wondered idly if she had any idea just how hot she looked with her clothes all knotted up like that. He thought about asking, which only showed just how dumb he could be, and bit his tongue.

She was wearing the same clothing as she had been this morning at breakfast except that now the knotted fabrics looped up to show off her very shapely calves to perfection. He swallowed hard. As if showing off her sleek legs wasn't enough, she had tied her shirt up so high that he could nearly see the bottom of what were now very obviously nice luscious breasts.

He grinned inwardly at his own thoughts. Funny how this morning he had thought she was too thin and not curvy at all. He would admit to liking her wild curly red hair, though. And her shimmering blue eyes were as mesmerizing as they were compelling. But her body, he'd told himself when he'd felt an instant attraction to her, wasn't that great. Now he wanted to laugh at his own stupidity, but he had reached the bottom of the stairs and she was watching him curiously with one eyebrow up.

She had a light sprinkle of freckles just over her nose and he wanted to know if she had any of those light brown spots on any of other parts of her body. He stopped that thought in its tracks and focused instead on her chin.

He cocked a boyish grin up at her and casually glanced down at her bare midriff. He swallowed a curse. That had been a bad idea, he chided himself. She was quite literally ripped. How she had managed to hide all those creamy and delicious curves and rippling abs under clothes he didn't know. Though he was trying to focus on something else he couldn't stop the tightening if his loins.

No freckles on her abs, he thought dumbly, before his brain began thinking of all the other places she might also have them.

Intelligently, he forced his dark eyes up and met her gaze instead. "I guess it's true, then, huh?"

Brooke stared at him, confused. "What is?"

He swept a hand to encompass the house and yard. "Dad, really hired you and allowed you stay here?" It was more of a statement than a question, but he let it hang in the air anyway. He saw the angry spark in her sapphire-blue eyes as she registered his tone and what he'd said. He watched the spark go cold and disappear just as quickly. His groin tightened heavily. Man, she was pretty when her eyes lit up like that.

Brooke squared her shoulders in defiance and then gave a very casual shrug. "Your father is very kind. I actually tried to leave several times this morning and yet somehow he managed to talk me into staying." She didn't know why she was letting him get under her skin, but she didn't like it. She squared her shoulders and her bright gaze clashed with his dark one. "He talked me into working for him and he generously agreed to *rent* me this place until I find another place to live or until he needs it for something else." She put plenty of emphasis on the word *rent.*

Cole could see that he was getting under her skin and it made him grin up at her. She watched him intently as he again tried to light that spark in her eyes. It was better if she was mad at him anyway, he told himself. That way he wouldn't have a choice but to keep his distance from her. Instinctively, he felt that she was a distraction that he really didn't need or want in his life. He raised one eyebrow in challenge. "Well, I don't see him here now and yet here you still are."

Just as he'd wanted, her eyes spit blue fire and her lips thinned into an unpleasant smile. She was definitely a proud one. He gave her a polite smile and waited for her response.

Her voice was low and cold as she said, "The only reason I'm still here is because I keep my word and I gave it to your dad." Her teeth were gritted together as she continued, "He pushed and pushed until he nearly drove me crazy trying to get me to stay here.

She groaned. "He wouldn't take no for an answer, even though I'm pretty sure your mom was mad at him and probably hates me." She rubbed her hands over her eyes tiredly. "I finally agreed to stay out of pure frustration and your dad made sure I shook on it and gave my word, so I can't back out now." The last was said quietly without anger or frustration.

God, she was tired. She'd really had a long day and it was only two in the afternoon. She looked down at Cole, daring him to judge her.

Instead, what she saw made her heart beat stop in her chest. He was staring up at her with that intense nearly black gaze and if she wasn't mistaken, he looked … she hesitated … almost hungry. She blinked and that look was gone replaced with a shuttered and untouched expression.

Cole forced a polite smile and willed his now heavy loins to quit throbbing. He adjusted his position to allow more room in his tight jeans. Looking up at her from this vantage point, he could see her long shapely legs nearly up to her thighs and it was distracting. Her abdomen rippled slightly in and out with every breath and he was having a hard time focusing on the conversation. He looked at the door behind her and his eyes darkened. "I know how convincing my dad can be," he said finally. "The worst part of it is that he is nearly always right because he's just so good, you know?"

She nodded her chin and gave him a friendly smile. She had nearly convinced herself that she had imagined that stark look of hunger when his gaze drifted back to her and she saw his eyes. He took two steps forward then and was standing eye to eye. She was still two steps above him and yet they were now about the same level. She swallowed nervously and then cleared her throat as she watched his black eyes follow the line of her throat before sliding up to warm her blue gaze again. She could see the hunger there in those gold-flecked black pools and her lips opened slightly in alarm.

She wanted to turn and run but didn't. Somehow as afraid as she was of hunger like that, she was more curious. Wanted to know what he was going to do next. He took another step up and she stopped breathing. He was watching her every move and waiting to see how she would react. She stood frozen on the top step. She had never in her life been so torn. One part of her wanted something from him, the other wanted to scream and run away. She blinked and forced air back into her burning lungs wanting him to close that last few inches and kiss her. Still, he waited. Watching her with those unnerving, unblinking eyes.

Others had used and abused her and her body and it had been terrifying. Fear engulfed her as she suddenly realized that he had the ability to steal her soul and that was far more terrifying than anything that could ever happen to her body. She let out a little whimper at that realization and his control snapped.

Just when she would have run, he stepped up and closed the gap between them tilting his head as he took her mouth with his in a hot demanding kiss. Her eyes squeezed closed and he deepened the kiss urging her mouth to open under his firm demanding onslaught. She resisted but only slightly and his long lean fingers came up to thread in her hair pulling her mouth tighter against his own. Her lips parted and the deliciously sweet nectar of her taste washed over his tongue with intoxicating madness. He growled low in his throat as her hands came up to settle around his neck, her fingers threading through his hair and pulling him closer to her. She pushed into him aligning her body tightly against his own.

He thought he was going to lose his mind when she tentatively brushed her hot sweet tongue against his. He hadn't even realized he'd wanted her to surrender to his onslaught until he felt her push into him, but the power of it surged through him like lightning sizzling in his blood and he lightly bit her bottom lip. She moaned and he starting moving her backward toward the house slowly at first. He was trying to make it to that bloody door before he took her right here on the front porch. He was so intent on the kiss that he didn't even notice when she started struggling against him.

Brooke was hot now and she wanted him to keep kissing her more than she wanted life itself. Wanted his taste to stay with her forever. When he had stroked his tongue across her lips demanding entrance to her mouth, she had melted down deep inside. She felt an unfamiliar throb between her legs and leaned into it curiously. He tasted like sin, hot and sweet and she didn't think she could ever get enough of that addictive male taste. She ached down deep in her belly and felt like her breasts were overly heavy and on fire. She brushed against him trying to put out those intense flames but touching him only stoked them higher. She moaned and rubbed her pelvis against him. He jerked and his arms turned to steel bands as he roughly molded her smaller feminine curves to his own hard masculine frame. He moved one hand between them to lightly brush her nipple and she surged against his hand.

Somewhere deep inside her, she felt fear begin and she stilled. Then she started shaking, she tried to swallow the terror that was working its way up to clog her throat now. She didn't want to stop now. Was angry at the fear even. Yet somehow, she couldn't seem to stop the tremors of fear that surged, leaving a metallic taste on her tongue. She tried to push him away, but he was holding her tightly against him roughly molding his hard body to hers. She tried to tell him to stop but honestly couldn't tell if it found its way out of her fear swollen throat. His tongue rubbed hard against hers and she tried to bite down on it, pure instinct taking over now. She couldn't breathe and couldn't stop the cloud of panic that had taken over her brain with a vengeance.

He pulled his tongue back before she got a hold of it with her teeth and groaned as her teeth merely scraped erotically across his tongue. She managed to get one hand free and a single tear ran down her left cheek as she pulled it back and slapped him hard across the face.

He jerked back looking stunned, confused, and God help her, hurt. He raised one hand to his cheek as though he could still feel the indentation of her hand there. She didn't wait for his response instead using his surprise to her advantage to jerk her body back and away. Tears of regret and fear and embarrassment ran in rivers down her cheeks as she stole one final look at his incredulous expression.

Something cold and terrifying slid into his eyes and she watched as his jaw hardened. She was only a step away but could see the red mark on his cheek where her hand had landed. She looked away as misery sunk in and whispered the only thing she could think to say, "I'm so sorry." Then she turned on her heels and ran. She opened the door and stepped inside, quickly closing it behind her and sliding the lock into place.

She leaned heavily against the door then and broke. Her shoulders shook as great sobs racked her body. She slid to the floor when her legs would no longer support her weight and took deep sobbing breaths as the reality of what she had done sank in. She didn't know how she could ever face him again, but she was going to have to find a way.

Cole cursed loudly in disgust at himself. Though he didn't fully understand what had just happened, he was pissing mad and his cock throbbed hard with need, which was almost laughable given the way that she had looked at him. He pictured her pale cheeks and the haunted look in her brilliant blue eyes before she had turned to run inside and he bit out a long curse again. His lips turned into a hard grimace of disgust at his own lack of self-control.

She'd looked flat-out terrified, which was a new experience for him and to top it all off, she had been the one that had apologized. He could hear her brokenhearted sobs on the other side of the door and his gut clenched inward. Despite the unusual urge he had to try to comfort her somehow, he forced his feet to turn and walk down the stairs toward his bike.

He wanted to hit something but bit back the anger that was directed inward. What the hell was wrong with him? He slipped the helmet onto his head and lifted the bike, sliding the stand back with a click. Then he stomped on the pedal much harder than necessary and breathed in as the engine roared to life.

Even as he pulled out of the driveway and onto the gravel road he spit out,

"Damn it all to hell." He had nearly lost control with her, which was only made worse by the fact that he definitely knew better. His dad would have been horrified if he had any idea what had just happened. A hard heartless grin stretched his lips inside the plastic face guard.

What was it his father had always said?

"No means no." That was it. He kicked a rock as he tilted the bike dangerously low and it went flying down the road to roll off one side. He couldn't ever remember being so far off base with a girl. Not even at sixteen. A low laugh slipped out, but he was far from amused.

He had, after all, been certain that she was as into what they were doing as he was. He would have sworn that she was as turned on as he was. Had he imagined it all? His brow furrowed as he replayed the events in his head, looking for the signs he had missed. He had advanced several times giving her plenty of time to step back or avoid the kiss. She hadn't moved an inch.

Anger surged for a moment because she hadn't given him any sign she didn't want him back, but then he remembered the sound of her gut-wrenching sobs. He'd heard the lock slide into place as soon as the door closed in an effort to protect herself. Even then all he'd wanted to do was push his way inside to make sure she was okay.

Then he'd have apologized for pushing it too far and they'd make up and take it slow. He grinned sardonically at his own stupidity. Even now his other brains were still trying to insert themselves into the equation. Considering that he was the one who had scared her half to death and had made her cry, it probably wasn't the best plan.

He glanced back in the direction of the old house consideringly. He could still go back and talk to her, try to make it up somehow. He shook his head forcefully.

The best thing he could do for her at this point was to take his sex-crazed self away from her and get back to work.

He'd find a time to apologize to her later, he promised himself. He was half a mile down the dirt road before it occurred to him to wonder how old she was. He slapped the front of his helmet in frustration as that thought left him feeling terrified. "Shit, Damn, Fuck," he cursed, as he sped the bike up fishtailing slightly before pulling easily out of it. He was twenty-one and she was maybe seventeen. To some people that was rape or at the very least sexual assault.

Then because he realized that if she pressed charges or called the cops, he had nothing left to lose, he laughed out loud. Wouldn't that just serve him right if he had just screwed up his life plans and wouldn't even be able to finish college unless it was from the inside of a jail cell.

He laughed harshly as the irony of that thought left a hole of concern in his gut. Considering that he had always had every opportunity in life handed to him, unlike many of his friends, who'd had to scrimp and save every dime and still take out piles of student loans just to go to college. He had always seen himself graduating early top of his class ready to take on the tech world. Now the image of him getting out of prison around the time he would have been graduating instead left an acrid taste in his mouth.

His lips twisted. He'd nearly raped the poor girl. Coming from her background, she probably didn't have a clue what was going to happen when he stepped up to her. She was most likely a young innocent girl that had been sheltered her whole life from men like him.

Cole thought about that for a long moment. He was honest enough to realize that had actually been part of the turn-on to him. The thought that those full pink lips had never even been kissed. His lips thinned into a merciless hard line as he admitted the truth. He turned the dirt bike onto the road at the corner of the field and headed straight toward the irrigation pivot in the center. He stood the bike on its kickstand and took off his helmet before turning to look off in the direction of the old house. He was going to keep his distance from her and hope for the best. With a little luck, she wouldn't press charges and he might actually have a life ahead. Mind made up, he squashed the need that still licked flames up into his gut and made an oath to himself. He would never touch her again. For that matter, he was going to stay completely away from her.

As he pulled tools from the metal box, he had left out here the day before, he sighed and thought about what had led to all this happening.

Around lunchtime Cole had stopped by home to grab a sandwich for lunch. His mother, Anne, who had also come home for lunch, was just leaving again and had seemed a little worked up. He'd been a little concerned so he'd asked if she was okay. She had shaken her head and confided to him that she was quite worried about his father.

Despite Cole's efforts to soothe her, Anne was determined that he was going through a midlife crisis or some such thing as he had been acting completely out of character all day. Then she had told Cole that he had hired "that" Reynolds girl on the spot and even offered to let her stay there with them in the house. That thought had Anne in quite the frenzy. Why on earth would Ivan take a chance on bringing a total stranger into their home, she wanted to know.

Cole could think of one very strong reason as he had never in his life seen his dad do anything that didn't appear to be the most kind and loving thing to do. He kept that thought wisely to himself as he listened to his mother rant at it all.

When she threw her hands emphatically in the air and said, "Now she's over at the old house, doing God only knows what." He had raised an eyebrow at that outburst but still stayed silent as he listened.

Cole had tried to reassure her. He'd reached out to touch her hand and smiled. "You know Dad, Mom. He is always out to save the world, one soul at a time."

Anne's hands flew into the air in frustration as she agreed. "I don't know why he always thinks it's his job to fix everything for everyone. Besides that, he has always at least talked to me before making decisions like this, but not this time."

Cole had hidden his smile, then said soothingly, "I'm sure Dad has a good explanation for everything." He'd glanced around then. "Where is he anyway? And why didn't you talk to him about all this?"

That had been a mistake. He had soon learned that his father had left with that "Brooke girl" and Anne hadn't heard a word since. Though she had called Ivan's cell, he hadn't yet called her back. She had glared at Cole then and marched out the door muttering under her breath, "If he wants to talk to me, he can call me back. I won't be nagging at that man."

He'd stared after her for a long minute before shrugging and heading to the kitchen for a sandwich.

Though the turkey and Swiss on rye was tasty, he couldn't really focus enough to enjoy it. His curiosity kept nagging at him, even though he told himself several times that he was much too busy to get involved.

He went ten rounds in his mind thinking of that strange but pretty girl with the all that red curly hair. In an effort to stay uninvolved he told himself all the things he needed to get done before the weekend. He reminded himself that he preferred to get it all done sooner rather than later so he could bug out Friday night but even that didn't do it.

He even reminded himself that he had big plans this weekend. But all to no avail. After washing the sandwich down with a tall glass of water, he hurried back outside fully intending to get back to work. He had just swung his leg over his dirt bike when he heard his younger brother call out behind him.

He turned and watched as Ryker make his way around the side of the big house and toward him. Ryker was muddy from his waist down and wearing a wide and a proud little grin. He looked up at Cole and asked, "Can I have a ride on your bike, Cole?"

Cole looked pointedly at all the mud and shook his head. "Sorry, little buddy, but you're all muddy and I don't want that all over me."

Ryker's bottom lip jutted out and he said, "But I'm all done with my chores and Mom says I can play now."

He looked hopefully up at his brother but then turned away as Cole shook his head once again. "Good job, buddy, I'm proud of you for getting the weeding done but you still need a shower and I have a lot of work to get done today."

When Ryker's shoulders slumped as he started to walk away, Cole caved. "Tell you what, Ryker, if you go get showered and hang out for a bit, I'll come back and give you a ride later."

Ryker turned with a happy smile. "Thanks, Cole. You're the best big brother ever." Then he turned and bounded up the curved concrete stairs.

Cole knew he'd been played by an eight-year-old but only grinned. "Don't take all that mud through the house or Mom will have it out with you!" He called out, though he wasn't sure if his brother heard him as he plowed through the door and disappeared inside.

Nothing he could do about it now. He turned back to his bike and stomped the starter and as the bike roared to life, he spit gravel and turned out onto the road. He was already half a mile down, heading the wrong direction up the road before he realized what he was doing.

He knew he should just stay out of it, but he just couldn't resist going to see if his mother was right and that girl was there at the old house with his father.

As Cole worked the wrench hard trying to loosen a bolt that was bound, his fingers slipped and his hand slammed against the heavy stainless-steel leg that held the pivot in place. He watched as a chunk of his finger was gouged off and then cursed under his breath. He was so distracted he had forgotten to put on his gloves. He reached for the leather work gloves as blood seeped slowly from the wound. He pulled the thick leather over his hands and went back to work.

With a grunt he loosened the bolt and thought to himself, if only he had listened to his own instincts earlier and stayed away from "that girl," as his mother had called her, he wouldn't be out here worried that his own sexual instincts had possibly cost him his future. He didn't want to think about it but the worst part was that fear that he had seen on her pale beautiful face. He couldn't stand the thought that he had been the one to put it there. His fingers tightened into a fist at his side as he cleared his mind of everything but the motor in front of him that he needed to get running.

CHAPTER 7

Brooke cried, crumpled there on the floor until her throat hurt and her eyes were sore and puffy. She cried for the pain of trauma in her past, and then, when she was done with that, cried for the shame she felt in how she had treated Cole.

She had, after all, wanted him to kiss her. Wanted it so bad in fact that her heart had been thumping wildly in her chest as he moved closer to her. He had given her every opportunity to back away and yet something deep and promising in those enigmatic dark eyes of his had promised pleasure and she hadn't been able to resist.

She had been struck hard with the heat and the passion of those moments in his arms. She would have happily kissed him all afternoon if not for that overwhelming panic that had risen up in her chest when his strong arms had locked around her waist and ground their bodies together. Even though that rough push against her feminine core was exactly what she had been needing, her brain had gone on alert. Then it had screamed until panic soared into every molecule of her bloodstream.

She hadn't meant to slap him, though. That had been pure instinct and she felt terrible. He hadn't deserved that from her, not after giving her that sinfully wanton and what she suspected could be addictive, taste of him.

She sat spent, still leaning against the door where she had collapsed. Her stomach grumbled loudly and she used her arms to push herself up to a standing position. She leaned her head back against the door and took a deep breath. Her stomach grumbled again, more loudly this time and she turned to walk into the kitchen in search of food.

Though most of the food left in the cupboards had been stale or long past expired she had seen an unopened pack of round buttery crackers and decided to give them a tentative try. She quickly ripped the package open and popped a round into her mouth before she could change her mind. She chewed and the bitter, stale flavor gagged her. She turned to spit it into the sink and then rinsed her mouth with the cool water. The water tasted refreshing, so she bent down and took a few gulps of the fresh well water.

Tossing the pack of crackers into the garbage, she turned and opened a can of corn. It wasn't out of date yet so she figured it would be okay. After a quick sniff to verify its freshness, she grabbed a spoon and took a bite. It was sweet and her empty stomach didn't seem to mind that it was cold. She walked over to the small round table and sat at one of the four wooden chairs around it. She reached for her note pad and the list of supplies she had been making as she cleaned throughout the day. She really needed to get a few groceries so she could survive until she got paid again.

Brooke sighed; her list of things she was putting off until that first paycheck was growing and she was beginning to worry that it was going to take several checks to get on top of things here. She looked around the empty kitchen and listed a few essential items below the supplies she had already added. She ate the whole can of corn but still felt hungry. She frowned, then reached for her car keys. If she ran to the store and got a few things now, then she could spend the evening finishing up what she needed to get done before work tomorrow.

She started the engine and then waited for a minute, praying, for the air conditioner to kick in and cool the hot interior. She stared dubiously at the ever-growing long list as she chewed on her bottom lip. She probably wouldn't have enough money for all of it, so she took a minute to rate the items from most important to least. That done she gave herself a quick nod and clicked her seat belt into place.

She pulled onto the crunching gravel road with nineties country blaring from the radio. She made the normally twenty-minute drive in fifteen.

The small town wasn't much to brag about. In fact, it really didn't have much more than a couple of gas stations, an auto parts store that also sold farm equipment, a small feed and hardware barn, and one small grocery store. Other than that, there was an old diner that had a bar off on one side and a large freshly painted white church. Across the road was the small though nicely built brick clinic that Anne owned and next to that was a cluster of brown brick buildings that made up the elementary school, middle school, and high school.

Brooke pulled into the first gas station as she had decided fuel was the most important thing as she needed it to get to and from work. After filling her tank up, she drove to the hardware store. She skimmed the lot quickly to make sure she didn't recognize any vehicles parked there before she pulled her car to the far end and parked.

She made it all the way to the door before the small gust of air reminded her that her clothes were still tied up in knots. She stopped and quickly worked the knots out trying to smooth the twisting wrinkles with her palms. She sighed, positive that it looked ridiculous, but there was nothing she could do about it now. Head held high, she opened the door and made her way quickly inside.

The clerk, a middle-aged woman with short spiky blonde hair looked up from behind the register as the little bell that was tied to the door jingled to signal all inside of a new arrival. The woman casually looked her up and down and then pasted a friendly smile on her bright pink lipstick covered lips. "Welcome to Handy's," she said in a friendly voice before turning back to look at the magazine she held in one hand.

Brooke had been in the store a handful of times with her mother. Her father had often sent Rebecca to pick up supplies and a few things they needed. Then it had seemed that people had always stared and then watched them as though they were animals in the zoo. Brooke could see the woman behind the counter watching her now as curiosity shown in her brown perfectly made-up eyes.

She felt uncomfortable but nodded politely and grabbed a small cart. Taking care to only get the things on her list, she gathered the items quickly and was soon back at the register. Two times she had glanced over and caught the woman staring at her while she shopped and she was feeling anxious and ready to get out of the store.

She stepped up and silently began loading her things on the counter.

"Hello, did you find everything okay?" the cashier asked in a friendly voice and Brooke found herself wondering if she had been mistaken about the woman judging her. Determined to start creating a better life for herself, she smiled and met the woman's eyes. "Hello, and yes I did, thank you."

When the middle-aged woman gave her a quick wink as she rung up her items, Brooke took a deep breath. She may as well start learning how to talk to people. She smiled again. "I'm Brooke. Are you guys staying busy today?"

To her credit the woman looked only slightly surprised at her attempt at conversation. Then she gave her smooth bob a shake and threw a quick eye roll in Brooke's direction. "Nope," she said before tapping a long fingernail against the counter as she watched her screen. "You're only the fifth person that's come in so far today." She sighed and then looked directly at Brooke. "It does usually get busier in the afternoon, though, so hopefully…." She lifted her hand in the air and crossed her fingers.

Brooke noticed her curiously watching her under her lashes again but this time met her gaze steadily. "I hope it does. It must be boring working here when it's slow."

The blonde nodded emphatically. "It sure does," she agreed. She watched Brooke for a long moment as though building up courage before asking, "You're one of those Reynolds kids, aren't you?"

Brooke felt her cheeks heating slightly and she lowered her head as she nodded.

The older woman held out her hand. "I'm Pam Openshaw." She waved a thin hand to encompass the north side of the valley as she continued. "My husband and I own a stretch of land just a few miles north of your family." She grinned warmly as Brooke shook her hand. "I'm sure you have seen us in passing."

Brooke smiled back at her. "Yes, I am familiar with Openshaw land. I've driven past you're place quite a lot. Isn't it that place with the double Quonsets out on the corner by the light brick house?" she asked politely.

Pam nodded and then tapping the register said, "Your total is $85.92."

She took the cash Brooke handed her and pushed a button that popped the cash drawer open with a loud ding. Brooke watched as she quickly counted out her change. She turned then and handed it to her with a smile. "There you go, Brooke," she said warmly and then opened her mouth as though she wanted to say something. Brooke reached for the bags but hesitated as her lips closed again.

Pam seemed to be trying to make up her mind about something and Brooke wasn't sure if she should turn and walk out or wait. She had just decided on the former when Pam burst out. "I worry about all you kids sometimes, you know? It seems like there is always so many people coming and going from your family's farm." She smiled as though trying to take the sting out of her words. She reached a hand out to gently squeeze Brooke's arm for a moment. "Isaiah, Benjamin and the older boys are all nice enough to us when we deal with them, but we just never see much of the girls and children, you know?"

Brooke nodded mutely as tears threatened to fill her eyes. Voice low, she said, "Yes I do know, ma'am." She forced a small smile. "I'd better get going, but thank you so much." She turned and hurried out of the store with her bags in tow before she started crying and made a fool of herself for the third time that day.

She was in such a hurry that she ran quite literally into her brother Isaiah, who was just reaching for the door handle as she came barreling out. She stared up at him feeling shocked and waited for his reaction. After a long moment he gave her a slight nod. "Brooke," he said.

She pasted a cold smile and nodded back at him. "Hello, Isaiah." She looked uncomfortably down at the bags she held and then back up at him.

"I just had to come pick up a few things," she rushed out and then with a little sidestep around him she said in the friendliest tone she could muster, "I'd better get going. I have a lot to do today."

He looked a little confused and turned to stare curiously after her. He'd thought she would have been long gone by now. He considered what to do for a moment as he watched her walk quickly to her car. Father had sent him in to pick up a few supplies from town, but he also thought their father would want him to keep tabs on Brooke. They couldn't have her running all around the valley and ruining their reputation after all. He hesitated but only for a moment before striding quickly toward her car.

He heard the engine roar to life and broke into a run, calling out to her. "Hey, Brooke, wait up!" He wasn't sure if she had heard him or not, but he suspected she just didn't care as she put the car in gear and sped out of the lot before he could get to her. He cursed low and then turned back to the store. He would at least be able to report back that he had seen her loitering here still in the valley.

Brooke sucked air into her lungs as she sped out of the gravel lot while watching him in her rearview mirror. Her hands shook a little and she held the steering wheel tightly to stop the tremors. She was nowhere near ready to take on her asshole brothers yet. She wasn't even ready to cope with seeing her mother or sisters let alone the bigot better than thou men. Her family was extremely complicated and running into them all over town was just not something she wanted to deal with.

She considered skipping the grocery store, but her empty stomach had her squaring her shoulders and going for it. She quickly scanned the lot before she pulled in as she didn't want to deal with any more family today. She didn't recognize any of the vehicles scattered across the lot and sighed in relief. She pulled her car around to park behind a large truck that would block the view of her car from the highway and reached for her wallet and list before climbing out. She would hurry in and very quickly get what she had to have and then be on her way back home in a jiffy.

That thought made her smile. She had a home. She thought of the small brick house she was going to be living in and it made her feel safe. She thought of everything that had happened that day and wondered with a little amusement how she didn't have whiplash.

If it wasn't for Ivan Burton being such a great person she would be long gone and out there searching still for a safe place to call home. She reminded herself to thank him when saw him again. Better yet she was going to thank him by being the hardest worker he had. She smiled as she dropped a frozen pizza into her cart, she was going to earn everything he had offered her and then some.

Groceries in hand she hummed a popular tune as she made her way back out to her car. She set a pack of crackers and a couple slices of cheese along with a rather green banana on the passenger seat to eat on the drive back to the Burton farm.

Things were really looking up for her. She had managed to get everything on her list and still even had a little bit of cash for extra fuel or whatever she needed. Excitement once again soared at the thought of getting back to clean the rest of the house.

The red brick house beckoned to her from the distance and then opened its arms in welcome as she pulled into the drive. She couldn't keep the smile off her face as she quickly toted in her haul. Feeling more energized now that she had eaten, she made quick work of the kitchen, scrubbing out the old whining fridge before sweeping and mopping the dirty floor. Feeling pretty great about what she'd accomplished so far, she allowed herself a ten-minute break and walked out the back door to look at and then walk through the yard.

There was junk and trash everywhere, but she squealed in pleasure as she found an old boombox radio sitting there on an old tin shelf just under the porch roof.

Reaching for it, she used her sleeve to wipe a thick layer of dust and cobwebs off the top before taking it into the now shiny kitchen. With a little hop in her step, she used a damp cloth to wipe it clean before setting it on the gray, chipped countertop.

She crossed her fingers and plugged it in, then reached hopefully for the power button. A loud buzzing sound popped and she grinned while quickly turning the dial until she found a local radio station. She put her hands in the air in a V shape and said loudly, "And just like that we have jams." Just because she could, she pumped one fist in the air to the beat and laughed aloud. Then she reached out and cranked the volume up before she turned and got back to work. She did a little twirl and a prance as she made her way to the bathroom with a cleaning pail full of bleach water and a scrub brush.

"Who's Cinderella now?" she asked no one in particular as she hummed happily along to the lilting soft rock hit that rolled through the house. Yes, things were definitely looking up.

CHAPTER 8

While it took the rest of the afternoon to clean the main floor of the house to her satisfaction, Brooke enjoyed the hard work as well as the results. Feeling parched, she pulled out a plastic cup and filled it with water, draining it several times before once again turning of the faucet.

She took a moment to survey her surroundings and the shiny clean surfaces with satisfaction. Then she turned to take the stairs two at a time down to the basement. She looked around at the dusty space with a sigh, as exhaustion settled in. She would clean the washer and dryer room but leave the rest for another day. She pulled out clean-smelling bedding she had thrown in the washer earlier in the day and turned, bounding up the stairs two at a time. She dumped it all in a pile on top of the mattress that was now covered in a clean white protector. If she could get the last few things finished for tonight, she would give herself permission to crawl into bed and pass out.

She yawned and looked down at her wristwatch. It was only seven thirty in the evening, but she hadn't slept much the night before in her car and she was so tired it felt like midnight. Her legs burned as she once again hurried down the wide staircase with cleaning bucket in hand. She made quick work of the laundry room. She wiped down the walls and then did a thorough sweep and mop before finally allowing herself to be done.

She smiled tiredly. Now she would just make up the bed, have a quick and easy snack, and then go pass out for the night. The freshly scrubbed clawfoot tub materialized in her mind and she smiled. Stretching out in hot water sounded like heaven to her aching muscles. Feeling a little energized by that thought, she hurried through the motions of making the bed and then quickly unpacked her small duffel bag.

She really hadn't brought much with her, so that was painless. Most of the clothing she'd had at home was heavy and uncomfortable besides being outdated and ugly. With new beginnings in mind, she had only packed a few of her lightest shirts, a couple of her nicer skirts and the one pair of jeans she had managed to buy secondhand under the radar of her parents. She had only paid two dollars for them and they weren't exactly in style, but they were in her estimation better than another dress or skirt and blouse combo.

She owned one pair of jade-colored silk pajamas, which she had brought but had chosen to leave the large stack of floral-patterned, old-fashioned, long-sleeve flannel nightgowns. At least she'd had several pairs of decent underwear, which was nice since she wouldn't have to spend precious money on that anytime soon.

She was planning to eat before she showered but changed her mind as she caught a glimpse of one sparkling silver clawfoot as she walked toward the kitchen. She turned and started water running and then she grabbed the one towel she had brought along and a set of clean underwear before hurrying back into the now fresh, lemon-scented bathroom. She peeled the damp sweaty clothing from her body and stepped into the soothing heat. As she lowered herself into the steamy depths, she leaned her head back and closed her eyes.

She gave herself a five-minute respite before reaching for the bottle of coconut shampoo she had bought earlier today. It was a luxury she had only experienced a few times in her life as she hadn't been allowed store-bought shampoo by her parents. The sweet but refreshing scent of coconut teased her nostrils as she worked up a nice lather in her thick hair. It felt soft on her skin as she scrubbed first her hair and then the rest of her body. Her scalp felt soothed as she worked conditioner through the lengths and she reveled in the softness of her curls as she used a black pick comb to work the tangles from her tresses before standing in the shower to rinse the conditioner out. She had bought a small bottle of rose-scented bubble bath but was too tired to use it.

Instead, she turned off the water and reached for the towel. She first wrung out her hair and then systematically worked her way down to her feet. Feeling refreshed and clean, she slipped into clean underwear and gently slung the towel over the brushed nickel rack before turning to leave. She saw the dirty clothes on the floor but didn't know what to do with them yet so she kicked them into the corner. She would pick them up later when she found something to use for dirty laundry.

She made her way quietly to her bedroom and was just pulling her pajama top over her head when she heard a car pull up to the house. Heart beating a little erratically, she hurried to the front room to check that the lock was latched. She took a deep breath, willing herself to go look out the window to see who it was, but her bare feet felt rooted to the spot.

She stood completely still and listened silently as she heard a car door slam shut. She heard footfalls as someone walked quickly up the stairs. Panicked, she looked around the room for anything she could use as a weapon but saw nothing. There was a firm knock on the door and she swallowed the golf ball-sized lump in her throat.

Please, please don't let it be Cole, she prayed. Then she closed her eyes for a moment as if that would somehow add weight to the inner plea. She stood silent for a long moment before finally calling out, "Who is it?"

Ivan stood on the other side of the door waiting patiently for her to let him in. He looked at the door in deep thought as she called out. Out here in the countryside many of the local people didn't even bother locking their doors at night. Knowing instinctively that it was both locked and that she was afraid to open it without knowing who it was bothered him. He brushed off his concern. She had been raised in a very different environment than his own.

He forced a jovial grin and called out, "It's just me, Ivan." He felt a little better when she immediately unlocked and opened the door without any hesitation.

She was clean and rosy cheeked as she peered out at him. He stood holding a large bag in one hand and a wide grin. She stepped aside, "Come on in." She held the door wide and then closed it gently behind him as he stepped into the room. He watched as she locked the door quickly. She turned as she caught a scent of something that smelled delicious and looked at the bag he held as her tummy complained with a growl.

He chuckled. "Well, I *was* just going to ask if you got some dinner or if you're hungry, but I guess your growling stomach answers that."

Brooke took one tempting sniff before attempting to remind herself that she wasn't a charity case. She forced a serious look at him. "While that is very thoughtful of you, sir, as I told you before I really am quite capable of taking care of myself." She eyed the bag he was holding and wondered what on earth was inside that could smell so good.

Ivan, suddenly aware of the room stared in surprise at what he could see. He let out a slow whistle. "Wow, you have really been busy in here." He stepped around her to give himself a good view into the kitchen and smiled. "You've really cleaned this place up. To be honest, I was a little sad at the condition of the place earlier. Anne and I lived here for several years before we built the new house, you know, and it was sad to see it so worn out." He grinned at her and his brown eyes sparkled. "It really looks great now."

He didn't miss her gaze, which was still going back and forth between him to the pack of food he now had tucked under his arm. He tightened his lips and squared his jaw. "Well, since you don't want the dinner I brought over, I guess I'll just head back home now. I'm sure you're tired and the chickens will quite appreciate the food for a snack." He paused as he was turning toward the door again. "I just wanted to check in and see how you're settling in and make sure you don't need anything else tonight."

He reached for the knob and fought back the grin as her eyes were now watching the food intently. "It looks like you have everything under control here, so I'll just be on my way now."

She'd looked horrified at the chicken remark and now moved to stand directly in his path effectively blocking his exit. He cocked one eyebrow down at her in question, holding back laughter.

Brooke held out a tentative hand toward the package. "I guess if it's just extra anyway, then I could help you out with it." Then her bright gaze slid up to his and she saw the teasing twinkle in his eye. She groaned and then lightly slapped his arm. "That's not fair," she complained as she snatched the bag from his arm. "I'm actually really hungry and I was just going to make some dinner, but this smells so good I would hate for it to go to waste." She held it up to her nose and sniffed; her eyes rolled back and then closed blissfully. "What's in there anyway?"

He was grinning down at her with a cheerful but bemused expression. He handed the bag to her and then held up his hands in warning. "It's nothing fancy, mind you. Anne ended up working late at the clinic, so I fired up the grill and made dinner."

She eyed him with obvious dubiousness before turning to walk quickly into the kitchen. She was pulling out a paper plate and napkin as he walked in behind her. She graciously grabbed a second one of each and offered them to him. He smiled a little sheepishly and said, "I did throw in extra just in case." He gave her a little wink and turned to walk to the table.

Brooke laughed aloud at that, pausing by a cabinet to pull out a pair of shiny if slightly mismatched forks. "I'll just bet you did," she teased. She filled a cup with water for herself and then politely asked if he wanted a drink as well. He shook his head as he planted himself on one of the carved wooden chairs at the table. She walked over and sat across from him. Then she set the bag in front of her. She reached inside and pulled out a large blue Tupperware bin and opened the lid.

Her stomach growled as she stared inside. The two huge seasoned T-bone steaks were still steaming and her mouth watered. She grabbed one with a fork and plopped it onto her plate before reluctantly handing the container to him. There was a second Tupperware bin in the bag and she reached for it. Her eyes widened at the large stack of grilled, seasoned potatoes next to a giant heap of garlic and pepper salted garden green beans. She raised one auburn eyebrow at him. "Not fancy, huh? I'd like to know what you eat on a good day, sir."

Her petulant tone made him laugh and she smiled back at him across the table as she loaded a large helping of each thing onto her plate. Lucky for both of them their paper plates were already situated nicely on a flat service because she was positive they wouldn't have held up to the weight of the food otherwise.

She slid the remaining food across the table to him and caught him staring dumbfounded at her heaped plate. She sent him a sweet innocent smile and batted her lashes. "Well, I'm hungry," she defended unnecessarily.

Ivan looked into the container at the somewhat meager portions she'd left for him and sent her a look of complaint. "I see you left a little for me. Thanks," he grumbled as he dumped the remainder onto his own plate. He couldn't be mad when he saw the look of sheer pleasure on her face as she plopped a huge chunk of potato in her mouth.

Brooke chewed it up slowly and then looked innocently at him as she said, "Oh, I'm sorry. I just assumed you had already eaten." She gave a pointed look at his stomach.

They both laughed then. They talked as they ate. Mostly Ivan asked a lot of questions about her family and growing up. He wanted to know how things had been for her as a child. She seemed a little hesitant about the subject but answered him anyway. She told him about her mother more than anyone and he got the sense that Rebecca was possibly the only family member who had been kind to Brooke.

She asked about his family, curious how many of the stories she'd heard were true. She asked about his grandfather and Ivan smiled warmly before telling her several stories.

She had just put the last bite of potato in her mouth when he asked in a serious tone. "What made you decide to leave home?"

She choked on the potato and then reached for her water to take a long drink, stalling while trying to think of an easy way to tell him the truth without lying but also without giving too much away. Finally, she shrugged and said simply, "I have wanted to leave for a long time, but it can be very difficult to actually do it. It takes money and money is hard to come by." She wiped her mouth with the napkin and continued. "I was torn up for a long time about giving my soul to the devil by leaving and because of that, I tried desperately to stick it out for my family." When he raised an eyebrow at that, she said ruefully, "I guess I always would have left sooner or later anyway, but this time my father decided he was through putting effort into saving me." She looked away then. "He actually kicked me out." Her eyes were downcast as she admitted the last.

Ivan scooted his chair closer to hers and reached his hand out to gently lift her chin so that her eyes met his. "Are you more ashamed that your father kicked you out or that you didn't get to make that choice on your own?" He waited calmly but determinedly for her answer.

She shrugged and tears swarmed in her eyes, "Both I guess." She lifted one shoulder. "It's one thing for me to decide to lose my place in God's kingdom by leaving his chosen work, but it's another thing altogether to realize my father has so little respect and love for me that he deemed me unworthy of being part of God's kingdom." She took a drink of water to steady herself. "How I feel about that really doesn't matter, though, since I would have eventually left either way." She was staring down at the table again.

Ivan's voice was soft and a little dangerous as he asked, "Do you want to know what I think?"

He let the question hang in the air, forcing her to look up at him. She finally met his brown-eyed gaze and nodded.

"I think that you are beautiful, and strong, and proud." He waved a hand to encompass the house. "You are obviously a hard worker and I know you have integrity, otherwise you would have taken off by now." One side of his mouth turned up at her guilty nod of acknowledgment of that statement before he continued. "In my book you are an amazing young woman and I know my God would agree with me on that. I believe that God loves us all and I don't buy all that bullshit about hoops we all have to jump through in order for God to accept us. Acceptance is a huge part of what love is and without it, love is conditional."

He smiled gently then and stood. "Now, come over here and give me a hug. I can't stand watching you fight all that baggage and pain alone." He held his arms out in invitation. Brooke stood and rushed gratefully into them. He held her tightly for a long moment and then pulled back to look down at her. "You, Brooke Reynolds, are going to be okay," he said.

"I know because I am going to make sure of it," he added at her dubious expression. "You are going to start now to live your life and be happy as who you really are, not as who some pompous asshole of a man has dictated you should be. And dammit you are going to let me help you do just that, understand?" He reached down to tuck a loose curl behind her ear and then stepped back.

"Now, we aren't going to talk about you being unworthy or a lost cause anymore. We are, however, going to focus on what you want to do with your life and what you want to create going forward, okay?" He waited until she nodded in understanding. "If anyone from your family tries to give you any trouble, Brooke, you just let me know and I'll handle it." His tone was fierce and hard.

He walked over to the door then, but turned back to her. "It's late and I'm going to go and let you get some rest, but I really mean it, Brooke. If anyone gives you a hard time you just let me know." His jaw was tight as he gazed intently at her until she finally nodded.

She felt like she couldn't speak as emotion clogged her throat.

He opened the door and stepped out before turning back again. He reached into his front shirt pocket and pulled out a card holding it out to her. "By the way, I forgot to mention that I had the phone company turn the service back on here as I assumed you don't have a cell phone yet." He pointed to the bottom of the black card with gold trim lettering. "This has both my home phone number as well as my cell number on it. Don't hesitate to call me if you ever need anything. Even if it's just because you need to talk."

Brooke closed her fingers over the smooth card and squeezed as it brushed her palm. He had the door halfway closed when she whispered hoarsely, "Ivan?"

He stopped and turned back. Tears were burning her eyes and the back of her throat as she said quietly, "Thank you. You really can't understand how much this all means to me."

He nodded and gave her a warm grin before bounding down the stairs and trotting toward his truck. He was whistling a happy tune as he opened the door and slid inside. He glanced back to see her still standing in the doorway. She gave him a little wave before she went inside and closed the door.

Ivan swallowed the lump in his own throat as he drove back toward home. For a week that had started off somewhat boring with routine it had sure turned around today. He felt the gratitude of all the beauty and love that he had in this life as he rolled down his window to take in the cool refreshing countryside air.

He found himself suddenly excited to be home with Anne and showing her how much she meant to him. The diesel engine roared as his foot pressed harder on the pedal as he sped towards home.

After Ivan left, Brooke felt tied in knots. She cleaned up the kitchen and washed the few dishes they had used. Then she wandered aimlessly through the house thinking of all the things she wanted to do to make it feel like her own. She tried distracting herself with crafting ideas and plans for the house but eventually realized that she would have to face the thing she didn't want to think about.

Ivan had been proud of her. He even seemed to care about her for some unexpected reason. She thought of all the kind things he had told her and she smiled. The problem however, was that she couldn't stop wondering if he would still feel the same way if he knew the truth. That one simple question plagued her until she finally made herself brush her teeth and climb into her bed.

The last thing she thought before she finally lost her fight with fatigue was that she really did like his version of God much better than her family's. That thought made her a little giddy. Was it really possible that God could be a kind and loving being that supported her instead of judging her? She didn't know if that was true, but she really wanted to believe it. She was smiling as her heavy eyelids drifted closed.

Ivan however took much longer to fall sleep. He lay in the bed long after Anne had drifted off. Her anger at him was well deserved and they both knew it. He had apologized for blindsiding her with Brooke but not for wanting to help a young girl in need. Anne was still irritated at him but had at least acknowledged his apology.

She had then railed quietly at him for bringing a stranger into their home and offering for her to live with them without even having a conversation with her first. Anne was, after all, concerned with the impact it could have on their boys.

He had promised to make it up to her and apologized yet again for blindsiding her. Then he had taken just a moment to explain what he had felt when he saw Brooke sleeping in her car and how protective he had felt of her.

She was concerned he was being used and ruthlessly told him that Brooke was not his child and therefore not his responsibility.

He'd gone cold then. He'd looked soberly down at her and quietly disagreed. "That is where you are wrong, honey," he'd said. "She may not be my flesh and blood, but I will damned well give that girl a fighting chance in life."

Anne pulled back then and listened quietly. She had only seen this kind of stubborn, quiet power in her husband a few times in their thirty years of marriage and every time it had been a blessing. One of those times had been when he'd quit his job to help out his grandfather not long after they had been married. She had wanted to stay in their small house and keep their secure jobs. She thought now of everything they had gained as a result of that decision and decided that she was going to try to be on his side this time. She ran her fingers gently through his thick hair as he talked about Brooke.

She murmured the occasional agreement when it seemed appropriate. He looked up at her when he finished and she saw the quiet determined set of his jaw as he vowed, "I will do everything I can to protect that girl and help her get what she deserves." He'd paused then, "I won't involve you and the boys if that's your choice, but aside from that agreement, you won't change my mind on this, Anne."

Anne smiled at him then and held up both hands. "Whoa there, I'm unarmed, and I'm on your side," she'd joked. She watched as the tension seeped away at her words and she bent down and kissed his nose.

Ivan had wrapped her in a tight hug then and in a low emotion-choked voice said, "Thank you for understanding, Anne. It means the world to me that you trust me with this."

She didn't bother to tell him that she disagreed with his assessment of the situation. Instead, she leaned into his embrace and kissed him deeply.

Ivan spent the next hour proving to her just how much he loved her and appreciated her support. She fell asleep content in his arms.

He lay awake thinking about the steps he could and would take to ensure that Brooke would always have a safe place that she could call home. While she had never actually admitted as much, he was fairly certain that she had spent much of her life on edge and afraid of each moment.

She was jumpy and un-trusting at nineteen and it didn't take a genius to see that there was trauma there. His jaw tightened at the thought of anyone taking advantage of such a courageous, loving young girl and her overwhelming kindness and generosity. He smiled in the dark as he remembered Brooke smiling while talking to Ryker and Dominic, trying even in her own discomfort to put them at ease.

Yes, she most definitely deserved to have someone on her side for a change. He stared up at the shape of the ornate light fixture that hung from the ceiling above their bed and made a decision. Tomorrow he would schedule a meeting with his lawyers. Satisfied that he had the problem all worked out, he rolled over and gently tucked Anne into the strong curve of his body before wrapping one arm gently around her waist and fell asleep.

CHAPTER 9

Feeling excited and nervous about her new job, Brooke woke up at five thirty and couldn't go back to sleep. By six o'clock, she had her hair braided back, was dressed in a button-down plaid shirt and blue denim skirt and was ready to go. She took a few minutes to eat a quick bowl of oats, and an apple and then glanced at her watch. Time was crawling, so she decided she might as well work on cleaning up the basement for a while before work. By the time she had hauled all the garbage from downstairs outside, the blue garbage bin by the road was overflowing with junk. It took a good ten minutes just to clear all of the spiders and their sticky webs from every corner and crack of the downstairs rooms.

She shuddered as she nearly walked right into the giant cat-face spider just outside the shower stall. She squealed as she backed up a few steps and then squished it with the broom before she thought better of it. The popping sound along with the egg-like sludge that ran down the wall had nearly gagged her. She had closed her eyes as she used a paper towel to wipe the wall dry and then used so much bleach on the wall the paint had started coming off on her brush.

After scrubbing the shower, she had just enough time to put together a lunch for later before leaving. The banana, peanut butter and jelly sandwich and full bright pink water bottle she had bought yesterday would have to tide her over until she got off work tonight. Grabbing the camo-colored lunch bag she had bought at the hardware store the day before she threw everything inside and rushed to the door. Keys jangling in her hand, she took one last glance around the house that was just now beginning to feel like home and smiled.

Then she carefully locked the door before bounding down the stairs and to her car with a bounce in her stride.

All in all, she had done pretty good at distracting herself from thinking of Cole today until she started driving. Then her mind replayed every instant of the day before as though in slow motion. Groaning loudly, she rubbed an embarrassed hand over her eyes. Brooke remembered plastering her hot aching body to his and that strange throb between her legs came back. Suddenly feeling overwhelmingly hot, she cranked up the fan in her car. Then she said something that she had never before dared to say in her entire life: "Damn it all to hell." The worst part was that she meant every word.

The closer she got to the shop, the tighter her stomach had felt. She was terrified she was going to be forced to face Cole. Though she felt excited and nervous at the same time she really didn't want to see him. How could she ever explain to him why she had reacted the way she had?

Panic settled in her chest and she found herself breathing hard.

She went over and over it in her mind, searching furiously for an explanation that would somehow magically make him understand. She found none. Finally, she gulped and decided the best she could do was to muster up a heartfelt apology for slapping him that way. She did feel bad for that and it would be easy to be honest about.

Brooke squealed into the gravel lot a little faster than she had intended and parked her car next to the Burton's huge three-story shop at 7:45 on the dot. The morning sun was bright in the clear blue sky, making the whole world seem fresh. She tilted her head back on to the headrest as she sighed away her nervous butterflies. She had never had an actual job working for anyone besides her father and brothers and wasn't altogether sure exactly how it was supposed to work. She opened her eyes as she took a deep breath in through her nose. "Here goes nothing," she mumbled under her breath as she undid her buckle and slid out of the car.

She reached for her lunch bag and took a quick sip of water before taking a deep breath again to build up her resolve. She could do this, she promised herself as she turned and strode determinedly toward the black steel door.

The shop itself was a tan, three-story monstrosity that would easily fit two large tractors side by side through the oversized, garage-style roll-up doors. She could see Ivan's truck now, though it was parked on the other side of the shop. She squinted in the morning sun, trying to see if he was inside. It looked empty, so she turned and opened the door to the shop, walking quickly inside.

The shop was only semi-lit, and so she stopped just inside the door waiting impatiently for her eyes to adjust to the dark interior. Ahead she could see the outline of what seemed to be a tractor hooked up to a baler on one side, though her vision was still blurry enough she couldn't be sure. Directly ahead of her was a large empty slot. She turned around to curiously survey the rest of the shop as her eyes finally adjusted. There was a gigantic green combine ahead with the front blades lowered to sit against the concrete floor. There were several tool boxes lined up against one cream-and-grease-splotched wall and next to them was a wide metal staircase going up to what appeared to be a second-level landing.

She turned back and saw two figures standing next to the baler on one side. One was bent at the waist with his hand tucked behind the wheel on the shaft. She grinned; he was fixing a sheared pin. For the first time this morning, she felt calm seep in. She knew this world, had changed a million sheared pins on balers. The other man turned toward her and was now watching her curiously as she stepped closer.

Neither man was Ivan and she swallowed her relief as she realized it wasn't Cole either. One man stood about what she guessed was five eight and the other was maybe even shorter than the first. She smiled at the man and then gave a quick nod of her head before turning to look around again. She wasn't sure exactly where Ivan had meant to meet with her. Not finding anyone else in the shop, she turned back toward the two men intending to ask them for directions. She nearly punched one of them in the face as he had somehow snuck up on her when she'd had her back turned. Her fist waved wildly in the air for a long moment before her brain caught up and she dropped it to her side.

He looked a little surprised, so she smiled. "I'm so sorry. You startled me, sir."

The man who she could clearly see now, was Hispanic with dark black hair, brown eyes, and a darkly tanned complexion. He looked at her hand and then at her face as a warm grin cracked his narrow lips.

He held out his hand and looked apologetic. "I'm sorry, I didn't mean to scare you, miss. I'm Luis." He spoke English with a heavy Spanish accent, which was a little hard to understand. He openly eyed her red hair with appreciation and smiled as he looked curiously at the blouse and skirt she wore. He shrugged and gave her a toothy grin as she shook his hand. "Mr. Ivan said you were coming and asked us to take you to his office when you got here." She caught barely enough of what he was saying to understand before he turned and walked away. "You follow me."

"Thank you," Brooke murmured as they walked across the shop and toward another door on the opposite side of the building that the tools were on. Silence stretched awkwardly between them, so she offered in a friendly tone. "I'm Brooke Reynolds, by the way. I'm new and just starting today."

He turned back to her with a flirty smile. "We are happy to have you here, Brooke. The men will enjoy a pretty face around here."

Brooke flushed slightly before meeting his eyes and smiling. "I'm sure" was all she could think to mutter in reply.

"Now, now, Luis, don't be teasing the young lady too much," Ivan chided with a grin as he opened the door in front of them and held it wide. He chuckled at Luis's look of concern before turning to give her a welcoming smile. "Good. You made it," he stated aloud. Then he turned back to Luis and said something in Spanish.

Luis nodded in agreement and then with a quick wave and a toothy grin in her direction, turned on his heel and headed back across the shop.

Ivan held the door until she walked through it. "The offices are all on this side of the shop," he informed in a steady voice. "Come on, I'll show you up to my office and you can fill out some quick paperwork before we get started for the day." She followed him into what appeared to be a large reception area and to their left Brooke saw a set of double glass doors that led outside. She raised one eyebrow as she took in the long rectangular room, which was painted a light gray with white trim. It looked modern and warm at the same time. Off to one side was a wall-to-wall painting of the valley near sunset with the mountains rising up in jagged lines in the distance.

On the other side was a tall granite counter that acted as a reception desk with a large clock on the wall behind it and several photos of growing fields. For the first time since entering, Brooke noticed the older woman seated on the other side of the counter and she started slightly.

The woman's fingers flew across the keyboard decisively for a long minute before she finally looked up. She smiled warmly at them and her gray eyes sparkled as she reached down and then held out a clipboard.

Ivan stepped over and took it from her as he introduced them. "Maude this is Brooke Reynolds. She's the one I mentioned will be starting today."

Maude laughed as she gave a pointed look at the clipboard he had just taken from her. "I figured as much," she said. She turned and gave Brooke a bright smile before saying jokingly, "It's a real pleasure to meet you, Brooke. God knows I am thrilled to have another female around this place."

She shook a finger at Ivan for just a minute as though scolding him. "Don't get me wrong I love working with all the big strong men we have around here and it is definitely quite handy when I need things moved around, but you know how it is. It just isn't the same as having someone who can keep up with a little stimulating and intelligent conversation." She gave Brooke a conspirator's wink that immediately made her feel warm inside.

Brooke couldn't help the smile that showed her dimple off to perfection. "I think I'm going to like you," she said honestly.

Ivan snorted at Maude and with one brow up, asked, "Is stimulating and intelligent what you ladies are calling gossip these days?"

Maude brushed off his attitude with a quick wave. "A little healthy gossip can be good for the soul." She turned to Brooke, then, "Don't you agree, honey?"

Brooke's smile widened. Though she didn't have a clue *how* to gossip, she couldn't help but side with those sparkling gray eyes. "I do look forward to such stimulating conversations," she said.

Both women laughed at Ivan's pained groan. He reached out with an exaggerated grip and tugged on Brooke's wrist. "Let's get you out of here before Maude is a bad influence on you."

Brooke threw an apologetic look over her shoulder, which only met with Maude's tinkling laughter as she was pulled firmly down a wide hallway.

Maude called out, "Don't worry, I'll catch you later, Brooke."

Brooke laughed and couldn't help noticing that Ivan picked up speed at the implied threat. When he turned to grin back at her and relax his pace, she returned it with a wide, dimpled smile.

He released her arm as they followed a long hallway with several closed doors before finally turning the corner to climb a wide sweeping staircase that took them up to the next level. She was curiously taking in the surroundings from various framed photos of working crews in fields to a gorgeous carved wooden emblem that stated The Burton Farms and Co. There was a photo of a large crew around spud equipment and a golden wheat field with five combines lined up with neat rows of straw behind them.

It was obvious to her that Ivan Burton took great pride in the empire that he had built. That pride somehow made Brooke feel safe and content. She found the nervousness gone to be replaced with excitement at how she could be a part of something to be proud of.

Ivan's office was a large square room with a huge window that looked out over the parking lot and then the fields beyond. There was a wide mahogany desk with a comfortable-looking black leather chair behind it. In front of the desk were three black leather armchairs and he invited her to sit.

She filled out paperwork as Ivan went over relevant safety issues and the procedures of the farm itself. He deftly explained protocol and what she was to do if she needed help with anything. Unlike most of the employees who had a crew chief to answer to, she would be reporting directly to him so he could track her progress.

He informed her that on occasion, however, he would send her out to work with a crew and when that happened, she would simply get help from the crew chief on the job. They spent nearly an hour talking about what she was proficient with before he told her that he was going to send her out to run one of the swathers for the day. It was something she had done often for her family and they needed more drivers.

She followed him outside to his truck once again nervously watching for Cole as they went. All the stress and worry she was putting herself through was for naught, however, as he was nowhere in sight.

She saw a tall dark-haired man climb out of a jeep and recognition tingled along her spine. She remembered seeing him somewhere, though she couldn't remember when. He walked toward them with an easy long-legged stride and a smile that lit his green eyes. He studied her with interest as she stood next to Ivan.

He hooked his thumbs in his pockets and grinned as he reached them. "Mornin', Dad," he said in greeting and suddenly Brooke remembered the picture she had seen of him in the Burton home.

Ivan smiled and held out a hand to squeeze his shoulder. "Morning, Jacob," he answered before he turned to face Brooke. "This is my son Jacob."

Brooke smiled and held out a hand. "Hello, Jacob, it's nice to meet you."

His green eyes warmed at her smile. "And you must be the infamous woman everyone was talking about at dinner last night," he drawled in a lazy tone.

Brooke glanced uncertainly at Ivan for a quick moment. "I'm Brooke" was all she said.

He was strikingly handsome with dark hair and a charismatic smile. His green eyes were inviting and intriguing at once and she liked him instantly. He didn't appear to be judging her, which was a great start and he smiled warmly as he shook her hand. "It's great to meet you too."

Ivan had already told her that Jacob was running the swathing crew for the day. She squinted up at him. "I guess I'll be working with you today."

It sounded like a question, so he nodded. "Yippers, we've been shorthanded this spring and Dad figured you probably had experience, so it would help out a lot if you can."

With introductions complete, Ivan turned and with a smile and a wave, walked back inside. Brooke turned to Jacob. "Okay, boss, what should I do next?"

He laughed out loud. "First of all, none of this boss business." He gave her a quick wink. "I like things a little more subtle." He turned serious then. "I already have most of the crew out there going, so we just need to go join them." He started walking away, so she followed. Jacob turned to look down at her. "We already moved all the equipment out there yesterday, so if you want to just jump in with me, that would be great."

Brooke hesitated momentarily before nodding at him. "That's fine but can you wait for just a minute while I grab my bag from the car?"

"I'll just pull around there and pick you up," he agreed cheerfully as he hopped up into his jeep. Brooke turned and jogged quickly around the shop and reached in to grab her lunchbox. She stuck her keys in the bag and carefully locked her car before turning back to get in his jeep.

Jacob informed her conversationally that he wanted to get the field done before they quit for the night. Brooke only smiled and nodded her agreement. He asked politely if she was settling in okay and then told her it could be pretty late when they finished.

Brooke turned and met his gaze for a moment as they drove. "Late is fine. I don't have anything pressing to do."

He parked on a corner near two still swathers and they walked together toward the equipment. "So, if you just follow me, you'll get the hang of it in no time," he assured her as he stepped up to one machine and then watched as she walked confidently to the other. He waited until he heard her machine start up before starting his own. With a little wave, they were off.

The field had an irrigation pivot on it, so they swathed in circles following the tire tracks. Brooke had obviously done this many times before as she followed behind and kept pace with him with no trouble.

They soon caught up to the other operators and all worked in unison.

Around one o'clock, Brooke saw a green car pull into the field next to Jacob's jeep and she watched curiously to see who it was. She held her breath a little as they came to the end of the field by the car. A plump dark-haired woman climbed out and then began unloading boxes. Brooke relaxed as soon as she saw that it wasn't Cole.

The drivers all followed Jacob's lead, finishing the row they were on before stopping one by one at the end of the field. Since she was the last one in the line now, the woman had already left by the time she pulled up and shut down her machine. She opened the door as Jacob came jogging over with an armload. He deftly climbed the small steps and held the plastic container out to her.

Brooke stared at his hand. "What is that?"

Jacob grinned happily. "Lunch is here." When she stared wide-eyed for a second, he added, "That was Isabel. She's Luis's wife and her and some of the other women take turns cooking meals for the crews."

"It's a way for them to make a little extra money as well."

He looked down at the container for a minute. "Looks like it's chicken enchiladas today." He smacked his lips hungrily. "I will say that Isabel's enchiladas are the best." He looked up at her for a moment. "She's used to packing enough for us big men so if you're not hungry or if it's too much for you to eat, I'd be happy to help you out."

Brooke shook her head and held the container behind her back. "I'm starving. I packed a banana and a sandwich, but I ate them hours ago." She smiled, amused as his hopeful expression faded. *Like father, like son,* she quoted in her head. Then she opened the lid to take a tentative sniff of the gooey, cheesy food inside. She'd never had enchiladas, but they smelled great.

He motioned to the other workers with one hand as he jumped down off the steps and said, "We'll all be taking a half-hour break to eat our lunch and then we'll get back to work." He started to walk away but turned back to pull an icy-looking cola out of his back pocket. His green eyes twinkled mischievously as he asked, "I guess you'll also be wanting this too, then?"

Brooke couldn't stop the laughter that tinkled out at his dramatically disappointed smile. "I'm sorry, but yes," she said as she jumped down to swipe it quickly from his hand before he could change his mind.

He laughed in good nature and with a wave, turned to walk off.

Brooke rubbed a hand against the sore small of her back trying to rub the tension out. Her muscles ached in response to her stretch and she moaned aloud. She wasn't ready to get back into the swather, so she walked around to a shady spot on the other side of the equipment. She leaned against the tire and crossed her legs at the ankles as she popped the cola open and took a swig.

Jacob came walking around to grin at her as he leaned back against the rear of the hopper. "I figured I may as well come keep you company," he said cheerfully as he stuck in his fork and came out with a huge bite. He followed the bite with a chug of his own opened can of soda. She was staring at him as he took another bite, so he shrugged. "I mean I'm totally fine over there by myself, but I wouldn't want you to get lonely over here in the shade."

She smiled at him. "Is that so? And am I to just take your word for it?"

He winked and shoveled another chunk of chicken filled corn tortilla into his open mouth. "How old are you anyway?" he asked without missing a beat and Brooke blinked.

"Nineteen," she said without any emotion.

He stopped eating just long enough to smile.

Brooke set down her fork. "How old are you?" she challenged in return.

He looked at her then as though to measure her reaction. "Twenty-three."

She nodded and quickly calculated how old that might make Cole. She wanted to ask him just that but before she could get herself in trouble, she shoved another bite of food in her mouth and followed it with cold soda. But that little insistent curious part wouldn't shut up and before she could stop herself, she blurted, "So that makes Cole, like, twenty-one?"

He stopped chewing and met her gaze, holding it for a moment before reluctantly nodding. He swallowed hard. "I take it you met him, then?" It was a statement more than a question but she answered anyway.

"Yes, I did. I met him at breakfast yesterday." She didn't mention that she had also seen him much later that day.

Jacob nodded and sighed, sounding a little disappointed. "I normally would have been there, but I was out really late the night before baling hay, so I slept in." He looked over at her. "I hope he was nice to you."

Brooke shrugged, thinking back for a long moment before finally replying vaguely, "He wasn't not nice."

Jacob laughed out loud. "That is a rather clever way to put it." His eyes twinkled green lights in that way he had and he said, "It sounds exactly like my brother." He shook his head in wonder. "All the ladies seem to flock to him and the best he can do is not be not nice." He glanced at his empty takeaway container with a frown and then looked at his watch. He wiped a hand across his mouth and straightened up. "You'd better hurry and eat that food before I decide to finish it for you." He took a threatening step toward her.

Brooke licked her lips and grinned. "What food?" she asked pleasantly.

Jacob looked down at her empty dish and then his gaze swung back up in astonishment. Despite her assurance that she was hungry, he really hadn't thought she would finish it all.

He frowned. "I only saw you take one bite," he whined in complaint.

Brooke laughed. "I told you I was hungry."

An appreciative smile broke through his disappointment. "I have never seen a girl eat like that." He met her blue gaze directly. "Especially not one as pretty as you." He bumped her shoulder with his own playfully. "I might just have to keep you around. Respect." He tugged on her long braid teasingly before he turned away. "I guess we'd better get back to work, then." He turned and gave her a little bow from the waist, then turned on his heel and strode off.

Brooke just stared silently after him. She couldn't think of a single comeback.

CHAPTER 10

The next three weeks flew by in a blur for Brooke. Despite her constant nerves when she thought of running into Cole, she showed up to work every day and went wherever Ivan instructed. Her concern, however, was unnecessary as she hadn't seen any sign of him since that first day. She knew he was around as Jacob and Ivan had mentioned him upon occasion.

By the second week, she was fully convinced that he was avoiding her and though she really did want to apologize to him she was also somewhat relieved at the end of each day as she drove home. She thought about hunting him down but instead used the excuse of exhaustion each day to give herself an out.

She spent most of the long days in the fields swathing alfalfa or running a planter alongside Jacob. When they weren't running all day, they spent the nighttime baling the hay they had swathed days before. She was really beginning to like Jacob and his easygoing manner. She spent so many days and nights working side by side with him that it had become obvious that he was interested in her. Though she thought of Cole, she found herself wondering about him as well. He was kind and fun and Brooke felt, for the first time in her life that he genuinely liked her for herself. That feeling was so new she couldn't help wondering about the possibility of more.

She often rode with him back and forth to job sites, and they flirted and joked around with each other easily. With Jacob it was easy and by the second week, she felt like they were fast friends. She learned from Jacob that he was only home from school for a few months out of the year, which he spent helping out his father who, it seemed, always needed all the help he could get. The problem Jacob told her in a cheerful voice was that whenever they finally got enough employees to handle all the work, Ivan expanded the business again.

Jacob, however, was in law school somewhere in California but flew into the nearest airport every chance he got to see his family.

Brooke found herself wondering if Cole also went to school, but after Jacob's reaction when she'd asked his age, she didn't want to ask. Jacob, she knew had already sensed that there might be something going on between her and Cole. The fact that Cole hadn't shown his face again since, had her questioning if she hadn't imagined the whole thing anyway. It obviously hadn't meant anything to Cole so she didn't want to add anything and make things awkward with Jacob as well.

Jacob actually seemed to like to talk to her and she felt the same way with him. He shared his plan to get his law degree and then come back home to the valley and open a small local practice. It was so far to drive into town for all the local farmers and small business owners and he thought it would be nice to have someone local that could handle their legal matters so they didn't all have to make the long drive into town every time they needed a legal document.

Jacob also told her that it was one of the only areas that he had felt he could actually be of help to his dad and he was genuinely interested in the law, so it worked well. The Burton farm and family paid a small fortune to keep a small firm in town on retainer. If he took over property purchases and all of their legal work, he could save his family a hefty amount in fees.

Jacob's openness and willingness to share in turn gave her the courage to talk to him. She shared her dream of creating a life free of the religious confines of her childhood. Brooke had often dreamed of a life without oppression, a life that was instead filled with laughter and love and choices made freely only because she wanted to do it. There was an obvious cultural difference between them and yet it didn't seem to matter. All that mattered to him was that she was happy and that she was excited about the life she was creating for herself.

He was constantly plying her with questions about her family. It was a subject she still had a hard time discussing, so she would pause, thinking deeply about her responses before answering.

She never complained, though, not even as she would talk of her father's cold disappointment in her. Or his temper at her not being exactly what he had demanded she be. When she talked of her siblings, she always turned sad. She shared that it had always felt like they distanced themselves from her because they didn't want to be tainted by her imperfection by association.

Occasionally he would reach out a hand and squeeze her shoulder in an effort to give comfort. More often, though, he would just tug her long braid and say, "You're all right, Brookie. In fact, I happen to think you are quite spectacular." He was the only person she had known that used a nickname for her, and though it felt special somehow, she felt the need to give him a narrow-eyed glare without true malice.

By her third week with the Burtons, she realized somewhat in surprise that he had somehow quietly become her best friend. After a particularly long and heartfelt conversation, she looked up at him, her expression solemn and said, "Thank you, Jacob." When he simply raised one eyebrow in question, she had been overwhelmed and looked away before forcing herself to meet his green gaze once again, "Thank you for being my very first friend."

His face warmed slightly, but he smiled. "It's absolutely my pleasure, Brooke." Then he gave her a mock bow and his eyes twinkled as he reached out to once again tug her braid. Looking more serious then, he held her gaze. "Thank you too. I have a lot of friends. Most of them are pretty great, but there is something really special here with you. I feel like everything that seems normal to me is like this big exciting adventure to you. You make the world seem bigger and brighter than anyone I have known and it gives me a fresh sense of gratitude for the abundance I've had my entire life."

Brooke smiled. "Your family has so much, but I'd also say that you all deserve it. You are such amazing people."

Jacob didn't try to kiss her, though he thought about it every time he felt the warmth between them. She was a bit younger than him and he still wasn't sure how she felt about that. Hell, he wasn't sure how he felt about that. He sensed in his gut that what she needed more than anything right now was a friend and he let that be enough. He had also recently realized just how much he valued their friendship as well.

She was an intelligent and dedicated worker. She never complained no matter how long the work days were. She worked nights without hesitation when the need arose and always pushed through 'til the job was complete.

Through it all she ate. She ate everything she packed into her lunchbox at the start of the day and then again, every bite offered to her by the three women that brought food out to the crew on most days. Jacob found himself staring in awe as she quickly and efficiently put away meal after meal. He finally joked that they might have to start deducting meals out of her paycheck just to keep up, but she had only smiled around a large bite of her burger. "That's fine," she agreed cheerfully. She paused with a bite halfway to her mouth. "It would be well worth it and I'd be more than happy to pay for good cooking."

Jacob had been unable to stop himself from reaching out to wipe a small splotch of ketchup off the corner of her lips. He'd given her a wide goofy grin. Her generosity constantly took him by surprise, so he raised his hands in the air. "I'm only joking, Brookie, you eat the same as all of us. It's just that you are so much smaller that I don't know how you fit it all inside there." He pointed to her flat stomach. "Don't tell Dad I joked about this, though, or he'll have my hide. He already complains constantly about how he feels like he's taking advantage of you with all the things you insist on paying him for."

Brooke looked surprised and then smiled grudgingly. "If it was up to him, he would just be giving me everything and taking nothing in return." She felt like she and Ivan were constantly bickering over money, so she understood Jacob's position.

Summer bloomed early with scorching heat during the day and the long cool nights were a peaceful welcome to the afternoon heat. Every spare moment she had was spent fixing up the old house. She repainted the main level of the house one room at a time. The kitchen she painted a cool blue that made the natural-colored oak shine in contrast. In the front room, she opted for a brighter cream color that felt warm and welcoming every time she walked through the door. In the bathroom she sponged on a blue and sea green, which made the walls shimmer against the bright white of the tub and fixtures. She added a painting of a dolphin encased in an elegant white frame that she hadn't been able to resist buying at a discount store in town. Her bedroom, she painted a very light and warm indigo because she had never really got the chance to have feminine things around her, added some white, purple, and yellow flowers encased in a delicately swirled white vase. She bought a brightly colored white, pink, and purple floral quilt that made her feel beautiful just by laying on it.

For the spare bedroom, she picked a creamy golden yellow that brought out the orange peel texture on the walls. Though she didn't know if she would ever have a guest, she painted it and bought a gray comforter that warmed up the room so it would feel clean and inviting.

Once she was satisfied with the way the upstairs felt, she'd started on the yard. The house itself was situated on a five-acre rectangular section of land. There was a large section at the back of the lot that was long since overgrown with willow trees and kochia weeds and splotched with flowered alfalfa plants. Directly behind the house was a large rectangular section that had been planted with grass at some point in the years past. Though overgrown, it looked thick and healthy. At the far corner of the rectangular yard was an old shed, which she opened to discover an old lawn mower, weed wacker, and a small but handy rototiller. There was also a whole variety of shovels, rakes, and hoes. Excited, she pulled out the mower, but it was out of fuel. She found a fuel can and drove to the nearest station to fill it. She fueled it and checked the oil, which was topped off before trying to start it. It took her several pulls of the cord and priming the pump an excessive amount before she finally got it started. Once it was running, it worked like a champ, though, so she didn't worry about it.

She mowed the grass and used a weed wacker to trim the edges. She started pulling weeds that had overgrown an oval section and discovered what looked like it may have once been a flower garden with a few loose rocks scattered around the edge. Heart pumping with excitement, she dug out the rest of the weeds and crabgrass and then drove happily into town to buy some flowers. She picked yellow and orange marigolds, purple, white, and pink petunias, and bright red lilies. By the time she checked out, her cart was overloaded and she grinned at the cashier who commented that Brooke was buying them out.

It took less time to plant them than it had to drive into town so by early afternoon she was finished and stood back with a water bottle in hand as she contentedly surveyed the results. It really was pretty, she decided with a happy grin. Daylight was going to run out eventually, so she turned back to the section of the yard still covered in weeds. She took a long drink of water and went back to work.

She was gradually weeding back the section of the yard just in front of the overgrown lilac and rose bushes that lined the back of the yard like a fence. Finally, too tired to keep going, she went inside to make some dinner.

The following morning, she hurried back out after a quick breakfast. She wanted to get the backyard done today as it was her last day off. She found old raspberry bushes and strawberry plants that had miraculously survived the weeds whose only goal appeared to be trying to choke them out and did a little happy dance. She cleared around them gently, giving them plenty of room to grow and breathe. She could see only a few berries beginning to grow on the vines but knew with some care, they would soon produce plenty of fresh fruit.

Finding the berries and the garden spot inspired her and she asked Ivan once again for the following weekend off work. Saturday morning bloomed warm and dry as she made the long drive into town and went to one of the local nurseries looking for seeds and garden plants.

Guilt tickled at her sensible nature at the thought of all the money she was spending, but she told herself that growing a garden would pay for itself in the long run. That helped a little, though it didn't entirely squash the tiny twinge of guilt she felt at spending more than half of her last paycheck.

The spending wasn't over, however, for as she was leaving the nursery, she saw a classy handmade whitewashed wooden picnic table that she imagined sitting at out in the backyard in the evening and couldn't resist buying it. She couldn't haul it in her car but would check with Ivan about borrowing one of the farm trucks to pick it up. She was confident that Ivan would agree to it, so she promised to come back the next day to pick it up. The nursery owner was thrilled at the sale and quickly agreed with a smile as she placed a sold sticker on top of the table.

After loading the plants and bags into her trunk, she slid into her car and started the engine. Wanting to make sure she had a way to pick up the table, she reached for the cell phone that Ivan had given her weeks ago. She looked up his number to call him and ask for the use of a truck. Tomorrow was Sunday and she knew most of the workers were off, so there should be several company trucks parked unused at the shop.

She got Ivan's voicemail and groaned before leaving a quick message. She would call him later if he didn't get back to her, but right now she was anxious to get her garden planted. She drove past a grocery store and pulled in to the lot with a heavy frown.

It had been well over a month since she'd started working for the Burtons. In that time, she hadn't had a period at all. She had found herself constantly worried though she prayed each time that it was the dramatic change in her routine that had held it at bay. With growing concern, she'd waited patiently for it to come to no avail. She had begun to fear the worst the last few days and with a heavy sigh she went into the store to pick up a home pregnancy test. She said a quick little prayer that she wouldn't actually have to use it when she got her period and shoved it into the glove box out of sight before driving home.

It took her the rest of the day to plant everything, but it was well worth it when she finally stepped back to look at the garden. She'd planted several tomato and pepper plants on one side. Across the back, she seeded in several rows of sweet corn and then two rows of potatoes in front of them. She was hoping to be able to put some corn up in the fall. On the other side of the tomatoes and peppers she planted squash, cucumbers, and green beans. Then through the center where there was a little shade from a tall willow tree that stood behind the roses, she planted long rows of lettuce, spinach, carrots, peas, and a short row of beets. The garden already looked so good, she joyfully thought of how great it would look in the following months. She turned on the heavy-duty sprinkler before she went into the house and got a large glass of lemonade she had left sitting in the refrigerator.

Humming as she walked back outside, she reached for her cell. Just as she'd suspected she had missed a call and now had a text from Ivan.

Got your message.

The truck is a go.

You're welcome to either of the ones by the shop

You know where the keys are.

She read it and smiled while using her thumbs to type a quick message back.

Thanks. You're a life saver.

I really appreciate it and if you want to take rent out of my check, I'm good with it.

Brooke knew before he even responded that he would refuse, but she had to try. She was constantly haggling him about taking more money from her and he would always respond by threatening to pay her more than she was already making.

He had in fact already insisted on giving her a raise after her first two weeks here. He insisted vehemently that her trial period was over and that she was already becoming one of his best employees. She'd given in and agreed but only when he threatened to keep raising her wage every time she gave him another argument. Her mouth had closed midargument and he'd grinned in victory.

It wasn't yet fully dark, so Brooke ate a quick sandwich with the lemonade and then hurried back outside determined to get the front lawn mowed while she could still see. Even though she rushed, she could barely see a few feet in front of her feet as she pushed the trusty lawnmower into the tool shed and then gathered up all the other tools she'd used that day and put them away. She closed up the shed and latched it carefully before walking tiredly into the house wanting nothing more than a good meal and a hot shower to wash away the dirt and sweat of the day.

She opted for the shower first and quickly slid out of her jeans and pulled the short-sleeved shirt over her head. She undid the clasp of her new lacy black bra and stretched her arms up with a loud yawn as it slid to the floor. God she was exhausted. She stepped under that hot spray and took her time with a long luxurious shower.

Feeling a little refreshed she stepped out and wrapped one towel around her hair, then set it on top of her head. She reached for a second towel and wrapped it around to secure it snugly just above her breasts. She rubbed a citrus scented lotion into her arms and legs as it seemed to make a difference with her light skin in the bright sun. She looked at herself critically in the mirror for a moment. She wondered and not for the first time if she should start wearing makeup and cut her hair. It sounded fun, but in all honesty, she just didn't have a clue where to start. She squinted at her reflection and made a decision. Tomorrow she would go buy some makeup while she was in town picking up her new table.

Feeling better about it, she opened the bathroom door and stepped out into the hall. There was a loud knock that sounded like it was coming from the front door and she froze. Fear slid into her belly as she remembered unlocking the front door earlier but didn't remember locking it again when she came in.

She glanced uncertainly down the hall as indecision slid across her face. Should she rush to the door and lock it or should she go straight into the bedroom and quickly get dressed first. She took two steps toward the door when she heard it open. Her throat closed and she froze as panic rode a wave all the way down her spine. She didn't even realize she had stopped breathing until she heard Jacob's warm voice. "Yo, Brooke? Are you home?"

Air swooshed back into her lungs and she turned tail ready to beeline it to the bedroom as she called out in answer. "Yes. Just a second. I'll be out in a minute." Her voice sounded a bit raspy and low and she fought back a cough. She was only halfway down the hall when she felt eyes on her back and swung back around to look behind her.

Eyes wide, she stared in embarrassment at Jacob who had come striding around the corner and then skidded to a quick stop while looking her up and down. Her eyes were round and she looked a little nervous.

He took in the towel, the fear that was written across her face, and the deep red blush that was creeping slowly up her neck and made a split-second decision. He gave her a purposely vacant but friendly smile and held his gaze on her eyes as he said cordially, "Well, I guess you didn't get my message after all."

She relaxed though only a little and he grinned. "Either that or you *did* get my message and are now trying to subtly tell me you want me." He wriggled his eyebrows in obvious exaggeration.

She relaxed her shoulders as her moist pink lips curved into a reluctant smile. "Don't tease me, you brat. And no, I obviously didn't get your message." She looked down at her towel pointedly, "Let me throw some clothes on quick and I'll be right back out." She turned and darted quickly into the bedroom, closing the door behind her with a definitive click.

Jacob grinned and mentally patted himself on the back for the depth of his integrity as he forced himself to turn around and walk away and into the kitchen. In fact, he was practically a saint, he thought with a little shrug. It had taken all of his willpower not wonder what exactly was under that towel as he watched her walk away. He was, after all, a man and Brooke Reynolds was not exactly unattractive.

Brooke forced herself to breathe even as she rushed about pulling out clothing items she would need. She had always been a fast dresser, but she wasn't sure she had ever thrown on clothes as quickly as she did now. Once fully covered in her green, full-length pajamas, she relaxed and pulled the towel from her head, shaking her curls to fall down her back. She tried to run her fingers through the wet curls but the tangles stopped them. With an impatient sigh, she grabbed a brush and started working it vigorously threw through the stubborn lengths until it ran freely from top to bottom without complaining. She glanced in the mirror she had placed above the long dresser and shrugged. There wasn't much else she could do. This was as good as it was getting for now and at least she was fully clothed.

She squared her shoulders and took a breath for courage as she went out to see what Jacob needed. She vowed to herself not to act embarrassed when she saw him again.

He made it easy for her. He was coming through the front door with an arm full of stuff when she entered from the hallway. She stared at him as though he had two heads.

He only grinned at her and winked.

She frowned. "What is all this?" she asked grumpily.

Jacob pointed one shoulder toward her back. "It goes with that," he said cheerfully as he shouldered his way past. She turned and was now gawking at the room. The brown suede couch that occupied the side of the room by the door had been moved as well as the old green recliner that had been against the wall across the room.

The chair was now next to the couch and in its place was a long brown table and a huge flat screen television.

Hands on her hips she turned to glare up at him. "Where on earth did that come from and why'd you move my chair?"

He set his armful down on the chair with a laugh. "So, I guess asking for your help is out of the question then?"

She stared critically at the chair he had moved to the end of the space in order to make room for the gigantic screen against the wall. "I'm not sure that's the best place for that."

He lifted one shoulder in a shrug and then grinned. "Well, I brought you a gift," he declared confidently. Her frown lines deepened and knowing she was going to have a fit, he rushed. "You can't be my friend and not have a flat screen to watch movies and television, Brookie."

She looked at the flat screen and then at him as one brow went up. "Fine," she said sweetly. "Just no sports." She fought back a grin as his face fell. When even his eyes looked sad, she laughed. "Just as I suspected. You're looking for a place to hang out and watch football, aren't you?"

He smiled wryly. "Only once in a while. We can watch movies and stuff too, though," he mumbled." Then he looked hopeful. "But maybe every once in a while, I can pop over and watch a game or two on Sunday?"

His face lit up a little at the last and she didn't have the heart to say no. Instead, she walked over to him and punched him lightly on the arm. "Maybe every once in a while," she agreed good-naturedly.

"It's a date," he said casually and then turned suddenly. "Hey, I forgot, I actually brought dinner over too." He grinned as her face lit up. He bumped her shoulder with his own. "I already ate, but I know how hungry you always are. Mom made this great pasta with garden vegetables and chicken tonight." He licked his lips. "It was scrumptious."

He lifted a large reusable bag from the top of the pile he'd dumped on her couch and held it out like a peace offering.

Brooke grinned. He could bring her a peace offering anytime he wanted. She gazed down into the bag happily and then her gaze flew back to his, suspicious now. There was an awful lot of food in that bag for one person.

He only smiled back at her and offered magnanimously, "If you go warm up the food, I'll get this thing up and running in no time at all." He waved a hand behind them. "With a little luck we can even watch a movie tonight." He rummaged through the pile. "I brought a jet pack here with me so we'll have internet right away, but you might want to eventually have it run right to the house. You'll get better service that way." She stared at him and the pile like he was from Mars and that great stack behind him was his spaceship.

She had no clue what a jet pack was, did in fact know very little about the internet itself. She now knew that she could type whatever she wanted into the search bar on her phone and it magically searched some invisible storage device for the information and then, voilà, gave it to her. How it worked and what kind she had was beyond her scope of knowledge, but he didn't need to know that. She turned as her tummy grumbled at the scent of the delicious-smelling food.

She made it around the corner before his words penetrated her ears. "I'm fine with a smaller portion by the way."

Brooke turned back and stuck her head around the corner to glare at him for a moment. "I thought you said you ate already," she muttered grumpily under her breath. He didn't respond, so she rolled her eyes dramatically and turned back toward the kitchen.

He grinned at her back. "I can always eat again," he offered as the aroma of fresh garlic and herbs filled the house. "Besides I wouldn't want you to feel rude or anything for eating in front of a guest."

He could hear her muttering something under her breath that didn't sound pretty and he laughed. He wasn't sure exactly what she said, but he did hear something about the "Bloody Burton men," so he backed away and didn't respond.

Excited to be both hanging with Brooke and setting up what should be a great television system, he whistled a happy little tune as he cut open one of the boxes and got to work.

Brooke emptied the bag onto the counter. There was a large container filled to the top with colorful orange, green, and yellow pasta. A smaller bowl was full of crisp green lettuce made into a Caesar salad complete with croutons and dressing. A foil-wrapped package that turned out to be parmesan sprinkled breadsticks was tucked in next to the Tupperware.

He had brought more food than she could imagine eating and she smiled happily, suddenly in a great mood. She warmed the pasta and breadsticks up and loaded large portions onto the new bright blue plates she had bought with her first paycheck. She stared at the heaped plates and wondered a little suspiciously just how much more he wanted to eat.

She was starving from all the yard work and would definitely be able to keep pace, so she let it go. She plopped a couple of noodles in her mouth to make sure it was hot enough and her eyes closed in bliss. They popped open again a moment later as it suddenly hit her that he might have brought so much food because he'd known how much she could eat lately. One side of her mouth turned up in a grin as she wondered if him thinking that was a good thing or not.

On the one hand, it was thoughtful of him and it pretty much guaranteed she'd have plenty to eat when he was around, which was absolutely a pro. But then she thought about how he constantly teased her about how much she could eat and a small self-conscious part of her wondered if he was secretly judging her for it. She finally shrugged at her own thoughts. Who cared what anyone thought about how and what she ate? She worked hard and needed the energy.

She dumped some salad onto some smaller plates and checked the pasta once again for the temperature. It was pretty good, she admitted and then forked in a large bite of salad to make sure the dressing was adequate. She had just reached for a final test on the pasta when Jacob called out. "Well, that does it, I'm all set up out here." There was silence for a moment before he said with suspicion, "Yo, make sure you save some of that food for me too, okay?"

Brooke harrumphed loudly and then with an evil little grin dumped half of his food onto her plate just to teach him a lesson. Feeling slightly better about the portions now she balanced two glasses of water and the salad plates in her arms and walked carefully back to the sofa. She quickly set them on the side table and went back for the pasta and breadsticks.

He gave her a quick grin when she walked in with the plates but frowned when he saw the difference between the two. Without missing a beat, he reached for the biggest one. Brooke sidestepped smoothly and gracefully landed a plate in his outstretched hand that had meager portions. "This one's for you, Burton," she said with a happy smile. When his eyes narrowed, she smiled sweetly. "Since you already ate, you know."

He knew better than to try taking her food away so he let it go with only a slightly cold stare.

He was the one who picked the movie for the simple reason that Brooke had only ever seen two movies before and had no clue which ones were good or not. They ate in silence as they watched what he called a great action film, about five movie stars that worked together as a team.

After her plate was empty, she got up to get just a little more food. The salad bowl was only about halfway full, so she decided to just bring it in and finish it off while they watched the movie. On her way past, she grabbed a couple of breadsticks and tossed them in as well.

Feeling content, she sat back down next to him and dug her fork in with her blue eyes fixed on the screen in front of them.

Within seconds she was fighting off Jacob's fork, which kept casually reaching for another bite. After trying to keep the food out of reach for a few minutes she finally sighed and gave up. Grudgingly she let him match her bite for bite. When the salad and breadsticks were gone, she sat back feeling contented.

Impossibly after twenty minutes, her stomach grumbled again and she sighed as she stood to go for more pasta. She pegged her fork into the now cold pasta for a quick nibble. It tasted just as good cold so she dumped the remaining breadsticks in the bowl and took it in the front room. The show was coming to a close as they neared the bottom of the dish. Suddenly she heaved a heavy sigh and exclaimed, "I'm so full, I literally can't eat another bite."

Jacob glanced at her and grinned as he took the dish out of her hand. He emptied the bowl in no time and licked his lips as he shoved the last bit inside his mouth.

The credits rolled across the screen as she yawned wide, suddenly sleepy. She tried to hold it back but couldn't and her eyes watered as she stretched her shoulders out.

Jacob grinned at her. "It's not even midnight, Cinderella." He smiled warmly down at her. She looked worn out but very content. He looked away. He was only putting off the inevitable by waiting. He turned back to meet her tired eyes with a sigh. "I'm flying out tomorrow."

Brooke felt surprise and then disappointment sink in but didn't show it. She crooked her neck so she could meet his gaze, asking quietly, "Where are you going?"

He smiled at her before answering. "I'm going back to California."

She frowned. "I thought you were planning to be home until August."

He nodded. "That was the plan, but then my professor called and invited me to participate in a summer workshop where a bunch of us students will be doing a mock trial." He held her gaze easily. "After we complete the mock trial, he's picking the top five students to take on the actual trial." She saw the excitement in his green eyes at that prospect and smiled.

"I'm guessing you are hoping to be one of the top five."

He looked away but then met her gaze again. "It would be really great to get some experience in the courtroom, but it also means that I could be gone for much longer."

Brooke wanted to be happy for him, knew that she should tell him to go and have fun. She searched silently for the words she knew she should be saying but couldn't find them. Finally, she sighed and said the only thing that felt real. "I'll miss you while you're gone." She reached out her hand to lay it on his arm.

Jacob stared down at her long slender fingers splayed out on his forearm for a long moment. His green eyes darkened slightly as he cocked his head to stare into her sapphire eyes. He held her gaze with his own as he leaned down slowly and murmured, "I think I'd like to kiss you if that's okay." He waited.

Brooke could see the gold flecks around the irises in his green eyes. She stared up at him. He felt safe and warm and suddenly she realized that she wanted him to kiss her too. She swallowed the refusal on her tongue and nodded.

His head came down slowly, giving her plenty of time to back out. She closed her eyes as he gently rubbed his lips against her own, softly at first and then harder as he deepened the kiss and waited patiently for the fireworks. He slid his fingers up into her hair and fused their lips together deepening the kiss once again. Nothing.

Jacob groaned. He really, really liked her, maybe even loved her and he had hoped they would have great chemistry. He felt her moving beneath him and looked down at her.

Her shoulders shook again. He stared in confusion at first as she tried to maintain a straight face.

His eyes narrowed. Was she laughing? He had never kissed a girl and made her laugh and he didn't like how it felt. He had just tried kissing the sense out of her and felt nothing. He frowned with disappointment as her shoulders shook again, harder this time.

Finally unable to contain herself, a little gargle wobbled out. The garbled sound only made her laugh harder but somehow the throaty sound of her voice soothed his frustration and he found himself first grinning and then finally laughing along with her. Tears streamed down her cheeks as she tried madly to calm herself.

Finally spent, she laid her head down on his shoulder. She smiled up at him and in a very matter-of-fact voice stated calmly, "While I admit I haven't been kissed very many times, I'm pretty sure *that*"—she pointed up at her lips—"is not the way I'm supposed to feel."

He didn't respond for a long moment and when he did finally speak, he sounded grumpy and disappointed. "While I don't think there is a man alive that would want to hear that, I can't disagree." He squeezed her chin with his hand and then his eyes twinkled as he stated, "And here I was thinking that maybe you were the one for me, Miss Brookie." He chuckled then. "I suppose we will just have to settle for friends, huh?"

Brooke tipped her head back and held out a hand to clasp his tightly. "Friends, then." She smiled and added somberly, "Best friends." He grasped her hand and they shook in mutual agreement.

He held on to her hand when she tried to pull it away and his eyes glowed mischievously as he stated, "I just feel like I should warn you, though, that my best friend is required to watch football and basketball with me whenever I want."

She laughed and shook her head in resignation, "Yeah, yeah," she complained. Then with a frown added, "I suppose you also think your best friend should like your Seattle team as well?" "Because I really like that team from San Francisco." She snapped her fingers a couple of times as though trying to remember the team name. "What are they called?"

Jacob only stared in horror as she tried to remember the name of his favorite team's greatest rival. Her eyes twinkled with amusement and together they laughed.

She lay her head on his shoulder once again and then murmured under her breath, "It's strange, don't you think, that you can be so sexy and good-looking, maybe even beautiful, and yet when we kiss, I feel nothing?"

Jacob scowled slightly at the reminder but agreed. "It is." He looked thoughtful for a minute before admitting, "I've thought I'm attracted to you since I first saw you there by the shop. I genuinely like your personality. I love how real and honest you always are and how you really don't seem to care what people think about you." He held up a hand when she opened her mouth to disagree with him. "I know you feel inadequate sometimes and maybe even insecure, but that's just because you're a fish out of water. But your choices and the decisions you make aren't affected by what other people might think. You just decide how you feel and then you roll with it. I'm actually a little jealous of that, you know?" He shrugged his shoulder under her head. "I admire you and I really hoped it would turn into more."

She nodded. "It would be so easy with us, wouldn't it?"

He smiled and nodded before changing the subject to something lighter. "So, Bestie, want to watch one last movie before I have to leave?"

Brooke nodded and hid her yawn as he generously picked another show that he proclaimed was awesome and everyone should see it.

She fell asleep on his shoulder somewhere between where the suited man who got in fights but always appeared to maintain his perfectly tailored persona throughout slept with one woman who turned out to be "bad" and the film was headlining him toward another woman who she supposed was the actual "good" one.

When the credits rolled down the screen, Jacob turned it off and then lifted her easily into his arms. He walked down the hallway and laid her gently on her bed careful not to disturb her. He smiled down at her wild red curls and then pulled the blanket up to her chin. Before he left, he leaned down and kissed her cheek and whispered softly, "Goodbye, best friend."

He washed the dishes from dinner and turned out all the lights before letting himself out and locking the door. He sat there in his jeep for several minutes watching the house while deep in thought before he put the jeep in gear and backed out of the driveway. Tonight hadn't gone at all the way he'd planned. He sighed, best to just keep moving. He could play the dating game some more. Exhaustion settled into his shoulders and he pressed the accelerator. He had an early flight tomorrow.

CHAPTER 11

Brooke woke up early on Sunday and couldn't go back to sleep. Not unlike the last four weeks she had two thoughts circling round and round her head vying for attention.

The first concern was this constant unshakable fear that she had managed stupidly to get herself pregnant. Her period still hadn't come regardless of her constant wishing for it.

The second concern was Cole. The image of his hard, slightly confused, and what she thought might have actually been pain in those bewitching eyes of his tormented her constantly. She groaned and closed her eyes, stubbornly trying to will her tired mind back to sleep. Like every morning since that one stupid kiss, sleep evaded her as soon as she opened her eyes.

She had first spent weeks on edge worried about running into Cole but as time passed without a glimpse, she began hoping she would run into him if only to clear the air. By week four she was actually just starting to feel angry because he obviously regretted the kiss and was now avoiding her instead of just telling her to her face.

She thought of the night before with Jacob and a happy smile stole across her lips before she remembered that he was leaving today. Her heart ached at the thought of once again being all alone, but she pushed it aside. Jacob had been the one constant good thing she had in her life and she was sad to see him go, even though she was proud of his accomplishments.

She had Ivan as well she reminded herself, trying to get herself excited. The problem there was that she had tried really hard to stay clear of Ivan over the last couple of weeks. Ever since she had realized she was causing a rift between him and Anne.

A few weeks back Ivan had sent her over to the Burton house to meet up with Jacob for work. Her main fear had been that she would run into Cole but instead Anne had answered the door. She had smiled politely and offered to go get Jacob for Brooke, but she seemed reserved. Brooke was already fairly certain that the older woman didn't much like her.

Though she didn't know why Anne didn't like her, Brooke felt disappointed and a little hurt. She didn't blame Anne for whatever she felt. After all, she was a stranger that had quite literally become an interloper in their happy little family whether willing or not.

Neither Ivan nor Jacob would even entertain her suggestion that she step back and get another job. She had suggested it a couple of times even though Brooke herself didn't really want to leave either. She would, though, if she felt like it would make things better. Since the farm was already shorthanded, she didn't want to leave Ivan in the lurch and so instead started avoiding him as much as possible.

The fact that Jacob had taken to her just as quickly and determinedly as Ivan had only made Anne that much more reserved about Brooke being in their lives.

Brooke hadn't told anyone the main reason she was avoiding Ivan however. Two weeks ago, she had spent the day helping Jacob move equipment across the valley. It had taken them most of the day to get all the balers moved over but since it was still a little earlier than she usually got off work, she drove back to the shop to make sure Ivan didn't have anything else he wanted her to do for the day. Jacob had told her to make an early night of it but she hadn't listened. Since Ivan was paying her a salary, she didn't want to take advantage of his generosity before checking in with him.

She got to the shop around four thirty but had run into Maude who was just leaving for the day. After they exchanged pleasantries, the older woman wanted to chat and Brooke hadn't had the heart to shut her up. It was nearing five when she'd finally said goodbye and hurried up to Ivan's office.

As she drew close to the door, she heard raised voices. She slowed her stride, not wanting to interrupt whomever Ivan was talking to. She hesitated outside the door for a moment but then turned to go when she heard Anne say angrily, "You had no right to do all of that for Brooke without talking to me first, Ivan. My God, it's like you and Jacob both have blinders on when it comes to that girl."

Brooke had frozen on the spot, and though she willed her feet to move away from the door, her curiosity won out, so she stayed to listened for a moment longer. She heard Ivan's chair roll back and knew instinctively that he had stood up. "I know we are partners in the business, Anne, and I understand that you are frustrated and that you can't seem to trust me with this." There was silence then before he continued sounding frustrated. "I did warn you that I planned to do whatever I can for Brooke." He sighed, sounding tired. "I honestly don't understand why you can't see her for what she is."

He paused and Brooke held her breath even as she willed her legs to move. "It is so obvious to me that she has been hurt and rejected by her parents and possible her entire family, hell maybe even abused." Ivan swore quietly. "As you know there really isn't any way of knowing exactly how deep her trauma goes unless and until she is willing to trust us enough to talk about it." His tone hardened. "I know you don't agree with my choice and I am sorry about that. I don't want this between us, but I've made up my mind on this and I have been clear with you where I stand. You can choose to support me or you can continue to be angry at me, the choice is yours." He sounded tired at the last.

Brooke turned with tears in her eyes to run unseen down the hall to the stairs. As she ran, she heard Anne's hard question, "And what if she is only here to take advantage of us, Ivan? Then what are we going to do?"

Brooke only heard the sound of his tired voice fading in the distance as she rushed out to her car and drove home. Tears ran down her cheeks and she knew she was driving a little too fast, but she slowed only when her car fishtailed slightly on the marbled gravel road before she slowed and got it under control.

She hurried into her little haven of a home and locked the door securely behind her before leaning against it and burying her face in her hands to sob uncontrollably. On the one hand she appreciated that Ivan was willing to take a stand for her, but on the other she genuinely cared for him and didn't want him to lose anything because of her. She mulled over everything that had happened in her life since that fated day when she had met Ivan. The question nagged at her relentlessly. *Was* she taking advantage of the Burton family?

She had thought her hard work and effort to make things better helped repay everything they had done for her but what if that wasn't enough? She groaned loudly and wiped her hands down her face in a useless attempt to dry the tears. Resolve set in and she straightened up. All she could do was try her best to make it worth it to Jacob and Ivan. Eyes clear, she turned determinedly and started working on the basement.

The next few days had been hard and she had considered packing her things and leaving several times. In the end, it was her word to Ivan and the fact that she didn't want to let him or Jacob down that kept her pushing through. At the end of the following week, she promised herself that if the price they paid to care about her was greater than the work she could do to make it up, she would leave.

She had confided to Jacob that she was considering moving on and he had helped to convince her to stay. He hadn't judged her. He'd just been honest and explained that besides them loving her, the farm was already shorthanded this summer and his dad was counting on her to be able to work through the harvest.

Maybe, she'd thought happily, that was the answer to her prayers. By staying and working hard to earn her place here she could prove that she wasn't here to take advantage of anyone. She hadn't brought it up again.

She avoided Ivan by texting him whenever she needed to talk to him. She adamantly did not want to get between him and Anne. She loved Ivan and wanted him to be happy. She had always respected Anne and hoped secretly that she could win her over. In a strange way, she supposed Anne had become her secret role model. She was, after all, a sophisticated, very intelligent, and graceful woman with a loving family. Brooke had only ever dreamed of having such things.

Perhaps that was why the mistrust stung so sharply even when Brooke could understand Anne's protective instinct for her family, even admired it.

That was a couple of weeks ago and now Brooke stretched out on her bed before finally giving up on sleep with a frustrated sigh. She felt an empty ache inside. Jacob was gone. He could be gone for months. She didn't know how long, and though she wanted her friend here with her, she couldn't help hoping that he would get one of those top five spots because that was what was best for him regardless of her missing him. Smiling at that realization, she reached for her cell phone. He probably wouldn't answer as he was on the plane, but she typed a quick message anyway.

Good morning Bestie.
Just wishing you good luck on your flight to LA
I'll miss you like crazy but I'm super excited your professor
recognizes just how intelligent you really are.
I'd tell you to knock 'em dead but I already
know you will.
Look forward to seeing you again in a 2+ months
to hear all the dets.
P.S. I really do love you, ya know. So, take good care of yourself.

Feeling better about the day already, Brooke hummed an old eighties rock tune as she slipped into skinny jeans and an aqua-colored square-necked tee that had little ties on the sleeves. She dampened her hair and combed determinedly through the tangles with a pick until it ran smoothly through. She nearly always braided her hair to keep it out of her way at work but today she opted instead to only braid the sides on front and pull them together with a clip at the back of her head, leaving curls to wind playfully down her back like a waterfall. She smiled at the effect. It was almost pretty she thought as she went to the kitchen to eat some breakfast before she went back to town for her new table.

Two eggs, two pieces of toast, and three slices of bacon later, she rinsed her plate in the sink and then filled a water bottle to take with her. She did a quick check through her new purse to make sure her wallet and keys were inside before slipping the water bottle inside with them.

She closed the door and was on the porch turning her key in the lock when a truck pulled into her drive. She turned with a smile on her lips. It froze on her face and then slowly faded. Cole sat behind the wheel of an ancient but good-looking dark blue pickup truck.

Her nervous gaze met his dark one through the windshield and an irritating electric surge shot through her middle and down her legs. Her smile faltered as she tried to look away but couldn't.

His intensely dark unblinking eyes held her gaze, captivated. He didn't smile. He didn't look happy to see her either. That, they could agree on. She didn't want to see him either, though she was curious what had brought him here. She felt anger rush up and looked down at the stairs as she slowly made her way down them carefully ensuring that she didn't fall on her face in front of him. Her legs felt rubbery as she made her way toward him. She heard the truck door open but refused to look up terrified that he might see what she was feeling.

She breathed calmly and willed the panic in her chest under control as she stepped gingerly toward him. Taking a deep breath Brooke lifted her chin and looked up as he slid out of his truck. She met his gaze again and forced a tight little smile. He was staring at her now with one brow raised curiously and she found herself wondering what on earth he was thinking. Her heart skipped a beat in anticipation.

He tipped his head in polite acknowledgment. "Brooke."

The one word was low and gravelly and Brooke wondered if he was angry or just grumpy. She cleared her throat loudly before grinding out his name. "Cole."

Her curiosity got the best of her and she raised her eyebrows. "What on earth are you doing here?"

She saw his in drawn breath and his nostrils flared slightly with what she could only assume was anger. She hadn't meant to sound rude and felt bad. Trying for a mild tone she forced another wide smile and stammered. "I'm so sorry, I didn't mean to be rude, it's just that I wasn't expecting anyone today."

It was a crappy explanation and she knew it. She was surprised and then oddly soothed when the anger in his eyes dissipated as quickly as it had come.

One corner of his mouth turned up into a vicious-looking grin. "What could you possibly have to be sorry about?" His tone was cold and hard and for some unknown reason it stung her.

Brooke stared hard at him, trying not to let him see her hurt feelings. She reached inside herself for strength and patience pulling at it like it was a roll of yarn. She shrugged, the best she could do was be as honest as possible. Hadn't she been waiting months for an opportunity to apologize to him? She gulped and rushed out. "I'm really very sorry that I slapped you before. I know it seems to be becoming a pattern with me as I was rude before and then again, I sounded rude just a minute ago. I'm sorry."

His gaze darkened and he stared incredulously at her as his jaw went taut. His anger at himself kept barely in check he ground out, "Do you really think that what I want from you is an apology?"

She shrugged helplessly and fought back tears. "I don't know what you want or what I can do." Her voice was quiet, then sounding as though she was pleading. "I just felt a little overwhelmed is all and I know I was rude and I shouldn't have slapped you like that. But it already happened and I can't take it back, so there really isn't much else I can do at this point except apologize."

He stared at her hard for another long second before finally turning his head to look away and toward the house. "That isn't exactly how this works, Brooke. For God's sake an apology doesn't just fix things like this. It is not okay. And to be absolutely clear it is an unforgivable offense." He looked down at his hands before turning his dark gaze up to meet hers once again. "I think it's a selfish thing to ask for forgiveness under the circumstances."

His gaze was hard again and Brooke's smile faltered. Her heart throbbed somewhere inside her chest and she raised her hand there now to rub at it. How was she supposed to make it up to him if she wasn't even allowed to apologize? She fought the tears back and nodded mutely at him.

Cole lifted a hand then and opened the passenger side door as he said quietly, "Good, then it's settled. We won't ever speak of this again and you have my word that I will never touch you again in that way."

Brooke stared up at him, confused once again. What exactly was settled? She wasn't well versed in these kinds of situations but hadn't he just told her that an apology from her could never make it up to him? Her heart ached at the thought of him despising her so much that he couldn't even stand to touch her.

She turned to stare numbly at the open door of the truck. Was he now expecting her to climb inside? She glared hotly as anger finally took over her mouth. "Am I just supposed to agree with you, be a good girl and hop to do your bidding now?" Her voice was pitched high, almost sounding shrill and she watched his jaw go tight again as his dark brown eyes turned black with anger.

She stepped back suddenly, unable to stop the fear that was now creeping up her spine. Did he mean to simply force her to go with him somewhere only he had decided they should go? How could this hard man in front of her be Jacob's brother?

She shivered as Cole growled low in his throat, "My God, woman, do you think that I can't control myself?" His eyes narrowed dangerously. "Do you think I'm actually stupid enough to try kissing you again?" He was fully pissed off now and she looked terrified.

The worst part of it was that he couldn't blame her for being afraid of him since he had nearly raped her. How could he have been so wrong about what he had thought was a mutual attraction. The problem was that even though the poor girl had every right to be afraid of him, it just didn't feel right to him.

He stepped forward to reassure her, but she stumbled back as he advanced. She looked as though she was going to turn and run, so he reached out and quickly closed the door again. His frustration had reached breaking point and he wanted to laugh at his own stupidity but instead he raised his hands into the air in an effort to calm her. She stilled then, staring up at him with those bewitchingly bright blue eyes. He leaned over slowly holding her gaze and his hands steady in the air.

It seemed that no matter what he did she wanted to run away afraid. She still looked nervous so he dropped his arms clenching his fists and groaning with exasperation and he closed his eyes as he took a deep breath. He willed his temper to calm and opened his eyes as he moved into a very relaxed, non-threatening position stepping back and away to lean casually against his truck.

She was watching his every move carefully so he forced a wide reassuring grin and said, "This is all just one big misunderstanding, Brooke." She raised one brow defiantly and his grin widened. "I should have been clear right from the start. My dad sent me over here to help you this morning."

Brooke looked taken aback but still watched him carefully. She didn't say anything but waited quietly for him to explain.

He shrugged. "Something about a table?"

A shiver worked its way up her spine in the aftermath of her nervousness and she couldn't stop the tremor that shook her shoulders. She stepped closer to him, feeling foolish now. "I see," she said as she realized she had jumped to all kinds of conclusions when he had only come at his dad's request to help her.

She stared at her feet. What had she thought? That he was going to haul her off to some remote place and take her as his own? A deep blush started up her neck. He hadn't even done anything to her that should warrant the level of fear that she'd felt. Embarrassed beyond words she mumbled, "I don't understand why he sent you too. I only asked him if I could borrow the truck."

Cole blinked unwilling to take offense at her obvious distaste at the idea of being in his company. He shrugged nonchalantly. "He woke me up and told me that he'd been planning to go with you himself but then something else came up that he had to handle." He ran a strong tanned hand through his hair. "Jacob left on a six o'clock flight this morning, so I guess that left me as the only choice." He grinned, looking charming and breathtakingly handsome.

Brooke shivered. She was feeling more foolish by the moment. On top of everything else, she had to quit thinking of him as attractive and sexy. He'd made it very clear that he wanted nothing else to do with her in that way.

He'd simply come here to help her. Hell, he probably hadn't even wanted to come but Ivan's stubborn nature most likely wouldn't have let him get out of it.

And she had treated him like the anger-crazed monster that she knew Richard was. She tried to smile at him, but it wobbled a little so she settled for a nod. "I'm sorry," she said, moving next to the truck and him. "I didn't realize your dad thought I was asking him for help. He shouldn't have bothered you since I am perfectly capable of going on my own. I was only asking to borrow a truck to haul it in."

Cole grinned sardonically. "I don't know if you've noticed yet, but Dad seems to have a particularly protective soft spot for you." She blinked and he chuckled. "He's no fool, so I'm fairly certain that he was well aware that all you were asking for was the truck." Since she still looked uncertain, he reached over and opened the door and then stepped back to give her a wide berth around him. "He would never let me hear the end of it if I'm not a gentleman now," he added an exaggerated bow with one eyebrow in the air.

Brooke couldn't help smiling at his expression but still hesitated. "I really don't want to interrupt your weekend plans, Cole. I'm sure this wasn't exactly how you intended to spend your day."

He shrugged and smiled. "It is now."

He hadn't disagreed with her so she hedged, "I really don't mind going alone." Her expression brightened suddenly. "Hey, I could just drop you back off at the shop to get your car." Another thought struck. "Or you could go inside and watch the game. Isn't there like basketball games every Sunday and Thursday or something? I remember Jacob telling me about that and he got a huge system all set up in there." She pointed to the house with a big smile.

Cole gave her a tortured frown. "It's football; that's Sunday and Thursday but not at this time of year. Basketball is more random but still going on." He groaned suddenly. "I don't know why I'm bothering to tell you all that. Damn it all, woman, will you just get in the truck before I'm tempted to pick you up and throw you in?"

She started looking nervous again so he sighed and called on what little patience he could muster. Somberly he met her gaze and asked seriously, "Are you too afraid of me to let me drive you into town and help you pick up some furniture?" He watched her closely as if measuring her reaction.

She shook her head adamantly. "Of course not, Cole! I just didn't want to be rude."

Unsure if he believed her or not, he nodded. "Well, I'm happy to help out a neighbor. And I have given you my word to keep my hands off you so…." He waited for her to capitulate. She still hesitated, so he added pleasantly, "By the way, this is my truck not one of the work trucks from the farm, so I go where it goes."

Brooke looked at the truck in surprise. It was a deep blue color that shimmered different shades when the viewpoint shifted. She stepped back, eyeing it curiously. It was an old truck, though she couldn't have said what year. It was old enough that without seeing the tag on front she couldn't even tell the make or model. It had a curved hood that sloped down to painted blue tire wells that curved over black with white striped tires. The bed was fairly short and narrow with the truck sides butting up to blue tire wells on the back end as well. She looked back up at him and smiled. "I thought you had a car."

Cole grinned at what had to sound like an accusation and said simply, "I do."

She stifled a laugh then. Of course he had a truck. And a car. And a motorcycle. Without another glance she rushed forward and climbed quickly inside before she could start laughing.

He most likely already believed she was nuts and if she suddenly broke into spontaneous laughter now, she might start agreeing with him. She bowed her head low to hide her amusement.

He reached out and tilted her grinning face up to confirm what he'd suspected. Heat spread from her throat and neck, slid into his fingertips, and began making its way up his arm. A memory of his mouth hard on hers with his hand holding her chin this way flashed like a camera lens.

Cole pulled his hand back as though he'd been burned. He swore harshly under his breath before turning to walk quickly around and climb into the driver side of the truck as he forcefully turned the key in the ignition. A rush of cold air blew from the vents as the fan kicked in and cooled him. The engine purred like a kitten as it came to life. Coldly determined, he placed one hand tightly on the steering wheel and one hand on the gearshift grasping it tightly in his fist. He glanced over and caught her staring across at him. Without another look he swore again and slammed the gearshift into reverse, backing smoothly out of the driveway and then shifting it into first without ever grinding gears.

It wasn't until Brooke cleared her throat loudly that he finally risked another look in her direction. She gave him a teasing smile and asked sweetly, "Has anyone ever told you that you swear a lot?"

He laughed aloud, but it wasn't out of amusement. "Would you believe me if I told you no?" he countered. Then with a self-deprecating grin said, "It really hasn't been a problem for me until now."

Brooke looked dubiously across the cab at him, which caused him to bark with laughter. He watched her face light up as she smiled in return. She looked radiant when she smiled and she had a great smile. It was one of those smiles that could light up a room and then make everyone who noticed want to smile right along with her.

He turned his gaze to the road and gripped the steering wheel and gear shift a little tighter. Better to keep his hands and brain occupied as much as possible. Lust made its way through his gut. How in God's name was he supposed to keep his hands off of her when she kept smiling like that? He gritted his teeth but swallowed the curse before it came off his tongue.

She laughed out loud and pointed at his lips. "See, right there, you nearly swore again." He looked at her sideways and then, unable to resist her charm, laughed with her at his own expense. She leaned back in the seat looking happy and relaxed. He looked over at her for a long moment in appreciation. She looked breathtakingly beautiful with all that red hair shimmering in the sunshine and her blue eyes twinkling brightly just above her gently curved but lightly freckled nose. She met his gaze and smiled. He sent a half smile back in response, but inside his head his brain chanted wildly. *Fuck, Fuck, Fuck….*

CHAPTER 12

The rest of the drive into town went smoothly. Cole stayed silent aside from answering the occasional question that Brooke asked. She asked if he was going to school. He nodded but didn't go into detail.

She rolled her eyes at his response. She sat on the seat next to him with her shoulders squared waiting hopefully for him to elaborate. When it became obvious he wasn't planning to share any more, she asked him where he went to school.

He gave her a sideways look before curtly telling her that he was going to tech school in Massachusetts. She hid her frustration when he didn't say anything more.

After several long minutes of silence, she sighed and asked if he minded if she turned on the radio. It was a decent and fairly fancy-looking radio that he must have retro-fit somehow to fit into the old truck. It was also equipped with a/c, which she was fairly certain hadn't been invented when the truck was made. He shrugged so she leaned forward and pressed the power button. Soft rock blared out of the stereo and she settled into her seat comfortably and sang along.

They drove in silence for the next thirty minutes with nothing but soft rock and pop hits to break the tension. Cole didn't appear to want to talk and Brooke was far too stubborn to be the only one participating in the conversation.

He spoke up once, though only when they got close to town. He glanced her way and casually asked, "Which exit should I take? I'm not even sure where we're going."

She motioned to the exit sign as they drove past. "Take this first one. It's that small nursery out on Yellowstone."

He nodded but said nothing else. If he didn't want to be friendly, so be it, she thought with a frown and let it go.

When they got to the nursery, the clerk recognized her and pointed to a side door. "It's out there. I had a couple of the guys haul it out this morning so it would be easier to load." Brooke thanked her and led the way outside. Cole looked at the sturdy table and turned to nod at her. "It looks pretty solid," he said with a little lift on one side.

She rolled her eyes. What was it with the male population? They always seemed to think it was their job to let the lowly women know whether or not they approved of such things. She went back inside to let the clerk know she was picking it up and asked if she needed to sign anything. Pickup form signed and tucked into her purse, she walked back outside.

Cole was hunched down in a squat while folding and unfolding the table top where the bench was attached. It was built so that the bench sides could fold in under the table nicely for storage purposes. It was one of the reasons she had liked it so much. He saw her there and stood. "It's a pretty cool design."

Brooke gave him a little smile and a nod. Together they lifted it and walked around the building to his truck. He had opened the tailgate before they went inside so they lifted it up and slid it inside the narrow bed. He hopped up onto the tailgate to ensure it was pushed all the way to the cab and then jumped down. He turned and opened the door to fold the truck seat forward just long enough to grab a couple of long gray tie down straps that he stored there.

Brooke watched as he tossed them over the truck bed and neatly secured the now folded picnic table. He gave her a quick but silent thumbs-up and walked around to open her door for her.

She almost laughed at the irony of it. It amused her to see that he had enough chivalry to hold her door open for her but didn't have the patience for the most basic polite conversation. She stepped around him and climbed onto the seat. "Thanks," she murmured a bit amused as he reached out and closed it behind her.

He walked around and slid into the seat next to her and she leaned her head back as she closed her eyes. The space somehow felt charged and a bit crowded as soon as they were both enclosed in the cab again. She opened her eyes and reached for her purse that she had set between them on the bench seat. Quickly unzipping it, she pulled out her water bottle and took a long drink.

Feeling his eyes on her, she turned to find him watching her. She swallowed, he sat perfectly still a mere two feet away not moving a muscle and in that moment her brain likened him to a predator. He reminded her of a panther sitting there like that, calmly watching her every move as though waiting for the perfect moment to pounce.

She swallowed again. Feeling a bit uncomfortable, she glared at him. "What?" She knew she sounded overly grumpy but didn't care.

He grinned and asked, "Aren't you going to offer me a drink too?"

She looked completely taken aback by his question, which only made his grin widen to a deadly level. She looked at her water bottle and then finally not sure what else to say, shrugged. "Why not? Cole, would you like some water?" she asked in mock severity. She leaned over with a little curtsy-like bow and held the bottle out toward him.

His eyes turned warm as he leaned over and casually snatched it from her extended hand. His fingers brushed against hers and the contact made her eyes close the merest bit. He held her gaze as he tilted his head back and slowly but completely drained the bottle.

Brooke wanted to look away. She really did. She even wanted to complain or make some smart comment about him rudely finishing her water. The problem however was that from this angle she could see his handsome profile with his black hair curling over the collar of his jade-colored button-down in the sexiest way. The ends of his short sleeves were like bands around his heavily muscled upper arms and she looked up and away in embarrassment. She watched as his throat worked with every swallow. His profile was sharp, maybe even a little aristocratic but the overall look was heart thumping and brain numbing. She remembered Jacob telling her that he always had the ladies flocking around him. That thought bothered her, though she didn't know why.

Mesmerized she watched as he shook the last few drops into his open mouth before lowering it as he replaced the cap on top.

She groaned dramatically. "You didn't have to drink it all, you know."

He gave her a devilish grin and tossed the bottle onto the seat between them. There was absolutely no sense in tempting fate or himself by risking touching her again. He placed his hands firmly in place again and started the truck. He turned and gave her a wink. "Don't sweat it, Brooke. I won't let you go hungry."

She lifted a brow curiously as he started the truck and pulled away from the curb. It was soon evident that he was heading away from the freeway, so she asked a little nervously. "Where are we going?"

He chucked her beneath the chin with his thumb. "We are going to get some lunch. I don't know about you, my dear, but I'm starving." He sent a lopsided grin her direction. "Besides that, it now looks like I owe you a drink."

Brooke couldn't fault that logic as her stomach rumbled in excitement. She nodded her approval as she smiled happily out the window at the thought of food.

He was watching her from the corner of his eyes. Suspiciously he asked, "How come you're so agreeable all of the sudden?" He sounded a little grumpy, so she flashed a toothy smile just to irritate him. It had its desired effect, making him frown. He fully turned then to stare at her as the truck came to a stop in front of the red light. "Seriously, what exactly are you so happy about?"

She closed her eyelids halfway and licked her lips in anticipation. "I'm pretty sure I heard someone mention food." She gave a little wiggle of her brows and met his dark eyes pointing with two fingers out at the now green light. "Light's green, cowboy, and you'd better hurry and keep that promise if you want my good mood to continue."

He let out a quick shout of laughter low in his belly before grinning widely and informing her, "I'm fairly certain that the simple mention of food has never gotten me out of a hot spot quite that quickly." He lifted a brow sardonically. "And I have four brothers." He shook his head. "I will definitely have to remember that this could possibly be the best way to get on your good side." To his surprise she only smiled and nodded seriously in agreement. Laughing, he shook his head and made a right turn onto the avenue he was looking for.

He took her to one of those old drive-in style burger joints. It was a local place that she had seen on occasion but had never been to. As they pulled in under the awning, a young happy-looking blonde girl came out with a pad and a pen to take their order. She had bright blue eyes, an upturned nose and a perky full-lipped mouth. Altogether a friendly looking face. Her expression lit up as she got her first good look at Cole. She gave him a quick flirty smile. Cole either didn't notice or didn't care because he only gave her a quick nod and then promptly announced, "We'll take two burgers with fries and milkshakes."

Brooke was fine with the basic items he ordered but wasn't nearly satisfied with the details. She leaned over to where she could peer up across at the girl and added, "That's fine but make mine a double, oh and also make sure it's a large fry." She threw a friendly smile at the girl who smiled back. "Oh, and also make my milkshake a chocolate one."

Cole was staring at her now with one eyebrow raised. She wasn't going to let that come between her and her food, though. Why would any intelligent human being let some other human being's disapproval get in the way of a good meal? She had never understood why some women thought they shouldn't eat actual food in front of people. She smiled sweetly up at him before saying quickly, "Oh and could you also bring me a bottle of water." She raised a cocked thumb and pointed it at him. "He owes me one."

The young blonde laughed out loud and scribbled on her pad again. She gave Cole a little look of sympathy and then stated, "No problem. I'll be right back with your total and your order."

Brooke dug through her purse and located her wallet. She pulled a twenty-dollar bill out and held the green toward him.

Cole shook his head and made no move to take it.

She stared at the stubborn set of his jaw. A little irritated at his general dismissive energy toward her all morning, she waved it in his face abruptly. "Come on, Cole, just take it. I cover my own food."

He didn't budge. Only turned a fraction to meet her gaze sideways with a little smirk. "What happened to, 'he owes me'?" he challenged mockingly.

Brooke groaned in frustration and unbuckled her seat belt to slide closer as she attempted to tuck the bill into his hand. "I was only talking about the water and you know it." His hand jerked back and away from hers as tingles went up her arm. More determined than ever now she dangled the money by his nose.

She turned her face up and became instantly aware of how close her face was to his. His eyes sparked with gold and she swallowed. She had been smiling as she waved the money and a curl had slipped out of her side braid to frame her cheek. The moment their gazes collided her smile faltered and nervousness lit her bright eyes.

Her face was tanner than when they'd first met and it looked good on her. Too good. He bit back a curse as he noticed that the square neckline of the lavender top she wore left her neck and a good portion of her shoulders bare before finally coming together just in time to curve down her arm at the sleeve. Her delicate button nose sloped up to sit elegantly between those bewitching sapphire eyes as though to taunt him.

In a taut, low voice he warned, "If you want me to keep my hands off of you, you'd better not flaunt yourself to me." It came out harsher than he'd intended and he felt a guilty twinge as she yanked her hand back and scooted quickly across the truck.

He didn't miss the look of pain in her eyes before she turned her head to look away and his gut clenched. He hated that he had caused her to hurt but was more determined than ever not to take advantage of her again. He sighed, better that her feelings get hurt than for him to find himself unable to hold back from kissing her again. The more time he spent with her the more he wanted to protect that warm, friendly, open, and trusting girl that she was. He didn't have to remind himself she was most probably underage; he was chanting that thought around his head nonstop whenever she was near as a reminder.

Brooke felt sad as she stared miserably through the front window in silence until the food was brought out. She was understandably confused and extremely frustrated. She felt a deep nearly overwhelming connection to Cole and she wasn't so pathetic she had to lie to herself and pretend it wasn't there. She also felt a deep unnerving attraction for him which she'd thought or maybe hoped that he felt too.

Though she knew it had hurt him and possibly pissed him off when she'd slapped him and run, she had also tried to apologize to him. She'd tried her damnedest to explain. She had tried nearly everything in her explanation except talk about Richard because she just couldn't do that. Not yet and maybe not ever.

The most confusing part of it all was whenever she was around him, she seemed to be constantly swinging back and forth between feeling awkward and inexperienced, only to find herself inexplicably aware of her own sexuality. That first night she had practically thrown herself at him, only to get scared and slap him before turning to run.

She breathed a quick sigh of relief when the waitress walked up with their order and promptly told them what they owed. The blonde smiled shyly up at Cole and then blushed slightly when he handed her two twenties and told her to keep the change. Brooke smiled and thanked her with a quick wave already reaching for the white paper bag filled with food.

She had already eaten a handful of fries by the time Cole got the old hand crank window rolled up. She graciously set the smaller box of fries and a burger on the seat between them careful not to touch him. She pulled her chocolate milkshake out of the brown cardboard carrier and took a long happy slurp before reaching down to pull his out and hand it to him as well.

She noticed with smiling satisfaction that the waitress had seen the wisdom and had also upgraded her milkshake to a large. She reached in the bag for more fries while she took another slug of shake. She popped a couple of the deliciously salty fries into her mouth and reached for the burger. She smiled, it had an oversized bun and was loaded thickly with lettuce, tomatoes, and pickles which she daintily removed with her nose scrunched in distaste. The two thick beef patties looked hot and juicy with cheese melted over the top of them and then dripping down the sides.

She stared at the monstrosity looking both excited and unsure. She didn't know if she could even fit her mouth over the top of the thick burger but she was sure going to give it her best. She gave a little sigh of satisfaction and opened her mouth wide, taking a bite. This was exactly the kind of dilemma she enjoyed. Sauce rolled down the side of her mouth and she licked at it quickly, trying to find somewhere to set her shake so she could dig out a napkin. Even as she set the shake precariously on the dash she moaned in pleasure and went in for another bite.

Cole had his burger opened and halfway to his mouth when he saw her picking out the pickles with a turned-up nose. He wanted to slide across the seat then and there and kiss her. He watched as she opened her mouth wide and attempted to take a chomp. Ketchup slid down her mouth and she began licking furiously at it as she tried to avoid a disaster. His jaw went taut and his loins tightened inexorably. Her shake wobbled on the dash as she reached for a napkin. He stared transfixed, his burger mere inches from his mouth as she multitasked between that huge burger, her fries, and then eventually once again reaching for the shake.

She moaned again and Cole forced himself to take a bite of his own burger, pickles and all. He had been looking forward to watching her struggle with the double burger, which he had long ago learned was a real challenge. Watching her take to it with such obvious excitement and gusto had his lips twisting in amusement. He thought of her taking to him with that same level of enjoyment and choked on the one small bite of burger he'd managed to take.

He reached for his shake, but she was already grasping it to set it in his hand with a look of genuine concern at his coughing. Their fingers brushed, leaving the now customary surge of heat crawling up his arm and tightening his loins even more. He had to stop thinking about her or it would soon be unavoidably obvious that he had a control issue where she was concerned.

Ten minutes before when she had asked for the double burger, he would have bet any amount of money that she wouldn't be able finish it. Now, he wasn't quite so confident. In fact, looking at the way she was lovingly devouring the thing, he might bet just the opposite.

He made himself look away then purely out of self-preservation, tried even to take a bite. He took another bite and choked again. From the corner of his eye, he saw her deftly take a bite of burger then throw three fries in with it while reaching to take a healthy slug of chocolate shake. He turned in slow motion to watch in horror as she gracefully situated that burger in her far hand, balanced the shake on her knee and leaned toward him to start casually pounding on his shoulder. All of this she did while still raising the burger for a bite. He swallowed and bellowed out a laugh. Since it sounded a bit like a cough, she pounded him harder.

His eyes teared up as she took another bite all the while never losing rhythm with the pounding. When she cast a concerned look at him around a mouthful of food, he couldn't take it. He slapped one leg hard, his shoulders shaking as he held his hands up trying to wield off another round of her pounding at him. It took her a moment to finally register that he was trying to hold her off as she had once again turned her focus back to her burger. She immediately stopped and shrugged as she leaned back to her side and reached for the shake before it could topple onto the floor.

As soon as she realized he was laughing, she turned to stare curiously across the seat at him. She finished chewing the bite in her mouth and asked casually, "What is so funny?" The question only made him laugh harder, so she shrugged and popped a few more fries into her mouth. She reached for her milkshake to wash down the fries while she waited for him to get it together enough to tell her what was so funny.

Her eyes narrowed suddenly. The way he was staring at her now made her feel like one of those monkeys in cages at the zoo and she frowned. He was holding his burger in one hand but she saw that it was barely touched. Discomfort put aside for more important things, her gaze zeroed in on it. Then like any concerned citizen would, she asked hopefully, "Are you going to eat that thing?" She looked at her own halfway eaten one and then back at his. "This was a pretty big burger, but I bet I could help you out when I'm done if you're not hungry." She promptly took another bite of her own.

His gut hurt and so did his face but with self-preservation in mind, he quickly moved the burger and his fries to the far side of the truck out of her reach. His shoulders shook again and he saw her hand rising toward him as though she wondered if he was choking again and needed assistance. He held his arm up to defend himself against her helpful pounding. A funny thought crept into his laughter-riddled mind. He honestly couldn't remember a time when he had laughed quite this hard. And most definitely never with a woman. That thought sobered him right up.

Brooke knew by now that he was laughing at her, she just didn't understand why. She had just been minding her own business and eating her burger until she'd realized he was choking. Then she had tried to be a good Samaritan and help him out. She shrugged. Cole Burton was a strange man.

By the time his laughter was well in check, her burger was gone and the giant pile of fries she was working on was considerably smaller. He wiped his eyes with the back of one hand, still holding his burger with the other. He saw her eyeing his milkshake and self-preservation kicked in once again. If he didn't hurry and eat, there was no telling what she might do to get her hands on his portion. He took a big bite of the burger and chewed as the lazy thought occurred that he might actually quite like her coming over here after his food.

He glanced over to find her watching him now as she popped in another fry. She raised one eyebrow at him, "Did you finally get it all out of your system?"

Cole gave her a dangerously appealing grin and took another bite. Best for all of them if he just stuck to his burger. One side of his mouth turned up in amusement as he silently thought, *not even close, sweetheart.* He didn't think it would serve either of them for him to elaborate on exactly *what* he had in his system. Wisely he ate in silence.

At some point she must have finished the fries because she wadded up the paper holder and dropped it in the white paper bag the food had come in. She was still watching him as she sipped on the chocolatey goodness of her shake. She was curious what had been so funny to him but hesitated to ask. What if he had been making fun of her? She didn't want to know that.

He kept holding his burger up against the window after each bite as though the window was hungry too. Between his shouts of laughter and that, she began to worry about his sanity. A little frown between her brows caused little wrinkles there. She watched him take a couple more bites and then return the burger to the window each time. The lines on her forehead deepened as she was struck by a thought.

Maybe he had one of those mental conditions like one of the books she'd read had talked about. Neither Jacob or Ivan had ever said anything, but could he? She tried to remember the name and the frown lines deepened again. Suddenly it popped into her brain and she almost said it out loud. She quickly slapped a hand over her mouth so it wouldn't come out.

If Cole really did have some mental problem, she was sure he wouldn't want her to mention it. He did appear to be normal sometimes too, so it could be nothing. He turned to look at her as he laid what was left of his burger against the window yet again.

She was frowning and had her hand clamped tightly over her mouth at the same time. Curious he asked, "Are you doing okay there?"

She nodded in affirmation and then quickly jerked her hand down and into her lap.

He watched her odd reaction with intrigue. She still didn't say anything, so he asked suspiciously, "Weren't you about to say something?"

Brooke thought quickly, trying without much success to think of anything she could say that wouldn't be rude. Suddenly, she broke into a big smile and turned to him to ask, "I was just going to ask if you are planning to eat that whole burger or if you want me to help you out." She smiled kindly, trying to appear helpful.

Cole grinned with amusement and lifted the burger, "This burger?" he asked.

She nodded.

He threw a heart stopping grin across the bench seat at her. "Sweetheart, in case you didn't notice, I have been trying my damnedest to hold this burger as far out of your reach as possible. I was honestly afraid that if I set it down you might take it as a sign that I was finished and inhale it before I had a chance to clarify."

He watched with satisfaction as her carefully crafted look of concern turned hot. She glared at him and then defiantly asked, "Why in the world would you think I would steal your food and eat it without asking you first." She gave an indignant toss of her head. "You obviously don't even know me. I would never do something like that."

His incredulous look was the only answer she got.

CHAPTER 13

They drove back home in companionable silence with country music playing softly in the background. When they got back to the house, Cole backed the truck into the driveway nearest the backyard. Excitedly, Brooke led the way around back pointing to the colorful flat stone pad she had laid. "It's going right there," she said as she turned to look at him. She had been thrilled when she found a huge stack of natural red, gray, and white flat rocks back behind the yard next to a couple of the trees there.

Cole looked stunned as he turned slowly while taking in the entire panoramic view of the backyard. Next to the house was a colorful raised garden bed with the same flat rocks stacked together around the edge to make a natural and yet eye-catching perimeter. There was a narrow rock pathway that started at the bottom steps of the back porch and forked off shortly after. One pathway led directly to the rectangular patio she was pointing at and the other wound around the small deck to follow the house to the edge of the driveway. From the patio the pathway curved in a pretty S-shape until it finally ended near the edge of what was already growing into a spectacular vegetable garden.

Rows of plants and hills dotted the garden spot in tidy and yet eye-pleasing fashion. He noticed the old raspberry bushes were now supported by new wooden stakes she had strategically placed in an attempt to help them grow straight and tall. The lilac bushes were trimmed back nicely and were just starting to bloom while the bright array of rose bushes already bloomed with pink and yellow rosebuds that opened in the sun. The grass was brilliant green, the kind of green that only came when carefully fertilized, and its freshly trimmed lengths added a soft smooth texture to the view.

Cole turned back to face her and stared down at her with one brow up in question. "Did you do all of this yourself?" he asked with a slightly disbelieving undertone.

She smiled widely and her head bobbed up and down as she turned to look around with pride. "Not too bad, huh?" she said joyfully. "This place really does have its charm." When he just stared hard at her, she shrugged. "I've been out here working on it whenever I get free time." She looked around for a minute and then back at him. "I still have a lot that I want to do, though, especially out in the front. All I've done up there is mow the lawn and trim out the weeds."

She pointed then to the gorgeous rock patio and asked timidly, "Do you think the picnic table will look okay right there?" She didn't give him a chance to respond before quickly rushing out, "I was originally thinking of putting a bench or two on that side." She pointed to the far side nearest the wood fence that ran along the edge of the yard. "But then I saw that white picnic table and I just couldn't resist it. I kept thinking how nice it would look right out here, so I bought it." She flushed a little with the admission.

Cole looked thoughtfully around the yard before finally saying with quiet admiration, "I don't think there is a place here that would look better." He grinned down at her obvious excitement. "I have to admit I'm surprised. I haven't seen this place ever look this good. In the last fifteen years that Dad has been renting this place out, I have honestly never seen it look like anyone cared about it." His eyes darkened as he surveyed it again and then met her eyes. "You really do love it here, don't you?"

Brooke's smile turned radiant and Cole had to force his gaze away before he lost the internal battle and kissed her again. In the warm afternoon light, her hair shone brightly. Her blue eyes were startlingly deep and luminescent with nature as her backdrop. Fresh pretty face aside, her nicely rounded butt sheathed snugly in those tight skinny jeans would have tempted even a saint. And he was no saint.

He made himself turn away as lust surged hard and hot. Determinedly he forced his body to move, walking quickly back toward the truck. He swore under his breath. If he didn't get that table unloaded and get out of here ASAP, he was going to lose the battle with himself and break his vow to both himself and her. His jaw hardened stubbornly as he lengthened his stride. Behind him he heard her breathing hard as she hurried her step trying to keep up with his fast pace.

They unloaded the table in silence and then together quickly pulled the bench seats out from where they had been tucked neatly beneath the table. That complete, they both stepped back to survey the overall effect. She beamed up at him again with that irresistible happy smile and breathed in wonder, "It's perfect." Then in a more somber tone she added quietly, "Thank you for helping me, Cole. I really appreciate you taking the time." She looked at her feet before adding. "I know I was kind of a pain in the butt, but I actually had a good time today too."

Cole didn't want to respond to her comment about a good time since he was concerned where it might go. Instead, he focused on her pain in the butt comment. He grinned as he tucked a loose curl behind her ear and said in a teasing tone, "The worst." He chuckled lightly and then more seriously added, "You're welcome, though." He looked around again at the yard and smiled. "You really do good work, you know." He chucked her under the chin gently again and then let his arm fall to hang at his side. He had already tempted the devil more than any sane man would do, so he stepped back and away.

"Well, thanks, Cole Burton; I think that is the first compliment you have given me. Now, I seriously owe you one." She smiled and wiggled her eyebrows.

Cole wondered how fast she would run if he told her every nice thing about her that he had noticed throughout the day. He glanced at her very fine ass and smartly held back a grin. Wisely he kept his mouth shut.

She looked at the picnic table brightly, having a great idea, excitedly she turned her face up toward his. "I know what! I should make you dinner and we can sit out here and enjoy it together," she offered with enthusiasm.

Cole ran his fingers tightly through his dark hair and started backing quickly away. He shook his head. "While I appreciate the gesture, that really isn't necessary and besides I have some things I gotta get done tonight." He lied, as images of her eating, started that damn surge of lust again.

Brooke studied his face with a slightly hurt and dubious look. "What on earth do you have to get done on Sunday?" she challenged.

Caught in his own lie, Cole only plastered a confident grin on his face before plunging determinedly forward. "I am right in the middle of a job for a friend and

I told him I would be finished today." He nodded politely and turned to leave.

Behind him he heard her say sarcastically under her breath, "Right, of course you did." He never looked back as he walked away. Didn't even acknowledge her remark, uncertain if he would have the willpower to walk away if he turned back now.

He tapped his horn and waved as he pulled away from the house. He revved the eight-cylinder engine up and spit gravel and sped away as though the devil was on his tail.

He'd been right all along, he thought with a growl of frustration. The best thing he could do for both of their sake's was carefully avoid anything to do with her. He still hadn't dared to ask how old she was and he wasn't sure he really wanted the answer. She was young and innocent either way. Much too innocent to handle the overwhelming animalistic sexuality that she naively triggered in him. He hit the steering wheel and swore loudly. Yes, it was much better if he never knew her age.

Unable to face the mundane thought of home and his family, he pulled up outside the garage and parked the truck. Nothing cleared his head or made him feel more in control than working out a mechanical problem that was difficult.

He strode inside, turning on the bright overhead lights as he walked past the switch. He paused for a long moment surveying the line of old classic cars that were waiting patiently for him to rehab them. Louisa, a '73 Porsche that had been wrecked on the front end and needed completely redone caught his eye. He gave her a sexy grin as he unbuttoned his shirt and shrugged it off. Chest covered by only the black tank that he wore beneath, he gathered tools and walked purposefully toward her.

Yes, he thought, Louisa would do quite nicely to help him work out some of the stress. His shoulders were slick with sweat, and he was still pulling apart her front end when Ivan came in several hours later with a plate of food. He nodded and took the wrench from Cole, trading it for the plate of food and continued where Cole left off pulling the second fender while Cole began to eat. It was, he knew one of the only ways for him to really connect with his son.

Jacob who had always been matter-of-fact and easygoing, tended to wear everything on his sleeve for the great big world to see. It had taken several years before both he and Anne had recognized that Cole was very different.

Unlike his older brother, when Cole had a problem, he was much more likely to bury his emotions inside and put his hands and brain to busy while trying to work through the issue. He could almost always be found out in the garage working on one project or another anytime he was frustrated or out of sorts. At least, Ivan thought with a smile, his second son had figured out how to turn his frustration into a lucrative enterprise.

Though Ivan and Anne had set aside a large chunk of money for each of their children in college funds, Cole had never touched a dime of his. For one thing, Cole had refinished his first antique car at the young age of fourteen. The burgundy 1960 Cadillac Coupe had been refinished from the tan leather seats to the chrome rims and white-walled tires when he was done with her. She had purred like a kitten when Cole had started her up. Jokingly he named her Clarice, which had then started his long-lived tradition of naming every old car he picked up.

A month later he had sold the car to a Vietnam Vet in town who had called out to him in the parking lot of a movie theater and asked him about the car. Cole being Cole, had just shrugged and told him he'd just finished rehabbing her. He was barely old enough to drive and although he had shown little interest in most of the modern sports cars that most kids were excited about, he'd spent months of long hours after school trying to have the car finished by his birthday when he would officially be able to drive it.

He had finished the car a week before his birthday and was thrilled to drive it into town. He'd been engrossed nearly to the point of obsession with the old caddie so when he'd called Jacob for a ride from town and had come home with an envelope full of cash instead of the car, both Ivan and Anne were worried about their son. When they approached him about it, though, Cole had simply shrugged and said in a no-nonsense voice, "It's just an old car and I can get another one and fix it up just as easy." He had smiled and then said, "It meant everything to that old vet, though. He's wanted one of those since he got back from the war."

The next day Ivan and Anne took him into the bank and helped him get both a checking and savings account. Cole put every dollar from the car into his savings account and stated rather matter-of-factly that if he just fixed and sold a few more cars by the time he graduated high school, he could easily pay for his own college.

Ivan had met Anne's worried gaze at his comment and they hurried to reassure him that he already had a large college fund so he didn't need to worry about it. Cole had smiled and nodded. "I know, but wouldn't it be cool if I could just have enough of my own money to cover it?" he'd asked, sounding both excited and determined. Neither of his parents knew what to say to that, so Anne hugged him tightly and Ivan gave him a proud pat on the back.

It hadn't even taken until the end of high school for Cole to save up enough for even an Ivy League education. It turned out he had an eye for cars that someone, somewhere wanted and was willing to pay good money for it. Even with the large amounts he made, he always gave the buyers a great deal compared to the market. That had his buyers talking to friends and soon strangers were calling to ask Cole if he had or could get a specific classic that they had always wanted. Sometimes he hauled them from old junkyards and sometimes he found them at auctions, but either way, he nearly always came through for his buyers.

Cole had eventually started taking other equipment apart as well to figure out how it worked before he would deftly put it back together in perfect working order. He seemed to have an insatiable appetite for understanding components and how they made things run.

Soon Ivan had asked him to work on some of the various farm equipment instead of sending it in to be repaired. Because he knew the value of Cole's time, he always paid him a decent wage. After all, it was possibly the only way for his teenage son to be involved with the operation of the family farm as well. Cole loved the work and was soon professionally repairing or instructing the farm mechanics on how to repair the equipment themselves.

Though Cole was always interested in new equipment, the old cars had never stopped. Ivan had long since lost count of the number of cars Cole had completely rehabilitated and then sold. He doubted even Cole knew that number. He also had no idea how much money his son had made over the years but knew it was a hefty chunk of money.

In the end Cole had needed neither the money from the cars he'd sold nor the college fund that his parents had started when he was only a toddler. In his junior year of high school an East Coast tech school had contacted him about a full ride scholarship opportunity that they wanted him to apply for. At his parents urging, he had agreed and went to a two-week STEM camp where the students were grouped into teams and asked to engineer and program the most efficient robotic equipment that could be used in manufacturing cars.

Cole's team had easily placed first in the exhibit and a month later a package had shown up for him offering him a full six-year scholarship for the engineering program of his choice. He had readily agreed, and then to Ivan's surprise had talked to his high school counselor about graduating early. Against his counselor's advice he took a few classes through the summer as he only needed a few more credits to graduate and was extremely excited to get started on his college education.

In the fall he had thrown his bags and a large red toolbox into the trunk of the '57 Corvette he'd recently finished, named Georgia. She was a brilliant shade of red with a wide white stripe down the center and complete with chrome accents on the front and rear bumper. He'd given his mom a quick hug and his dad a handshake with a shoulder bump and reassured them that he would call when he got to the college campus. He had seemed altogether too grown-up that day.

Anne had cried softly when his car disappeared in a cloud of dust on the recently plowed gravel road. She turned and laid her head against Ivan's shoulder. "Do you think we did okay with him?" she'd asked sadly. When Ivan smiled down at her, she wiped her eyes. "He just seems so distant sometimes, as though he's in his own little world."

Thoughtfully, Ivan stared down the road where the car had gone. "I think he's strong and intelligent and, to be honest, I think sometimes with children who are born that way, there is little raising to do. All that was necessary of us was to love him through it all and we have both done that part well."

That seemed to reassure Anne and make her feel better. Until the following day dawned and they drove Jacob to the airport. He was headed for California and a bright new future there. She had cried spontaneously through the following week at the thought of not one but both of her eldest boys gone off to start the next chapter of their lives.

When Cole came home for Christmas a few months later, he called for a ride from the airport. When Ivan drove to pick him up at the airport, he'd asked him about Georgia. Cole had given him a rather vague look before eventually smiling and answering, "Oh yeah, I sold her a couple months ago. I do have a new car I'm working on, though." He'd flashed an excited grin and told his father all about his latest endeavor named Lucille.

Ivan asked him how school was going to which Cole shrugged. "Same as ever, I guess."

Ivan chuckled. "So, all As and a 4.0 GPA, then?"

Cole nodded absentmindedly. "I have been wondering, though, if there is any way I can just buy an apartment or small house?" He looked out the window at the passing fields. "Campus housing is so crowded, and I don't really have a good place to work, so I end up doing it in the parking lot." He turned to meet his father's sideways look. "I know I'm not eighteen yet, but I wondered if you or Mom could maybe sign with me and then sign it over once I am."

Ivan cleared his throat. "I can talk to your mother, but first I just want to say that buying real estate is expensive, and once you sign, you have to be able to make the payments or it really isn't worth it. Are you sure you're ready for that, son?"

Cole didn't smile or argue, just stated facts. "I'm paying a lot for campus housing now. I've looked up some different options and I wonder where I have plenty to buy something outright with my savings if that wouldn't be better than having money go out of pocket. It would be a good investment since the housing market there is on the rise, so I could potentially make a good sum when I sell it in six years."

Ivan didn't know what to say, so he only smiled and nodded. He wouldn't, however, deny that his own eyes filled with tears if only for a moment. Somehow Cole had become mature and responsible in his own stubborn way. He promised to talk it over with Anne but somehow knew Cole would find a way to do what he wanted, with or without his parents' help.

When Cole came home for the summer after his first year of college, he was grounded and content. The new house with the full garage underneath the two-bedroom home was working out great. He drove home, though it took four days to do it. He drove an old classic Ford truck that he'd found and rebuilt. Unable to think of a suitable name, he kept the truck. For while he couldn't in good conscience give the truck a girl's name, he also couldn't seem to come up with any other name that really suited the truck. He drove into the yard of his family home feeling refreshed and excited to be home again. Little did he know that the truck was going to be one of the only constants in his life over the following years.

The next three years began to take on a similar pattern. For with the exception of the truck, every other vehicle he rebuilt came and went without a moment's hesitation. The girls on the East Coast came and went in somewhat of the same pattern begetting a long string of girls that chased him until he asked them out.

Relationships with the opposite sex, however, he'd soon discovered were definitely not his strong suit. The girls were needy and clingy, and though in the beginning of the relationship they found it sexy that he fixed cars, they soon became angry at what they saw as a weird attachment. When the relationships turned sour, he broke up with them. It didn't, after all, seem healthy to be constantly questioned about why exactly he needed to spend all that time in his garage.

By his twentieth birthday, he had tired of the constant flirting and hanging all over him that women seemed prone to do when he was around, so he swore off dating. Some of the girls he'd dated moved on with other friends and students, though a few of them came back to try to get him back when they realized many of the other guys were disrespectful and immature.

He agreed only to new friendships with them but insisted that they weren't a good match. He found himself socializing less and less instead, spending more time working on cars and other pet projects he had in his garage. Despite his mother constantly asking if he'd found someone special, he shied away from dating except when he was too attracted to someone to ignore it. Then he was very clear that it was only casual dating and went home to his house alone every night afterwards.

It was shortly after his twentieth birthday that he'd come across the broken-up '67 Mustang. He'd first seen her in an old junkyard he drove past. He got online and searched for hours until he finally found an ad by the owner who simply wanted her gone. Something about her rusty broken body had touched him. She had been in a terrible accident where she had rolled several times before finally ending up wrapped around what had to have been a large tree.

Her entire body was wrecked and she had spent ten years sitting in the back lot of an old shutdown body shop. Cole knew even as he looked her over that he would be better off walking away. He knew he would spend more time and money fixing her up than she was worth, but something about her called to him. Grin on his face at his own fixation, he'd reluctantly had her towed to his garage. One section at a time he had worked on her, replacing more parts than those he kept of her original body.

Several times he had even tried talking some sense into himself and letting her go. He nearly gave up on finding some of the rare parts he'd needed to finish the job, but in the end, he couldn't just let her rot. His gut told him he should paint her something bright and catchy as that seemed to be popular with his buyers. In the end, however, he had settled on a light silvery blue that seemed somehow to give her the elegant glow of class that she deserved.

By the time he had her purring like a kitten, Cole knew that he was going to keep her. He still hadn't named her as he was more determined with her to find the perfect name. Just like his truck, however, the name seemed to shift just out of reach of him as though quietly taunting him from the distance. He drove her home during spring break that year.

As he pulled into the driveway, his mother hurried out with a happy smile. She gave the car a quick once-over and him a welcoming hug before turning back to smile at the car. "So, who do we have here, Cole? Does she have a name?" she'd asked teasingly.

Cole had shoved his hands into his pockets as he looked with pride at the her now-shimmering elegant body and shrugged. "I'm not sure yet."

His mom made a little loop around her in an effort to connect with her son before circling back to Cole. "She is very pretty. A little more understated than most of the cars you rebuild," she said and smiled at Cole who nodded and smiled back.

"She really is, isn't she? I think I might actually keep this one, Mom." He looked as surprised at the admission as Anne who raised an eyebrow as though to say. *Finally.*

Anne ordered him to stay where he was and hurried back inside. She reappeared a moment later with a large camera hanging from her neck on a strap. She smiled at his groan and ordered him to stand by the car so she could take a quick photo or two. Knowing his mother wouldn't give up until he let her take some pictures, he grinned easily, turning in resignation to lean a hip against her curvy, silvery blue body.

Now, though, as Cole ate and Ivan worked. He thought back to each of the homecomings since Cole had first gone away for school. He loosened a bolt and then angled his head around the open hood to get a good look at his son. "Is everything going all right, son?" he asked evenly.

Cole grunted around a bite of chicken with rice.

Ivan gave a little laugh before turning solemn. "I know you like to come out here and work a lot but you do usually at least come inside for meals unless you have a lot of thinking to do." He made the statement in a quiet steady tone.

Cole set his loaded fork back onto his plate with a clink. "I'm okay. Just thinking about all the mistakes I've made in life and wishing I could undo them or somehow make them up."

Ivan's right brow shot up as he dropped the wrench and walked around to face Cole. "I hope you know how proud I am of you, Cole."

Cole didn't meet his dad's eyes. "I know." His voice was a little unsteady. "I also realize that you and Mom haven't been a hundred percent privy to everything I've done in the past few years."

Uneasiness settled on Ivan's shoulders. "What are we talking about here, son?"

Cole did meet his gaze then, feeling angry at himself. "I have made a lot of mistakes. There were so many girls that I could have treated better. Girls I ignored or just didn't give enough attention to. I'm sure you know how it is. You weren't always married to Mom."

Ivan sighed. "You're right in technical terms, son, but I like to think that I was always married to her somewhere deep in my heart. I like to believe that all of the failed relationships I had before failed because I was secretly always looking for your mother. When I found her, I knew. Nothing else mattered at that point but that she was there with me and it was what I had always been searching for." He held Cole's gaze as he said quietly, "I don't know exactly what you're beating yourself up for, son, but I know you are a good man. I also know that when it's right for you, you'll know. All the other relationships between that may feel like mistakes but are really just stepping stones to help you find what you're looking for."

Cole pulled his gaze away and stared hard at the hood of the old car. "I suppose you're right. I know what you and Mom have is special now that I've tried to have relationships that have failed miserably."

Ivan chuckled. "Your mom and I are good. Just don't go deluding yourself that any relationship exists that doesn't have its challenges and hardships because they all do. It's when we know the challenges are worth it that defines its value."

Cole smiled fleetingly. "I get it. I just don't know what it all means for me yet."

Ivan laughed and set a hand on his shoulder. "None of us do, son. When you get it all figured out, though, come clue me in too, oh, and welcome to manhood," he added with another chuckle.

CHAPTER 14

Brooke spent all her spare time over the following two weeks working out in her front yard in nature. She loved the fresh air and working with the soil and plants. It seemed to ground and support her even with the turmoil she experienced when thinking of Cole.

She hadn't seen him since he'd helped her with the table, but that fact really didn't surprise her. At this point it was pretty obvious that he couldn't stand being around her and truly wanted nothing to do with her. Though her heart ached at that realization, she admitted even to herself that it was probably for the best, especially given that two more weeks had passed and still she hadn't bled.

Whenever she found her mind wandering to thoughts of him and where he was, she reminded herself sensibly that getting involved with anyone under the circumstances would be unwise. Still, her heart ached and she admitted, if only to herself that she really wanted to see him again. Every day felt like the dark clouds overhead swirled ever closer as though a promise of struggle and hardship was on the horizon.

It was on a bright Saturday morning that she finally worked up the courage to take the pregnancy test that had been sitting inside her closet unopened. She read through the instructions and then followed them carefully. As she waited impatiently for the two-minute timer to ring, she focused on breathing calmly in and out. When the timer went off, she jumped a little, nerves on edge before reaching for the stick and peering into the tiny plastic window for the results.

She did a double take when she saw the positive result. She blinked hard and looked again before sinking down heavily to sit onto the toilet. Fear surged first and then frustration as she wondered how she had stupidly managed to end up in this predicament. When the frustration settled, she cried. She cried for the loss of her own innocence and childhood. Then she cried for the innocence of the unborn child inside her. She cried great gulping sobs until she was physically spent and emotionally exhausted.

When the tears finally stopped, she stood and ran a hot bath. She slid into the bubbly water and soaked until her hands and feet were waterlogged with deep wrinkles before finally pulling herself up and out of the water. Exhausted she wrapped a towel around herself and her hair and walked numbly into the bedroom. She collapsed onto the bed clad only in the towel. The towel parted at the bottom and her stomach peeked through.

Suddenly intrigued she stared intently at her stomach trying to tell if it was any bigger than it had been before. She tried to imagine a bump there but couldn't. Her stomach still looked flat and ridged, so if there was a change, she couldn't see it. She tugged the towel together as a lifetime of being told endlessly to be modest settled inside. She rolled over to her side to get more comfortable and fell promptly into a fitful sleep plagued with dreams of wandering endlessly while looking for a home. She slept all afternoon and through the night getting up only when hunger settled its growling way inside, so she couldn't sleep any longer the following morning. As she walked down the hall still clad only in a towel, she took a chapter from Cole's book and let out a long string of curses.

The following week went by in an emotional blur. Though she felt guilty every time she talked to either Ivan or Jacob and didn't tell them the truth, she just couldn't seem to find the words. Since Jacob texted her every day to update her and ask about her day, she ended each working day racked with guilt for not having told him. Somehow, she just couldn't bring herself to tell him something so life changing in a text. She would have to admit the truth eventually as it wasn't exactly something she could hide forever, but she just wasn't quite ready to face their disappointment yet.

The next week, morning sickness kicked in with a vengeance and she began feeling sick all the time. She woke up feeling sweaty and clammy, though her appetite stayed strong. She found herself throwing up after nearly every meal. She managed her morning sickness by making sure to eat long before she left for work in the morning to give her stomach plenty of time to accept or reject her breakfast before leaving for work.

On Thursday morning Ivan overheard heard her throwing up in the shop restroom and immediately told her to go home for the day. Brooke refused to go, calmly reassuring him that she was fine to work through whatever she had. She couldn't exactly afford to take every day off that she felt sick after all and had to be ready for the long haul with her pregnancy, though she still hadn't had the courage to tell him about it. He eventually caved and let her work but only because her color already looked better to him.

It was the following Saturday, which just happened to be the weekend before July 4th, that she next saw Cole. Ivan had cheerfully reminded her that he and Anne were throwing their annual company, friends, and family barbecue. He had already told her that every year they invited all of their employees both from the farm and Anne's clinic. She hadn't responded to her invitation yet and Ivan jokingly informed her that it was mandatory, though she knew it wasn't.

It was rumored to be quite a large affair as they also invited all of their closest neighbors and friends to come join in the fun. All of the workers had been talking excitedly about the event for weeks now. Brooke thought of spending her Saturday at home relaxing and wasn't sure she wanted to attend, but Ivan wouldn't take no for an answer. He stubbornly insisted that her attendance was a must and she couldn't exactly beg off without telling him why she felt like relaxing so much. Hands tied, she finally agreed to show up at least for an hour or so. Ivan beamed happily down at her. "You won't regret it. You'll see." Since he seemed so sure of that fact, she let his confidence reign.

Brooke had never actually been to a barbecue and in reality, had absolutely no clue how she was supposed to dress. She'd looked up what clothes to wear to a barbecue on her phone and got such a wide variety of dress that she gave up on that information source.

She had a soft white sundress with delicate little plum-colored lilies embroidered in curving rows along the bottom of the skirt around the hem as well as a curvy row that ran across the bodice just above the high waistline of the dress that she had splurged and bought recently. It was sleeveless and the skirt flared out slightly and ended a few inches above her knees. She didn't have anything else she could imagine wearing it for, so she decided she may as well wear it now. Besides she would soon be round and who knew if the dress would ever fit her again.

She had a pair of medium-heeled strappy sandals that where silver and seemed like a good match with the dress that she pulled out of her closet as well.

Though she had finally taken a pair of scissors to her hair to cut off the bottom two inches of split ends and uneven hair, she still wished she had gone to a salon and had it cut professionally. She had finally taken the time and spent a rather large chunk of money on a bag full of all the makeup a young woman at the department store assured was absolutely necessary. She still hadn't yet worn any of the makeup, however, feeling uncertain about the application. Though the same young lady had also given her instructions on how to apply it, Brooke felt clumsy and awkward.

Deciding that it was now or never, she spent Friday night watching makeup videos for application and blending. Even with all the videos, it took her an hour and a half to get ready. The makeup kept smearing in a very unfortunate way that the video had forgot to mention and it took several tries before she was finally somewhat satisfied with the results. She still didn't look all sleek and beautiful, but it did look okay.

Her bright blue eyes were accented by both the mascara she'd applied as well as the blue and pink eye shadow she'd neatly blended to make the color pop. Her skin was now clear and slightly tanned so she'd only used a light powder to gently hide her freckles and added a warm glowing rose blusher. She had completely avoided the bottle of goopy-looking nude slime since she was sure using it would cause more damage than good in her hands.

With a little sigh she stepped back and stared curiously at her new reflection in the mirror. It was a little strange to see herself that way. That somewhat pretty-looking woman staring back at her looking slightly older and almost like someone else entirely. She smiled a little and then added a light rose-colored lip gloss to finish the look before gently smacking her lips together the way she'd seen the girl in the video do.

Feeling more nervous than usual, she quickly slid the lip gloss in her purse so that she could reapply it later if she needed to. Strapping the sandals around her slender ankles she glanced down at her watch and shrieked. The makeup process had taken much longer than she had expected. She had planned on showing up plenty early so that she could help with anything Anne or Ivan might need. It would also have given her a chance to adjust to the environment at their house before too many people showed up. She sighed anxiously and hurried out the door. There wasn't a whole lot she could do at this point except hurry and get there.

It was early afternoon when she parked her car next to a minivan she didn't recognize and walked quickly toward the house. The gate to the backyard was open and she could hear children laughing and shouting joyfully. Self-consciously she brushed a quick hand down her skirt, smoothing it as she neared the open gate. Heart thudding loudly in anticipation, she took a deep breath and held her head high with a smile as she stepped through the white vinyl gate.

It hit her all at once like a sensory overload. The smell of hot dogs and burgers sizzling on the grill. Several children were running and playing beneath a large maple tree and she watched as one small but quick young girl playfully tagged Ryker before turning to run off. She took in her surroundings seeing Ivan and Luis standing together behind two rather large-looking grills. Next to the grills stood a long table overloaded with bowls of food and packages of treats and cookies. At one end were large boxes filled with eating ware. On the other side of the grill were two huge tubs of ice loaded with water and a variety of soft drinks. Just behind it and set high in the air just out of reach of little children was a third tub that looked like it was filled with beer and a variety of other alcoholic beverages.

From the corner of her eye, she saw Anne trying without much success to get the children lined up for a game and Brooke watched her for a moment as she wondered what it felt like to be a mom. Her hand went to her stomach to lay flatly there until she realized what she was doing and quickly dropped it to her side.

Women stood around in small groups, visiting with glasses of wine or other soft drinks in hand. Most of the men stood in a large circle not too far from the grills and she suspected that they stood just close enough to include Ivan and Luis in the conversation. She quickly scanned the throng looking for Cole. He wasn't there and she breathed a sigh of relief.

She wanted to turn and leave. Felt completely out of her comfort zone. She didn't, however, want to let Ivan down after all he had done for her. She looked around hesitantly, unsure where to go. Should she go talk to Anne and see if she wanted help? Should she go get food? Unable to decide, she stood rooted to the spot looking frantically around.

It was too much to deal with. She turned back to the gate ready to bolt but a strong hand clasped her arm and stopped her midturn. She knew instantly who it was. She gulped and turned nervously to meet his dark eyes. Heat seeped into her arm and worked its way up into her cheeks as she studied him. She couldn't help herself. She wanted to stop but couldn't help her perusal as she drank in the sight of his rugged good looks.

His hair was longer than the last time she'd seen him. She liked the way it curled rebelliously down his neck to tease at his collar. He was wearing a peach and blue square patterned button-up that made his dark eyes look black. He had his sleeves rolled up to his elbows which made his muscular arms look fit and strong. His cream-colored slacks narrowed down to rest lightly on the shiny brown leather shoes on his feet.

She felt a surge of heat start in her core and reminded herself that she was not to get mixed up in anything right now. She glared up at him suddenly angry. "What do you want?" she asked through clenched teeth.

His lips stretched into a wide grin. He took his time looking her up and down critically before letting his gaze collide once again with hers. She glared hotly again and tried to yank her arm free. He held it firmly and she couldn't help noticing the ripple of muscle in his forearm next to her own. She forced her gaze away and reminded herself that she was pregnant with someone else's baby. Anger was better.

It did indeed piss her off that he thought he could avoid her for weeks at a time without even a thought and then come over to invade her personal space and tip her entire world on end before turning away again completely unaffected. He had been doing that very thing since that first day and she suddenly wanted to stomp on his toes. She refrained, of course. What kind of lady stomped on even a demon's toes after all?

He held her gaze, which at this moment was sending blue shards of anger at him. He was turned on as hell and her angry little rebellious nature wasn't exactly helping the situation. He hadn't meant to touch her or even acknowledge her tonight. But then he had seen her walk through the gate and pause. He'd turned back to the friend he was talking to not recognizing her at first. But then all that red hair teased at him and he swung back to confirm his suspicion as recognition hit.

He'd quite literally felt like someone took a bat to his gut when he studied her gorgeous face and all that thick curly hair tied at her nape but still curling down her back. And then, God help him he'd caught a glimpse of her shapely legs. He meant to turn away then, to force his mind off her and back to his conversation. His friend whistled softly, "Who is that pretty young thing?"

Cole growled something low and his friend laughed. He turned then and saw her looking around and knew instinctively that she was nervous. It was obvious by her flexing fingers that she felt out of place. Still, he'd planned to ignore her. His sanity quite literally depended on just how well he could ignore her.

He saw her hand settle on her stomach to calm her nerves. She looked terrified and instinctively he knew she was going to run. Knew it the same way he knew when a motor was running smoothly or that it had a nasty little tick. He took several quick strides barely reaching her side and grasping her arm firmly as she turned to flee. "Going somewhere, Brooke?"

It chafed at him that she hadn't even noticed him a few feet away while he had been aware and watching her since she'd stepped through the gate. He turned and nodded quickly at his old high school friend as he had walked away a bit rudely in the middle of the conversation. His friend chuckled and saluted him in understanding and a bit of envy.

When she turned to look up at him, he saw the fear in her eyes before she shoved it aside and let her temper flare. He had never known how sexy a temper could be, but he definitely liked her when she was angry. He felt the strange caress of that hot spark that lit blue fire in her eyes. He knew he shouldn't be looking at her, noticing those long shapely legs, or the snug fullness of her breasts beneath that tight frothy white fabric. He knew that he was playing with fire even as he stepped closer. Unfortunately, it didn't stop him.

She was glaring up at him again and tugging on her arm. The devil inside him had him leaning down to breathe against the sexy slope of her neck, "You look good enough to ravage, my dear." Heat flared between them again. Purely out of self-preservation and to keep himself from kissing those rosy pink lips he asked with one eyebrow up. "Did you do something different with your hair?"

She gave him a firm but dainty shake of her head. He had a lot of nerve. She felt her hands tighten into fists and realized she wanted to shake him. She wanted to get her strong little fists right up under his collar and really give him a good shake. What on earth was the matter with him? One moment he was kissing or flirting with her only to turn around the next and spend weeks at a time completely avoiding her. She took a deep breath as she tried and failed to calm her soaring emotions.

She swallowed her anger and in a saccharine sweet voice gave him a flirty little bat of her lashes. "Not at all, Cole. In fact, all this, is exactly what I wear with every guy I go out with." The anger inside had at least dissipated her shyness now and she smiled sweetly up at him. "Now, if you're done manhandling and ogling me, I'm going to go over and say hello to your mom and dad before I leave." She turned on her heel and walked away without a backward glance.

A hot surge of anger simmered in his gut as Cole watched her walk away. He suspected she was just messing with him but had she really been going out with a lot of guys? He ground out a curse. It shouldn't matter to him who she chose to date. In fact, it was probably a good thing since it gave him even another reason to stay away. He strode back to his friend and talked him into a twenty-dollar game of pool. It was best that she be out of his sight. His friend, Mike Bauer agreed and they grabbed a couple more beers before heading inside to the pool table.

Brooke quickly beelined it toward Ivan with a curse on her tongue, no thanks to Cole. She stopped to give a friendly smile and say hello to a couple of women she recognized who were standing together in a small group while visiting. She warmly thanked them for all of the great food they'd brought out to the crew. She awkwardly introduced herself to the women she hadn't met.

Luis's wife, Isabel, smiled warmly and nodded before turning to translate the quick conversation for the other woman she was standing with. Brooke gave them all friendly smiles as she shook her hand and then in turn the other women's hands as Isabel told her their names. Content that she had done her social duty, she smiled again and waved as she informed them she was off to say hello to Ivan.

She only made it two steps before being waylaid by Maude who latched on to her arm with a conspiring announcement. "Brooke honey, I'm so glad you're here." She gave the younger woman a quick wink. "And here I was starting to think I was going to have to endure this entire mundane thing by myself!"

Brooke smiled and kissed her rosy cheek. She stepped back to get a good look at Maude's colorful flowing top and black dress pants. Somehow the older woman had managed to look both classy and warmly inviting in the simple getup. Bright blue dream catchers hung from her ears and accented the outfit perfectly.

Brooke smiled again. "You know I would never allow that, Maude," she stated laughingly. As if the woman had ever endured a dull moment in her life. "You look lovely today." Brooke cast a quick glance around the yard again. "Where is Frank anyway?"

Maude shook her head as though unable to believe what she was about to say. "Would you believe that he is out working today instead of being here with me?" She gave Brooke a deep frown and then followed it with a grin. "I told him it's not going to be my fault if some dashing young man comes and sweeps a great catch like me off my feet while he's off working."

Brooke laughed aloud. Everyone who knew Maude had heard an abundance of lovely stories about her loving husband of thirty-five years. She was constantly telling anyone who'd listen about the many sweet things Frank did for her. "As if, Maude." She gave another little laugh. "Well, I will happily try to sweep you off your feet if it makes you feel any better. I'd love a catch like you," Brooke teased as she squeezed her hand warmly.

Maude just wriggled her brows suggestively. "Now that, is something to consider, my dear. He's not here to see it and who would dare to tell him anyway?"

Brooke chuckled again and gave her another peck on the cheek. "You are a terrible example, you know?" she teased. She looped her arm through Maude's as they made their way over to Ivan.

Ivan did a quick double take and then whistled lightly as he reached one arm out to give Brooke a quick hug. "Well, don't you look lovely today," he said and then frowned thoughtfully. "It's going to make my job a very difficult one tonight." He saw Maude then and smiled as he bent to give her a kiss on her cheek. He whistled lightly and grinned. "I'm going to be very busy trying to keep the young men off the two of you tonight, aren't I?"

Maude looked sufficiently pleased but Brooke only flushed slightly and changed the subject. She glanced around the space. "Do you need me to help out with anything?" She sounded hopeful, which made Maude laugh.

Ivan looked horrified at her offer as he gave a pointed look at her white dress. He shook his head and smiled. "I wouldn't dream of wrecking that dress and today is a good chance for you to relax and get to know some of the neighbors." In a quiet tone, for her ears alone he confided, "Everyone has been talking about the new girl that's working for us. I think it's high time they all meet you so they can quit pestering me about it." He chuckled and skillfully turned some burgers over on the grill.

Maude who was listening a bit unrepentantly to every word he said, tugged gently on her arm. "Great idea, boss. I'll just take her around now and start making some introductions."

Brooke dragged her feet as she was propelled forward by the surprisingly strong grip of the older woman. She threw a begging look at Ivan as she was whisked away and got only a shrug and a grin in return.

The next few hours flew by as she was introduced to so many neighbors and friends of the family that she could no longer keep all of their names straight. Several of the young men asked her to save them a dance for later and she smiled and cheerfully informed them that she wouldn't "be here that long, but thank you so much anyway."

She didn't notice the slightly insulted and somewhat disappointed looks that followed her as she went on her way. Maude, however, kept saying, "Poor guy, he looks like you took his puppy, and Oh that one was really upset, hon. Are you sure you don't want to at least give him a shot, dear? He is quite handsome and his daddy is a good man."

Brooke would only shake her head and smile. "I am not looking for a man right now. My life is very complicated as it is."

One of Maude's brows rose at the comment and she turned those intelligent eyes on Brooke to ask, "What is so complicated about your life, dear?"

Brooke shrugged. "Everything! I don't know what I want to do with myself yet long-term and I'm still trying to figure out how I even fit into this world."

Maude gave her a long hard stare. "Is that really all that's going on, dear? You have seemed a little more stressed of late."

Brooke forced a smile and held the older woman's gaze steadily. She was afraid

Maude would see right through her if she let anything slip. "I never really believed I could get away from my family and now that I have, I feel like I'm constantly trying to figure out where I fit."

Maude didn't want to let it go but wisely did, asking only, "Are you sure there isn't already some young man that you're hung up on, Brooke?"

Brooke stared blankly and then shook her head.

Maude continued to watch her with that piercing stare for a long moment. "I've introduced you to several young men who are kind and very good-looking and I haven't once seen any interest on your part."

Brooke only shrugged. "Like I said, I'm not looking to make life more complicated right now. Now, can we talk about something else, please?"

Maude wisely closed her mouth and nodded.

They got huge plates of food and found a place to sit. She had just set her plate down and settled on a bench at one of the picnic tables when Ryker came running up and wrapped her in a bear hug. She smiled warmly down at him and then invited him to sit by her to eat his food. He nodded cheerfully and then promptly turned to yell across the yard to Dominic that he was the luckiest after all since he got to sit by Brooke.

That of course started a loud argument that ended with Maude who was originally seated to one side of Brooke to be nearly shoved off the bench as Dominic shouldered his way between them and stated with great authority that he was older and therefore should have first dibs on sitting with Brooke.

Maude squealed, and then, as she was righted by Ivan, who had just walked up, only turned to call him a handsome young brute, which didn't exactly tame his ego as she ruffled his hair fondly. Then she wisely removed herself from the table altogether and claimed a nearby lawn chair. After Maude left, all the young boys came over vying at once for the opportunity to be near their friends and also to take part in determining who was most suited to sit with Brooke. A loud discussion ensued, which had everyone gathering around to see what all the commotion was about.

Brooke tried several times to remove herself only to be overcrowded by the large group of boys. She finally gave up and focused instead on eating as she watched with curiosity the young men reasoning out who was truly best suited to a seat at what had been dubbed Brooke's Table. She grinned openly at a few of the illogical reasonings of the prepubescent boys while she enjoyed the burger and potato salad. She didn't notice the crowd that had gathered until she stood and reached for her drink, which was now across the table from boys pushing and shoving while vying for better position. She froze with the cold soda can in hand as a crimson blush worked its way up her neck.

Nearly every person in attendance stood circled around with differing looks of amusement, interest, and even a couple of parents who looked horrified at their child's behavior but couldn't make their way through the crowd to stop it.

She sat heavily back down and reached for a cookie. All she could do now was let it play out. The conversation took a wild turn as the boys began fighting about who got to dance with her the most times tonight. Brooke's plate was cleaned off now, but still hungry, she reached for a forgotten plate of chips and salsa nearby and started eating that.

To her surprise it was Anne who finally made her way over to save her. She gave a loud whistle through her fingers and hurried through the gap made as boys turned to see where it had come from. At the table she threw quick smile at Brooke, and turned to tell the once-again noisy boys that she needed to borrow Brooke to help her in the house. Brooke stood and gratefully extracted herself as noises of complaints ensued as she followed Anne away. It was the warmest Anne had ever been to her, and though she didn't understand why or what had changed, she wasn't going to question it right now.

Anne turned and smiled again as she opened the back door for them to step through, "Boys will be boys as I'm sure you know," she said. "Give them about five minutes or so and they will be on to the next exciting adventure." She waved a hand at Brooke. "I'm sure you know all about that, though. You have brothers, right?"

Brooke beamed and nodded. "Yes, I have six of them from my mother and way too many cousins to count."

Anne smiled at her as she made her way to the fridge. "You seem comfortable with the kids, so I figured you must have experience." She opened the fridge to pull out two large bowls and set them on the counter. "We ran out of potato salad and fruit salad." She offered kindly in response to Brooke's curious look.

In that very unfortunate moment, Brooke's stomach chose to heave. She turned green and quickly asked if she could use the restroom, afraid she was going to lose her lunch all over the kitchen floor. Anne pointed in the general direction of the hall and Brooke bolted. She barely made it to the toilet before her stomach heaved again.

She spent a good fifteen minutes in the bathroom after throwing up just to make sure it wasn't going to happen again. She used her hands to splash cool water on her face and rinse her mouth out. She took a couple extra minutes to tuck some wayward curls back into the knot she had formed on the back of her neck. She applied a fresh coat of lip gloss and then opened the door with resolve. She was going to find Ivan to tell him thanks before she left for home. He had finished grilling lunch a bit ago and had been making the rounds visiting with their guests before the fight.

She came out of the bathroom and heard laughter down the hall. Curiously, she turned towards the sound, but then she heard the low timbre of Cole's voice. She stopped midstep and turned back toward the kitchen. She was not in the mood to get into anything with him again. She had wondered where he had gone since he'd disappeared shortly after their conversation.

She frowned as she turned the corner into the kitchen. She had to stop this infatuation she had with him. Hadn't he made it very clear that he didn't want anything to do with her? She shook her head in frustration; she needed to get away from him and get back home where she could think more clearly. With strengthened resolve, she moved quickly into the kitchen and toward the back door. She jumped in surprise and spun when Anne quietly asked, "Can I talk to you for a minute, Brooke?"

She'd thought that Anne had gone back outside by now with food replacements.

She glanced at the bar and saw that the bowls were gone. She swallowed, feeling suddenly uneasy as she turned to meet the older woman's direct unsmiling gaze. She nodded mutely.

Anne smiled then and motioned with her hand toward a chair by the long mahogany table. She sat across from the chair and waited patiently for Brooke to join her. Brooke dragged her high-heeled sandals reluctantly as she moved over and sat down.

Brooke forced her gaze up and put her hands in her lap as she cleared her throat. "What were you wanting to talk about?" she asked, sounding every bit as nervous as she felt.

Anne held her gaze and then to Brooke's surprise reached out a calming hand to clasp hers. "Ivan had mentioned to me that you had a bug the other day." Gaze steady she watched Brooke who only nodded her agreement.

She sighed and then smiled, trying instinctively to put Brooke at ease. "I saw you throwing up out by the shop yesterday when I drove past," she admitted with a gentle smile. Brooke still didn't offer anything, so she continued. "As you know, I am a doctor." She hesitated as the younger woman simply nodded miserably at her. "I'm aware that I could just be jumping to conclusions here, but I am wondering if you are pregnant?"

Brooke nodded jerkily as tears swam in her bright eyes. She looked miserable and couldn't bring herself to meet Anne's gaze now. Anne already hadn't liked her and who knew how she would feel about her now that she knew the truth.

She blinked rapidly trying unsuccessfully to clear the tears away and forced her gaze up to Anne's knowing green one. Fully expecting to see condemnation and even anger in Anne's green eyes, she was surprised as she saw only compassion. Guilt surged for not telling Ivan or Jacob sooner. She lifted her shoulders and prayed for courage as with a firmer voice she quietly said, "I have been meaning to tell Ivan and Jacob, I really have."

"I wasn't sure that I was pregnant until a week ago, and since then I haven't been able to bring myself to admit it out loud to anyone." She looked down at her hands for a minute and then guiltily rushed out, "I swear I would have told them eventually. I've just been building up the courage. I'm sorry." She turned her imploring gaze to Anne's.

Anne watched her face for a long moment before finally saying, "I believe you, Brooke." Then she asked gently, "Do you know how far along you are yet?"

Brooke nodded and then shook her head immediately afterwards, which made Anne laugh. Her laughter made Brooke blush so Anne immediately forced a calm smile of encouragement instead. "What I mean is that I know when my last cycle was," Brooke offered. "And I think I have a pretty good idea about when my due date might be, but I don't know the exact day yet."

Anne asked for the start date of her last cycle and then quickly did the math in her head. She met Brooke's eyes and noticed that she looked more curious than scared now. Calm was good, Anne thought and squeezed Brooke's hand with her own again. "That would put you right around eleven weeks. Which puts your due date somewhere in the middle of January."

Brooke seemed pleased with that bit of information as she finally smiled a little.

Anne hesitated but finally asked, "And do you know who the father is?"

A stricken look of fear crossed Brooke's face before she could stop it. She nodded. "I do."

Anne waited patiently but Brooke didn't say any more, so she asked, "Does he know about the baby?"

This time there was no mistaking her look of fear as Brooke shook her head adamantly. "No." She mouthed the one word. In a hoarse whisper she said, "And he can never know."

Anne didn't know what to make of that, so she simply made Brooke promise to make an appointment at the clinic or with another doctor soon. After Brooke agreed, Anne squeezed her hand once more before letting it go. She stood then, looking down at Brooke to say quietly, "You need to tell Ivan, Brooke, mostly because he deserves the truth but also because you shouldn't be maintaining the same level of workload while you're expecting."

Brooke looked up in surprise; she had foolishly assumed that Anne had already talked to Ivan. She nodded her head emphatically. "I will. I promise. Thank you for letting me be the one to tell him. I know you didn't have to wait for that."

Anne gave her a quick nod and a smile. "I know I haven't been very involved with you, Brooke, but it looks like my husband and children think the world of you. I don't see how I can stay out of it anymore, so I just want you to know that I am on your side now."

Brooke stared across at her as questions surged unanswered through her mind. She smiled and nodded. "Thank you so much, ma'am.

Opening the sliding glass door, Anne turned as she said seriously, "I should warn you, though, if you are planning to hurt in any way or trying to take advantage of my husband or any of my sons, all bets are off." She stared hard at Brooke's now-pale face. "Pregnant or not, I will do whatever I have to do to protect my family." She left the threat hanging in the air as she turned with a friendly smile, walking out to visit with their guests.

CHAPTER 15

Brooke stood on trembling legs and hurried quickly back to the bathroom. In the rectangular mirror her skin looked pale and gaunt, which made the freckles stand out despite her light makeup. She thought of Anne's fierce expression as she had given her the warning. A helpless tear slid down one cheek and she brushed it away in frustration as she fought off the overwhelming emotions that were bubbling up.

She took a deep breath, attempting to calm herself. She could not afford to fall apart now. Scratch that, the baby growing inside her could not afford for her to fall apart. She took another painful gulp of air. Anne was right about one thing, she had to admit. She *had* been taking advantage of Ivan and Jacob. Though not intentionally for they had made it difficult for her anytime she wouldn't allow them to help her. With a miserable feeling of regret, she swiped away another tear. She absolutely agreed with Anne that it was unacceptable to take advantage of their kindness. She smiled harshly as she found herself once again agreeing with the woman. Ivan and Jacob would never stop trying to help her out. She could see it clearly now. Her only choice at this point was to go away. Somewhere far enough to ensure that neither one of them would or even could help her out.

Brooke forced her mind from thoughts of the home she had been creating and her friendship with Jacob. Heart throbbing at the thought of not seeing him again, she reached into her purse and pulled out her phone. She turned it on and looked at her checking account, puffing out her cheeks as she worked out the math in her head. She had been saving most of her paychecks and was now grateful as she would need every penny of it when she left here. She had enough savings to find a small space to rent and buy groceries for a couple of months, but she would have to be able to get a job right away.

She put one hand on her stomach and smiled through the tears. They would be okay, she thought and with a hand splayed warmly over her belly button, she looked in the mirror at her reflection and forced a smile. Yes, they would be okay. She would make sure of that.

Mind made up, she let herself out of the bathroom and hurried up the hall and through the kitchen. She could hear Cole laughing again and her heart throbbed again as she paused to listen for a moment before walking determinedly away. After today she would never see or hear him again.

She lifted her chin and squared her shoulders as peace settled inside. From now on, every decision she made had to be in the best interest of the baby growing inside her. That thought led to the sudden realization that she completely understood the fierce look on Anne's face when she had threatened her because of her family. She smiled, happy to know that Anne felt that way and would take care of Jacob and Ivan and look after them with that same level of intensity.

She made her way blindly through the crowded backyard determined to make her way to Ivan. Brooke was waylaid by several people stopping her to ask friendly questions or make little jokes about how many young men she was seeing at once. It took her a frustrating twenty minutes to finally extricate herself from the group of young men and young women who had stopped her to once again offer several invitations to events they were planning nearby. At this rate the dance would start and finish by the time she finally got to have a word with Ivan. She swallowed a groan as yet another man stepped in front of her to offer his name and ask for a dance later. She politely thanked him and told him she was leaving right away but promised to save one next time.

Ivan saw her coming toward him and met her in the center with his usual warm grin. He shook the hand of the man he was talking to before saying something funny and turning to walk toward her. She fought back emotional tears as she realized this would be the last time she saw him and pasted a warm smile on her lips. He reached her and put one arm companionably around her shoulders as he squeezed. "I haven't seen much of you today," he said as he smiled down at her. "Come to think of it, I haven't seen much of you for the past few weeks. How are you doing, Brooke?"

She forced a smile. "I suppose that's because we are both so busy." She easily sidestepped the issue of his wife not liking her.

Ivan turned serious as he took in her pale face and neck. "Are you sure you're okay?" he asked quiet enough that others standing nearby couldn't hear.

Brooke shook her head miserably. "I was actually wondering if you have just a minute to talk to me." She looked around at the throngs of visitors a little guiltily. "I know it's not a great time what with all of your guests, but I promise to take only a second."

Ivan turned without hesitation urging her along with a hand on her elbow as he guided them to an empty, and somewhat shady spot near the tall white picket fence. He looked concerned now as he moved to face her.

Brooke saw Anne across the lawn and hesitated. Three middle-aged women were standing near her and laughing. Anne was nodding and smiling politely to the group but watching Ivan and Brooke. Their gazes collided and held for a brief moment before Brooke turned to look up at Ivan.

She didn't know how to say what she needed to say. He watched her with his warm brown eyes as he waited patiently for her to find her tongue. She licked her suddenly dry lips and plunged in. "I wanted to let you know that I'm pregnant," she blurted awkwardly. She watched him, waiting with a thudding heartbeat for the disgust that she knew was coming. Waited patiently for his anger to lash out at her. His eyes widened slightly in surprise, but the warmth was still there. He didn't say anything at first, so she hurried to explain. "I found out last week and I know I should have told you right away, sir." She looked at her hands, which were now tightly grasped in front of her. She was wringing them together as she finally admitted, "I'm so sorry, sir. I knew that pregnancy was possibility when I first met you. I just didn't know how to tell you and honestly I hoped that I wasn't." Her voice trailed off and when she finally did look up at him again, the anger was there.

His jaw was hard, his eyes narrowed, and in alarmed dismay she heard his heavy breathing. She backed up a step and held her hands up between them. "I really am so sorry, sir." She didn't dare look at him so instead, just whispered hoarsely, "I'll go now." She tried to push quickly past him, but he moved to block her exit. She closed her eyes as she waited for the blow to come.

Nothing happened. She opened her eyes. Ivan wrapped her in a tight bear hug and pushed her head down on his shoulder. "There now," he said in a low soothing tone. "It's all going to be okay. We will figure it all out together."

Confused, Brooke leaned her neck back to look up at him. His jaw was still hard and she saw the anger there in his deep gaze and yet his touch was gentle and soothing. Suspiciously, she asked, "You aren't angry, are you?"

A flame sparked in those dark eyes and she watched him intently. He took a deep breath. "Oh, I'm angry all right," he said viciously as a cold chilling grin spread his lips. "Just not at you." He chucked her gently under the chin. "Never at you, Brooke."

At the moment he was thinking of driving over to her family's farm to give her father a not very kind piece of his mind. He didn't know all the details yet, but at the very least the bastard had sent his pregnant daughter away to handle it on her own. For that alone, he wanted to pop the guy a couple of times.

She still looked nervous as she watched him intently, so he forced his jaw to relax and smiled down at her. "The only thing to do about it tonight is for us to go enjoy the party." He gave her a light squeeze before he stepped back. "Tomorrow we can sort out all of the details, okay?" He turned. "Why don't we go get a drink and we can relax for a bit before I fire up the grill again for dinner?"

Brooke shook her head feeling rooted to the spot. "Thanks, but I think I just want to head home for now." She rubbed at her temples. "I have a bit of a headache," she lied. Though now that she thought about it her head did actually hurt.

Ivan looked worried but nodded. "If that's what you really want, I suppose I won't try and talk you into staying." Silently he held out his arm to her. "Come on, I'll at least walk you out."

She smiled gratefully and took hold of his arm. Anne met them as they started across the patio. She looked back and forth between them before asking quietly, "Is everything all right?" Ivan held her gaze for a long moment as though making up his mind about something before smiling warmly and saying in a jovial tone, "Brooke just has a headache and wants to go home and rest for a while." He grinned disarmingly down at Anne. "I'm going to walk her out and I'll be back."

Anne looked pointedly at Brooke for a minute, who piped up, "I'm fine to walk myself out." When Ivan started shaking his head, she smiled. "Really, Ivan, you should go spend some time with Anne." She nodded to Anne and said graciously, "Thanks for inviting me over to the barbecue. It really was delicious." She forced herself to walk away without looking to see if he'd followed her or not. She weaved her way quickly through the crowd. She could see the gate ahead only a few yards now and her gaze latched onto it as she pushed determinedly through a throng of teenage boys. She smiled at Zack and moved quickly past.

She made it through without interruption and sighed with relief as she neared the fence. The gate opened and a tall dark-haired man walked inside. He paused to look around the yard for a minute before moving forward. Brooke muttered an apology and smiled vaguely at a woman she bumped as she brushed by. The man was still standing there and suddenly she realized he was looking straight at her.

She met his liquid green eyes and her own widened in recognition as a wide smile spread over her face. She moved around another young boy who was tilting an icy cold root beer to his lips.

Jacob met her fast stride as she made her way around the final group of guests between them. His arms lifted open and she ran into them as his arms closed tightly around her. A warm tingle moved through her numb limbs and she raised up on her toes to kiss his cheek happily. Someone whistled out loud and the crowd went silent. Her stomach sank.

Brooke tried to pull away feeling self-conscious now, but Jacob only tightened his grip while leaning down to whisper, "It'll be okay. Just let them have their fun." He released her just long enough to lift one arm to nudge her chin up. "I've missed you, Brookie," he said, grinning happily down at her. Behind her, she heard someone calling for a kiss so she laughed and raised on her toes with a wide smile as she plastered a kiss on his cheek again. Someone booed to the right side of them and that made him chuckle as he stepped back and released her. He whistled softly. "Just so you know, you are looking mighty fine today, Bestie."

Brooke punched his arm lightly and accusingly complained, "You didn't tell me you were coming home today!"

Jacob grinned. "I didn't know for sure until a couple of days ago, and I wanted to surprise everyone." He smiled at his mom as she hurried over and gave him a tight hug. Then Ivan was there and he shook Jacob's hand even as he pulled him in for a quick hug. A line of people began gathering to say hello to Jacob.

He didn't miss the curious as well as slightly disappointed looks on the faces of several of his good friends as they said hello and then looked curiously between Brooke and himself, obviously thinking they were together.

Brooke however was oblivious to the men but shivered as she met Anne's unwavering stare. She tried to smile, but it trembled unsuccessfully on her lips. She knew in her heart that she should have slipped out while Jacob was busy greeting people but her heart demanded she take in this final moment. Soon all she would have of him were memories. She looked away from Anne as Jacob took her hand and pulled her toward the drink table.

He reached for a cold beer and then asked her what she wanted before bending down to open a ginger ale as he held it out to her. She lifted the can to her lips and took a sip. It was cold and refreshing and she sighed as the ginger settled her stomach and tingled against her tongue. She turned to thank Jacob for the drink and stopped midturn.

Cole stood just outside of the back door of the house watching them with one brow up. Or to be more correct, he watched her. His jaw was taut and his eyes sparked with anger as she met his gaze. His stare felt like a hard challenge and she shivered again in spite of the warmth of the afternoon sun that touched her shoulders.

She felt Jacob bump her shoulder and in relief turned to chide him for trying to spill her drink. He only grinned. "God, it's good to see you again. I really missed you."

Brooke could only nod and agree as she fought the tears that threatened. She drank in the sight of him as they strolled over so he could load a plate with food. The comforting feeling of having him by her side again soothed her as the afternoon progressed.

She had a very lovely afternoon. Jacob walked her around with him introducing her happily and sometimes even reintroducing her to his friends and acquaintances. He always introduced her as his good friend, and though raised eyebrows and suggestive looks made her slightly uncomfortable, Brooke found herself quite enjoying the event.

So long as she avoided Anne and pretended not to notice the way Cole kept staring at them from across the yard, she could almost forget that her life was once again about to fall apart. She promised herself to take it all in and enjoy this last opportunity to have a good time with her best friend.

Cole eventually came over and said a curt hello to Jacob who had met his brothers cold stare in somewhat surprised but unfazed challenge.

Brooke simply smiled kindly and said hello to him as well, which had only seemed to anger him further. He had nodded curtly at her before walking off, but Brooke hardly felt like it was warm. Just what she had done to make him angry this time she didn't know. Apparently, she had done something that offended him.

She turned back to Jacob just in time to see his amused look as he watched Cole stride away hands in fists. He turned to give her a searching look and asked under his breath, "When exactly did that happen?"

Brooke feigned innocence and with a shrugging laugh, he let it go. He'd pester her about it later, she knew, but was grateful for the momentary reprieve now. With any luck, she would be long gone before she had to have that conversation with him.

The sun faded behind the mountains turning the sky brilliant yellows, orange, and red as Ivan fired up the grills again. The men brought out stacks of thick steaks and a huge tub of marinated chicken and began loading it on the smoking grill tops. Brooke watched as Ivan disappeared into the house again and then returned with a platter heaped full of barbecued baby back ribs.

Jacob asked her to come with as he joined his dad at the grill. Though neither of them would let her do anything to help, she still enjoyed joking around with them as they tied white aprons around their waists and took to grilling. Even Cole's bad mood couldn't keep his manners from showing as he soon wandered over as well, grabbing an apron as he turned and lit up a third grill. Despite his deep resentment of her, he nodded as he took the platter of ribs near her and deftly laid them out on the grill.

Brooke felt her pulse flutter when he stepped up close to her and she wanted to slap herself for her own stupidity. Though she wanted to make her excuses and go right then, she refused to let his sullen mood take these last few memories of Jacob and Ivan away from her. Feeling warm she turned to ask if there was anything she could do to help. Three matching cold looks had her lifting her hands in surrender as the men continued loading the savory-smelling meat onto the racks.

She turned and caught Cole's sideways stare. Uncomfortable, she asked if any of them wanted a drink. Ivan asked for a beer and she quickly grabbed one and popped the top before handing it over. Jacob held up his half empty bottle and grinned. "Maybe in a minute."

Cole didn't respond at all, which made both Ivan and Jacob shoot him twin looks of irritation.

Brooke walked over and grabbed another beer anyway. She popped the top and set it next to him with a loud plink. Cole looked a little surprised and Ivan and Jacob laughed as she stormed moodily back to where she'd been standing before. Cole could take a hint after all as he grabbed the beer and tipped it toward her in a silent salute. He met her sparking eyes with his darker stare and said politely, "Thanks for the drink."

Ivan watched Cole for a long while in silence before finally asking casually, "Are you having a rough day, son?"

Cole shrugged nonchalantly. "No more than usual."

Ivan exchanged a look with Jacob before turning back to study him again. "Well, I know your mother and I have both taught you manners. Until today I have never seen you be anything less than a gentleman, but today you seem a bit on edge." He smiled pointedly. "Did you run into any hiccups with the new car you're working on?"

"Nothing I can't handle. Just the usual." He shrugged again and then forced a grin. "Sorry, I guess I'm just in a bad mood today." He threw an apologetic look Brooke's way.

Ivan wasn't sold, but it was apparent that his son didn't want to talk about it, so he kept his mouth shut. A sneaking suspicion surfaced that his son's cold attitude was somehow related to the beautiful redhead that was standing in front of them. He grinned but hid it. *Wouldn't that just be the best damned thing?* he thought. He started whistling a happy little tune and got twin looks of curiosity from his sons before he wisely shut up and changed the subject back to the food.

People soon began lining up with clean but empty plates, asking for juicy hunks of meat. Anne started carrying out bowls of mashed potatoes and gravy and Brooke hurried over to help her. Once the last bowl of salad had been uncovered and set down, she went back over to stand with the men as they loaded plates high. Both Ivan and Jacob kept insisting she should go get a plate. She insisted right back that she would wait to eat with all of them. Cole frowned at that bit of information, but didn't say anything and didn't look directly at her, so she chose to believe he was frowning at something else.

Once the lines were gone and they had large platters of extra cooked meat prepared, they pulled off their aprons one by one to heap plates of their own and headed toward a semi-empty picnic table. Brooke grabbed several bottles of water and offered them to everyone at the table. While the nausea from earlier had long since faded, she was nervous about a repeat of that so she ate very slowly and only put a small amount of food on her plate. Her irritation surged, as she found both Jacob and Cole watching her with obvious concern.

She shook it off with a small smile as Anne came over to sit by Ivan's side. He threw a warm arm over her shoulder and pulled her close as he planted a moist kiss on her lips. She smiled up at him and then turned politely to visit with everyone at the table. Zack soon came over to sit with them and Brooke found herself looking around for the two younger boys. It would, after all, be nice to have one last evening with them.

One by one they came over and to her great relief weren't fighting anymore and didn't repeat the fiasco from earlier. She teared up as she felt at once like she was home and yet displaced. She casually wiped her eyes with the napkin as she realized that this would be the last time she would be with them all.

She soaked it in. At one point she even bravely asked Anne about her work and how her clinic was doing. Jacob announced that he and his team had indeed won the lawsuit they had taken on in their law clinic. Ivan congratulated him with a proud grin and Cole bumped his shoulder and smiled. Anne stood and walked around the table to give him a big hug.

Jacob looked at her then as though waiting for a response. She didn't give him one, didn't say anything at all. Curiously he asked, "Aren't you happy for me, Brooke?"

She met his gaze then, hers steady. "Of course I am. I just never doubted that you would. I already knew that you did," she said in such a matter-of-fact tone that everyone laughed. She looked up and met Anne's gaze. To her surprise Anne was smiling warmly back at her. An icy sliver of pain melted inside her heart and she smiled radiantly. Perhaps, she thought, this was the perfect way to end the night.

It didn't end after dinner, however, as lanterns were lit around the patio and a band began setting up equipment next to the house. By the time they cleared their plates away, a few people were already starting to dance. Jacob grabbed her hand and pulled her onto the dance floor with him. She reluctantly followed, though she warned him in no uncertain tone that she didn't know how to dance. He grinned with a twinkle in his eyes and said laughingly, "That's okay, I don't have any doubt that you'll be great at it." He gave her an exaggerated wink and she laughed.

He taught her the basic two-step and then tried several times to show her the country swing. After several dances, he reluctantly whispered, "I guess I better give you a chance to dance with some of the other guys that are currently giving me cold looks."

She laughed as he led her off the floor. She glanced around and then laughed again as he led her to a chair. "Ha-ha, Jacob, I don't see anyone giving you dirty looks here."

He grinned back at her and threw a thumb over his shoulder. She turned to follow it and met Cole's hard unsmiling look. She smiled cheerfully at him and then turned back to Jacob. He looked around them, then and said in a conspiring murmur, "Besides, we wouldn't want anyone to talk."

She laughed at that and several heads turned to watch as her tinkling laughter filled the space. Jacob got them both bottles of water and Brooke had barely taken a sip when a young man she thought was named Jack came up and asked her to dance. She smiled and nodded and then took his offered hand as she warned gently, "As long as you don't mind teaching me. I really don't know how to dance." He beamed a proud smile and nodded as he swung her around and held her gently in his arms as he occasionally gave her tips on the steps.

She danced until she was sure that her feet were going to fall off. Several times she saw Jacob on the floor dancing. He would grin at her over the shoulder of his own female partner and then swing them around on the concrete pad until they were dizzy.

Brooke couldn't help noticing that there was a large crowd of women fluttering around Cole and trying to flirt outrageously with him. He only smiled at them and leaned against a tree asking none of them to dance.

One girl finally got up the nerve to ask him outright, and he gracefully swung her around the floor. Brooke avoided looking at him as he floated by with the girl in his arms. She did, however, have to ask her current dance partner to repeat himself as she hadn't heard a word of his sentence.

After several dances with Ivan, Anne walked over to stand by Cole and he graciously asked her to dance.

Brooke had just finished dancing with a tall blond who re-introduced himself as Rand and passed Cole as they left the dance floor. He met her gaze and nodded but didn't smile. Rand, however. smiled endlessly as he explained that he had gone to high school with Jacob and Cole and then began telling stories of the old days. She urged him to walk her toward the drink table and asked politely what he did. After a long refreshing drink of cool water, she looked around the yard and thanked him as she turned and quickly walked away.

Several people had obviously cleared out now because the crowd was beginning to thin. She saw Jacob on the dance floor with a tall brunette with long legs and a pretty smile. She waved in response to Jacob's questioning look and turned to search for Ivan. He and Anne were on the dance floor again swaying slowly together and she smiled. She took one last long look around and turned toward the parking lot. She would just slip out and head home; after all, she had a long day ahead of her tomorrow.

She moved into the shadows near the fence as she made her way quickly toward the gate. She adjusted her purse on her shoulder and squinted as she reached for the gate handle. Her fingers found it and closed over it as she tugged hard on it. It didn't budge. She grunted and put her weight behind her as she pulled once again. It still didn't move. She cursed aloud and took a step forward bending to look closely at the latch in the dark and that was when she saw him.

He grinned sardonically and his smile shone white in the dim light as he stepped from the shadows and away from the gate toward her. All night long he had watched as she laughed and danced with every guy who asked her. Every touch and smile she gave made him feel grumpier. Now, he advanced with all that built-up frustration of wanting something he couldn't or shouldn't have.

She sucked in a breath and backed up a step. He followed. She glared up at him hard, though she wasn't sure if he could see her. "Excuse me please, Cole. I'm just heading out now." Brooke tried to step around him but misjudged the distance and caught her foot on his shoe. He reached out and caught her easily with one strong arm that shot heat through her dress everywhere it brushed.

She looked up at him through the darkness, curious as his intense gaze captured hers, then held it for a long unreadable moment. She started to pull away, then hesitated as he opened his mouth. In an achingly tender voice, he said simply, "Dance with me."

Brooke wasn't sure that she could have pulled away even if she'd wanted to. Even this, she thought, would be her last goodbye with him. Relaxing, she let him take her hand and followed his lead. To her surprise he didn't turn toward the lantern-lit dance floor but instead pulled her deeper into the shadows. He wrapped one arm firmly around her waist as he pulled her body up tight against his and swayed gently to the rhythm of a slow country ballad.

The song ended and the band moved smoothly into a song with a different beat. He said nothing as she fumbled her feet clumsily, trying to find the rhythm. Instead, he placed one hand lightly against the small of her back and gently put pressure to move her forward and then lightened it to allow her back again. He was so smooth; she soon found the step and he twirled her around and around in tight circles. Her face filled with pleasure and she smiled up at him. "What is this dance called? I really like it."

He looked down at her beautiful face and stilled his urge to kiss her. "It's a waltz," he said, his face devoid of expression.

Brooke smiled. "Well, I think it's one of my favorites already."

He nodded politely, but his expression went blank and his jaw tightened perceptibly as he asked in a low but intentionally impersonal tone, "What in the hell is going on between you and my brother?"

Brooke gulped and then quickly pasted a smile and shook her head, saying just as impersonally, "Nothing." His gaze narrowed visibly and she sensed that he was once again angry with her. Stepping back and away she hurried to soothe him, "We're just friends is all."

Wasn't it ironic, she thought, that he didn't like her or want anything to do with her and yet here he was also trying to protect his brother from her as well? She smiled bitterly up at him. "You have nothing to worry about, Cole. I know you don't want me to have a relationship with Jacob and I give you my word that I have no intention of that." She lowered her head in defeat.

She felt his warm breath against her cheek as his hand tilted her head back and up as he replied, "Damn straight I don't." He said it harshly and then he took her mouth in a hungry kiss that sent shivers down to her toes. His tongue slid against her own as she opened her mouth to object to his constant hot-then-cold act.

She forgot why she didn't want him to kiss her and leaned into him as he deepened the kiss. She grasped tightly on to his muscled shoulders as her legs turned to mush beneath her. That heavy familiar ache started deep inside her body and she instinctively moved restlessly against him trying to get closer to him.

Cole pulled back suddenly, releasing her in an instant. She nearly collapsed but held steady as she turned and leaned against the fence as pained confusion lit her flushed face. She tried to see his eyes now, but it was too dark. She heard him take in one unsteady and ragged breath of air. Then he turned and said calmly, "Hello, Jacob."

He nodded at his brother who Brooke now noticed for the first time was standing a mere few feet away. Then he turned and strode away without a second look at her.

Jacob was grinning knowingly. "Nothing there, huh?" He moved closer as he informed her, "I didn't mean to interrupt. I just couldn't find you, so I was going to check and see if you had left already." He lifted his eyebrows in mock surprise. "Imagine my surprise to find my brother all over you like that."

Heat flushed her cheeks and, unable to think of a suitable comeback, she muttered for what felt like the hundredth time that day, "I'm sorry."

Jacob grinned. "I bet. Though I may be inclined to think your sorrow has more to do with my interruption than the fact that I found you with him."

Brooke shook her head emphatically and a curl fell into her eyes. She brushed it back impatiently as she met his amused gaze. "It's not like that." Her voice broke and she swallowed. With a very confused and slightly injured smile she explained, "Your brother really doesn't like me. I honestly don't know why he keeps kissing me. He really does seem to hate it and he always ends up pissed off at me afterward." She rubbed a tired hand across her hair.

"I wouldn't take it too personal," he said lightly as he moved to place his arm around her shoulders comfortingly. "He can be a real prickly bear sometimes." He gave her a wink. "Plus, I'm guessing you must really get under his skin if he's getting all pissed off. He hates it whenever anyone does that." He turned a crooked grin down at her.

She hugged him. "Thanks, Jacob, now I think I'm just going to take off. I'm bushed," she admitted honestly with a little sigh.

He nodded and gave her hair a little tug as he said good night and held the gate open. He released it and walked away, but Brooke caught at it before it closed. She stood there for a long moment looking around at each of the Burtons and thinking about how they had all changed her life forever. She didn't see Cole anywhere and with a sad little smile thought that, even that fact seemed to sum up their strange relationship. With one final look around the lamp-lit patio, she moved through the gate and walked quickly toward her car.

She walked under a circle of light that blossomed out from a fixture on the side of the house. She stepped quickly back into the darkness and because her eyes were still adjusting, searched instinctively for her car. She thought she saw the white outline and moved quickly across the driveway.

She never even saw his fist coming, only felt sharp pain and saw brilliant spots of color before darkness took over as his blow connected to the side of her head with a sickening pop. With a quiet swoosh, as though someone was shaking out a sheet, her body folded and she collapsed soundlessly onto the concrete.

CHAPTER 16

When she regained consciousness, Brooke felt a strong arm wrapped around her just below her breasts from behind. Her sandals dragged roughly across the concrete. She struggled up against the arm in confusion. *What had happened?* She tried to clear the cobwebs from her aching brain.

Her head throbbed and with a little cry she lifted her hand to rub it against her temple. Her mind cleared and with the sudden clarity came choking terror. She tried to turn her head to see who had ahold of her but white spots formed as pain surged again on the right side of her head. With a breathless whimper she pleaded, "Please stop. Just let me go." She tried to push up onto her feet, but he jerked her hard before she could gain purchase.

In a low familiarly controlled voice he asked, "Why on earth would I do that, sweetheart. Have you already forgotten that you're mine?" He chuckled maniacally. "And I thought I taught you so well last time we were together."

Brooke raised an arm, tried to get an elbow in his ribs. It barely bumped against him.

He squeezed her chest tightly and laughed low as the air left her lungs and she fought for breath. "Things will go a lot easier for you if you don't fight it, Brooke. You know how this works. Did you really think you could escape me?" His throaty chuckle sent another wave of terror down her spine. "I guess I will have to do a better job of teaching you this time."

She stopped fighting instantly, felt his grip loosen but only by a fraction. She took a long deep breath, filling her lungs with oxygen. Then with a quick little prayer for good luck she used every ounce of fight she still had in her body and screamed. He fumbled to try covering her mouth and she got one foot straightened solidly against the concrete and shoved back against him trying to break loose. Her head bucked hard against his chin and she heard him curse vehemently just before everything went dark again. Her last thought was that she shouldn't have screamed. She had no idea what he would do to anyone who came running to her rescue.

The next time Brooke woke up, light prickled painfully against her eyelids and made her head throb uncontrollably. She moaned and then in surprise realized that her hands were free to hold to her temples. She heard a low in-drawn breath and opened her eyes to look frantically around the dimly lit space.

"God, Brooke are you awake?" It was Jacob's worried voice and she relaxed a little, though fear still permeated her breathing.

She looked around dazedly, she was laying over on one of the cherry wood and wrought iron benches that she knew sat on the front porch of the Burton's home. The porch light shone brightly against her throbbing head, lighting the porch and making bright spots behind her lids. She squinted and looked up at Jacob who was leaning over her with concern to carefully study her head. "What happened?" she asked dumbly, her words slurred.

Jacob shrugged as he gently touched the bump on her head. "That's what I was about to ask you," he said in frustration. "I was walking past the gate when I thought I heard a scream. I ran out here and saw someone dragging you toward a truck. I only got a couple of punches in before he left you behind and ran off. I couldn't see him very well, but he climbed into a truck and drove off." He helped her sit up fully as he ran his fingers through his hair in frustration. "I wanted to go after the guy, but you were crumpled on the ground and I couldn't even tell if you were breathing at first so I carried you over here to check on you," he said as he sank down on the bench next to her. "My God, you had me really worried there for a minute."

She tried to smile, but her head throbbed and she finally just reached a hand out to touch his shoulder. "I'm sorry. I'm okay, though. I promise."

He stared at her for a minute before asking in frustration, "Who was that guy?" He ran another hand through his already messy hair. "Did you get a good look at him? Was it somebody we know?"

Brooke looked him calmly in the eye and shook her head. "I tried to turn around, but I never did see his face." She hadn't exactly lied, she told herself guiltily. She really hadn't seen his face. "It was probably just someone who got a little too drunk and wanted to keep the party going," she suggested. Even she heard the foolish unlikely reality as she said it and didn't continue.

Jacob stared down at her in obvious concern. "I better go get Dad and Mom. We need to call the sheriff and get someone out here to take statements and we need to get you checked out."

Brooke shook her head quickly. "Please don't, Jacob." She looked down at her hands in shame. "I really don't want anyone fussing over me right now. I just want to go home and get some sleep," she pleaded.

Jacob wasn't convinced, so she forced her shaky legs to stand and smiled at him as he stood ready to catch her if she collapsed. He frowned. "I really don't like the idea of some creep wandering around these parts and taking advantage of women," he said through gritted teeth.

Brooke put a soothing hand on his arm. "I understand that, Jacob, but we don't have anything on him anyway, so I'm not sure what good it will do to talk to the sheriff." She forced a smile, though her insides felt like rubbery Jell-O. "Besides I'm not sure this was just your garden variety creep looking for women to beat up. Whoever he was, I'm guessing I was his target."

Jacob looked hard at her and then suggested, "Maybe I should at least go get Dad and see what he thinks." Brooke grabbed on to his hand and held it tight as he continued. "We really ought to have Mom come take a look at you to make sure you're okay."

Brooke wouldn't let him go. She held on tightly and begged, "Please, Jacob, I really appreciate you coming when you did. Lord knows what could have happened otherwise." Her eyes filled with tears with the truth of her words. "I'm so embarrassed, though, because I wasn't paying enough attention. I should have been more aware and on the lookout, but I really am okay. I promise," she said again when he still didn't look convinced. "All I want right now is to go home to my own bed and get some sleep." She held up a hand when he looked ready to argue again. "After I get some rest, we can talk more about it and decide if there is anything else we can do," she lied, knowing that by this time tomorrow, she would be long gone and whoever had attacked her would no longer be a problem for the Burtons.

He caved when she lifted a hand to her head again with a groan. He took her arm in his. "Okay, but I am going to follow you home and make sure you get settled in safely before I come back and talk to Dad." His tone left no room for argument, though in truth Brooke was relieved for that.

She had been trying not to think about going home alone and taking the chance that *he* would be there. She hadn't thought he would come after her like this. She pursed her lips together tightly. She had underestimated him once again. He'd threatened to always come after her, of course, but he was also a weak pathetic bully and she had thought he would just let it go once she was out of sight. She swore silently that she wouldn't underestimate him again. She knew reasonably that if he had found her here at the Burton home, the chances were pretty good that he knew right where she was living. She shivered as that thought came and went. Had he already been watching her? Panic soared and she took in a deep gulp of the cool night air.

Jacob held her arm as they walked slowly down the stairs. He helped her to her car and then told her to wait for him while he went to get his jeep so he could follow her.

Her mind raced and she breathed heavily. Did he somehow know she was pregnant? She shook her head as though trying to calm herself. It was insane to think he could know. There was absolutely no way he could have known. She'd barely found out herself and only told Ivan and Anne. Unless he'd broken into her home while she was away and seen the test she'd taken, she really couldn't see any possible way that he could know. She thought back over the last week as she drove home with Jacob's jeep close on her tail. She had been very thorough at locking her home up both at night and when she left each time and she hadn't noticed broken locks or any evidence of a break-in.

Brooke sighed. He had likely just been watching her from a distance. Even that was creepy as hell and for the first time since she had decided to leave earlier tonight, she was happy that she was going. She didn't say anything to Jacob as he stepped out of his jeep, only opened her trunk to pull out a bat she had put in there for protection. Not that it had done her any good.

Jacob raised an eyebrow before flashing a quick grin and together they walked up the steps to her front door. She examined it carefully for a moment before sliding her key in and turning the lock. It didn't look tampered with. Jacob shoved her behind him as soon as the door was open and walked in front of her inside. She followed closely on his heel. Together they made their way through the house, checking every room, including the closets as they went. Finally satisfied that they were alone, he turned to her and gave her a tight squeeze. "I'm really glad you're all right." He looked serious then. "I'm pretty sure you have a slight concussion, so you should set a timer to wake up every couple of hours to be safe."

She faked a yawn and told him that she was tired, so he said good night and told her to lock the door behind him. He waited until he heard the click of the lock sliding into place before turning to jog back to his jeep.

Brooke waited until the crunching sound of tires grinding against gravel faded before pulling down her luggage and quickly loading up her meager belongings.

She cried a little as she looked around the warm house that had become home in such a short time. With a daring little hop, she grabbed the bat and walked out into the backyard. Even in the dim moonlight it looked refreshing and beautiful and she smiled through her tears. Her dreams of time spent playing with her child here in this yard flashed and then slid into the distance as she forced herself to let it go.

She went back inside, carefully locking the door behind her. She glanced around the small but tidy kitchen. She didn't have time to pack her few decorations or the rest of her household items. With a wistful sigh, she hoped that whomever happened to live here next would appreciate the effort and love she had put in to the place. She couldn't talk to Jacob or Ivan. She was sure that they would try talking her into staying, and especially now with Richard on her tail, she couldn't afford to take that risk. She also couldn't be sure she wouldn't cave at their stubborn insistence and she was determined to create a life where she wasn't taking advantage of anyone.

She pulled a notepad and pen out of a kitchen drawer and sat at the small round table. She chewed on the end for a long minute while trying to sort her feelings into words.

She wrote letters to Ivan and Jacob and then signed and folded them. Before she could forget, she pulled her wallet from her purse and pulled out all her cash. She slipped it under the fold of the letter to Ivan. Finished with that, she slipped the letters into her purse and picked up her heavy bags. She tossed the bags into the back seat and then angled the bat next to them.

She walked through her home for the few short months she'd been here one last time before locking it up. Anxious, now that she was ready to go, she stopped on the bottom step to look around the front yard. Tears streamed down her cheeks as she made her way quickly back to her car. Even without the added problem of Richard, Ivan and Jacob deserved so much more than having her take constant advantage of their unyielding kindness. It was what was best she assured herself as she drove away.

She watched her rearview mirror carefully for headlights as she sped towards the shop. Using the key Ivan had given her the first week here to let herself in, she made her way slowly through the dark shop up to his office on the second floor. She didn't want to turn on the lights and draw attention to herself, so she stumbled through the dark up the stairs and down the hallway. Moonlight shone through the windows illuminating the desk. She sat in his chair as she quickly wrote Ivan's name on the top of one letter and set it on his desk before doing the same with Jacob's. Then she pulled her cell phone out and laid it as well as both the keys to the shop and the keys to the house next to them before turning and quietly leaving. Ivan would find them when he came into work Monday morning, she knew. She took an extra minute to make sure the shop was locked up behind her and then climbed into her little white car and drove away.

She stopped on her way through town just long enough to get fuel. Then she took several side roads to make sure that no one was following her. She looked in her rearview mirror with a heartbreakingly sad smile as she pulled onto the interstate and headed north. This was, after all, the valley she had lived in one way or another her whole life.

CHAPTER 17

Jacob didn't like leaving Brooke alone at the house, but he knew from experience that his parents were going to have quite a mess to clean up after the party. Just as he'd expected, the last of the late-night stragglers were leaving as he pulled up and parked his jeep by the house. The band was loading up their equipment while Zachary and Dominic were walking around picking up garbage from the lawn when he entered through the back gate. He saw his father disappear inside with a half-empty tub of drinks and hurried to haul another. Cole had set a lantern by the grills and was busy scraping and cleaning them. Jacob threw a knowing grin at him but didn't say anything as he walked past with a half-empty cooler.

Cole only gave him a cold look and went back to scraping.

It took nearly an hour by the time the band had finished up and left. The backyard had been tidied as well as it could be in the dark. He knew from years past they would have a little more to do in the morning when it was light again, but for tonight, it was all they could do. Cole disappeared inside and Anne took Ryker in the house to put him to bed. Dom and Zack followed closely behind with big yawns. Though his instincts were screaming at him to call the cavalry in, he honored Brooke's wishes. He said good night to his dad and went in to bed himself.

Before he crashed, he pulled out his phone and tried calling Brooke. He was still feeling a little uneasy about her being alone in the old house and wanted to reassure himself that she was okay. It went straight to voicemail. He considered calling in the cavalry again but something about the way Brooke had been acting teased at his mind and he hesitated.

He lay down, putting his arms behind his head. She was fine, he told himself for the hundredth time. She had most likely just turned her phone off so she could rest without being interrupted. It took him a long while, but he finally managed to relax enough to fall into a fitful sleep.

He woke up early as the sun peeked through the wooden blinds. He reached for his phone before he climbed out of bed and tried calling her again. He got her voicemail and again figured she was probably still home sleeping. She had looked extra tired last night. Groaning as he stretched, he went into his en suite bathroom and took a long hot shower. He dressed comfortably in shorts and a V-neck T-shirt and went to the kitchen to find Ivan, who was scrambling eggs as bacon sizzled and popped in a pan nearby. He told his father good morning and started setting the table. With the table set, he turned to his father. "Mom up yet?"

Ivan nodded with quick smile. "Yes, but she wanted to take a shower, so I offered to get breakfast going." He set down the spatula and reached for a mug of coffee before taking a long drink. Without speaking, he reached into the cupboard and pulled out a mug, filling it nearly to the top before offering it to his son in companionable silence. Jacob nodded his thanks and took a sip of the hot liquid. It burned his tongue but also soothed his head from all the beer from the night before, so he took another sip. They stood there for a long minute, sipping hot coffee together. Then Ivan turned and started stirring the eggs. "It's really good to have you home, son."

Jacob grinned. "It's good to be home." He looked around the kitchen and met his father's gaze. "I really miss everyone when I'm gone." He looked across and met Ivan's eyes. "How are things going with the farm? Have you had enough help since I've been gone?" He hadn't liked leaving his father and his brothers to handle everything without him, in the middle of their busiest season, but Ivan had insisted that they would be fine.

Ivan smiled and nodded. "It has been good. The hay has been thick and we've had good luck getting it in before the rain comes." He reached for his coffee and took another sip before continuing. "Brooke has sure been a godsend. I swear that girl can outwork most of the men." He chuckled and then pulled the eggs off the stove before turning to give Jacob a sideways look. "By the way, I've been meaning to ask you, is there something going on between you and Brooke?"

Jacob swallowed his coffee. "Not exactly," he said in an intentionally vague tone. Then unable to hold it back, he grinned in amusement. "Though not for lack of trying."

Ivan chuckled. "Yesterday it sure looked like the two of you are close." He looked at Jacob with questions in his warm brown eyes. "I'm fairly sure that the whole valley now thinks that the two of you are a thing."

Jacob laughed then and stared quietly into his coffee for a minute. "I had hoped we would be," he said honestly and with evident disappointment before looking back at his father. "She's beautiful and I genuinely admire her spirit. She really likes me too," he said and a dimple appeared with his grin.

Ivan watched his son closely as he listened. Finally, impatiently he asked, "So then, what's the problem?"

Jacob gave a bitter laugh and looked deadpan into Ivan's curious brown eyes before answering with unyielding honesty. "There just aren't any sparks."

Ivan raised a somewhat surprised eyebrow at that revelation. "And you know this how?"

Jacob grinned and set his coffee down on the counter. "Because I kissed her."

A low grunt behind them had both men turning as Cole walked in. He had grease stains down his arms and had obviously just come in from the garage. He stared coldly at Jacob, his jaw ticking for a long moment before turning to the sink to wash his arms and hands without a word.

Jacob hid his grin behind his mug.

Ivan hid his own grin as he turned and carefully loaded a huge stack of bacon and eggs onto a platter before covering it with a topper. He cheerfully told Cole good morning as he pulled out bread and popped several slices in the toaster. Then he casually pulled down yet another mug and filled it for Cole, handing it to him before turning back to butter the toast.

All three of the younger boys came in long before Anne finally made an appearance. Ivan had already poured a cup of coffee and added cream and sugar and handed it to her as she walked in. She smiled gratefully and took a long drag, closing her eyes in bliss before turning to tell everyone good morning.

They ate the way they usually ate. With everyone talking all at once and also trying to keep up with everything everyone was saying at the same time.

Jacob picked up a piece of bacon and bit half of it off, chewing as he pulled out his phone. He'd texted Brooke and asked her to call him when she woke up. He'd also left several voicemails for her to call him at this point and he wanted to make sure he didn't miss her text response. He stared in frustration at the blank screen. There was nothing there. His gut tightened with concern as he stared down and willed the damn thing to ring. One by one the noise around him subsided and he glanced up. Every member of his family with the exception of Ryker was watching him with avid curiosity. Jacob forced a nonchalant smile and took another bite of bacon.

Cole was staring hard at him, his gaze cold, angry, and if Jacob wasn't mistaken, jealous. He grinned in response, which only pissed his brother off. He watched Cole's hand tighten to a fist and his grin widened. His younger brother definitely had a pretty strong case of the Brookies. He wanted to laugh at his own joke but worry plagued him again.

He found himself looking at his phone again to check the time. It was nine o'clock and he didn't think Brooke would still be asleep at this point. As far as he could tell the girl never slept past six o'clock. Fear curled its way through his gut. *What if she'd had a bad concussion from last night? What if she had been in worse condition than he realized?*

He didn't realize he was frowning until his dad spoke up. "Jacob, is there a reason you're frowning and can't seem to put your phone down?" His father's calm voice brought him back to the moment and he looked up, though the frown continued.

"I'm sorry," he said to no one in particular. "I just asked Brooke to call me first thing this morning when she woke up."

That statement caused a variety of reactions from his family. Cole scowled and clanked his mug down on the table, which made both Ivan and Jacob grin in spite of the situation. Anne's brows raised in concern because she was very worried that her eldest son was getting far to invested with a very pregnant Brooke. Dominic and Ryker both started talking over the top of each other to ask with excitement if Brooke was coming over today.

He shook his head at the boys, which had Ryker sticking out his bottom lip in a pout. He smiled to reassure his worried mother, ignored Cole altogether, and turned to meet his father's concerned look.

He sighed loudly and set down the phone. It was time, Jacob decided, to tell him what had happened the night before. Brooke could get mad at him if she wanted. At this point he was so concerned he didn't care. He hadn't been able to silence the worry he'd been feeling all morning and he needed to do something about it. He set his fork down with a clank. He glanced at Cole quickly before turning to hold Ivan's serious gaze. "Something happened last night after the party and I'm pretty worried about her," he admitted.

He watched as his father and mother exchanged a long look before looking back at him. Ivan met his eyes again. "What happened?"

"She left toward the end of the dance last night," he began and took a quick glance at Cole before he continued. "I saw her just before she went and said good night. I should have walked her to her car, but she said she was fine and left. I was thirsty from dancing so I got some water to drink." He took another deep breath before he continued. "I saw Dominic chasing Ryker and I followed to make sure they weren't going get into a fight. I was walking by the gate after the boys when I heard what sounded like a scream." He looked at Cole for a minute. "It sounded like Brooke, so I hurried out to see if she had left already."

"Instead, I saw a dark-figured man dragging something heavy that looked like a woman, so I ran over to them." Cole stood up then, his hands in tight fists as he listened to Jacob.

"I ran toward them and when I got close, I could see her white dress. The man had his arm around her waist and was dragging her toward a truck. I think it was a gray full-sized pickup." He hesitated for just a moment. "Anyway, I ran over and gave him a couple of good hits on his sides before he dropped her. He ran to the truck and jumped in before I could stop him. Brooke was lying on the ground and I wanted to make sure she was okay or I would have gone after him."

Ivan looked furious now and Jacob avoided looking at Cole altogether. He had a pretty good idea how his brother might be feeling right about now. "Why on earth didn't you come get me?" Ivan asked with barely concealed rage.

"Hell, I had just walked away," Cole growled fiercely obviously mad at himself. "I should have walked her out myself."

Jacob held his hands up. "I had to make sure she was okay first," he said and looked to his mother who also looked worried but was patiently waiting for him to finish. "I got her up on the front porch and was checking to see if she was injured when she came back to." He shuddered as he remembered his fear in that moment when he had been wondering if she was still alive. He had been prepared to check for a pulse when she'd opened her eyes.

Cole glowered down at him with rage evident in his nearly black eyes. "There had to be at least ten of us around that could have helped you."

Once again Jacob raised a hand to subdue them before they could pass judgment. "She had a huge bump on her head where he'd hit her, but she seemed fine otherwise. She was shaking and scared. I tried to tell her we needed to get help, but she kept insisting she was fine and kept trying to stand up so I couldn't just leave." He looked at Anne. "I told her I wanted to get you to check her out, but she wouldn't hear of it." He turned back to Ivan and Cole who were both standing now. Cole was now pacing up and down the length of the table. "I told her I should get Dad and call the sheriff." Ivan nodded at that.

Jacob continued, "She said she was embarrassed and tired and since she didn't know the man and hadn't seen his face, the sheriff couldn't do anything about it anyway." He took a deep breath. "She did have a point there." He shrugged. "Honestly, I was afraid she was going to try getting in her car and leaving alone if I left her to come get you guys. You know how stubborn she can be." He aimed that statement at his father and Ivan nodded in agreement. "She asked me to just keep it between us and that if she remembered anything else, then we could call the sheriff this morning. That's why I've been trying to get ahold of her. I really think we need to get the sheriff down here and get them looking for the guy."

Anne spoke for the first time. "Was she nauseated at all?" Everyone turned to listen to Jacob's answer.

He shook his head. "She didn't seem to be. She walked to her car okay and I followed her home." Before anyone had time to say anything, he hurried to finish. "I checked in the house and no one was there. The locks hadn't been tampered with and the windows were all still closed and locked, so I told her to call if she needed anything and came back here to help you clean up."

Ivan sat down heavily again. "I'm sure everything is fine, son. She probably just turned her phone off so she could get some rest." He reached a hand out and squeezed Jacob on the shoulder. It was obvious that his son really cared.

"I still think you should have told us what happened," Cole said through his teeth. "Maybe there was something we could have done to catch the guy." He ran agitated fingers through his long hair. "Hell, at the very least we could have watched the house through the night to make sure the asshole didn't come back for another pass at her."

Anne looked pointedly at Cole and then the younger boys. "Cole, I know you're upset. We all are, but is it really necessary to use that kind of language around your brothers?"

He apologized absentmindedly, then started pacing again.

She met Ivan's worried gaze and understanding passed between them. She nodded at his worried look. She would have to go do a thorough exam to make sure both Brooke and the baby were okay.

Jacob stood and took his plate to the sink before checking his silent phone once again. "I get that I probably should have done more last night, Cole, but I honestly don't know what good it would have done. She didn't know the guy. It was most likely just a random attempt to rape her."

Cole's gaze narrowed. "What exactly makes you so sure that she didn't know him?"

Jacob shrugged and met Cole's heated look steadily. "I asked her several times if she saw his face or knew him."

Cole muttered something low under his breath that all the adults were pretty sure was a curse.

Anne said nothing but turned and sent the two youngest boys off to play a game. She began quietly clearing the table.

Cole stopped pacing suddenly as he made up his mind. "I'm going over there now to make sure she's okay." He gave Ivan one quick nod and turned toward the front of the house. Jacob stood quickly nearly toppling his chair in the process. He caught it before it fell and righted it as he called out, "Hold on, Cole, I'm going with you."

They took Jacob's jeep for the simple reason that it was parked just outside the house. Cole was silent on the drive to her place. He remembered her innocent terror after he had attacked her the first time and closed his eyes in self-hatred. If she was that scared of the kiss with him when she had seen it coming, he couldn't imagine how terrified she might have been at being attacked in the dark. He felt sick. With as scared as she had been then, there was no telling how skittish she would be now. He swore.

Jacob smiled. "She'll be okay, Cole," he assured with confidence.

Cole only nodded silently in return.

They pulled up to the house and skidded to a halt in the gravel driveway. Her car was gone from its usual spot but everything else looked normal. Cole hopped out and jogged quickly to the door. He rapped his fingers against the oak three times and waited. There was no response. He swore low in his throat and tried the knob. It was locked. He banged on the door again, harder this time, but they heard nothing. He watched as Jacob walked around the house to check the back door. He raised his hand to bang again and then stopped midair as he remembered what she did every time she was scared.

He swore again. He knew in his gut that she was gone. Knew that she had indeed left them. He cursed aloud and hit the side of the house once before he turned and stalked down the steps to stand by the jeep. He looked around the yard with appreciation, noting that she had added some shrubbery and a long colorful flower garden to the pretty little front yard as well. Somewhere deep inside, he felt empty but he stilled himself and that feeling. Cold settled over his heart like a vise and he smiled harshly.

He turned as Jacob came back around looking as confused as he was worried. "Maybe she went into town," he said, but it sounded more like a question than a statement.

Cole laughed bitterly. "I hate to break it to you, bro, but she's gone." When Jacob just stared blankly at him, he repeated, "She ran." He turned without an explanation and climbed into the jeep. "We'd better go tell Dad and let the sheriff know there is some creepy guy hanging around these parts that needs caught."

Jacob reluctantly slid into the seat next to him, unsure whether to believe Cole or not. "What makes you so sure?"

Cole smiled coldly. "That's what she does when she's scared."

Jacob sighed. "I get that, but why didn't she call me or something so I could help her?" he asked and then more to himself than Cole said, "It just doesn't make any sense."

Cole raised an eyebrow at Jacob. "She knew you would have tried talking her out of it," he said confidently. He grimaced then before admitting with self-derision, "Besides, I think it's half my fault because she was definitely afraid of me."

Jacob shook his head. "I don't think so, Cole. I talked to her a little last night and she didn't act afraid of you, only said you didn't like her but kept kissing her anyway or something like that."

Cole turned to look out the window in silence. He wasn't about to make things worse by telling Jacob what had happened.

Ivan met them in front of the Burton house and Jacob quickly told him that her car was gone and the house was locked. He listened with concern as Jacob told him they had knocked several times. He looked at Cole then, who had been silent. He was standing still as a statue while Jacob talked. His eyes were unnervingly cold and looked black against the bright sunlight, his jaw was taught with tension. Ivan met his cold gaze with concern. "What do you think about it, Cole?"

He didn't make any expression, didn't move a muscle. He looked his father straight in the eye and with certainty said, "I don't think anything." He wasn't fazed by the raised eyebrow as he stated calmly, "She ran away." A tick started in his jaw then, and Ivan watched as it moved into his tanned neck.

"Well, we can't just assume that. I called the sheriff and I'm going to meet up with him over at my office. I'll fill him in so they can find her to make sure she's okay." He turned to Jacob. "Keep trying to get through to her. I'm sure she'll call us soon to let us know that she's all right." He stopped next to Cole and put a hand on his shoulder. "We'll find her," he said simply and with quiet confidence.

Cole shrugged. "Maybe, maybe not," he replied without emotion.

He turned and watched as his father drove away in his truck. Jacob pulled out his phone again and swore vehemently as he obviously got her voicemail once again. Cole didn't say anything only turned and stalked across the wide drive and into the garage where he could think the best. He walked over to lean a hip against his silver Mustang. He pulled out his phone and opened up the map. With cold precision he studied the map from his location and outward. With a frustrated growl he asked no one in particular, "Where the hell did you go, Brooke?"

Getting away from him was one thing. He could understand why she might want that. The problem was that he needed to know that she was safe at the very least. That and it really pissed him off that she was leaving his father and Jacob high and dry. Yes, that was the reason he was going to find her, he told himself. Once he knew she was okay and could give her a piece of his mind about leaving his family in the lurch, then he could let her go for good. He climbed into the car and tapped the control to the overhead garage door.

Jacob wasn't in the driveway anymore as he sped away without a second thought. With a little luck he would be able to catch her before she got too far. His gut clenched. He had to find her before she got so far out of reach that he couldn't.

CHAPTER 18

Ivan met Sheriff Hanover out by the side of the shop. After shaking hands in warm comradery, Ivan led the way up to his office. As they walked, he asked the sheriff about his wife and daughter and offered a friendly smile as he was assured that they were doing well. He stepped into his office and immediately saw the phone, keys, and letters that were sitting there on the top of his desk where they wouldn't be missed.

He frowned as concern for Brooke's well-being swelled heavily. Apparently, Cole understood Brooke pretty well if he'd pegged this one right. He motioned to two chairs in invitation before walking around the desk to sit down. He thanked the sheriff for coming out and explained in detail what had happened the previous evening.

Sheriff Hanover had several questions as well as wanting a full list of everyone who had been invited to and attended the barbecue. He asked to speak with Brooke and Ivan quickly explained that she had left and he hadn't been able to get in touch with her today. The sheriff scrunched his eyebrows together at that bit of information. "And you're sure she didn't know her attacker?" he asked.

Ivan shook his head. "I really can't say for sure. I do know that's what she told Jacob several times."

The sheriff nodded, his brow still furrowed in deep thought before meeting Ivan's gaze. "I gotta say that it seems unusual for her to take off, afraid or not, if she really believed it was a random attack." He met Ivan's eyes and held his gaze for a long moment. "You should know that in the twenty years that I've been a cop, I have rarely seen a case of abuse where the victims didn't have at least some familiarity with their attackers. It does happen, but it's rare, especially this far out in the countryside." He hesitated for a long moment and then finally asked, "Do you think there is any possibility it could be something related to her family?" He turned to look out the window for a long thoughtful moment. "I've gotten a few calls over the years about the Reynolds," he admitted. "And while nothing ever really came of those calls, I've heard the rumors." Looking uncomfortable he added, "I don't like to give much clout to rumor, but I have to wonder if it was a family member who possibly wanted her back at home." He met Ivan's worried gaze again.

"I don't know for sure, but I don't think it would be her family," Ivan mused. "She told me her father had told her to leave and that her siblings always took his side."

The sheriff raised an eyebrow at that information. "Well, I'm going to have to go out there and talk to them at the very least to try to get this all sorted out."

In a very serious but quiet voice, Ivan said, "You probably ought to know that she's pregnant." He hesitated a moment to let that sink in. "She didn't want her family to know and I would appreciate your discretion with this. I just thought you might need to know in case it's related in any way."

Sheriff Hanover agreed to keep that information as need-to-know only and after a few more questions and a promise from Ivan to send over the guest list, they shook hands and he left.

After Ivan walked him out, he headed slowly back to his desk and sat down heavily. He'd seen letters with both his and Jacob's names on them. It wasn't a good sign. That, along with the phone she'd been using since she started working for them made him inclined to believe Cole. He sent a quick text to Jacob to let him know that she had indeed left and that he should come meet with him at the office. Then he turned and slowly opened the letter. A wad of cash fell out and he stared down at it in exasperated amusement as he read:

Dear Ivan,

I know this isn't how you wanted things to go and I am really sorry about that. I really appreciate everything you have done for me. In many ways you have been the only real parent I have ever had. I know you are not my father but you cared for me and offered me a safe place to call home and I feel like in some ways you are like a father to me.

By now I'm sure that Jacob has talked to you about what happened last night… While I was terrified and very glad that Jacob got to me before that man could get me into his truck, I need you to know, that wasn't the reason I left. Truth be told I had already planned on leaving tonight before he even came after me.

I have come to care very deeply for you and your family and will miss you all forever. You and Jacob have shown me what it feels like to be loved and accepted for myself. I never knew that kind of unconditional love was possible and I am extremely grateful to you both. I will remember it always and forever. I look forward to loving my own child in that same way.

I have felt continually guilty ever since that day when you took me home for breakfast. You have given to me constantly and unconditionally and I'm not really sure that I deserved it. I feel that I have taken advantage of both yours and Jacob's generosity for far too long and the guilt has become more than I can bear.

Please tell Anne that I am sorry. I never meant to take anything away from your family or your relationship with her, though I know it weighed heavily between you.

My heart is heavy as I know that I can never repay you for what you have given me and done for me but I left what little cash I had. I'm sorry I couldn't leave more but I have to have something to keep my child safe and build a future. The cell phone is yours and I left that as well as the keys to the home you let me enjoy for a while. I tried to leave it in better condition than it was when I moved in. Hopefully someday I will be able to pay you what I owe and I hope you can be patient as I have no idea how long it will take.

I know you didn't want this for me, which is just another testament to the good man that you are, but I simply can't keep going through life knowing that I am taking advantage of two of the people I love the most. I couldn't talk to you or Jacob because I knew you would try to convince me to stay. It's just the way your very giving personality is. I'm glad you have Anne to watch out for you so less kind people won't take advantage of your generosity. I also understand why she didn't like me very much and if there is any generosity left in your heart for me, I hope you won't hold it against her. She really does have yours and your family's very best interests at heart.

I wrote a letter to Jacob and I was hoping you would give it to him. You are both so alike and I fear that he is going to take my leaving the hardest so please help him to understand that my leaving is in both of your best interests.

This is off topic I know, but I don't want to forget to tell you. I agree with you about God, by the way. My whole life I was taught that God judges us and judges everything we do. If we don't fit inside some box that is determined by some man then we won't make it to heaven. I like your god much better and it has given my heart great peace to feel like it's okay to choose the life that I want for myself without fear of hell. I thought when I first met you that my soul was damned for eternity because of my bad choices. While I still have a long way to go, I now have hope that my soul can be once again whole and beautiful. For that, I owe you my life.

I don't know where I am going from here yet but I do know that my life will be better because I have known your family. Maybe someday when I have my life all figured out, I can come back and visit knowing that I also have something to bring to the table.

Please don't be mad at me for leaving you in the middle of the busiest season. I wish I could have done more. I'm sorry I didn't have the courage to tell you I might be pregnant sooner and I appreciate you not judging me for it. It is a very complicated situation and I didn't want to get you and Jacob involved in it at all.

Once again, thank you for giving me a glimpse of what a healthy beautiful life can be. It gives me something to look forward to with my own child.

I love you. I will miss you. And I will forever remember all you have given me.

Your friend, Brooke.

Ivan swallowed the lump in his throat and then his eyes narrowed as he re-read the parts about Anne. He wracked his memory for anything that would have led to her assumptions before finally setting the letter down.

He heard Jacob coming up the stairs and stood as he came in. "Come in and sit down for a minute, son," he said as he walked over to the window to look out.

Jacob stared curiously at him as he turned and walked back around his desk to sit. "Cole is right," he stated quietly. "Brooke left." He held up the keys and cell phone and then with a sigh the letter with Jacob's name on it. "She left this for you." He held it out like an offering.

Jacob reached for it, disbelief written across his face. "Why on earth would she leave? She loved it here."

Ivan sighed. "I'm guessing she explained it in the letter much better than I can." He held up his own letter still reeling.

Jacob bent down and opened his own and read.

Dear Jacob,

Please don't be mad at me. The decision to leave was one of the hardest I have ever made. I love you and I didn't want to be without you in my life. Scratch that I mean our lives. I'm pregnant, Bestie. I know, it's a big surprise! I didn't know for sure until a week ago and I wanted to tell you in person, though it didn't quite work out that way. I had planned to tell you when you got home, but then you got home early and I got so carried away in the moment that I forgot all about it. I didn't know the father well and it was from a one-time experience that I had hoped would end differently.

I know you're going be angry at me. You can't help it, so just let it come and then let it go when you're ready. You are one of the most giving and fun people I have ever met. I've loved our talks and texts and every minute we've spent together was special to me. In my heart you will forever be my best friend. I have many brothers and yet you are the first one that felt like you cared for me that way. Thank you for that.

I love you and have felt for a long time that I have been taking advantage of a very generous family and I feel that it's time for me to go out and try to make it on my own. My child deserves it. I want to bring my baby into a world where I know I can take care of myself and him/her. I know you and Ivan would have gladly helped me out, but it wouldn't be fair of me to ask that of either of you.

Thank you for being my first real friend in a world where all I had known was loneliness. I actually really wish we could have been more. Can you imagine how cool it would have been if we also had crazy chemistry? Too bad we were only meant to walk this life as friends.

I'm sorry I didn't confide in you about my pregnancy. I can see now that it would have been so much lighter of a burden had I shared it with you from the first moment I wondered. I hope that one day you can forgive me and even feel the warmth of our friendship again.

I will be back one day when I have more to offer and feel that I can hold my own. I promise. When I come, please try to be ready to talk it through. I know you have another year of school, but I also know that you will finish on top and I am already so proud of you. Don't be afraid to grasp the moment! Sometimes you get so caught up in taking care of everyone that you forget to live each moment for yourself.

Try to find someone who can love you the way I do but also makes your heart beat faster and your heart melt. I know I saw several girls tonight who would be thrilled to go out and maybe one of them is the right one for you. Don't be afraid to give them a shot.

On a less personal note. I don't have the money to pay you back for the TV, but I am hoping that you are okay with just taking it back so I don't owe you for that at least. I left the keys with your dad.

Be happy. I love you. And last but not least don't forget about me.

Love Always Your Bestie,

Brooke.

Jacob finished reading and turned an incredulous look toward his father. "Can you believe this garbage?" he asked.

Ivan gave him a little smile.

"She basically said she had no value and it sounds as though she believes she wasn't pulling her own weight around here." Jacob paused and breathed through his frustration. "I know I haven't been here for a while, but before I left here, she was working her ass off."

Ivan nodded in agreement. "I was actually planning to give her another raise soon because she was doing such a great job."

Jacob hesitated for a minute looking several years older than he had yesterday before asking quietly, "Did you know about the baby?"

Ivan rubbed his hand across his eyes and then through his hair. "She told me about it yesterday," he admitted tiredly. "She acted like she was expecting me to blow a gasket and be angry at her." He met Jacob's eyes, so much like his mother's. "I admit I wanted to go give her father a piece of my mind, but I wasn't angry with her at all." He frowned. "Maybe if I had handled it differently, she wouldn't have gone."

Jacob shook his head at that. "I don't think so, Dad. I think she had already made up her mind to go by then. See, look at this." He held out the letter for his father to read.

Ivan read the section thoughtfully and nodded his agreement. "It does sound like she had already made up her mind," he agreed. He turned suddenly to look at his son. "Did she happen to tell you who the father is?"

"No. I was wondering if you knew." Jacob looked disappointed. "I wish she had told me."

Ivan nodded in understanding. "Me too." Then in frustration. "I don't think we have any way of finding her. She left her phone." He met Jacob's worried frown with his own. "Not unless she contacts us."

Neither one of them were inclined to believe that would happen after reading her letters, but they kept that to themselves.

Jacob stood and, looking at the door, asked quietly, "Where do you think she got the idea that she was taking advantage of us?"

Ivan shrugged. "It was likely partly because she didn't feel she held any value to her own family." He didn't add more, but he had been wondering the same thing. Try as he might he couldn't quite rid himself of the suspicion that he knew exactly why she had felt that way. A sliver of anger cut through his sadness and then slowly grew.

He was going to have a very long honest conversation with his wife. But first he needed to cool off. He wouldn't be doing anyone any favors by storming in with his anger in top gear.

CHAPTER 19

Cole drove until it was dark, heading eastward first for a long while before turning back and driving south. He didn't really think he was going to find her tonight, but he had way too much pent-up frustration to go back home. He thought of the many projects he could get lost in back at the farm but for the first time in his life found he lacked the interest.

He had gotten a text from Jacob hours ago confirming that she had indeed left and that she also left her cell phone with their father. He swore and hit the steering wheel as he threw the damned phone down on the seat. The cell phone was the easiest way that he could have tracked her. He still didn't know exactly why it mattered to him that she had left, but he was really pissed off at her.

He thought once again of the fear on her face just before she had run in the house and locked the door and he cursed again. Just the thought of some guy putting his slimy hands all over her last night made his blood boil. Again, he wasn't sure why it mattered so much to him unless it was simply because he wanted her. Had wanted her since that first time when he'd seen her standing in the kitchen in her prudish clothes. If he wasn't going to take away her innocence, he for damned sure wasn't okay with some other asshole taking it. The only thing that bothered him was that he just didn't understand why.

Watching her at the party the day before, flirting and talking to all those men had been infuriating. And if all that flirting wasn't enough, she had swayed those curvy hips and sashayed to song after song with a whole bunch of horny guys. Some of them had even been his friends but wasn't that how he knew exactly what they were thinking?

He tortured himself with memories of how she'd looked the day before as he turned his car around and headed back toward home. Her red hair had been twisted around and tied at the back of her neck leaving those irresistible long curls bouncing freely down her back. Her deep sapphire eyes had bedazzled more than one of those so-called gentlemen she'd danced with.

He groaned in frustration. Why in God's name did he even care? He had never been the jealous type. Wasn't sure he would have even cared if one of his girlfriends had slept around on him. Girls were easy. It had taken very little on his part in his past relationships. The girls had always done most of the work and had seemed more than happy to do it.

He had usually got busy again at some point with a new project and when they asked him for more time, he'd simply been honest. He had a project that meant a lot that he needed to get done. He didn't know if they understood or not, hadn't really cared if they did if he was honest about it, but eventually they had all moved on and he had been fine with that.

He drove home slowly. He didn't know why, but something about all of it felt off. Though he had always been different than Jacob, he always knew his parents loved him. He had always looked forward to coming home whether his family knew it or not. Usually, he felt excited to have good home cooking and see his younger brothers as well as Jacob and his parents. He liked working on his projects in his home garage. Now, however, he felt nothing. Wasn't even sure what to do with himself when he did get there.

With a speculating thought he pulled off the road at an all-night truck service station. He went inside and grabbed a cold Coke before sifting through a stack of paper maps on a side table. With a nod he grabbed a map of Idaho. He started toward the counter but then inspiration hit and he turned back and grabbed several more. Based on what little he'd heard from his dad, she couldn't have too much money and would likely want to get a job quickly. Satisfied with his choices, he paid for the maps and the drink and then headed home.

Jacob was standing in the kitchen when he walked in, so Cole casually slid the maps into the inside pocket of his leather jacket. He grinned at Jacob's glum look. In a mocking drawl, he asked, "So I was right, then? She took off?"

Jacob glowered and then lowered his beer to look at Cole. "She left a couple of letters to explain it."

Cole laughed low and harsh. "Of course she did. So, what did little Miss Brooke say was the reason she left?" he tossed out with a perfectly mastered unaffected grin.

Jacob watched him for a long minute before he shrugged. "Just that she didn't want to be a burden and that she felt like she needed to figure out how to carry her own weight."

That surprised Cole, who raised eyebrows in disbelief. "She didn't think she was working hard enough?" He stared at the Coke in his hand for a minute. "She out-worked all of the farmhands we have."

Jacob nodded. "I know. I know she always felt like Dad did too much for her. I'm just not sure what finally set her off after the last three months."

Cole watched his brother take a long drag of his cold beer. "Have you seen what she did with the yard at the old house?"

Jacob looked up in surprise. "I didn't even notice when we were over there this morning. I was so worried about her."

Cole smiled. "Well, she has done a lot with it." He watched Jacob nurse his beer for a moment. "So, what are you going to do now?" Cole asked casually. He wanted to know once and for all exactly how involved Jacob had really been with her despite both of them having sworn that they were just friends.

Jacob shrugged. "Not much else we can do, I guess. She left her cell phone anyway so it won't do any good to try getting in touch. She wants to do it on her own and I honestly don't see any way of changing her mind." He looked straight at Cole then. "At least we know she's safe. And if we don't know where she is then chances are good that the guy that attacked her last night won't know either if it turns out not to be a random act."

Cole met his brother's eyes without blinking. "That is one way to look at it," he said lightly before turning and heading down the hallway toward his room.

Jacob stared after him knowingly. He turned and smiled when Anne entered from the back door.

She smiled sweetly and went to the fridge to pour a glass of iced tea before joining him at the table. "How are you doing with all of this, Jacob?" she asked gently as she took a sip of tea.

Jacob had come straight home after reading the letter. He had rushed to tell his mother about Brooke leaving and how frustrated he was. She had squeezed his hand in understanding.

In truth she thought it was probably for the best. Her eldest son was already far too taken with the girl. Especially now that they knew she was pregnant. She didn't think it would be good for any of them if they got too involved in the situation. However, she knew her son wouldn't feel the same, so she kept her opinion to herself.

"Have you seen your father?" she asked.

Jacob shrugged. "Not since earlier. He told me he was going to get some paperwork done when I left the shop."

Anne glanced at the clock, concern on her face. She hadn't heard anything from Ivan since he'd left early in the day and it was unusual for him not to keep in touch. "Well, I guess if I don't hear anything soon, I'll give him a call."

Ivan walked in as she was finishing her sentence. He didn't smile but gave Jacob a curt nod. He turned to look at Anne and she knew instantly that something was very, very wrong. She stood and moved toward him haltingly. He turned toward the door. "Anne, could I have a word with you in private?" He didn't wait to see if she followed. He strode determinedly out onto the porch and let the door swing shut behind him.

Anne followed him a bit reluctantly. She had barely closed the door behind her when he advanced angrily. "I have gone over and over it all day," Ivan said coldly. Then he reached into his jacket and pulled a letter out. He thrust it at her. "What in the hell is she talking about?" he asked as his normally warm brown eyes flashed hot with anger.

Anne paled, she had rarely seen Ivan this angry and never ever had it been at herself. She took the letter from him and risked a look up at him. "Is this the letter from Brooke?" she asked carefully.

Jaw tight, he tipped his head once. He watched her in silence until she moved under the porch light and opened the letter. Cash fell out and she scrambled to pick it up. She glanced uncertainly at him before she started reading again. Her face was stiff and unreadable as she scanned the pages. When she was done, she stared down for several seconds before turning to face him. "I'm not sure what you mean," she started to say, but Ivan stopped her with a cold look.

She stared up at this ruggedly handsome face of the man that she had loved for so many years and for the first time in a very long time felt unsure of herself.

He met her gaze with unbending will. "I thought we had come to an understanding with this Anne." She looked away and he took her silence as a rebuttal. "I was very clear with you that I was going to be a part of Brooke's life and that I feel very strongly about this." He ran an agitated hand through his gray-speckled dark hair. "I already talked to the lawyer and got things all settled on my end." He took a deep breath trying unsuccessfully to calm his temper. "I won't lie to you. I simply don't understand why you have such a big issue with this." He looked at her pleadingly for a minute and that look hurt worse than the anger had. "You are normally the most loving person I know and I really don't get how you can't see her for what she is."

Anne met his gaze then, her own temper rising to the surface. "You have no idea what that girl is up to or where she has been," she challenged. "I know you and Jacob both think she is always upfront and trustworthy but you just brought her into our lives without knowing anything about her."

Ivan's jaw hardened again and his voice was low and icy when he responded. "We have already been over this. What kind of life leads a nineteen-year-old girl to be sleeping in a car next to the ditch?" he asked with obvious frustration. "And to think that you have somehow gotten it in your head that we need to protect our kids from her? In the last three months that girl has become a great friend to Jacob. She has helped me and the workers tremendously with all the work we've had around here without a single compliant. She tried to talk *me* out of giving her a raise. Does that sound like someone who is trying to take advantage of me?"

He had raised his voice again, and she backed up a step.

"I get that it might not seem that way, and I understand why you might even have a soft spot for her," she said in a trembling voice. "But honestly did you have to give her property and set up a trust for her?" She took a deep breath and then in a rush asked, "With everything you have given her, why wasn't it enough for her? Has it crossed your mind that she might have left with the intention of trying to get you to give her even more when she 'comes' back?" Anne was just as angry now too.

Ivan looked sad and tired then as he looked down at her cheeks that were flushed with anger. "My God, Anne, are you even listening to yourself." He held her gaze steadily. "I never even told her about putting the deed in her name or about the trust." He let that sink in good before he continued. "I was waiting to tell her when I could come up with a way to convince her to accept it." His arms folded stubbornly across his chest. "I fully intend on going down to the lawyer to also set up a trust for her unborn child first thing tomorrow."

Anne looked taken aback. "She doesn't know?" she asked.

Ivan shook his head and with a bitter smile said, "That girl has too much pride to accept anything more than a paycheck from me. And even with that she insists that I pull out rent and utilities on the old house or she threatens mutiny. She tried to give Cole money for rent when he took his truck to town to haul something for her. I get why a person needs to be careful about such things, but, Anne, hear me when I say, Brooke Reynolds has done nothing but give since she got here. In truth it has been all I can do to get her to accept what little I have done for her."

Anne was stunned. "Why didn't you tell me all of this before."

Ivan smiled coldly. "I did. You just didn't hear it."

One thing still troubled her and she asked in a gentler tone, "And what about her pregnancy. Doesn't it bother you that she wasn't upfront about it from the beginning?"

Ivan turned away from her then. He couldn't even look at her as he quietly answered, "No, it doesn't, and frankly I would have thought you of all people would be more understanding about that." It was a low blow and both of them knew it. Anne had gotten pregnant shortly after they'd started dating. She had been terrified to tell her parents. In the end, however, she hadn't had to tell them as she had miscarried at ten weeks.

As Anne thought about everything he'd said, her eyes filled with tears at the memory of that painful time. "I do understand her fear," she said finally. "I did talk to her yesterday and told her that she shouldn't take advantage of you and Jacob and that I wouldn't stand for it. But I also offered to see her at the clinic for a checkup." She took a deep breath. "I'm sorry, Ivan, I know that's not what you want to hear and that you care about her, but it's the truth."

Ivan turned back then. "I don't know what the situation was with her pregnancy. Hell, for all I know she was raped." His voice was low and hoarse and when he said the last Anne looked away in shame.

She hadn't even considered that. She stepped closer to Ivan and put a hand on his tensed arm. "I am really sorry, Ivan. I never should have insinuated that she was selfish and taking advantage of this family. I can see now that I might have blown this all out of proportion."

Behind her she heard a sharp in-drawn breath. "You told her what?" Cole who had just walked up asked with an incredulous frown. Each word got louder and more enunciated as he finished.

Anne turned in surprise. Though she loved all of her children equally as well as unconditionally, Cole had always been the one that she understood the most. They'd always had an easygoing relationship where they seemed to just get how the other felt and what they were going through without words. She met his dark eyes and to her surprise they were cold with anger. The small smile died on her lips. She turned back to Ivan. "I will let it go and I will apologize to her when we she comes back," she promised quietly.

Ivan brushed her hand off his arm and looked directly at her. "That is both an overdue and presumptuous offer. We may never see her again." He turned to walk into the house and then, changing his mind, turned instead toward the back gate and his truck.

With nowhere left to turn, Anne finally faced Cole. "For the record I may have told Brooke that she shouldn't ever take advantage of your father and Jacob," she confessed in a heavy-laden voice.

Cole watched her for a long moment. "Why would you think she was taking advantage of them anyway?" He knew his mother well and he knew she would never have treated anyone that way if she hadn't been truly concerned for her family.

Anne looked up hopefully. Cole didn't look as angry now. She took a deep breath. "Ever since your father first saw Brooke, he has been determined to look out for her. He actually went and opened a trust in her name." She frowned in consternation. "I admit that worried me a bit, but then he also had the deed to the old house along with the water rights for that property transferred into her name."

She sighed. "Next thing I know, Jacob is completely taken with her as well." She looked down at her feet. "I must confess that I actually started wondering if Brooke had come here with a plan to use her charm to take advantage of us from the start." She rubbed a tired hand across her temple. "I didn't know that Ivan had never actually told her what he had done, so I thought she was just taking it all in stride," she admitted, miserable now.

Cole reached out a hand and touched her shoulder. "It's all going to work out,

Mom." He promised with steely determination. His mother had enough to deal with, without his own anger, judging by his father's angry departure. He patted her gently again and then with a narrowed gaze vowed quietly, "I am going to find her and fix all of this." Then he turned on his heel and walked into the house.

Anne stood staring after him in perplexed curiosity. What exactly was he going on about? She wondered as she turned and looked toward the gate Ivan had stalked through. And exactly how long was Ivan planning to punish her for her mistakes? A sad little laugh escaped her lips. It seemed that ever since Brooke Reynolds had entered her world, everything had changed. Was it a good change? she wondered to herself or was it simply a warning of things yet to come? The moon was high in the sky as she trod with heavy feet and heart inside to make sure the younger boys had indeed gone to bed. She lay in bed alone for long hours waiting for Ivan to come or for sleep to take her into its oblivious warmth.

CHAPTER 20

The following week went by one long taxing day after another in the Burton home. Ivan hadn't come home Sunday night much to Anne's everlasting frustration. It was the first time in all their years together that they had spent the night apart and she hadn't been able to sleep much at all. He had come in for breakfast and a quick shower before heading back out to work on Monday morning. Though his temper had cooled off some he still didn't understand his wife's harsh judgment of Brooke nor her obvious lack of trust in him when it came to the situation. He had hoped that their trust in one another would have made up the difference and yet it appeared to be the driving force of the wedge between them.

Each day went slowly as they waited patiently for any word from the sheriff or even from Brooke herself. Neither was inclined to call, so the men went out and worked long hard days in the fields and Anne spent extra time catching up at the clinic.

Each day ended with Cole disappearing to the garage to do whatever it was that he was working on. The discussion at the dinner table usually consisted of Jacob and Ivan talking about how neither Brooke nor Sheriff Hanover had called yet. Then everyone sat picking at the food until they all gave up and excused themselves. After excusing himself Jacob would head to bed and Ivan would go to the guest bed despite the hopeful look on Anne's face each evening. Hours into the night Cole could be heard coming in late to take a quick shower and hit the sack.

Ivan and Jacob had both cared deeply for Brooke. They had also offered their trust and love to the troubled girl without reservation. Anne truly wanted to understand how a young redheaded girl that wasn't even here any longer could have caused so much upset in what had previously been a very stable family life. Even Zachary who had appeared the least attached to Brooke had been upset to learn of Brooke's departure. Ryker still continued to ask every night when Brooke was coming home despite being told countless times that she may never even come back at all. He continued to pout and refused to believe it.

With her family in complete upheaval, Anne tried without success to make it up to Ivan. She made his favorite dishes for dinner and wore the perfume he'd given her on their last anniversary. She apologized countless times even though she still didn't exactly understand how one young girl could have made such an impact in three short months. Ivan was still angry with her and very concerned about Brooke's being gone, which, it seemed he blamed her for. He wouldn't budge regardless of the many attempts she made to make it up to him.

In the end it was Cole who finally got through to both of them. He had been disappearing every night to work on one of his projects, which had honestly been a relief to Anne. He was the only one of her family who didn't keep bringing Brooke's name up and didn't seem to blame her at all for what had happened. She was glad that he at least was his old self, working tirelessly on his cars.

The weekend went by quietly as Ivan and Jacob opted to work through it. Both found it easier to stay busy than sitting around wondering where Brooke would have gone. As usual Cole once again disappeared to the garage so Anne took the boys shopping and to a new movie that had just come out.

Monday morning started the same way the previous week had gone with everyone eating breakfast in silence except for the occasional comment or complaint about Brooke. Ivan began clearing the dishes and Jacob stood to help. Cole sat watching his parents and Jacob in quiet frustration. In a rare moment of determined disgust he stood and stated, "All this crap is not helping anyone with anything." He looked his dad in the eye pointedly. Then he turned to his mother. "Would you come with me, Mom?" He asked the question in polite respect but the somber authority in his voice left no room for argument.

She nodded and stood stiffly. Cole strode out the door and Anne followed after throwing a questioning look at both Ivan and Jacob as she passed them. Jacob shrugged and looked toward the door and Ivan just looked silently at her with one eyebrow up.

Cole's car was parked by the front door and he walked around to open the passenger door for his mother before walking back around to climb inside. Anne reluctantly closed the door and buckled her seat belt. A long week of bearing Ivan's anger and dealing with the constant upheaval of Brooke's leaving had her exhausted and on edge. She turned to Cole as he started the engine and shifted into first gear. He was silent as he pulled out onto the road.

Anne wrung her hands in frustration. She was well on the verge of giving her son an ever-loving piece of her mind when he finally spoke.

"I know that you don't get why everyone is so worked up about this," he said with quiet confidence. "I'm going to help you understand who Brooke really is because this family is falling apart and you and Dad really need to get your shit together." He shifted gears and glanced sideways at her. "I want you to be able to see this from Dad's point of view because he is never going to see it your way," he said simply.

Even though Anne wasn't sure she wanted to see Ivan's point of view right now, as she was becoming quite angry herself that he had let the situation drag on this long, she nodded. After all, her son was telling her it was time to work things out. If one's own children were telling them there was a problem, it was time to shut up and listen. "Okay, then, show me."

Cole smiled and her heart warmed. There hadn't been many of those around as of late. "Dad is a good guy as you know and tends to be overly protective of anyone that he thinks needs protection. We all live in this world where Dad has pretty much made life easy for all of us." He saw her mouth open and quickly added. "I know you were a big part of that too. But the point here is that none of us has really had to do a lot to survive. We all have everything we could ever need or even want." He took a deep breath searching for the words. "We've grown up in this valley with good people and good friends." He changed direction. "We have all heard the rumors about the Reynolds family." He looked at her pointedly until she nodded.

"So here you have Dad and his very protective nature who comes upon a young girl parked in one of our fields sleeping in her car. At first, he thinks she is probably just sleeping off her fatigue. But then he begins to realize she looks emotional and washed out. The next thing he notices is that she is jumpy and scared. Then the realization hits him as he sees what she is wearing, that she is most likely one of the Reynolds kids."

He glanced over at her again and pulled onto the shoulder of the road and stopped the car. "So now here's Dad thinking of all the rumors he's heard and trying to piece it all together with his own dealings with Mr. Reynolds when he finds out that Brooke has been kicked out of the only home she has ever known. He starts wondering if she is even capable of coping with the real world and this has him worried. Then Dad being Dad and not wanting to let a young girl drown in an unfamiliar life he's not sure she has been equipped to deal with, he brings her home for breakfast and decides to offer her a safe place to land while she figures things out."

Anne nodded in understanding, so Cole continued. "As it turns out, this girl is extremely intelligent and a very hard and diligent worker, which would have been enough on its own. But then she has this stubborn streak of pride that won't allow her to accept any charity or help from others unless she feels that she can somehow repay it or make it up to that person."

Anne was staring at him hard now, a curiously searching look in her green eyes. "I didn't realize that you had much at all to do with Brooke, Cole." It was more of a question than a statement and Cole looked away.

"I didn't," he agreed quietly. "But that doesn't mean that I don't see where Dad is coming from."

Anne watched his carefully guarded expression. "And giving her a trust and even some of our land and the home on it? That is just what you do in such a case?"

Cole shrugged. "It's only money to us. All of that would mean so much more than just money to someone like Brooke. It would essentially be a safe place to call home."

Anne nodded at that revelation. "I can see that." She looked at his profile in curious consideration. "Why are *you* telling me all of this, Cole? This last week you have seemed to be the least affected by all of this."

Cole had turned to meet her gaze but looked away again. "To be honest I'm sick of watching two people who have loved each other since before I was born fight and refuse to work it out."

Anne swallowed as her eyes blazed. "That's not fair, Cole. I *have* been trying to work it out with your father, but he refuses to deal with me at all," she said harshly.

Cole turned an intelligent, knowing look on her. "You and I both know that you're also holding a rather large grudge about this. The truth is that you can keep apologizing and pretend that you feel bad, but Dad knows you too well to fall for that crap when you obviously still feel justified in your actions." He smiled kindly to lighten the truth of his words. "I want you to imagine yourself in his shoes and think of a young girl coming to you. I know you would want to help her. It only bothered you because it seemed like Dad was willing to risk his relationship with you to help Brooke. So, you've been fighting like crazy and trying to make him choose you." He held her gaze. "In truth Dad loves you very much and only wants you to see what an amazing person Brooke is. He wants you two to be a team and help her together."

Anne's face fell and honest tears filled her eyes. "I think I knew that all along and the truth is I would have been more open to all of it if he had ever actually asked me for my opinion or respected me enough to listen to my concerns."

Cole countered calmly, "His point, though, Mom, is that you wouldn't have even had any concerns if you had chosen to be involved in it from the start instead of being mad about Dad slighting you in some way."

Anne laughed through her tears and nodded. "Okay, you got me there."

Cole smiled and pulled back on the road. "Brooke is a proud, very innocent girl that really did deserve any break in life that she could get." He turned and pulled up to the old house. "I want to show you something," he said as he opened his door and then walked around to open his mother's too.

Anne slid out and looked around in happy surprise. Over the years the old house had become run down and had been a slight source of sadness to her because of the many wonderful memories they'd had here as a family. The whole place looked clean and tidy now. The old bricks were clean and bright and she wondered if Ivan had hired someone to come out and clean them. The old stainless-steel windows were shiny and clear of the hard water stains of past and recent years.

Anne had quit coming over here when she realized it was depressing to see their old place slowly going to pot. Now the grass was green, and a vibrant and colorful array of flowers bloomed together in a rock-circled bed in the sun-brightened front yard. The front porch was bright white with a fresh coat of paint and the concrete had been swept and washed. She smiled and turned to Cole. "When did your father have all of this done?" she asked in wonder.

Cole slid his hands into the pockets of his dark blue jeans. "He didn't," he said simply as he watched his mother's face while waiting for her to understand.

She scrunched her brows together in confusion. Then suddenly her smile fell and she looked around again and then up at him. "Brooke did all of this?"

He nodded with a quiet but proud smile.

"When would she have had the time to do all this?" she asked in disbelief.

Cole shrugged again. "Evenings and weekends best as I can tell." He hesitated before adding, "That girl could really work." One side of his mouth curled into a crooked grin as he said, "And eat."

Anne looked confused then. She wasn't what sure eating had to do with any of it, but this was Cole's moment. "I had no idea she was doing all of this." She walked over to look down at the freshly weeded flower garden as her own memories of this place swelled. "We have been renting this place out for years and no one has ever kept it this nice," she mused.

"That's what I meant about this place being a safe home for someone like Brooke." Cole grinned then. "Come on, I want you to see the back of the house too."

They walked around the house and Anne stopped to stare in amazement. "It's so beautiful," she said as she suddenly remembered Brooke's words, *I tried to leave the house in better shape than it was* she'd written in the letter to Ivan. Anne's smile faltered.

By the time they had walked through the house and Anne saw the fresh paint and warm tidy décor, she was in tears. It was obvious that it had been done with love by someone who cared deeply.

Cole didn't say anything as he held the car door for Anne once again. He didn't see any point in making her feel bad now that she understood. They made the drive home in silence. As they pulled into the driveway, Anne asked quietly, "Why did you show me all of this, Cole?"

His face was stiff and expressionless as he responded, "I just wanted you to know why Jacob and Dad like her so much so you can understand their pain."

He walked her to the door before he turned to go.

His next stop was to his father's office. He said hello to Maude as he walked past and she smiled warmly. He found his father at his desk staring at the phone in frustration. Cole knocked lightly on the open door. His father looked up and nodded, so he entered and took a seat leaning back into a casually relaxed position. He nodded at his dad and watched him force a smile. "What do you need, son?"

Cole was silent for a long while. He met his father's gaze, held it there. "You need to forgive Mom," he said.

Ivan started muttering something and Cole wondered if he was swearing but didn't ask him to repeat it.

Instead, he held up a hand to silence him. "I don't really care what problems you both have with each other right now. You need to fix it," he said simply and with almost cruel honesty. "We are going to find Brooke and we will make sure she is all right and when we do that, you and Mom are going to be on the same page with everything."

Ivan just looked at him, a stubborn glint in his brown eyes.

Cole's gaze was harsh and unbending. "I know that Mom let you down and she broke your trust, but in her defense, she really thought she was protecting this family." He held a hand up again as his father started to speak angrily. "The truth here is that you hurt her too and you broke her trust first by not asking how she felt or listening to her considerations through it all. I know you love her, Dad, and I know she is going crazy from you trying to punish her for this. You need to stop. And you need to go home until you work things out. Being at war with each other is only making all of this worse. What is the point of bringing Brooke home if we're all at war with each other?" He stood up then, gave his father a quick respectful nod, and then walked out.

Ivan stared after him for a long while. Slowly, a wide smile lifted his lips and the week's worth of un-shaven stubble that covered his chin and cheeks. "Damn, that boy is smart," he said aloud to no one in particular. Then he reached for his hat and settled it on his head as he headed out to his truck and drove home.

Anne was crying when he entered their suite. She sat on the brightly colored floral chaise at the end of their bed that faced the smart flat-screen television hanging on the wall. He walked over to her and with a heavy sigh sat down next to her. He reached out a strong arm and clasped her hand in his. "I'm just going to assume that our very intelligent son also had a very honest and direct conversation with you as well," he stated in a slightly amused drawl.

Anne smiled back at him and nodded. "I am so sorry that I refused to see the kind of person that Brooke really is." She looked across the room and said honestly, "I was just so mad that you had already decided what you were going to do and that what I thought didn't even matter." She looked back at him her eyes swimming with unshed tears. "I wanted to believe she was selfish and looking for someone to take advantage of because I was hurt and I wanted you to be wrong." She looked down at her hands, ashamed to admit the truth.

Ivan pulled her into his side. "I hear you and I am sorry that I didn't give you a say with any of it. I saw a broken girl that needed someone to care about her and for the first time in a long while, I felt excited. Here was someone that I could truly make a difference with. I felt a surge of peace and I knew that I got to do it." He rolled one shoulder. "I realize now that I should have trusted that you would also want to help her out and just asked what you thought we should do."

An incredibly beautiful smile dawned as Anne admitted honestly, "I really don't know how I would have felt, though. I hope that I would have wanted to help her." She looked worried at that confession and Ivan chuckled.

"I have no doubt now that you would have," he reassured as he pulled her gently into his arms.

They talked for a long time about trust and love and the best way to handle the mess they had created together.

It was one o'clock in the afternoon when Anne finally rose, reluctantly saying that she needed to go make sure the boys had gotten lunch. Cole was in the kitchen making a plate of sandwiches and had already tossed a fresh garden salad. He nodded politely at both of them before silently continuing to make sandwiches as his parents went to set the table. They all worked in companionable silence.

After the food was on the table and Ivan had called the boys in to eat, they sat. Anne loaded a healthy portion of salad onto her plate and quietly said, "I hope Brooke has found a doctor and set up an appointment for a checkup." She was thinking out loud and missed Cole's narrowed look.

Ivan nodded. "I'm sure she'll figure it out. She's a smart capable girl," he said reassuringly.

A frown wrinkled her forehead and she sighed. "Truth be told, I really wish she was here. I would feel a lot better knowing that her and the baby were here where I could keep an eye on them."

Ivan nodded in understanding.

Cole froze with his fork halfway to his lips. "What do you mean her and the baby?" he asked hoarsely.

Anne smiled at him with a curious look. "Brooke is expecting, dear." She set her fork down. "I'm sorry, I just assumed that you knew."

Anger hot and raw surged through him. "Brooke Reynolds?" he asked.

Ivan was watching him closely now. "She found out shortly before she left, but apparently she was expecting when she first came to work for us."

"That's impossible. She's still just a young innocent girl," he insisted in a determined tone.

Ivan smiled at Cole. "She's nearly twenty, so not completely naïve, Cole." He grinned at Anne. "In fact, I seem to remember a few girls you had on your arm long before you were eighteen and we didn't judge you."

Cole looked at him in obvious frustration. "That's not what I meant."

Ivan and Anne both raised an eyebrow across at him. He forced a smile at both of them and carefully cleared his face of all emotion.

Inside he felt the fury growing. *How in God's name had she gotten pregnant?* He laughed inwardly at his own stupid question. He was quite familiar with the way she had gotten pregnant and it had nothing to do with God. An image of her naked body with all that long fiery red hair tangled with some loser of a guy made him choke on the lettuce he'd just stuck in his mouth. A frown creased his forehead as he quickly swallowed some water to wash it down.

With a bitter smile, he realized that she was probably in love with some other guy and that explained why she had pushed him away. Thinking through his own stupidity, he smiled in self-derision. Here he had been thinking she was such an innocent little thing when in reality she simply hadn't wanted him. He laughed suddenly and stood, leaving his half-eaten plate where it was as he stalked out of the room. *Had she run off with the other guy?* He swore savagely. He was going to find her if it killed him. He would damn well make her face him and admit the truth.

Anne stared after Cole and then turned to Ivan and asked, "What in the world was that about?"

Ivan grinned and shrugged. "If I had to guess, I would say that Cole has a thing for Brooke."

Anne shook her head in denial and then stopped short. "You really think so?" She almost sounded hopeful. "But he hasn't really had any interest in girls since he left for college."

Ivan nodded. "No, he hasn't," he agreed with a cheerful smile.

CHAPTER 21

It took Brooke two days of driving to make it to the small town in Montana. She spent the first night in a town nestled between big buttes in the mountains and after heavy consideration about spending her savings bought a prepaid cell phone at the department store there. She was going to need a way for people to get ahold of her if she wanted a job.

The next day she drove straight through the main part of the city. She finally stopped in a small charming town twenty minutes out of the northern Montana city in the early afternoon. *It's beautiful here*, she thought with a hopeful smile. There were green meadows of tall grass surrounded by large swaths of deep green evergreens and large lakes with beautiful homes at their edge. This was indeed a place she could see herself eventually calling home. Her heart ached and she thought of the home she'd left behind. She couldn't think of that now, she reminded herself. She had to look to the future. Valiantly she squared her shoulders and pushed away the painful memories. She had to be positive for the baby.

Originally, she had been planning to go to a larger city in northern Montana, but when she got there, it felt busy and overwhelming. She stopped and bought a map since her phone was one of those flip kind. There was a small town just twenty minutes out of the city and she drove to it.

Now she drove down main street looking around in avid curiosity. She needed a fresh shower and a decent meal after the last day of driving and nothing to eat but road snacks. She parked in a grocery store parking lot and pulled out the new phone. In the short time that she'd had a cell phone she had come to feel dependent on it.

She couldn't do much with the flip phone, so she looked around to see if there was one of those ancient phone booths and a phone book. Seeing nothing, she sighed and pulled back onto the road. She was going to have to drive around and see what motels she could find.

She found one motel just off main street but kept driving. Farther up the road and toward the mountainside, she came onto a small inn. It was a picturesque and cozy little place. She pulled in and parked feeling immediately drawn to the place. A middle-aged woman helped her get checked in and handed her a key with the room number. With a friendly smile she told Brooke to let them know if there was anything else that she needed. As she walked to the door to leave, she saw a little sign that announced the inn was a family-owned business.

Brooke smiled back at the receptionist and waved as she walked back outside with a key in hand.

The room was clean and airy with gorgeous vintage-style furniture and a bed that felt ridiculously comfortable to her sore muscles. She took a hot shower first and then went in search of food. She found a small café and parked in the lot. It was across from the grocery store and she made a mental note to ask about work there after dinner.

She felt a little self-conscious as she went inside the café. A man with light brown hair and who looked to be somewhere in his forties met her at the pulpitlike hostess stand and asked if she wanted a table for one. She nodded with a smile and he took her to a small cozy booth by the window. She sat down and looked curiously at the menu while he poured her some water.

The man had just left when a young blonde waitress came to take her drink order. Brooke asked the waitress what was good and was told that most people ordered the meatloaf. She ordered that with an icy Coke and a garden salad with ranch. The waitress seemed friendly enough, so when she stopped by with her Coke, Brooke asked her how she liked her work. The waitress shrugged indifferently and said it was fine for a job.

Brooke laughed and thanked her. Her food came and she made quick work of it while she looked through a wanted paper that she had seen and snatched at the front of the restaurant. Noticing that the restaurant had a bright sign in the window that said they were hiring, she asked for a job application before she left. The waitress assured her cheerfully that someone like her could probably get the job right away and Brooke promised to return in the morning with the application completed.

She slept for twelve hours straight before she finally forced herself out of the soft mattress. She ate a muffin she'd picked up at the grocery store when she got an application there and drank some rather weak coffee before heading out of her room for the day. She had paid for three nights at the little inn upfront and was hoping to have a job and a place to stay by the end of those three nights. She didn't want to blow all her savings on a room for the next few weeks.

She dropped off the application at the restaurant but didn't see the waitress from yesterday anywhere. She drove around the town for several hours stopping to fill out applications for a gas station, another grocery store, and one fast food burger joint in the middle of town. With nothing left to do for now, she drove back to the inn.

The middle-aged woman who had checked her in the day before was out with a cart cleaning the rooms when she got to the hotel.

A little bored, Brooke kindly offered to help her. The woman looked at her like she was nuts so Brooke assured her with a smile that she would love to help out while she was here since she didn't have anything better to do. The woman looked down the long line of rooms needing serviced and finally nodded. She carefully instructed Brooke on exactly what to do in each room. The cleaning and replacing of linens went quickly with both women working together and with her work done early, the woman—who introduced herself as Janae—offered to make them some fresh tea or coffee in the lobby.

She told Brooke to sit in the lobby and rest as she disappeared into a back room. She reappeared a few minutes later with a tray of small sandwiches and cookies and set it on a table in front of Brooke. She disappeared inside again and when she came back, had a tray stacked with a small teapot and a french press full of hot coffee. Cream and sugar sat to the side of the round white mugs.

Brooke thanked Janae warmly as she sipped some great peppermint tea. They talked together about the weather and just how nice the day was.

Janae thanked her for the help and kindly asked what Brooke was doing in town. Brooke cheerfully informed her that she was moving to town and was looking for work and a place to stay. The older woman smiled and mentioned all of the people that she knew were looking for help, ticking them off her fingers like soldiers. They spent the afternoon talking about local opportunities and all of the fun local entertainment available before Brooke finally excused herself and went back to her room.

The following day Brooke woke early and went to two different interviews. Then she drove to some of the places Janae had recommended and got more applications. She returned to the inn just in time to help Janae do all of the cleaning once again. They visited over tea and a light lunch afterward much like the day before. While they visited Brooke offered to help outside with some of the yard work that appeared to be overdue.

With a little laugh after the offer Janae said, "Maybe you should just stay here and help us out with upkeep on the place."

Brooke hesitated. "I swear I'm not trying to wrangle a job from you. I just like to stay busy you know?"

Janae smiled. "I know that, honey, but if you wanted to help with some of the chores around here it would be worth it to us and you can stay here free for as long as you want to."

That offer was too good to turn down so Brooke hastily agreed. She spent that evening weeding and then replanting a large rectangular raised flower garden just outside the inn's lobby.

It was around dinnertime when the café finally called and asked if she could come in for an interview. She hastily agreed and set it up for the following morning. Since she now had at the very least, a temporary place to stay she was content to wait and see if she could get the job. The burger joint had already offered to hire her, but she had really liked the waitress at the café and the thought of working with her made Brooke feel hopeful for the future.

After a long interview the manager of the café told her she was hired before she even left the building. One of the grocery stores had also called to offer her a position stacking shelves but she thought she might be able to make more money waiting tables if she could only get good tips. Plus, she thought, it would help her get through her social discomfort.

With a happy little skip in her step, she made her way back to the inn. Once again, she helped out Janae with the cleaning who then told her that she and her husband owned the small inn and were thrilled to have a little help without having to spend money out of pocket. Brooke happily informed Janae that she had gotten a job at the café and would start tomorrow. Together they worked out a schedule for Brooke to do some of the daily chores around the motel when she wasn't working at the café. It was the beginning of a warm friendship and it made Brooke feel a little better about her circumstances.

The next few weeks flew by in a rush as Brooke first trained and then started waiting tables on her own. Since most of her shifts were in the afternoon, she would get up early and clean all of the main areas of the hotel and do some work outside before she went to the café.

Between staying for free at the inn and getting most of her meals from the restaurant, she had to spend very little. When she could afford it, she made a doctor's appointment for a checkup. The doctor referred her to an OBGYN who then informed her that they needed to run a full list of tests just to make sure everything was good with her pregnancy. Brooke readily agreed.

Her second appointment went well and all the tests had come back positive. Between the baby, the inn, and work Brooke managed to stay so busy that she barely had any time to miss the Burtons.

Janae told her all about a local high school that offered free classes that she could take to get her high school diploma if she wanted it. Brooke was so thrilled, that she called the next morning and signed up for the class.

While her family had done home schooling in an effort to keep their children from interacting with unholy people, it wasn't legal so she didn't have a diploma. She had always wanted to go to public school but hadn't been allowed. She was excited and thrilled to have another opportunity to get a diploma now.

The weeks went by in a blaze turning into months and in what seemed like a flash she was taking her high school exams and then passing them with decent scores. Both her friend and coworkers Jill and Janae insisted they take her out to celebrate her achievement.

Together they drove into the city to a nice steak house. It turned out to be a lovely evening with good friends and laughter. Though Jill had pertly informed her that it was strange for one of her best friends to be so much older than she was, Jill herself also liked Janae and their little trio was born.

It was that night when Brooke finally confided her pregnancy to her friends. It was also the first time she had talked to anyone except the café manager and the doctor about her pregnancy. Though both Jill and Janae were obviously curious about the baby's father, they didn't push when it seemed to make Brooke uncomfortable.

Jill suggested that they throw a baby shower a little later on and Janae agreed and offered the hotel lobby as the venue. Together they made up a guest list. There were, after all, a few other friends she had made at work that they could invite as well.

Brooke was relieved when she finally started showing, though she wasn't happy about spending money on clothing items that allowed more room for the baby to grow. She was eighteen weeks along and had just outgrown the waist of her jeans when the doctor cheerfully informed her that she was having a baby boy. It was the day after her twentieth birthday and she felt like it was the best gift she had ever received. She cried as she thought of running and playing with a cute little boy. She thought of Little League and bikes and long hikes in the mountains. She was so excited she went to a baby store and bought a cute little blue onesie with a bright red fire engine on the front.

They soon had weekly girls' nights planned with cold drinks, snacks, and lots of laughter. Sometimes, it was the three women only and other times they invited several more friends to join. Brooke began to settle quietly into an acceptable life. Her heart ached as she thought of the Burtons every day and still missed them with a lonesome throb that might accompany a lost limb, but her life was good and she found herself chanting that thought again and again. The girls' nights and her friends did help to fill the void after all.

It was just such a night on a cool evening in September when she finally shared the truth of where she had grown up. The Burtons had already known her family, so she hadn't had to tell them, but here in this small town in Montana, no one had heard of her family. For a while, it was nice not to have that stigma of interest from those who didn't understand, but as time went on, she found herself wanting to talk about it with her friends.

Janae and Jill tried multiple times to set her up on dates. Jill with ex-boyfriends or guys she'd known her entire life and Janae with nephews, neighbors, and friends' sons. As they sipped cider on the deck outside the inn, Janae was once again trying to set her up on a date with her nephew. Brooke was already shaking her head in denial as a vivid image of Cole planted itself firmly in her mind. It wasn't, of course that she was stuck on him or even that she wanted only a relationship with him and no one else. It was the simple fact that whenever anyone talked to her about men or dating, his face would settle into her mind's eye solidly, and she remembered their kisses. Sometimes it took days for her to stop thinking about him again only to start up again as soon as someone mentioned dating.

Today she remembered that last day at the barbecue and those few stolen moments in the shadows with him. She lifted her hands up in self-preservation. "Please, can we just not do this again, Janae?" she asked as she met her friend's serious gray eyes.

Janae looked concerned. "Honey, I'm just a little worried about you is all. I haven't seen you show any interest in anyone since you've been here." She smiled gently, "You don't want to spend your life alone, do you?"

Brooke gave her a frustrated smile. "I just don't feel like I can be making choices that complicate my life right now." She placed a hand on her rounding belly.

Jill jumped in. "That's exactly the point, Brooke. Soon you will have your son and your whole life will be about being his mom and how are you going to find the time to date then?"

Brooke groaned impatiently. "I know that it may seem strange to you both, but I am still trying to process my life up to this point and I don't feel like adding a random guy to the mix, is going to help."

Janae's gaze narrowed in on her. "Is this about being pregnant at twenty, hon?"

Brooke wanted to agree with her but couldn't get herself to lie. "Not exactly."

That statement had even Jill, who was busy picking lint off her sweater looking up and zeroing in on Brooke. "I sense drama," she said matter-of-factly. Then she leaned toward Brooke and propped her gorgeous face on her hands and grinned. "Spill."

Both Brooke and Janae laughed. Then Janae seconded the command and Brooke found herself quietly telling them about her family and the strange life she had grown up in. Both women looked slightly shell-shocked and then proceeded to ask a million and one questions. Though she felt a little uncomfortable, Brooke was happy to share if it meant not talking about men.

Another month and several more attempts to set her up on dates had her finally admitting she had known someone that she cared about. She didn't mention Cole by name. They hadn't really dated anyway, really only had a few stolen kisses and a grumpy Cole to show for anything. She did, however, mention that she had met a guy before and that she wasn't quite over him yet.

No amount of pressure from Jill made her feel inclined to tell them more, so even though they dug, she gave them nothing else. Brooke had only given a very generalized description of Cole and even that was simply a ploy to get Jill off her back.

Her tummy grew and with it the full realization of what it would mean to be a mom. She started looking seriously for a place with more space. After all she couldn't just live at the motel forever.

Janae suggested wisely that she at least check with a couple of banks to see if she could get approved to buy a small place of her own. "What could it hurt", she'd asked several times. While Brooke didn't think that was really a possibility, she finally agreed for Janae's sake. To her surprise after running a basic credit check and then verifying her work income, she was approved right away.

Still somewhat in shock she called a local realtor that both Jill and Janae had suggested and set up some showings for some of the smaller houses around town. She wanted a two-bedroom place with a nice little yard so the first couple of townhouses just didn't feel right.

They spent three busy weeks looking at two-bedroom houses as far out as the next town over. She was ready to give up on finding the perfect place to buy after the three exhausting weeks, but her realtor begged her to look at one last property that had just come on the market. Knowing her next step was going to be looking at apartments to rent she agreed. She really didn't want to rent but also knew that she would if that's what it took to have a place before the bug came. That was what she had started calling her unborn son as she hadn't yet come up with a name for him.

She beat the realtor to the property and knew before they even went inside that it was the one. It was at the end of a long road lined with pretty little houses and pretty little yards. It had a long driveway that wound through a small field of grass that was skirted with pine trees and bushes. It was a cottage-style house with whitewashed rough wood siding and warm blue shutters against the windows. There was a red brick chimney on one end of the house and she could already imagine fires on cold winter nights as it snowed outside.

It had a rather small backyard, but the front yard, with a full acre of grass, by far made up the difference. The price was a little higher than she'd originally wanted to pay, but the bank quickly approved it and with her savings from the past several months she should be okay to make the slightly higher monthly payment. Just to be cautious she asked the realtor to wait for a day for her to think about it before she put in an offer.

When she woke up the following morning, excitement permeated the fresh morning air, so she cheerfully called and had him put an offer in on it. They closed two weeks later, and she found herself the proud new owner of what would be hers and the bug's home.

The thought of home appealed greatly to her but she had to wipe tears as her memories of the old house in Idaho flooded in. She had imagined having her baby there and having Jacob and Ivan nearby to be role models for her child. She put it all firmly out of her mind. That was before, now she had to focus on moving forward and taking care of herself and her child. She knew if she called them now, they would want to try helping her and take care of her, which was why she had left in the first place. They deserved someone who could give them more. Her friends here were kind and loving but weren't always trying to take care of her financially.

The weather began cooling down drastically and stacks of firewood grew large as most of the locals began prepping for the coming winter. As they cut wood, she repainted and then searched far and wide for cheap furnishings to fill her home. She moved out of the motel as soon as she found a suitable bed for her bedroom. Once she was living there, she had more time on her hands and spent it happily refinishing an old beautifully carved crib and matching diaper station/dresser that she found at a local garage sale. When she finished, its weathered-white antique style was both classy and warm.

She found an old rocking chair near a dumpster and sanded it down by hand. Jill insisted on staining it for her as the toxicity of the cherry stain wasn't good for the baby. Gratefully, Brooke accepted and agreed to make dinner in return. They made a fun afternoon out of it with a fresh salad, sandwiches, and icy cold, fresh-squeezed lemonade that Brooke prepared while her friend did the painting. They ended the evening with a movie on the small television that Brooke bought off an online market place for fifty bucks.

Counting her pennies, Brooke carefully worked out a plan to financially cover both the downtime of her maternity leave and the cost of a newborn baby. She was careful with every dollar she spent. She spent a couple of her weekends working a section in the backyard to prep a nice spot that she planned to use to start a vegetable garden first thing in the spring.

As her baby grew, her heart ached more at the realization that Ivan, Jacob, and even Cole wouldn't be a part of his life. At least not now. Though she had believed that distance and time would have healed her heart from wanting Cole, the opposite had happened instead. She missed all of them more than ever but found herself constantly thinking and even fantasizing of Cole being near her. The murky heat-filled dreams she had of him always made her feel conflicted. For though he had kissed her and she knew that she liked him, it had always appeared that he didn't like or want her in return.

As the first snow fell, Jacob was the constant warm spot in her heart. She finished all she could do in the house and yard for now and was left with too much time on her hands to think about her lost family. She picked up her phone countless times intending to call him, but she always talked herself out of it. At this point she wasn't even sure he would want to hear from her. After all, she had quite literally run away in the night.

She called her mother once, knowing that Rebecca was the most likely of her family to be worried about her well-being. She'd told her that she had found a good job and had some friends and that yes, she was indeed pregnant. Rebecca had cried at that confession. Brooke reassured her that she was fine but refused tell her mother where she was living and merely said that it was a really nice place.

When the fall session at the community college started, she signed up for a few classes along with Jill to ease her boredom. She would be having the baby in January, after all, and would be long done with fall classes by then. Because she loved growing things and desperately wanted to know her way around the business world, she took an agri-business crash course that would give her a degree after a year. She would have to finish the classes in the summer, of course, after her son was born and they'd had a chance to adjust, but she felt that it would be worth it to her in the long term.

When the second snow storm rolled in over the mountains in October, she found herself wondering curiously if there was any snow in the valley yet. It seemed that the closer she got to her delivery date the more she found herself dreaming of being back home there. She missed the valley with its variety of crops laid out in miles upon miles of square sectioned acreage. She missed the Burtons desperately and to her utter frustration found that she missed Cole the most.

She still hadn't been able to think of the perfect name for her baby, so she continued to happily call him her bug. He would need good male role models and she couldn't imagine any better role models than the Burton men. They were kind and generous and full of integrity. It wasn't to be, she knew, but couldn't seem to get her imaginings under control as she was forced to spend more and more time indoors. Maybe Jill and Janae were right and it was time to start dating, she thought and then laughed until she cried as she stared down at her now-protruding stomach. As if anyone would want her in this condition!

On November first she caved during a particular melancholy mood and called Jacob. She wasn't sure what to expect when he answered, but she pushed Send anyway. He could be mad, or disappointed, or even worse, hate her enough to be completely over their friendship. For one thing it had now been longer since she'd left them than she had actually spent on the Burton farm. She let it ring twice before losing her nerve and ending the call.

She felt huge all the time now even though the doctor told her that she was a good size. She felt stressed about needing a name for her son but still couldn't seem to settle on anything she liked. She briefly considered naming him after Cole. Thankfully she thought better of that idea since if she did ever actually get the courage to go visit them again it might be strange and awkward.

It was getting harder to waitress and she found herself feeling exhausted more often than not as she hauled trays to tables and bins of dirty dishes into the kitchen. Since she had been able to get on a healthcare plan through the state as a single mom, her birth plan had been settled with her doctor. She planned to go to a small birthing clinic with spacious birthing suites with their own small pools available for those who wanted a water birth.

Brooke didn't know what she wanted as she had never had a baby before. She figured that if it was available, however, she could do it if she wanted to when that time came. She felt panicked and wanted to call Jacob and beg him to come be her birthing coach. She called Jill instead, who was a great stand-in but could also be a little dramatic. She comforted herself by remembering that he would likely be back in law school by now and quite possibly wouldn't want to come anyway.

When Jill freaked out after watching a real birth video at her birthing class, Brooke let her off the hook. She took Janae to lunch and asked her if she might be open to being there with her. Janae had, after all, had five of her own children and that experience seemed like a good idea. Janae was touched and honored at the request and committed to it without hesitation. Her confident easy manner was a comfort to Brooke.

At night she sat in front of the little fireplace and watched the flames swirl and leap as she wondered how her life had become so complicated. In silent misery, Brooke tried to content herself with all that she had created in the months since she had moved to this beautiful town in Montana. After all, she should be proud of herself for how far she had come. Instead, she always ended the night thinking of the Burton family and wishing she could somehow connect her two lives together. She didn't want to lose her friendships here by going back to Idaho and yet she didn't really feel fully content here either.

CHAPTER 22

Richard Lotell Jessup looked down at his phone and studied the message his private detective had just sent him. He had spent the last several months searching, hunting, and following every thread he could find that might lead him to Brooke.

He was fucking angry at the bitch for evading him for as long as she had. Though he admired her tenacity and knew it was only a game between them, he felt used. Now, he had the first real lead he'd been able to get right here on his phone.

He read it again and laughed hoarsely. Soon, he thought soothingly, he would have her with him and only then could he take his time with her. He'd found her when she left before and he would again. It wasn't a question of if so much as it was when.

In the beginning when she had first run away from him and her home, he had enjoyed the fun little game. He could chase after her and when he found her, they would have a good laugh about it. She would be as charmed that he had taken her bait and followed her, as he was that she was teasing him this way in the first place. Bottom line was, that then she would be his.

He grinned. She already was his, but at that point she would happily submit to him and then meekly do his godly bidding. Brooke Reynolds had been promised to him years ago by her father, after all. As far as he was concerned, he owned her. Her father had called him and made a quiet little deal where Richard would do some expensive work for her old man, and in return, he would get that feisty little redhead he'd had his eye on as a bride. She was the shining prize at the end of a long bit of hard work.

Brooke had been sixteen going on seventeen at the time and hadn't been thrilled at all when she was introduced to him as his fiancée. She was cold and unfriendly to him right from the start. That didn't really bother Richard, though. He was perfectly capable and most definitely man enough to handle and train her. Besides he got along quite well with her brothers and that fact had softened the blow of her rejection. It really didn't matter what the little minx wanted anyway. She was the property of her father and he had contracted her to Richard to be his property.

He spent hours watching her on the farm imagining what that luscious figure would look like when he bared her. He admitted that he felt a dirty little thrill every time he imagined the kinds of things he planned to do to her. He knew it would take time to break her and train her to do all the things he wanted her to do to him in return. It didn't matter, he was a patient man. He felt a surge of pleasure as he thought of ways to punish her as he taught her what he liked. Growing hard at the images he stroked his need and smiled as she sashayed past him taunting him with every step.

The only issue he'd run into was that her father, John Reynolds was a hard man and hadn't trusted him to finish the job he'd agreed to. Because of this utter lack of trust, old John had insisted the work he was doing be completed before the wedding nuptials were exchanged. It would, he told Richard with a hard knowing smile, give him something to look forward to, after all.

The job was to build a large shop for the man. Richard had been in construction for several years now and had a small crew that was more than capable of such a job.

For such a straightforward project, the work had dragged on far longer than Richard had ever anticipated. As though lady luck herself was against him, one disastrous thing after another had come up. They spent weeks prepping the ground for the concrete. The concrete they laid for the foundation of the large shop had been wrecked in some weird unknown way as it dried, making it useless. With ease he adapted and rented all the equipment needed to take out the ruined concrete before he could again replace it with new. That process was slow and tedious and took much longer than planned. A month later, when the framing supplies had been delivered, they opened the pallets to find the lumber unusable as it was cut and split, rendering it useless as well. He took it in stride and reordered the supplies raising such a stink with the delivery company that they agreed to redo the order as quickly as possible.

When the order didn't come on its scheduled day, Richard called in an angry huff only to find that they had mistakenly canceled it again. With a frustrated chain of curses, he had them start it again. The next year went by much the same with disaster after disaster striking, and though he had made John pay the financial price for those mistakes, Richard had paid a high price on a much more personal level as he felt taunted constantly by the blossoming young redheaded Brooke.

It took him way too long to figure out the truth. She had gotten him with that he admitted with a lusty grin. He wasn't sure why he hadn't seen sooner that it was Brooke causing the disasters in an attempt to prolong their engagement, smart little minx that she was. At first, he had been shocked and then he'd laughed in delight.

She was proving to be a much greater challenge than even he had thought. With gleeful excitement he set his trap. He'd had a semiload of sheet rock delivered to the project and then waited patiently in the dark. She had asked for this, practically even begged him and he was happy to comply. He had felt truly alive for the first time in his life as he leaned against the outside wall of the shop in total stillness waiting as she dragged a water hose over toward the stacks in the dark.

Hidden in the shadows, he moved only when she turned on the faucet and was holding the spray nozzle up and ready to ruin the entire lot of materials. He was careful not to make noise as he stepped out and walked silently toward her. In a low voice reeking of amusement and glee he said, "I thought I might find you out here, my lovely."

She whirled in surprise and fear blossomed across her moonlit face. She could barely make out his shape through the darkness but didn't need to see him to know who he was. She would have recognized that shrill nasally tone anywhere. Fear crawled down her spine like a lizard on a tree branch.

He had terrified her from the first moment they met. The way he watched her across the yard gave her the willies. He stepped closer now and without thinking she pulled up the nozzle and hit him square in the face. It was the first mistake she made and she knew it the moment his large powerful form surged toward her even blinded. For over two years, she had been dealing with him ogling her anytime they were in the same place. He stood and watched her like a predator watched its prey, eyes heavy lidded. It was creepy and she didn't like it or him.

She tried to sidestep him but forgot where she was and stubbed her foot on a stack of sheet rock. Stumbling forward she grasped at anything she could find to hold on to for balance. Her hand settled on something flat and with a gasp of relief and air she lurched forward just as his hand touched her arm. She slipped right through his fingers and ran for the shop looking frantically for somewhere to hide. It was the second mistake she made. The doors had all been hung, but she soon realized that the knobs were still missing and she had no way to lock him out. She ran through the large open room to the stairs that lead up to a large loft above. Hoping to find some where to hide or maybe even a tool she could use as a weapon.

She stopped at the top of the stairs and a scream welled up inside her. Eyes wide, she searched but there was nothing but a large rectangular open space that looked way too clean even in the slight light cast by the moon glowing through the huge windows. She turned to run back downstairs, but it was too late. He was grinning as he made his way slowly, step by step up to her. She tried to scream then, but her throat closed and all that came out was a tiny whimper. She backed into the room, looking frantically for an escape that she already knew wasn't there.

She swallowed the lump in her throat, knowing suddenly that her only way out was to talk him down.

His mouth was twisted into a terrifying grin and he looked almost proud. That thought threw her off a little as she tried to offer a small smile. "I'm sorry, Richard," she managed to whimper. "I shouldn't have done that, I know."

He laughed and took another careful step toward her. She backed into the wall, feeling utterly cornered now. "No, my dear, you really shouldn't have." He agreed in a gleeful tone. She stared at him in confusion. She thought he'd been angry but all she saw now was what appeared to be crazed pride and unsettling joy.

With a forced hopeful smile, she said, "I promise I won't do it again."

He tilted his head back as though studying something interesting. He cracked another wide smile and his eyes glittered as her blood ran cold. He lifted a finger to wag it at her. "I suspect, my dear that you have been responsible for a great deal of naughty things." He laughed again and she wondered if he had lost his mind. "I should have known sooner. I blame myself for that."

Brooke's smile wavered and then fell. Unable to be still any longer and feeling like a cornered rat, she worked up a force of courage and stepped forward. She nodded and then tried to walk around him as she said quickly, "I'm sorry again. I will make it all up to you." She saw him move but kept walking. "If it's all right with you, I'll just head back home now."

His hand snaked out and grasped her arm tightly as he yanked her hard against him. "Not so fast, you naughty little girl," he said and to Brooke's utter horror, she could feel his erection through her layers of clothing pushing up against her stomach. Her hands shook as she tried to push him away. Though she was still a virgin, she had read enough romance novels to know that meant he was turned on. With a sinking feeling she thought in terror of what it could lead to.

His arm tightened around her waist and he ground her stomach painfully against his body. "I think I'm going to have to teach you a little lesson, my dear." He smiled down at her as though it was a longtime joke between them.

Again, she tried without success to shove away from him. When he didn't budge, she thought desperately for a way out. Suddenly she narrowed her eyes and glared up at him. "My father is expecting me home any minute and he will come looking for me if I don't go now," she threatened. "If he finds you like this, there is no telling what he might do to you," she lied.

She had climbed out the bedroom window to come here because the outside door creaked much too loudly to slip out. Her entire family was most likely fast asleep in their own beds right now. Not a single soul cared about her or would come to her rescue even if they did find her missing. The truth of that hurt and tears shone in her eyes as defeat settled between her shoulders.

Richard admired her spunk even as he looked forward to molding her to his will. He knew she was lying. He gave her a dark frown to show her that he was the one in control; then he said very quietly, "I don't believe you, Brooke. Your father more or less sold you to me as the highest bidder, so he wouldn't blame me for taking what's mine. Especially under the circumstances. You are mine and I fully intend to teach you exactly what I want you to be."

Brooke shook her head. "We aren't even married yet and you know that even touching me like this is a sin before marriage in our teachings."

A slow amused smile dawned as he leaned down mere inches from her face. "With everything you have put me through, I'm sure God will understand. I am, after all, a man and men are weak. Another way to look at it is that we would already have long since been married if you hadn't been sabotaging every phase of my building project." He nodded as though it all made sense. "Yes, you are already mine even in the eyes of God," he finished with a cold nod.

Brooke used every ounce of energy she could muster and fought then. She kicked at his shins and clawed at his eyes. It didn't matter as he quickly snagged her wrists and held them high above her head then rubbed her hard against his chest. He wrapped one leg tightly around hers and took them to the floor landing on top of her and knocking the air from her lungs. He kissed her hard, cruelly prying her lips open with his teeth and tongue to taste the tangy sweetness of her spirited nature.

She bit his tongue and he slapped her hard. Her freed hand came up and took a chunk out of his neck with her fingernails as she went for his eyes again. He cursed, he really wanted to take his time with her to teach her a lesson, but she was making it impossible. He had been watching and lusting after her for far too long already and he wouldn't be held off again.

He grasped both of her wrists in one of his hands and yanked them once again above her head. Her shoulder popped and she screamed once before biting down on her lips, stubbornly refusing to let him see her pain. He nuzzled her neck and she thrust helplessly against him once before his chin came down hard against her head. He swore aloud as he bit his tongue from the force and kneed her hard in the belly.

She cried out in pain and thrust up against him in an effort to get away and he nearly came in his own jeans. He reached down and yanked her dress up as he thrust his hand between her legs and ripped her underwear off without much effort. He reached out and undid his fly, released himself from the tight jeans he wore. With a last hard yank at her buttoned bodice, he watched as one of her breasts popped free and he lowered his head to taste the innocent bud. She bucked again and twisted hard as he raised up over her to hold her still.

She lifted her head to his shoulder and bit down hard on the flesh between his neck and shoulder joint. He growled in pain and slammed his head into her own. She went limp and in desperation he shoved her legs apart and took her. He came over and over in waves as she stirred back into awareness.

He heard her sob and felt her body start to shake under his weight. He rolled off of her slowly and in a relaxed lecturing tone said, "The sooner you understand that you are mine and that I can take you anytime I want to, the better things will go for you. I will let you go now this time and I'll even give you the time it takes me to finish this job for your father so that I can take you away from your family while I teach you how to be the wife that I need. If you ever try anything like this again, I will take you again and again until you can no longer stand or fight."

It was a cold promise of what was to come, she knew and she heeded every word as she launched painfully to her feet clutching her torn shirt together at her chest. She wisely resisted the urge to kick him hard on her way past. She couldn't afford to piss him off or let him get the upper hand again. She ran home without looking back, terrified that at any moment he would be there following her.

She let herself quietly into the house. Holding back a sob she quickly grabbed a nightgown from her drawer before rushing into the bathroom. Blood ran heavily down her thighs as she undressed and climbed into the hot cleansing spray. Her shoulders began to shake and tears ran unchecked down her pale cheeks. She scrubbed every inch of her body again and again until the water ran cold. She stepped out and dressed quickly using a pad to soak up the blood.

She looked at her gaunt reflection in the mirror and swore that she would never allow something like this to happen again. She lay in bed feeling numb and then eventually her mind began to race. She closed her eyes as she remembered what it felt like when she woke up and he was on top of her, warm sticky liquid sliming against her thighs and she cried again.

Once again, her mind raced; for though something terrible had just happened, she began to wonder if she could use it to finally get out.

When the rising sun cast shimmering light across the wall, she rose and dressed. The house was still quiet, so she took a moment and quickly loaded her bags with the few things she would want to take with her. She dropped them carefully to the ground outside the window at the back of the house as two of her sisters lay sleeping a mere two feet away.

She knew what she was going to do now and a ghost of a smile crept over her face as she realized that Richard Jessup had actually given her just the excuse she needed to finally get away for good. Plans made, she went into the kitchen and helped her mother prepare breakfast. Her father and brothers soon crowded in and her sisters stumbled out of their bedroom to all partake of the breakfast she'd helped to prepare.

No one thanked them for the meal, not that it surprised her as that was just the way of it. Her father offered a lengthy prayer of his family's submission to God's plan and they ate. She waited patiently for her father to finish eating and quoting scripture and then asked him if she could have a personal conversation with him and her mother.

He didn't look happy at the request but told her that if she got her chores done for the day and there was still time, she could come find him.

Brooke finished her chores numbly. Twice she caught Richard watching her from a distance and shudders sent tremors down her back. She didn't even complain when two of her brothers came and insisted that she was to do their chores as well. After all, they were the men and it was the last time she would ever do it for them. It was five o'clock in the afternoon before she finally finished with her work and walked, exhausted back home.

She checked to make sure her father was in his office and then went in search of her mother. She found her in the kitchen making applesauce from large crates of apples they had picked a week before and asked if she had time to come with her. Rebecca Reynolds nodded and with a worried frown asked if she could finish up what she was doing first. Brooke agreed, not because she was okay with waiting but because her mother was already overworked and taking a break now would mean more for later.

As she helped her mother finish cleaning up, she thought of what she was going to say to her parents. Together they washed their hands before turning to go. Once inside the office, she stood unable to calm her nerves enough to sit. Her parents both sat and stared up at her with blank expressions as they waited impatiently for her to speak.

Brooke took a deep breath, twisted her fingers together and told them what Richard had done to her. Her mother gasped in horror and then moved to hold her hand, but her father only got angry. Brooke watched as he flexed his fingers and then squeezed them into fists. Silently she wondered if her last memory of him was going to be him beating her, but she didn't budge. He didn't hit her and she wasn't altogether certain if he was angry at Richard for raping her or at her for not still being the pure virgin that was worthy of his love or a bargaining chip.

After a long while, he asked her why she had been out at the new shop in the first place. He harshly accused her of being impure and wanting to be with Richard out of wedlock. She held his gaze with courage and calmly explained all she had done to slow down the building of the shop because she didn't want to marry Richard at all. He stood then and before she could step back, he slapped her hard across the face.

She had, after all, cost him thousands of dollars as well as the months of delay. Eyes narrowed to hard slits, his lips curled in anger and he coldly told her to get out and never come back. She left without a backward glance. She took only enough time to tell each of her siblings she was leaving. The younger boys and her sisters she hugged tightly. Despite what they all thought of her, she did actually love them. She simply couldn't stay here living this way. Alone she walked out the back door and calmly picked up the bags she had loaded that morning and set them in her car. Rebecca was waiting by the car with tears in her eyes and Brooke reached out and hugged her.

Neither of them spoke. Despite feeling like her mother cared for her, they both knew that her mother would never walk away from her father or what she saw as the Lord's work. They held on to each other, and then Brooke calmly kissed her on the cheek and whispered goodbye as she turned to climb into her car. Her mother grasped on to her hand and slipped something inside and closed Brooke's fingers over it. "It is all I have," she said simply and tears welled up in Brooke's eyes as she looked down at the small wad of cash.

"Thank you, I love you, Mother," she said and with her last vestige of courage, she closed her door and drove away.

It was dark as she made her way down the long dirt road and Brooke was exhausted. She hadn't had a wink of sleep the night before and it was already getting late again tonight. It didn't matter as she had nowhere to go. She drove until her tears blinded her and she was forced to pull off the road.

CHAPTER 23

While Brooke worked to create a new life for herself in Montana, Cole searched tirelessly for any clue as to where she might have gone. He spent his days working on the farm and his evenings searching. He didn't talk to his family about her. Only listened when she came up in the conversation. Occasionally Jacob complained about missing her and his dad would wonder out loud how she was doing. The sheriff found nothing. He hadn't been able to find anything out about her attacker and Brooke herself seemed to have vanished.

His mother worried quietly about Brooke wanting to help the situation she felt partially responsible for, but didn't know what to do. Still, Cole said nothing. He listened to all of them only nodding in answer and then went back to searching himself. His evenings and weekends became road trips as he searched state by state looking for any sign of her.

He checked even the small towns, stopping to ask people at gas stations and motels if they had ever seen her. He had a picture of her he'd stolen from Jacob's phone and was counting on her uniquely stunning looks to stand out in their memories. Harvest season came and he slept very little, choosing to spend what little spare time he had searching.

Fall semester came, and though the world was plagued with virus, he was somewhat grateful for it as fall semester came with the only option of school being online courses. He only had a few remaining classes to complete before he graduated with his masters in engineering and he really didn't want to waste time going back to Massachusetts anyway. He signed up to complete his course with the fall semester and put his house there up for sale.

It was early October when Cole finally got his first real lead in his search. He'd driven north into Montana that weekend and after the fifteenth hotel finally found a receptionist near the Montana border that remembered seeing Brooke with her long bright curls. He resisted the urge to cheer and instead thanked the woman and left. He walked across the street to a bar and bought himself a congratulatory beer.

His excitement was short lived as the receptionist didn't know anything about where Brooke went and the rest of the weekend went by without any new leads. When Sunday night came, he was forced to drive all night in order to get back home in time for work on Monday morning.

His parents had begun to worry about him and had both told him so. He'd smiled and reassured them that he was fine and then had gone back to work. He hadn't seen much of his family since Brooke had left and he understood their concern. Truthfully, he was a little worried about himself. As the anger at Brooke's dismissal of his advances faded, he found himself wondering why he was still looking. He didn't, however, admit as much to his parents who believed he was burying himself in work.

His gut told him that Montana was the key, especially after talking to the woman who remembered seeing Brooke. He turned all his focus there, but it was long tedious work as he soon realized just how big the beautiful state actually was. It was early on a Tuesday that he was studying his map of Montana and all the pins that showed the places he'd checked, when a quick knock sounded at his door. He walked over and opened it a few inches to see Jacob standing on the other side.

Cole raised an inquiring eyebrow at Jacob and asked, "What's up?"

Jacob shrugged and stepped forward as though he intended to brush past Cole. "I just wanted to talk to you about something."

Cole held his ground, but Jacob took another step forward and finally Cole stepped back and reluctantly held the door open. "Come on in, I guess," he muttered, looking less than thrilled.

Jacob walked in and stopped dead in his tracks. Cole had always kept a very tidy room, even when they were kids. Jacob had always liked it because his younger brother had often cleaned up behind him as well. Eyes wide, he surveyed the room.

The main part of the room itself looked the way it always had with light gray walls trimmed in white, with classy photos and paintings scattering tidily across the walls. His bed was a black wooden monstrosity that matched his somewhat black personality. Down one side of the long room was a small gray and black leather couch that faced a sixty-inch flat screen that hung on the opposite wall.

Now, however, the opposite wall had been completely cleared of décor. Jacob stared in stupefaction at several large state maps stapled floor-to-ceiling down the wall. There were sticky notes and pins pasted all over some of the maps. A little intrigued by the inner workings of Cole's mind he stepped closer and saw the maps were set in the geographically correct place. In the center of the wall Cole had drawn a large red star and Jacob noticed that it was around their farm. Blue and yellow pins marked hundreds of places surrounding the farm and going out. He saw a lone red pin somewhere in Montana. Not knowing what to say, he studied it for another long moment before finally turning to look at Cole who now stood with his thumbs in his pockets while he watched his brother's face, his own carefully expressionless.

"My God," Jacob said, "is this where you've been disappearing to all this time?"

Cole didn't speak, only looked at him.

"Mom and Dad have been worried sick about you and frankly so have I." Jacob raised a hand to run it down the wall. "I thought you were, like, depressed or something but this...." He looked back at the wall for a long thoughtful moment. "This is more than depression. What is all of this?"

Cole shrugged. "Just a little project I've been working on."

Jacob snorted. "A little project?" He stared hard at Cole and then suddenly turned back to the wall as he realized exactly what was going on. With a brilliant smile of disbelief, he turned and met Cole's shuttered gaze. "My God, you're looking for Brooke." It was a statement more than a question, but he waited for Cole to deny it anyway.

Again, Cole shrugged his shoulders. "I might have been curious where she took off to," he admitted reluctantly.

Jacob laughed aloud at Cole's admission. "Curious?" He laughed again. "I knew you had a thing for her, bro, but this...." He paused to encompass the wall with a wide sweep of his hand. "I didn't know you had it this bad."

Cole watched his brother with an unreadable expression. He shrugged again and tucked his thumbs deeper in his pockets. "I wouldn't say that," he denied. "It just really pissed me off that she came around and got everyone worrying about her and then ran away without a word."

Jacob grinned knowingly. "I wasn't aware that 'everyone' was worried about her. I literally haven't heard you say a single word about her these past few months."

Cole's lips twitched, and he couldn't hold back a lopsided grin. "Not all of us have diarrhea of the mouth, bro," he mocked.

"Touché" was all Jacob said with a little shake of his head as he turned to carefully study the map. Curious he asked, "What are the blue pins for?"

Cole turned to face the map as well, pulling his hand from his pocket to point at a section of blue. "Blue is all the places I've gone to but haven't seen any sign of her, but it was too late to actually talk to people."

Jacob studied the blue pins with a raised eyebrow, looking impressed. "You went to all these places in the last few months?" he asked.

Cole nodded.

"And the yellow pins are…?" Jacob let the question hang in the air.

"The yellow pins are all the places I've gone that I've actually talked to people and showed her picture around but they hadn't seen any sign of her." Cole stated in a steady voice. He could feel Jacob staring at him from the side, but he used his many years of practice to ignore his brother.

Jacob turned back to the wall and moved closer to study the lone red pin. "And what is the red pin for?"

Cole grinned widely. "That is the first real lead I've gotten. I went there last weekend and after showing Brooke's picture around several fuel stations and motels, I finally found someone who remembered her coming there a few months back. She spent the night there in the hotel."

Jacob studied the pin that was located near the Montana border as something teased at the back of his mind, but he couldn't seem to center the thought. "Well, it looks like you have been busy," he muttered under his breath as he stepped back and away. He waited for Cole to look at him before he added, "From now on I go with you, though."

Cole shrugged. "We'll see how it goes."

Jacob rolled his eyes. "No, we won't," he said in frustration. "From now on I go with!" He turned away before Cole could argue as he turned to leave. He turned back at the door. "Oh and, Cole?" Cole looked up to meet Jacob's serious eyes. "You need to tell Mom and Dad that you're okay. They don't have a clue why you dropped off the face of the planet and they're worried." He turned and walked out, closing the door quietly behind himself.

Cole turned back to the wall. He was getting close. He could feel it. He could feel her. He groaned in frustration. What in the hell was wrong with him? He could deny that he felt something about Brooke forever but denying it didn't make it true. He looked at the surrounding cities in Montana, concentrating deeply. He ran a finger north because he imagined she would want to be farther away. *She would have wanted a small town*, he thought. Somewhere that she wouldn't be dealing with too many people but not so small she would stand out too much. "Where are you, Brooke?" he asked aloud to himself.

For all his feeling close to her, the following weeks went by with him trying unsuccessfully to find any other connections. He was standing at the map and he'd just put several blue and yellow pins around the Helena area. He swore as he heard a quick knock only a second before Jacob came walking in.

Jacob looked excited. "Hey," he said as he walked quickly toward the map. "So, something was bugging me the last couple weeks after I saw that red pin," he rushed out. "It took me a while to figure out why, but it came to me just now." Jacob reached into his pocket and pulled his phone out. He quickly unlocked it with his fingerprint. "A couple of weeks ago, I was in the middle of a test online and I got a random phone call. It only rang twice." He was typing quickly on his phone as he spoke. "I remember it because I figured I'd send it to voicemail, but then it quit ringing, so I didn't have to. At the time I just thought it was probably a spam call since it was a random out-of-state number." He found what he was looking for and held the phone out toward Cole. "See, look it's right here."

Cole took the phone and stared down at the missed call notification. He raised an eyebrow at Jacob. "Okay." He glanced at it for a minute and was about to give it back to Jacob, but then he did a double take. "Wait, is that a Montana area code?" He pulled out his own phone and typed it into Google.

He grinned and looked across at Jacob who was nodding. "It is," he answered his own question. Then unhelpfully he said, "Montana only has one area code, though, so it still doesn't narrow it down much." He took a deep breath and looked at Jacob who had been getting rudely interrupted. "You're thinking that she tried calling you and then hung up?" he asked.

Jacob nodded. "I think she did. I think she tried calling me and then changed her mind."

Cole laughed without amusement. "Damn, girl probably thought she didn't have enough to offer you yet." Then he looked at his brother again. "So, did you try calling the number?"

Jacob's expression turned to disappointed. "I did." At Cole's impatiently questioning look he shrugged. "No one answered and the voicemail wasn't set up."

That didn't really mean anything to Cole, but he didn't share that sentiment with Jacob. "Send it to me so I can see if I can track anything with it."

Jacob nodded and, using his thumbs, quickly sent the contact to Cole's phone.

Cole seemed preoccupied after his announcement, so Jacob left to meet a friend in town for drinks. As soon as he drove off, Cole went to look for his father. Ivan was out mowing the lawn and he turned off the loud motor as his son walked up.

Cole smiled respectfully at him. "I know it's short notice, but I need to take off for a couple of weeks."

Ivan's warm smile faded and his brows raised in concern. "Okay. Where are you going? Is everything okay with you, son?"

Cole shrugged. "I just need to get out for a bit. Decompress, you know?" Guilt surged as he used the fact that his parents had been worried about him to get what he wanted.

Ivan smiled, looking a little relieved. "Okay, I don't see what it would hurt."

Cole grinned in response. He would have left whether or not Ivan had been okay with it, but he preferred to keep his parents happy whenever he could. He thanked Ivan and turned to walk back to the house. Quickly he threw a few changes of clothing into a bag along with a dop kit and a role of cash. He needed to drive too far this time and now that he was closing in on her, he wanted to spend the time focused on finding her without being distracted. He would be taking his final exams soon, but he could do those online if he needed to. With that thought in mind, he tossed his textbooks and laptop into a padded backpack. He tossed the bags into his Mustang and went back in to say a quick goodbye to his mother and brothers.

Ten minutes later, he was pulling onto the highway heading toward northern Montana. *With any luck,* he thought a little nervously, *I'll find her within the week.*

CHAPTER 24

Brooke was excited about the baby shower that her friends had planned for her, but she also felt apprehensive. Though she was getting better with social events and that part of it wasn't a challenge so much anymore, she wished more than anything that Ivan and Jacob could be here for this. It felt wrong somehow to have something so big in her life that they weren't a part of even after all these months.

After she had moved into her new home, all three women decided it was best if they had the baby shower at her house since it would be easier than moving everything over there later.

Janae showed up hours before the shower was to start, to help prepare things and Jill was close behind her. Brooke turned some fun party music on the Bluetooth speaker she had bought recently and while they worked, they danced. They visited and laughed as they smeared different candy on diapers for a game of identifying what was in the diaper. When Jill asked Brooke about her parents, Brooke stopped what she was doing and met her friend's eyes. "As you know they didn't want me around anymore."

She didn't say any more, but Jill persisted. They spent the remainder of their prep time discussing how strange it must have been to be raised in a religious cult that way.

The baby shower went off without a hitch as they served heaped platters of small sandwiches, crackers, and cheese, and a variety of cookies. They set colorful bowls of potato chips out for snacking as well as a large garden salad for a healthy snack. The games were all fun and interactive and it seemed that even the few men that had come with girlfriends and wives enjoyed themselves thoroughly.

As Brooke opened gifts all the women oohed and ahhed and talked about how cute every item was. She was extremely touched by everyone's overwhelming generosity and told them so. For a girl who had never even been given a simple birthday gift, she was aghast at the mounds of cute clothes, blankets, and even accessories given to her by her friends. She thanked them each as she opened them and then again as they all helped haul them into the small nursery.

It was a cold day in early December and she had a fire burning cozily in the hearth. Slowly the guests trickled out after the eating and games were done and she thanked them each and gave them little gift bags she had prepared as they left for home. Soon everyone was gone except her and her close friends. Janae, Jill, and a couple of the other girls that worked at the restaurant with her sat around sipping cider and talking about the harsh winter to come.

Brooke excused herself for a moment and went into the bathroom for a quick break. After she used the toilet, she splashed cold water on her face and washed her hands before walking back out. She was walking toward the front room when she caught a glimpse of a particularly soft blue blanket with a giraffe and an elephant playing together embroidered on one corner. With a little sigh of pleasure, she turned into the nursery and with tears of gratitude in her eyes once again looked lovingly through the gifts. She was holding another blanket against her cheek to feel the softness when Janae stepped through the door with a big smile.

Brooke heard her come in and turned with a wide smile. "Everything is so beautiful and amazing," she said as she looked down at the huge pile of gifts.

Janae nodded and stepped up close to put a hand on her shoulder. "It really is," she agreed. Then she leaned close to Brooke's ear and said quietly, "Your young man is here."

Brooke looked at her friend in confusion not understanding in the least what she was taking about.

Janae grinned and shrugged and for just a moment, Brooke wondered if her friend was trying once again to set her up. Anger flushed her cheeks as she had been clear with them about wanting this time for herself and the bug. Janae held up her hands at Brooke's fierce look. "There is a young man at the door asking for you and if I'm not mistaken, I think he's your Cole."

Brooke shook her head in denial. "You are most definitely mistaken. Cole wouldn't have any reason to be here. Besides that, I haven't even told any of his family where I am." She turned to walk out of the room, saying assuredly over her shoulder, "I'm sure it's just a delivery man or some such."

Janae followed closely on her heels, and so when Brooke came to a sudden stop in the doorway of the airy front room Janae bumped into her from behind. They both stumbled and then hurried to steady each other, laughing a little embarrassed.

From across the room Cole said in a low calm voice, "Hello, Brooke."

She wasn't exactly sure how she felt about him being here and a myriad of emotions crossed her face before she finally forced herself to smile and say calmly, "Hello, Cole."

His dark eyes were unreadable, but he had a small mocking smile on his lips as though he had some secret that she might want to know. He looked better than she remembered, which was saying a lot since his handsome face had been forever etched in her memory. He wore a black leather jacket over dark brown jeans and brown leather shoes. His hair looked like it hadn't been cut since she'd last seen him and it curled down his neck now. It was tucked neatly behind his ears as though he'd run his fingers through it before coming in. She remembered him doing that a lot and groaned inwardly. He was every bit the sexy fiend that she had tried to forget and worse.

Janae cleared her throat, and with a start, Brooke looked back at her. She had forgotten her friends were there. "Oh, I'm sorry," she mumbled. "Cole, these are my friends, Janae, Jill, Rachel, and Jordyn." She pointed to each of them as she said their names and didn't miss their curious smiles as she pointed them out to Cole.

He smiled charmingly around the room at them and nodded. He had been watching her house for hours now, waiting patiently for her guests to leave. He'd thought most of them were gone when he finally got impatient and knocked. Apparently, some of them had driven together as there were only a couple of cars left in her long driveway.

"Ladies, this is my uh, an old acquaintance of mine," she finally finished awkwardly, "Cole."

Janae clapped her hands together in joy. "I knew it," she exclaimed and then quickly made up some excuse about her son needing her and left after giving

Brooke a tight hug.

Brooke rolled her eyes in amusement. Janae's youngest son was twenty-three and quite capable of taking care of himself. But she hugged her friend and thanked her once again for everything before she rushed out the door.

Brooke's younger girlfriends were much less inclined to leave and feeling a little awkward she turned to Cole. "We have all been eating for hours, but there is a ton of food left if you would like some."

He nodded and gave an appreciative look at all the leftovers, "I haven't eaten since breakfast, so I would much appreciate it." There was a distinct twinkle in his eye as he took the plate she offered and started putting food on it.

Every eye in the room was on him as he took his loaded plate and intentionally sat on the chair that was closest to Brooke. He wasn't exactly sure why he liked that she was so obviously uncomfortable with him, but he did. It made him feel downright cheery, in fact. He could feel all eyes on him so he turned a warm smile toward her. "Thanks for feeding me," he teased lightly under his breath, "I'm surprised there's any left."

Brooke blushed and then looked around the room nervously. Unable to sit this close, she smiled shakily at him before getting up and hurrying over to the table loaded with food. "I should probably start putting all this away," she muttered.

Jill laughed at her friend and stood up. "So exactly how do you two know each other again, Cole?" she asked curiously. It was obvious that the two of them had history and they hadn't been able to get much detail from Brooke. Maybe the devilishly handsome man that was making her friend so nervous would give her more details.

Cole chuckled and took a bite of sandwich. "Brooke used to work for my family," he said casually not wanting to give the woman any idea that he wanted to have a conversation with her. He wanted them all to go away, though he would never have been so rude as to tell them that.

He watched Brooke as she bustled around. He was a little angry that she was still every bit as beautiful as she was before she'd left. Maybe even more so. Her red hair had been cut a few inches and layered to flow down her back elegantly. Her eyes were still that bewitching sapphire color that he loved. Her face, which was the tiniest bit fuller than before was flushed, her cheeks rosy and healthy-looking. He avoided looking at her body for both of their sakes.

Oh, there was no doubt that she was still curvy and very sensual but that large bump swelling her belly out made him a mite uncomfortable. Made him remember that maybe she wasn't so innocent as he had once believed. He felt hot desire followed closely by a deep surge of anger. She had really played him all those months ago.

She had taunted him and flirted with him only to push him away because she obviously had someone else. Where, he wondered idly, was this other guy anyway? She was obviously very pregnant and the guy should be here taking care of her, shouldn't he? He swore inwardly. It wasn't really any of his business, which didn't seem to matter because he had no intention of letting it go.

She was wearing tan slacks that curved nicely over her bottom and he felt himself harden in response as she bent over the table to lift a tray and haul it away.

That was a bad road to go down he remembered and pulled his gaze away to look at the other women in the room. Two of them sat watching him with avid smiles. He smiled politely but a little coldly and they looked away.

The awkwardness finally urged the rest of her guests to leave, and Brooke hugged them each in turn as she thanked them one last time for their gifts. Cole nodded politely at them as he polished off a large stack of crackers and cheese. He found himself wondering if he would still be attracted to her when she was pregnant. He quickly changed his line of thought.

With a reluctant smile, Brooke closed the door behind the last of her friends. She took a deep breath and turned back to face him. He had stood again and was watching her with what looked like quiet amusement. He wondered what she was going to say now that her friends were gone.

She met his eyes and then quickly looked away. "How did you find me?" she asked with a resigned sigh as she walked over and sat on a rather ancient-looking couch.

Cole chuckled. "Don't sound so delighted," he teased. "And to think I actually thought you might have missed us." He took the safe route with the *us* part.

Brooke stood again and started stacking dishes. "I did" was all she said.

His smile faded and he moved over to give her a hand. He looked pointedly at her belly. "It looks like you might have forgotten to tell me some key information."

Fire lit those blue eyes like twin flames of ice and he was reminded again just how beautiful she looked this way. "Because we had so many close conversations?" she spit out. "We barely even talked when we were in the same room. I'm not even sure what I was supposed to say," she continued in a sarcasm-laced tone. "Oh hey, thanks for kissing me, and by the way, I might be pregnant with someone else's baby." Her voice was a little high pitched now as she continued. "Or thanks for helping me haul that picnic table, and did I happen to tell you yet that I just found out I'm pregnant and I'm now thinking of how me and my child might sit out here for evening picnics together," she finished with a very disrespectful mocking bow.

His hand shot out and held hers as he pulled her toward him. That familiar fear surged in her expression and he swore. "Stop looking at me like I am the Grim Reaper," he commanded through his teeth.

She actually smiled at that and then even relaxed a little. "I'm not looking at you like you're the Grim Reaper, Cole. I'm looking at you like you terrify me, because you do," she said honestly and followed it with a short laugh.

Her eyes were sparkling now and before he could think better of it, he bent his head and took her smiling mouth in a deep slow kiss. He pulled back again when he really wanted to wrap her up in his arms and take her into the bedroom. His eyes nearly black with desire, he stared down at her slightly dazed expression. Her lips were pink from his kiss. He resisted leaning back down and stepped back. Well, that answered that, unfortunately he wanted her more than ever pregnant or not.

Brooke looked up at him and couldn't help laughing. "I'm glad to see nothing has changed with us." She looked pointedly at his back. "Wait, why are you still here? Isn't this where you usually swear at me and then stalk off?"

He didn't blink. Wasn't fazed by her comment. "Isn't this where you normally turn tail and run?" he countered in a lazy drawl.

She put her hand against her heart and laughed. "Touché."

They stood looking at each other for a long awkward moment before she turned and once again began clearing the table. They worked side by side in silence packing food into the fridge and washing the dishes afterward. Neither of them said anything unless it was related to the chores at hand. He asked where her dishes went and she responded but added nothing else.

When the dishes were clean and the table had been moved back into the kitchen, the chairs folded and stacked against a wall, he said quietly, "I gotta go grab something out of my car, I'll be right back."

She heard the door click shut behind him and actually considered sneaking out the back. She could go hide out somewhere for a few days until he got bored of waiting for her to come back. He had a life, didn't he? He had to leave at some point. She laughed at her own immature impulse. It was time to be a big girl now.

She was going to have a son soon. Her hand rubbed lovingly over her belly in a gentle caress. It didn't seem to matter anymore how she had gotten pregnant. Oh, how she loved the innocent baby boy growing inside her. She would love him and cherish him forever she vowed solemnly. Unlike her, he would grow up knowing his mom would do anything to protect and care for him. She couldn't simply leave now she had to think of him first.

She heard the door open again and walked out to meet him. He had bags in each hand, which he calmly walked over and plopped on the couch. She stared at them with open curiosity. He smiled a warm disarming smile and walked past her. He held a six-pack of beer in his hand and something else. He walked into the kitchen and put the beer in the fridge after pulling one out. He held out a box as she followed him. "I don't really know what you drink, but I've heard this is good for pregnant women," he said in the gentlest tone she had heard him use.

She took the box and looked at it. It was a red raspberry blend of caffeine-free tea. It touched her that he had cared enough to bring something for her. "Thank you," she said softly as she pulled a mug from a hook on the wall and started water heating in the teapot on the stove top.

He opened his beer and took a long drink and then came over to stand by her. "How far along are you?" he asked in a low, emotionless voice.

Brooke turned from the stove to smile nervously up at him. "I'm about thirty-seven weeks."

He didn't miss the hand she placed lovingly there. He wanted to be mad but couldn't resist smiling back. "Who is the father?" he asked bluntly, forcing a casual tone.

She stilled immediately and fear crossed her face before she carefully cleared her expression and shrugged. "Someone I used to know" was all she said.

He stared hard at her. "And does he know that you are about to have his baby?"

She shook her head quickly. "No, he doesn't and I'm not going to tell him. He isn't any part of my life and I plan to keep it that way."

That at least seemed to take away the edge off his anger, though he wasn't sure why. So, she didn't want anything to do with the guy, huh? He couldn't disagree with that logic.

The pot whistled and she deftly poured a mug full and then added one of the tea bags he'd brought. She walked over to sit at the table. "So, how is everyone?" she asked uncertainly. She wasn't sure if it was okay for her to ask since she had been the one who left.

For some unknown reason Cole wanted to put her at ease. He smiled. "Jacob is good. He'll be graduating at the end of the school year."

He told her about Ryker, Dom, and Zack and how they asked about her all the time, which brought a warm smile to her soft lips. "I've missed everyone so much," she admitted in a wistful tone.

He grinned again. That worked great for his plan. Funny how he hadn't realized until now that he had a plan. He took a swig of beer as he said, "They miss you too. Dad is always telling everyone that he knows you're fine and you'll call when you're ready." He met her gaze, held hers with his own. "Mom, has been worried sick about you. She was afraid you wouldn't get the care you needed during the pregnancy."

Brooke looked away at the mention of Anne and a lump of emotion swelled in her throat. "I'm fine. I got a doctor here as soon as I got settled." She smiled sadly. "I don't think she could have been too sad when I left, though. She really didn't like me, you know?"

He reached out, lifted her chin to meet his gaze in that oh-so-familiar way. "She has since come to realize what the rest of us already knew."

Brooke didn't smile now just stared up at him. "And what is that exactly?" she asked with a carefully guarded expression.

He rubbed a thumb across her bottom lip. "A very kind and very generous person that isn't afraid of hard work … or food," he added as an afterthought.

She smiled at the last. "I really, really miss Jacob."

He frowned at that. "Do you have a thing for my brother or something?" he asked with barely controlled frustration.

She nodded earnestly. "I really do. I have, like, this really strong friendship thing with him." She watched his face harden and then relax as a small grin turned up one corner of his sexy and very kissable lips. She looked a little surprised as she said seriously, "I never thought I'd say this, but I am really glad you came, Cole."

He just watched her with those dark, unreadable, gold-flecked eyes. "I'd have come sooner, but it took me a very, very, long time to find you," he said it simply, but with a shuttered expression.

She looked guiltily at the table. "I didn't want to take advantage of your family anymore."

He snorted. "And you honestly believe that all that hard work you did along with all the time and energy put into the old house wasn't enough to make up the difference?"

Confused now, she watched him. "Your mom made it sound like what your dad did for me was worth far more than what I was doing. Not to mention all that Jacob did for me."

"I don't think she had a full understanding of exactly how much you were doing." He smiled casually and changed the subject. "So how about this place?"

Her face lit up. "It's mine. What I mean to say is that I'm buying it."

He smiled right back. "Good, then you won't mind if I stay for a few days before I take you back home."

Brooke's eyes widened in alarm. She opened her mouth to speak and then closed it again. She wasn't exactly sure that she liked where all of this was going but didn't have a clue what to say to him.

CHAPTER 25

Richard stood outside the small house and watched as that dark-haired asshole from Idaho kissed his woman. Anger seethed just beneath the surface and he wanted to rush in and beat the guy to a pulp. He wasn't sure how long the guy had been here, but he'd watched him go inside shortly before the rest of the guests had departed, which had postponed his plan.

He had gotten into town late the night before. He had come by the address his private investigator had given him, but the house was dark with no sign of anyone inside. After waiting impatiently for a couple of hours, he booked a room at an inn nearby and decided to get some sleep.

As he watched them through the window, he smiled. When he got his way, he wouldn't be getting much sleep for the next few days. He chuckled at his own dirty joke before starting his gray truck and driving away.

Brooke didn't know it, but she had quite literally missed him by minutes. She had worked the late shift at the café the night before and helped close up, so hadn't gotten home until around eleven thirty, which was a mere five minutes after Richard had driven away.

After a much needed eight hours of sleep along with a late breakfast of fresh coffee and a large stack of pancakes that he got at a small local café, he drove back to her house to watch her. He had seen her there through the windows talking and laughing with a couple of other women. He watched and waited patiently. He could take them all, he knew, but he really didn't want all of them. He laughed low in his throat. All he really wanted at this point was a good long stretch of alone time with his feisty little bitch of a bride.

Brooke laughed at something the older woman said and a glint of anger lit his beady eyes. He had forgotten how beautiful she was when she laughed and he didn't like that she was sharing that with a random stranger. He smiled widely as though there was a secret joke between them. After all, she would soon have laughter only for him. The image of her smiling and laughing as she served him a hot homemade meal and he graciously told her something funny flashed in his mind. *And that*, he thought, *was exactly why he had tracked her down.*

Her father had curtly told him that she was used goods and he may as well look elsewhere. Richard had only smiled at that. He was, after all, the one who had used her. He hadn't bothered to finish the job he'd been doing for the stupid old man. John had long since lost all control of his daughter so there really wasn't any point in it. It was up to Richard now to see that she did what she was destined to do.

The first time he saw her belly he stared in horror at the offensive bump. He'd thought she looked bulkier but hadn't wanted to believe it. It took her answering the door several times to let in more guests before he finally forced himself to face it. A burst of pride and joy had lit his face then. Of course, she was pregnant, he was truly a man after all. He laughed out loud in crazed laughter. It had only taken him one little thrust inside her to create a life. God must really be on his side and believe in his strength and wisdom. Another thought occurred shortly after. Maybe *he* was one of God's most chosen sons sent to earth to make the world right again.

His joy over the child and his woman was the thing that gave him the patience to wait for all her guests to leave. He had watched from his truck window for hours. He had made the occasional trip to the bushes to get a closer look and relieve himself, but the chilly weather didn't permit him staying out for long. Around three o'clock, he left to get some lunch. He was certain he could be back long before her party was over and he hummed a hymn as he pulled away.

When he came back, he saw the blue car parked there in her driveway. He thought it looked familiar but couldn't place it. He could see someone sitting inside the car as though they were watching the party too. He laughed; he sounded paranoid now. Why would someone else be watching the party from out here? He blamed Brooke because he had been chasing her for months with no release.

A few of the guests trickled out and the person in the car sat up tall. Richard stared hard; he could see that it was a man now. Doubt trickled in, but he pushed it away. She was his. The baby she carried was his. It became a chant inside his tired mind.

Richard actually considered going over and talking to the guy. Maybe he could teach him a lesson. He decided to wait as more guests trickled out. There was nothing to worry about, he told himself, though he clenched his fists tightly.

He leaned his head back against the seat and closed his eyes for a minute. He dozed and when he woke again most of the cars were gone. Richard rubbed his cold fingers together and started his truck for some heat. He took caution to make sure the headlights didn't come on when he started it. He stared in disbelief as the guy immediately unfolded his tall form from the car and doubt rushed in again.

He bit his lip and cut marks into his palm as recognition took his breath away. It was definitely one of the guys from the party in Idaho where he had tried to take Brooke with him. It wasn't the man who had hit him but maybe a brother?

Fury rose sharp and hot. What if Brooke had been with this man when she lived nearby him. He ground his jaw together causing pain to shoot up into his ear. If this guy really was the father, he had no choice but to take care of him.

He watched as the older woman from earlier let the man in with a big smile. She looked like she recognized him as she hurried to get Brooke. Richard opened his door and slid silently out of the truck. It was getting dark now, so he crept closer to the house for a better view. He could see Brooke in another room and watched as the woman went in and talked with her for a while. Soon they both left the room only to return to the front room where the man had entered. Several other women sat around visiting and he hoped, unconvinced that the man was there for one of them.

He saw the surprise on her face when she saw the man and he relaxed. She obviously hadn't been expecting him. The room was obviously uncomfortable with the man in there and he laughed quietly. He should have known she wouldn't have done that to him. She was his. She had to know that.

He went back to his truck and the warmth of the cab. He turned and grinned as one of the women hurried out to a car and drove off. He looked back at the house. And then there were four, he thought with a little sigh of relief. His time was almost here. He frowned as the three remaining women left but the man wasn't with them. He watched with frustrated impatience now for the guy to get out of there so he could go in and claim his well-deserved prize.

His heart stopped when he saw the man lean down and kiss her. He swore indistinctly as he slid out of his truck again and hurried around the side of the house to watch as they moved into the kitchen. They laughed now and talked as though they were close friends. A single tear rolled slowly down his cheek turning to ice in the frigid air before it could drip off of his chin. The joy he'd felt at the idea of being a father slowly ebbed as reality sank in.

This man was obviously the father. Was this a test, he wondered as he looked up at the star-riddled sky. It had to be. God was testing him to see if he would strike down this evil sidekick of the devil. Richard stepped into the shadows at the edge of the yard just in time to be hidden when the man came out and jogged quickly to the light blue car. He grabbed his bags and an armful of stuff before quickly jogging back inside. In painful horror Richard watched him casually toss them onto the couch before they went back into the kitchen to visit some more. A silent scream sounded inside his head.

He grasped at his temples trying to shut it out. He couldn't watch anymore. Angry and hurt he hurried back to his truck and started the engine as he climbed inside. He looked up at the sky again. Of course, he would fulfill his duty to God. He would come back tomorrow with a plan.

He looked sadly at Brooke's face again before he turned the truck around to go. They would all have to die now, he thought. He would not, no, could not put up with another man's leftovers. That would be impure and he was one of God's chosen now. He wouldn't go against the word of God. He drove away without another look, already planning ahead to his next move.

Jacob was extremely pissed off at Cole. Not only had his brother taken off without him, he had completely ignored Jacob's calls for the first two days. He would have got in his jeep and followed his fool of a brother into Montana, but he didn't have a clue where he was headed.

His exams were coming up and his school had called to let him know they were scheduling the bars and needed him to fly out to California at the end of the semester. He swore as he once again got Cole's voicemail.

Cole finally answered his call on day three only to inform him that he hadn't found her yet and was still looking. Calmly Cole told him he should focus on his education and his final year of school. Jacob had wanted to slug his brother but once again had no clue how to get to him. In angry disbelief he pointed out that Cole was actually set to graduate before him and that he should also be focused on his finals to which Cole had confidently insisted that he had everything under control and school would be just fine.

Jacob hung up only when his brother promised to let him know if and when he found her.

Jacob went to his father then, feeling like it was high time that Ivan knew what was going on. Ivan and Anne were actually visibly relieved when Jacob showed them exactly what Cole had been doing. They had been worried as he had been cold and standoffish for months now. To realize he had actually been focused on this gave them some sense of relief as it was very Cole-like.

Cole's two-week road trip rolled into three as Jacob waited impatiently for information. He flew to California for his exams and got home again a few days into December. Cole texted again that he was still looking and not to worry. Jacob read the text with an ironic grin as his plane taxied toward the airport.

The next day Cole sent him a brief text that said: *I know where she is now but don't bother coming. Will bring her home with me.* Jacob responded, *where is she?* Insightful as ever, Cole sent him a laughing emoji and told him it didn't matter because he had no reason to come, which only pissed Jacob off further.

CHAPTER 26

Brooke lay in bed stirring restlessly against her sheets. She was unusually hot and kicked off her blanket in frustration. She could hear Cole in the other room his fingers typing in a steady rhythm on his laptop.

He had made himself at home after dinner and a couple of beers. Though she still wasn't sure exactly how he had found her, it didn't really matter all that much since he was already here now. The painful loss of him and his family that she'd been trying not to focus on these past months was now a constant ache under her breast. She missed Jacob and Ivan and God help her, even that old house she had called home for those few warm beautiful months. She liked this house okay, even liked the town here pretty well, but it just didn't feel like home the same way.

She avoided thinking about how much she had missed Cole since he was now in her living room camping out on her couch for God knew how long. The fact that he was here at all made her jumpy and nervous. Which in turn only made her more determined to ignore him until he got back in that sexy old car of his and drove away. She couldn't afford any more drama with him right now. She rubbed her stomach and rolled onto her side forcing her eyes closed determinedly.

Cole had talked earlier as though she was just going to climb into her car and go back to Idaho. She couldn't do that she knew. She had worked way too hard building stability here. Sure, she had managed to buy this house and save up a little, but it was hardly enough to go back to the Burtons feeling like she had something real to offer in return.

But oh God, did she love the thought of seeing her friends once again. Her eyes popped open as she heard Cole close the laptop with a click and she turned over onto her other side. It was a chilly night and even with the fire burning brightly in the other room and the furnace running, she could feel a draft. She burrowed back under the covers she'd just kicked off and willed herself to go to sleep.

An uneasy feeling stirred just under her skin and she shivered, unable to put it at ease. She sighed loudly. What on earth was the matter with her? Why couldn't she sleep now? She had been sleeping alone in this house for months and had managed to sleep just fine.

She rolled over again and the baby kicked against her bladder. She groaned loudly, now she had to go to the bathroom. She threw the covers off again and slid her feet into the soft slippers she always left on the side of her bed.

The hardwood floors were often cold on her bare feet and she hated sleeping with socks on. She made her way quietly down the hall to the one bathroom there on her tiptoes. The living room was silent now and she didn't want to wake Cole up. She turned on the light only after she softly closed the door. She quickly took care of business and then turned off the light before opening the door and walking on tiptoes back out into the hallway.

From the corner of her eyes, she saw a shadow and jumped. Heart beating wildly, she swung around fully intending to hit whatever it was.

"It's only me," Cole assured her quietly as he stepped closer to her in the dark. "I didn't mean to startle you; it just seems like you are having a hard time sleeping."

The statement was casual and offered gently so Brooke didn't bristle at it. He almost sounded concerned as he added, "Aren't expecting mothers supposed to get extra rest?"

Not sure how to respond to that question, Brooke smiled in the dark. "I'm sorry if I'm keeping you awake," she mumbled apologetically. "The baby is doing gymnastics tonight and it's a little hard to sleep through." She smiled again but couldn't tell if he could see it. She turned toward her bedroom door. "I'll just go now and let you get some rest. I promise to try to be quieter."

She nearly missed his low nearly inaudible response, "I'm not sure I'll be sleeping tonight with the image of you laying in that sexy little nightgown in the next room."

She ignored his under-the-breath comment since she really had no desire to explore that subject. "Good night, Cole." She murmured and hurried into her room closing the door almost all the way and hurrying to her bedside.

Even from across the room she could heard his low-voiced challenge: "Chicken."

She smiled and hurried back to firmly close the door behind her. She slid back under the covers and closed her eyes once again willing sleep to come. An hour later she rolled over and tucked a pillow between her knees still trying to relax when she heard soft footsteps coming down the hall. Moments later she heard a soft knock on the door.

She held absolutely still for a very long moment, waiting for another knock or for his footsteps to recede back down her hallway. When she heard neither, she slid out of bed and tiptoed quietly to the door and opened it. There was just enough moonlight shining through her bedroom window for her to see him leaning casually against her doorjamb with his strong bare arms folded across his chest. He was wearing a black tank that fit too snugly to her way of thinking as she could quite literally see his contoured abs through the lined fabric. His snug black knit shorts did nothing to hide the slight bulge there.

She gulped and then took a deep breath and looked up to meet his gaze, black now in the semidarkness. "Did you need something?" she asked politely. The little wobble in her voice gave away her discomfort, which only pissed her off.

He shook his head and grinned widely. "I can hear the springs in your mattress creaking from the other room even with the door closed." He straightened up and away from the wall, which put him too close. "I remember when my mom was expecting, she would always get a lot of back pain in the last trimester and I thought it might help for me to rub your back for a while to help you fall asleep."

Brooke stared up at him in utter disbelief. "You aren't actually suggesting that you rub it in my bed, are you?" She sounded so horrified at that thought that he actually laughed, the sound low and warm.

He held both hands up and grinned. "I promise to keep my hands to myself. I just can't sleep with those springs making all that constant pinging." He stepped through her doorway and put his hands on her shoulders and gently pushed her toward the bed.

She moved ahead of him reluctantly and then sat on the very edge of the bed. He reached over the top of her and lifted the covers to lay them softly over her as she lay back and away to avoid brushing against his arms and chest. He chuckled low in his throat again and walked around the bed. "You're looking at me like I'm the big bad wolf and you're a tiny little sheep," he teased.

She both felt and heard his weight as he lowered onto the bed next to her. She stiffened instinctively as he reached for her shoulders and began squeezing gently and rubbing his knuckles back and forth from side to side. It felt so heavenly that she relaxed and rolled over onto her side exposing her full back to him and his magical fingers.

Cole cursed himself inwardly. Her shoulders were strong and slender and her spine curved down sensually. What exactly had propelled him to give her his word that he would keep his hands to himself? Her back sloped elegantly in to her curvy waistline and he swallowed. She was wearing an emerald green camisole that shimmered and slid against her curves. He felt himself harden instantly but forced aside his urge as he rubbed his way gently down her back. He dug his knuckles in and gently massaged her lower back as she moaned in ecstasy.

He couldn't help himself. He imagined making her moan just like that in so many pleasure-filled ways his erection pushed painfully against the restricting band of his shorts. He cursed silently at himself. Pregnant or not, she was a damn fine woman and he would have to be dead not to react.

He ran his hands up and down her back wickedly enjoying what he could touch of her body long after her relaxed breathing told him she was asleep. Desperately, he forced his hands away and started to move away. She gave a satisfied little moan and tucked herself up against his warm hard body. He sucked in a ragged breath and willed his racing pulse to slow down before he lost control. He tried once again to move away from her purely out of self-preservation, but she threw one leg over him and snuggled close again. With an inward groan and a quick prayer for stamina, he gave in and gently wrapped one arm around her waist holding her close and a bit protectively.

It took him another very long and very painful hour to finally relax into sleep.

Brooke dreamed of him. She dreamed that he kissed her tenderly on her neck and pulled her close. She snuggled up to him in the dream even knowing that it wasn't real but only a dream. He touched her hair and that familiar warm tingle started between her legs as her breasts felt hot and heavy. He lifted her breasts then in his strong working hands as he kissed one lightly at its budding center and then turned his head to kiss the other. She arched her back thrusting them out toward him again wanting more.

She jerked awake and two realizations hit her at once. The first was that she was not alone as she could feel his body pressed tightly against her back. The second realization was that he was awake and extremely hard and erect held tightly against her bottom. She froze feeling panicked for just a moment. His low voice calmed her somehow.

"Good, you're awake. Do you think I can have my arm back now?" He pulled away gently, though he allowed his hand to slide up her side and over the side of her breast once as he pulled it from her waist and sat up. "I really don't think I could have handled you moaning like that and rubbing against me much longer." His tone was low and raspy.

She scrambled back and away, quickly pulling herself up to lean against the wooden headboard. "I was not doing that," she denied, but her voice was husky from sleep and his gaze only narrowed on her lips. She looked away from his and took a deep breath.

He watched her lazily with one eyebrow raised. She had absolutely been rubbing against him. It was in fact what had woken him up. He had been on the verge of giving her exactly what she wanted when she finally woke up. He wasn't, however, feeling inclined to point it out again. He cursed at his own unyielding gentlemanly manners.

If he had any brains at all he would have just taken what she was offering. He groaned aloud. The only reason he had held back was because he didn't think he could stand to see that same look of terror on her face yet again. He stood and stretched with a yawn. "Hungry?" he asked, determined to be a gentleman.

She nodded mutely. His bare arms were sleekly muscled and bulged as he stretched them wide. His shoulders and chest were nicely rounded and sleek with hard-muscled strength. She forced her gaze away from him as the heavy throb between her legs grew. She wouldn't allow herself to look any lower. She met his gaze, which was dark and knowing.

He smiled and looked down at her legs, a look of genuine appreciation there. She followed his gaze down and squealed as she realized her camisole had risen up to tangled around her hips leaving her legs completely bare all the way up to her lacy white underwear. She blushed a deep crimson red and hastily tried to pull it down. It wouldn't pull as she was sitting on it so she scooted off the bed to frantically tug it down.

Cole was sure in that moment that he was an absolute saint. For all that she was trying her best to cover up, it was actually so damn sexy that he was having a hard time not walking around and taking her into his arms, conscience be damned.

Finally, a little desperately he pleaded, "Brooke, please hold still." He looked pointedly at her breasts, which were bouncing and trying to push their way out the top of her sleek nightgown as she tried without success to pull it down past her knees. She froze. A painful grin turned up one side of his mouth. "All that wiggling about is going to have me losing control, and I don't think either of us want that right now. My word is only so good." His voice was low and desperate and he ran his fingers through his long hair to keep them busy.

Like a deer caught in headlights, she raised her gaze to his. She folded her arms over her breasts self-consciously. "I'm sorry. Most of my nightclothes don't fit well anymore and I get so hot and sweaty at night that I don't like wearing anything too heavy," she explained, though she wasn't sure why she felt it so necessary.

Cole laughed hoarsely. That information was truly the last thing he needed to hear because now he was imagining her full sleek body slick with sweat in her bed. He closed his eyes and took a long deep breath. "Here is what is going to happen," he said as he opened them again and met her nervous gaze. "I'm going to go into the other room and get dressed and then I'm going to go make you some breakfast." He smiled. "You take your time getting ready and I will see you in the kitchen." He walked quickly to the door.

He was halfway down the hallway before he heard her say, "Uh, Cole, that might be an issue. I don't really have a lot of groceries on hand right now because I usually eat at the café." He didn't dare test the boundaries of his self-control, so he kept walking anyway. It was best to give himself a good long while to cool off before he had to face her again, he thought with a self-mocking grimace.

CHAPTER 27

Brooke only took twenty minutes to get dressed and ready for the day. She picked a warm blue sweater top that gathered at her sides and under her breasts to leave plenty of room for the bulk of a pregnant belly along with a pair of snug-fitting black slacks. She slipped on some sleek black pumps that were low heeled and comfortable.

She would be on her feet all day at the café and didn't want to have aching feet an hour into her shift. As always, her makeup was lightly applied, barely enough there to accent her fresh look. She brushed through her hair and then loosely braided it, leaving a few small tendrils loose to curl around her face. She looked in the mirror and shrugged. It wasn't great, but it would have to do.

She grabbed her bag off the long table by her bedroom door and took a deep breath before she walked out to the front room to face Cole. He stood as she walked in and took a moment to look her up and down with an appreciative smile.

She gave him a quick nervous smile. "Why do you always look at me so intensely?" she asked under her breath. "It makes me feel like I put my clothes on inside out or something like that." She looked quickly down at her clothes to make sure they were indeed fine.

Cole chuckled low in his throat. "Feel free to turn them around if you'd like." His eyes twinkled and he wiggled his brows suggestively, which had the desired effect as Brooke burst out laughing.

"You really have no shame, do you?" she accused lightly. She hadn't missed just how nice the soft gray shirt he wore hugged his hard sexy shoulders and chest. His black jeans hugged his thickly muscled thighs and narrowed slightly down to his calves and slightly over his gray leather boat shoes. She swallowed and pulled her eyes intentionally back up to his laughing gaze. "I wish I could stay here with you and hang out all day," she lied, "but I have to be at work by nine." She faked what she thought was a pretty sincerely disappointed face.

Cole grinned. "Right." He turned his expression to a calm understanding one. "That's okay. I think it'll be all right since I have every intention of going with you." He held up his hands when she would have disagreed. "I have to study, so I am bringing my laptop along. After I eat, I'll sit and drink coffee while I work."

Her mouth closed again with a snap unable to think of anything to say that wouldn't sound rude. She looked at him uncertainly. "Well, I work until five, so I don't think you'll be wanting to be at the café that long."

Cole shrugged. "If I get done before that, I'll just head out for a bit and then come back to get you after your shift is over."

"I can drive myself," she insisted with a spark of temper. Him being here was already a lot to deal with and though she was much more comfortable with him than she would have guessed, it was still bizarre that he, of all people, had come here to this little town and was now inserting himself solidly into the life she had built. She stopped a groan before it escaped her lips. "I'm sure you have things you want to do," she said haltingly, though it ended up sounding like a plea.

A wide charming smile that touched his eyes spread and made the gold specks in them sparkle. "And take the risk of you running away again while I'm not paying attention?" He clucked his tongue and wiggled a finger at her, but his teasing tone made her smile. The serious and challenging look he sent her after that heart-stopping smile had her nerves tingling with awareness.

What on earth was he planning to do here anyway? she wondered. He couldn't exactly stay here forever. He had a full life somewhere else. Suddenly she remembered his comment from the night before. "*Good, then you won't mind if I stay here a few days until I can take you back home.*" Flustered, she met his gaze. "You can't just stay here in Montana, Cole. You have a life back home and I have worked too hard here building one for myself to just pick up and leave it all behind."

His gaze was steady and unyielding. "My life is wherever I choose to be and right now I choose to be here with you and *when* I choose to go...." He paused for effect. "...you will be coming back with me." He informed her in a steady confident tone. She looked like she was about to argue, so he clicked his tongue again. "After you come home and see the family again and, of course, apologize to them for leaving without notice in the first place, then we can all decide the best thing from there."

She raised her chin stubbornly as shards of blue sparked in her eyes. "I have a plan. And I can't just drop work and take off on some last-minute whim because you decided that you want me to. I'm having a baby, Cole." Brooke rubbed at her stomach pointedly. "I have to think of my son first."

He stared hard at her stomach. "It's a boy?" he asked.

She gritted her teeth in frustration as a small growl erupted. "That is not the point, Cole," she ground out waving her hand wildly in the air. "Not all of us can just do whatever we want whenever we want to. Some of us have to work hard for what we get in life and be really smart about how we do it."

His gaze didn't waver at her unspoken challenge, though he did give her a small smile. "While I'm fairly certain that was meant to be a jab at me because I happen to have a very intelligent and very wealthy father, I'd like to point out that I haven't taken a dime from my parents since I was maybe...." He stopped to think about it for a minute. "...fourteen, so the money part is irrelevant. As to the other part of that statement, *I* happen to think you are a very intelligent woman who is capable of creating anything you choose to create." He looked around her front room. "Take an honest look at yourself for a change, Brooke. In the last eight months, you have managed to create not one but two homes as well as two decent jobs of which either would both support you and the baby."

When he turned back to her, his face held only honest sincerity. "Let's be honest here, Brooke, at this point, the only reason for you to not come home with me would be if you really don't want us in your life." He gave her a minute to think about that before finishing. "And if that is your truth, then you are on your own with all of it because I won't be the one going back to Jacob, Ryker, and my dad to tell them to quit caring about you since you don't give a damn."

Horror filled her eyes at his words before they filled with tears. "Don't care?" she mumbled. "The only reason I left was because I care and love your family too much." She looked away for a minute and then turned back to stare angrily at him. "Damn you anyway, you don't have any clue how I feel."

He was grinning down at her now with that damnable knowing grin and she realized a little too late that he had backed her into the very corner he had been aiming for. "I really don't see the problem, then," he stated casually as he picked a piece of lint off his shoulder. "And if any of this is about what my mom said to you, she has since realized just how valuable you were to us all. Also, you may not know this, but nearly every one of our employees complained when you left." He obviously knew she didn't know since she hadn't been in touch. He plowed on. "And don't even get me started about Ryker and Dom. They have nearly driven us all mad because they ask at least once a day when you're coming back home." He knew he was pushing his point but couldn't stop. "Jacob spent the first month after you left stomping around in a grumpy miserable funk, and my mom and dad fought nonstop for weeks."

Brooke stared up at him wordlessly, looking dazed and a little disbelieving. "You don't honestly expect me to buy all that do you?" she asked.

Cole held her gaze steadily. "You should," he said calmly. "It's only the truth." His gaze never wavered on hers and Brooke finally looked away.

"Even if all of that is true and I did want to come back to visit, I have responsibilities here." She looked back at him. "I'm buying this house, my job is here now, and I even have a birthing plan all of which are here." She smiled sadly. "I can't just come back with you."

Cole nodded. "I get it. You have a lot riding here and a lot to think about. Why don't we get you to work before you're late and we can talk more about this later?" He smiled as he opened the door for her. A rush of frosty air slapped her in the face as she stepped carefully out onto the icy porch. She saw exhaust streaming out behind his car and in surprise turned to look back at him.

He gave her a lopsided grin. "I started it earlier, so we don't freeze our asses off while we wait for it to warm up."

She nodded and murmured thanks under her breath. A bit reluctantly, Brooke climbed into the door he held open for her and he closed it securely behind her. He walked around and stood just outside the door for a long moment before finally folding his frame inside. He turned to her. "Is that truck one of your neighbors?" he asked with his brow furrowed.

Brooke glanced in the direction he was pointing. An unfamiliar silver pickup was parked a short distance behind them. She shrugged. "Not that I know of. I don't recognize it." She turned and met his concerned gaze with curiosity. "Why?"

He shook his head and grinned. "I'm sure it's nothing," he assured her. His gut clenched and he sighed. He'd noticed that same truck last night, though it had been parked much closer to her house. He had assumed it belonged to one of her many guests, but it was still here. It hadn't been there, however, when he'd come out to start his car, but it was back now. He brushed it aside; it was probably nothing. He turned his car around and pulled past slowly, looking curiously into the cab for a glimpse of anything. To his relief there was no one inside and nothing stood out except the fact that it had a Utah license plate. That wasn't too uncommon, he assured himself; after all, he was here and he had Idaho plates. Most likely it was just someone visiting from the south or someone who'd recently moved here. He put it firmly out of his mind as he turned his focus to driving on the icy roads.

Brooke gave him directions and thirteen minutes later, they were pulling into the paved lot of the café. Cole jumped out and hurried around to open her door and took her elbow securely as she stepped out. The lot was snow packed and slick. Even wearing shoes with good traction wasn't enough against the snow-packed blacktop, so he kept a tight grip on her arm as they made their way to the entrance. He held the door for her and she stomped the snow and ice onto the rug inside the door before smiling and saying hi to the guy standing behind the host's desk.

She quickly introduced Cole as a friend and asked if they could sit at a side booth to eat before her shift. He smiled pleasantly and shook Cole's hand as he handed her a couple of menus. "You can just seat yourselves."

Brooke thanked him and soon they were both seated with menus. He helped her take off her coat before unzipping his and doing the same. He watched her over the top of his menu as she studied the breakfast portion. She pretended not to notice as she stared blankly down at the tabletop. She knew the menu by heart, but Cole made her nervous the way he always watched her so intently. She wasn't about to admit that to him, though, as she was sure it would make him happy.

CHAPTER 28

Breakfast was delicious. Jill appeared at their booth and took their drink order of coffee and orange juice and then rushed off to get them. She smiled at Cole and said hello before turning her back to wiggle her brows suggestively at Brooke. She looked pointedly at Brooke and then Cole again as she commented in a friendly voice, "I see you're still here in Montana, Cole."

He nodded and gave her a friendly smile.

She hurried off but not before giving Brooke a quick wink and a suggestive little smile. Brooke rolled her eyes.

They ate their pancakes, hash browns, and eggs in silence. Though not an uncomfortable silence. Brooke found herself watching him as he watched her and hid a smile. She scraped the last of her food from her plate into her mouth and glanced at his half-eaten plate. He still had one egg and a pile of hash browns left. She eyed them but only for a split second. He deftly scooted his plate out of her reach.

She frowned in displeasure.

He grinned. "Oh no you don't."

She planked her fork unceremoniously onto her own empty plate. "Come on now, I'm eating for two these days, you know," she said as though that explained everything.

Cole chuckled. "And why do I get the distinct feeling, that being pregnant only slightly affected your appetite?"

She glared down her nose at him. "I eat way more now," she said seriously, trying unsuccessfully to convince him.

His eyes went wide and he stared across at her in mock horror. "Are you saying that you get even hungrier than before?" he asked.

She slapped his hand as Jill walked up. She looked between them. "Well, I don't mean to interrupt you two, but can I get anything else for you?" It didn't escape Cole's notice that she directed the question to him.

Brooke answered, "No thanks, I gotta start my shift soon."

He and Jill exchanged amused smiles. He looked pointedly at Brooke. "We'll just take a piece of pie and one of those cinnamon buns I saw on the front counter if it's not too much trouble," he countered in a friendly drawl.

Jill laughed and nodded as she turned to leave.

Brooke stared hard at him until he met her gaze. "I guess someone is hungry today," she grumbled as she looked pointedly at his still uneaten egg.

Cole made a big show of cutting a big bite and shoving in his mouth before smiling sweetly. "I am," he said and smacked his lips together.

The pie and cinnamon bun appeared on the table between them and Jill waved as she hurried off to take care of another customer. Brooke looked down at the pie and then back up at him. Defiantly, she picked up her fork and went for a bite. He didn't pull it away like she'd expected him to, which surprised her. She smirked across the table. "I thought you weren't going to share with me."

He looked down and then back up at her. "Oh, I ordered those for you, sweetheart, out of self-preservation."

Brooke rolled her eyes. "I'm not *that* hungry," she announced as she cheerfully took another forkful of the crispy apple pie.

He reached out and wiped a crumb off her lip. "Okay. I just wouldn't want the two of you to go hungry," he said quietly.

She stilled and searched for something witty to say. Her mind was blank so she took a small bite of the gooey cinnamon bun. She watched as Cole took a small bite of one and then the other. He smiled in approval. "Not bad." He set his fork down and watched, entranced as she inhaled the rest. His heart gave a little offbeat thud, but he brushed it aside. There was no point in worrying about something he couldn't control.

After every plate at the table was emptied, Brooke pulled out her wallet. He stopped her with a cold look. He pulled out a couple of twenties and set them on the table with the bill. He told her cheerfully to get to work before she was late and she rose reluctantly and headed into the back. She disappeared for several minutes while Cole sipped at a fresh cup of coffee Jill poured for him. She batted her lashes playfully and asked if he was sticking around for a while.

He told her yes and pulled out his laptop. She kindly told him the Wi-Fi password and pointed out an obscure outlet under the table as she cleared away the dirty dishes. She turned to leave with the loaded tray in her arms but then turned back with a serious look on her face. "Look," she started. "I don't know exactly what the story is with you and Brooke." She paused to study one of her long delicate pink and green nails. "But she means a lot to us here. I don't know if you're the baby's father or not and I try not to judge. I just don't want to see her hurt," she rushed out protectively. "If you are the father, then I'm glad she finally told you and I admire you for showing up. Brooke has had a lot of tough experiences as I'm sure you understand. She is a really good person and a great friend and she deserves the best."

She courageously threw him a friendly smile. "Anyway, I just needed to say that there isn't a person around here that she hasn't done something really nice for, so if you're going to stay you better be good to her. And if you're planning to leave again you should do it now before she gets hurt again." She turned with her load to walk away.

Behind her Cole smiled. "I couldn't agree more," he said more to himself than to her receding back. He didn't see the wide smile that lit up Jill's face as she walked quickly back into the kitchen.

He opened his laptop to a project he had but couldn't focus on the screen in front of him. He picked up his coffee and took a sip deep in thought. So, she hadn't told her friends who the father was either? He frowned suddenly as the realization hit him that it hadn't bothered him for Jill to think he was the father. He had almost felt honored at the mistake. He shook his head at his own dumb lack of sense.

Determined to put the subject away, he turned his focus to the laptop and logged in to the school website again. He really didn't need his grades to fall right before graduation and he still had a couple of projects to do before he was ready for his exams.

He didn't raise his head again until he heard Brooke's friendly tone as she welcomed a couple at a nearby table and took their drink order. He couldn't help his instinct to keep one eye on her and the other on his screen.

She was warm and friendly to everyone it seemed and it was undeniably obvious that she made everyone feel welcome. Her customers appeared to love her and she kept close tabs on all her tables and what was going on. She rushed a large stack of napkins to a family with two small children as a cup of chocolate milk was overturned by the young boy before they had to ask. She kept drinks refilled and rushed the food orders out while they were still hot.

She chatted a little with the more friendly customers and left the introverted ones to themselves after making sure they had everything they needed. She was very insightful, he thought and he was a little surprised that even in a job as simple as waiting tables her intelligence and attention to detail gave her an edge.

A couple of hours went by before the café slowed down a bit and she came over to ask if he needed anything. He nodded his thanks at the fresh coffee and suggested she sit and rest if she had a minute. She had been on her feet and rushing around nonstop since her shift started. She smiled and curtly informed him that it was the job before waving and heading over to check on three men who were seated near the front entrance.

Her tips showed her care and popularity with the locals. He raised one eyebrow when he saw a guy pay his bill with a fifty and tell her to keep the change. She smiled warmly at him and assured him that was way too much, but when he insisted, she thanked him and graciously pocketed the large tip.

Cole finished one of his assignments and closed the laptop for a minute as he took a drink of coffee. He hadn't actually told his family that he had found her yet but knew they would be calling any day now to check in. He didn't want to lie to them, but he was also worried that they would just jump in and drive up here if they knew exactly where she was. He didn't want to examine wanting her to himself too closely, so he put it aside.

There was also the issue of that guy who had attacked her and tried to take her. While the sheriff hadn't been able to find any leads and no one had seen or heard anything else since, he worried. He shrugged inwardly and admitted once again that it was a small selfish part of him that wanted her to himself. He couldn't stand the thought of watching her and Jacob as they did everything together while he stood on the outside. But all that was beside the point.

Resolute he shot a quick group text to Jacob and Ivan. "*Just checking in. I found her now. Can't say where, so don't ask. I'm planning to bring her back to visit soon. Will let you know when.*"

He knew it would bring up all kinds of questions but what the hell. Jacob would just have to deal with it. Just as he'd suspected, his phone went off as soon as he clicked Send. After the third buzz he sighed and lifted the phone again.

Jacob: *Where is she????*

Jacob: *Is she okay?*

Jacob: *Does she want to come back?*

Jacob again: *Hello???? Cole???*

Jacob: *Answer me bro!!*

He gave a resigned sigh and lifted his thumbs.

Cole: *She is somewhere safe. She is very, very, pregnant but healthy. She has a nice little place she is staying. She misses you guys. I will have her call you ASAP. I'm working on getting her to agree to come for a visit, wink, wink.*

Cole: *Oh and by the way Jacob stop texting me every two seconds. I'm trying to study.* He ended the text with an exploding angry emoji.

Then grinned and once again turned his phone over. Let Jacob take that because he needed to get some things done. With a cheerful grin he reached into his pocket and pulled out Brooke's phone that he had stolen from her purse while her attention was on the dessert. He lifted it and hit the power button hopefully. The screen lit up and he slid a thumb up to unlock it. Bingo. She hadn't locked it. He grinned and went immediately to her contacts. The first thing he did was add his own name and number in there, then he shot his own phone a quick text from her. He took a selfie of himself with a big cocky grin and saved it as the contact photo. He took a second to set up her contact info on his own phone as he watched for any sign of her. She was still in the kitchen, so he took a minute to add a "find my phone" app and connected her phone to his. He wasn't going to take any chance of her running away from him again. He glanced up and smiled as she walked over to check on him. He lowered her phone to the seat beside him and smiled up at her.

She frowned. "I can't believe you're still here waiting for me. You really should go do something fun or really anything at all besides sit here all day. There isn't any reason for you to be waiting here."

He looked very serious as he answered. "On the contrary. I'm quite afraid that if I let you out of my sight, you're going to find a way to disappear and that it will take me another five months to find you again," he countered softly.

Brooke rolled her eyes in dramatic exasperation, "Oh for God's sake, Cole, I'm eight months along and I literally work in a café. Where on earth would I even go?"

He stared her down. "Where indeed? You see, I once knew this girl that had the most unholy habit of running away every time she got scared. She was pregnant and didn't have much to her name and yet she disappeared into the blue." In a quiet serious way, he continued despite her rolling eyes. "I had to search every town, state-to-state looking for any clues as to where she might have gone. Funny thing, though, I finally had a small stroke of luck and located her." He gave her a chilly smile. "Now, I'm going to make damn sure she doesn't up and slip away in the night again."

She sat down heavily and met his dark angry eyes. "I didn't leave because I was scared," she insisted with a stubborn tilt of her elegant chin. "I left because I had been taking advantage of Jacob and your dad and your whole family and I needed to know that I could take care of myself and this baby." Her eyes lightened as she put a protective hand on her swollen stomach. "I have no reason to leave again," she said, putting emphasis on leave.

One corner of his mouth turned up. "While I'll admit that is great news, forgive me if I'm a mite hesitant to simply take your word for it." His eyes darkened suddenly and she saw a glint of anger as his jaw tightened before he shuttered his expression. "Would you believe that you had me thinking you were some innocent little thing for a while?"

He looked suggestively at her stomach and then back up and Brooke felt as though he had slapped her when he continued coolly. "Obviously, you've been around that block a time or two."

She paled but fought the tears that threatened. In a cool tone she said, "I never told you I was innocent. Whatever assumption you made about that was your own." Steadier now, she raised her head to look at him. "I never asked anything of you, Cole. I honestly don't even know why you're here. You are quite literally the last person in the world that I thought would come looking for me, so please forgive me if I'm a little stressed out by it."

He met her gaze for gaze and the anger he felt drained away as he took in her eyes shimmering with unshed tears. "I'm sorry," he said and sounded sincere. "The last thing you need right now is to be more stressed. I only want to help you make things better," he said sincerely again and she couldn't help but believe him.

She smiled brightly and reached out to touch his hand. "I can see that. I gotta get back to work, but I'll drop some lunch by in a few minutes," she promised as she stood. "Any special requests?"

He shrugged and gave her that irresistible grin that she loved so much. "Surprise me."

Brooke smiled back at him and then walked back into the kitchen to check on her orders. She had tables to wait and customers to take care of, but before she left the kitchen, she took just a minute to put in a lunch order with the chef for Cole.

Cole reached for her phone again and scrolled through her contacts quickly sending a few more of them to his own. He stood and stretched before strolling casually toward the back of the restaurant where the restrooms were located. He stepped through the double swinging doors that led into the kitchen from this side of the restaurant and looked around. He spotted her bag right away and with a little grin slipped her phone inside.

He used the men's room quickly before going back to his table. When he sat, he stared down at the plate that was loaded with a huge grilled cheese sandwich and seasoned steak fries. Next to that plate sat a glass of water, a side salad with ranch and a big bowl of soup. He looked around the restaurant for her but didn't see Brooke anywhere. Jill noticed him looking around and winked from across the room.

He quite literally felt like a king as he picked up his fork and dug into the salad. The grilled cheese was crispy on the outside but melted cheese squeezed out when he took a bite. The salad was surprisingly fresh for a small café, with fresh crisp lettuce and baby spinach sprinkled with chunks of cucumber, tomato, and carrots on top. The chicken enchilada soup was flavorful and savory with melted cheese on top and tortilla chips. Even the fries were decent. They were topped with a garlicky spice mix sprinkled on top of crisply fried potatoes. He noted with a little smile that she had even set a small bowl of fry sauce next to the plate. Though he hadn't thought he was hungry, he finished the food because it was delicious.

Another twenty minutes went by before he saw Brooke again. She looked in mock surprise at his empty dishes as she came over. "Apparently we have a big eater in the house today," she teased. It worked a dimpled smile out of him as she cleared the dishes.

Cole thanked her and asked for the bill. She laughed in his face. "It's on me this time, cowboy. And there really isn't much you can do since I'm not going to bring you a ticket."

He smiled and motioned her closer as he leaned in as though to tell a secret. Deftly he slipped a hundred-dollar bill in her apron pocket as she leaned in playfully. "I can always ask for your manager, miss," he threatened in a quiet voice.

Brooke laughed delightedly and then forced a worried look. "I guess if you really must, sir."

She was smiling as she walked away. Jill had obviously been busy texting their friends because they all started showing up for "lunch." Interestingly enough, though, they all kept asking her questions about Cole like why he was here? And were they a thing? Oh, and had he spent the night at her place?

Brooke laughed breathlessly as she tried to ward off all the curiosity. The last thing she needed was for her friends to think something serious was going between her and Cole. They would all be let down when he got bored and went home. She assured all of them that he was just here for a quick visit and would soon return home. She tried not to feel guilty about their disappointed acceptance.

It was when Janae came in with her husband that Brooke finally decided she needed to put a stop to it. She answered all of Janae's questions a bit too quickly, which had her friend smiling with excitement. When Brooke set their order on the table, she leaned toward her and confided, "I think that boy is in love with you, dear."

Brooke shook her head sadly. "No Janae, I'm sorry but that just isn't possible." She turned and glanced at Cole before saying quietly. "Cole doesn't really even like me. He just likes to play around with me when he gets bored."

Janae didn't respond to that accusation, but her doubtful expression said what she wouldn't.

Around two o'clock, Cole disappeared for a couple of hours but then returned to sit at the same booth when he came back in. He ordered some more coffee and went back to work on his computer. It wasn't until five when she turned in her tips and was counting through them that she found the hundred-dollar bill. She stared at it suspiciously. She couldn't remember anyone paying cash with a hundred today.

She laughed as she took off her apron and grabbed her bag to leave. She tucked the bill into the pocket of her slacks planning to wait for the opportunity to return it.

CHAPTER 29

Richard watched them from the swarm of trees and bushes while that bastard and his woman went about their morning as though it was the most casual thing ever. Anger was a putrid burn in the back of his throat. Why had she done this to him? A sad tear formed at the corner of his left eye blurring his vision and he blinked it away. They'd had such a bright promising future in front of them and now she had gone and ruined everything. His fingernails made oozing bloody cuts in his palms as he watched them climb into that stupid blue car and leave. He hurried to his truck and climbed inside but not before they were a block away.

He followed them from a distance keeping several cars between himself and them. When they pulled off the highway and parked at the little restaurant he had gone to for breakfast the last couple of days, he chortled in amusement. Wasn't life such a funny and mysterious thing. He could have run into them by accident at any point and yet he hadn't. He parked at the edge of a grocery store lot just across the street and watched as Brooke and her little sex pal made their way carefully inside.

The fucking loser even held her arm in protection and wore an expression of concern as they crossed the ice. Richard sighed. Poor little Brooke didn't have a clue that all that gentlemanly shit was just a big game so the guy could get what he wanted from her. Richard could appreciate what he wanted from her; after all, didn't he want the same thing?

He waited patiently for a long while for them to once again emerge from the restaurant. His coffee ran out and his overstretched bladder complained. He looked around his truck before reaching for an old Gatorade bottle that was settled inside his door. He didn't even take his eyes off the restaurant as he unzipped and relieved himself quickly, re-capping the bottle before tossing it down on the passenger side floorboard.

One hour turned into two and frustration began to seep in. What in the holy hell was taking them so long? A few possibilities nagged at his brain. Maybe they had seen him following them, after all, and had ditched the car and snuck out a back door. "Fuck, fuck, fuck!" he chanted as he stared hard at the café door willing them to step out. It had crossed his mind that this could possibly be where she was working, but that wouldn't explain why that dickhead was still inside. He gave it another long fifteen minutes before sliding impatiently out of his truck. While he didn't want her to know he was here until he was ready to surprise her, he did need to know that they were actually still inside.

He crossed the street and strolled casually inside, pausing to let his eyes adjust to the dim interior before walking over to the vacated host stand. He glanced around trying to appear casual about it as a man walked up to stand behind the host's desk and was now watching him curiously. He smiled and nodded politely as he scanned first one side of the long table and booth spotted café and then the other. He nearly missed the man seated in a back booth with his head down staring fixedly at a silver laptop.

Richard had been looking for a couple that was seated together so his gaze passed over and then swung back as he saw the guy look up and directly at him. He froze momentarily before forcing a little nod and making himself turn toward the host. He had been watching them even before she had left Idaho but they didn't know that. There was no reason to freak out as the man wouldn't recognize him as anything other than a stranger. He smiled at his own careful nature. It was in that moment that he saw her.

Brooke had on a light blue shirt that showed off way more of her delectable body than any man should be okay with. There was a little black apron tied around her bulky stomach and she was smiling at a family as she waited patiently for their order. He wanted to stare. Wanted to sit down and watch her but unfortunately that just wouldn't do.

He turned without a word to the host and walked quickly back outside lowering his sunglasses to his nose again as he stepped onto the sunlit blacktop. He made his way back to his truck but not before a quick stop in the grocery store behind him for some cold drinks and a few snacks.

The day dragged by slowly but he made the best of it as he meticulously made a plan. Richard grinned as he stared down at his phone. By this time tomorrow night that asshole would be dead and Richard would have her all to himself. He frowned and slid lower in his truck seat when Cole came out of the restaurant. He watched through the slat of his steering wheel as the guy walked over to lean on his pristine little sports car and talked on the phone. It was over an hour later before the guy finally tucked his phone back into his pocket and sauntered back inside.

Richard relaxed and sat up straight, laughing out loud. He knew everything about them and yet they hadn't even noticed him. Of course, they hadn't because, after all, God was on his side. Amusement warmed him up almost as much as the thought of his neatly made plans.

It was after five in the afternoon before they finally left the café and drove to her home. He followed them just a little closer this time much less afraid of being seen now. Obviously, the guy was too dumb to know when he was in danger. Richard rubbed his cold fingers together as he watched them go into the house together.

Satisfied that they would stay in for the night, he turned his truck around and drove away. He needed to go to the hardware store for some choice items before he turned in for the night. He would need to make sure he was well rested for everything he had to do tomorrow. Plan securely made, he turned on the *Phantom of the Opera* soundtrack as he drove into the city for some supplies. Happily, he hummed along to a song about the darkness.

Jacob was tied in knots. Three times he had started walking out to his jeep, fully intending on driving to wherever Cole was. The only problem, was that he didn't know where that was so he would end up walking back inside. He had called and texted Cole several times throughout the day to no avail. Cole was definitely ignoring his calls at this point and only responded to his texts with cryptic one or two-word replies.

Jacob was really starting to get pissed off by early afternoon when he tried calling yet again only to get his pigheaded brother's voicemail. In frustration, he scowled down at his phone, "Dammit, Cole call me back. I don't know what in the hell you're thinking about or doing, but I need to talk to you."

It was around three when his phone rang and he saw Cole's face pop up on the screen of his smartphone. He bumped the button with his thumb and lifted the phone to his ear. "Finally, bro, what the hell is going on?"

He could hear the cool amusement in Cole's voice when he responded, "Hello to you too, Jacob."

Jacob swallowed the curse that flew to his lips. "Where are you?" he asked impatiently, grabbing his keys and walking out to his jeep. "I'm coming to you."

Cole chuckled. "As I said the first fifty times, there is no need for that. I'm making all the arrangements now and I will be bringing her home soon."

Jacob stopped walking. "She agreed to that?" he asked in surprise.

Cole laughed again. "She will" was all he said.

That seemed to put his brother in a slightly better mood so he only sounded slightly irritated as he complained, "I have been trying to get you on the phone all day. Why haven't you been taking my calls?"

"You really are quite the nag, you know," Cole accused lightly. "I told you everything you needed to know this morning and you have still been calling and texting nonstop. I've been busy."

Jacob gave a frustrated little laugh. "You haven't told me much of anything and you know it. I couldn't find any new info on the wall in your room and I finally realized you covered your tracks so I wouldn't know. I would have followed you all the way out there if I had any clue where you went." He smiled. "By the way, how is she doing? I want to talk to her."

"You'll be able to talk to her as much as you want soon" was Cole's only response.

They talked for a few more minutes with Jacob promising utter vengeance if Cole didn't have Brooke call him by tonight. Cole had planned to have her call him after work but changed his mind just to spite Jacob. He didn't respond to the threat before hanging up.

Jacob turned and went back into the house to give his parents an update. Both his mom and dad had asked him several questions that he had to admit he didn't have the answers to. It irritated him that he hadn't been able to get any information from his younger brother.

He didn't have anything better to do and he couldn't just sit around driving himself nuts, so he called up a girl he had been seeing and asked her to go to dinner and a movie with him. He took a shower and put on a gray shirt and blue jeans with a tan jacket and shoes before jumping in his jeep to go. His mother waved and smiled from the front porch as he drove off.

His date was gorgeous with brown hair and warm gray eyes. She was tall and slender and had dressed in a long cream-colored sweater dress that was complete with leggings and tall warm boots. She had a wide black belt cinched tightly at her slender waist and was wearing a black leather and fur-lined jacket for warmth. She laughed at all of his jokes and flirted with him with smiling eyes. Her name was Shyla and he had met her at a state fair in the fall. They had gone out a few times casually in the past few months, but he really wasn't interested in much these days.

Though he knew she liked him, she wanted more from him than he was willing to give, and he just couldn't get into it. He groaned inwardly at his own bad manners as he realized she had said something and was staring across the table at him waiting expectantly for an answer. He racked his brain trying to remember what she'd said. His memory was blank and so he gave her a good-natured grin. "I'm sorry, what did you say? I was so taken by how gorgeous you look today that I completely missed it."

She blushed and smiled pleasantly. "I was just asking how things are going with law school now that everything has been switched to online because of this virus."

He smiled and nodded. "It's not too bad. Obviously, it's much easier going to class in person and the workshops suck online, but I'm managing,"

There was a long awkward silence where it seemed that neither of them had anything to say. The server came with their food and they were both relieved. The rest of their dinner went quickly. They drove over to the movie theater in silence. Most of the shows available were reruns since the virus had kept producers from making new shows. Jacob picked an old classic and they took their seats just as the previews ended.

After the show Jacob drove her back home and left her at her door without so much as a kiss. They both knew it was over as he climbed into his jeep and drove off. Jacob hit the steering wheel in frustration as he thought of Brooke. He didn't know what was wrong with him lately. He had spent the summer going out with several different girls but had found he simply had no interest in them. Since he had gotten close to Brooke, he couldn't seem to find interest in any of the other women he met.

There were those that he felt a physical attraction to, but he couldn't stop judging the shallow things they did. That thought was frustrating, for though he and Brooke were great friends and she was definitely great with stimulating conversation, it was evident that they seriously lacked chemistry. She was beautiful and he was a guy, so he knew he could push through that, but then there was the whole thing with Cole who seemed to have some kind of jealous streak where she was concerned. It had been maddeningly obvious that sparks were flying when he'd found them kissing after the barbecue, though he suspected that neither Cole nor Brooke liked that fact.

The thing that worried Jacob the most was that he wouldn't be able to find someone that was as real and deep as Brooke was. Since they had become friends, he had realized that he wanted something more serious in his life than the shallow flirting that seemed to come with the territory with other women. He wanted a woman who was so vibrant and powerful she didn't need to flirt or play games to get what she wanted in life. He ran his long lean fingers through his short hair in frustration.

More than anything he wanted to see Brooke and talk to her again just to know that she was okay. He could worry about women later. He frowned as he parked his jeep and went back inside. There didn't seem to be much here for him lately either. A little desperately he wondered if he should take that job offer of a clerkship that was over in San Francisco.

He smiled at his mother as he walked past the door to the front room where she sat on the couch looking at her phone. It was definitely something to think about. The only reason he hadn't already accepted was because he didn't want to leave his father to handle the farm alone. On the plus side it would be a great experience for him to get to see the law on that level. He sighed as he opened the fridge for a beer. He would have to decide soon.

CHAPTER 30

While Brooke slipped into her room to change out of her work clothes, Cole rummaged through her kitchen cabinets looking for anything edible to make for dinner. He found some pasta in the cupboard and some chicken breasts in the freezer. With a triumphant cheer, he put some water on to boil and started the chicken thawing out. While he was waiting, he dug through the freezer for some vegetables and finally found a bag of broccoli florets.

He heard a thumping sound and walked over to the archway between the kitchen and living room to look around. Brooke was bent over working at the fireplace. His eyes nearly crossed as he checked out her very fine round ass. He grinned and stilled the urge to go over and put his hand on her. His jeans felt a little snug and he adjusted himself for better comfort before he wisely forced himself to turn back to the kitchen and dinner.

The water was boiling, so he dumped in the box of penne noodles. Then he steamed and cut the broccoli into bite-sized chunks. The chicken had thawed so he rubbed a mixture of garlic, salt, basil, and paprika seasoning over the breasts before laying them together in a hot skillet. He dumped the water off the pasta and then put some butter to melt in a saucepan while he looked for milk. The fridge was empty but he did find a couple things of canned milk and he poured it in with a shrug. He added some dried minced garlic, salt, and pepper and turned it on low to simmer. After a long search he found a bottle of outdated grated parmesan cheese.

Knowing it was the best he was going to find, he measured a cup of it and stirred it into the saucepan. He looked up when he heard her come in. She was staring at the messy kitchen in avid curiosity and he gave her a cocky grin. "It's just about done," he assured her and looked around at the mess. "I'll clean it all up." For a girl who liked to eat as much as she did, her cooking and shopping skills left a lot to be desired.

She smiled and sniffed. "It smells delicious. I know I didn't have anything that smells that good in the house," she said and looked around suspiciously.

Cole chuckled. "I'm just throwing some pasta together with a creamy garlic sauce."

She watched in awe as he pulled out a pasta spoon and tossed the penne with the sauce. Then he reached for a pan and dumped the broccoli in and tossed it. He turned off the oven as he pulled out a pan with garlic toast. It looked like he'd sliced what was left of the sub rolls from the baby shower and spread butter and garlic salt on them. Brooke smiled happily as he carefully set two of the hot chicken breasts on a cutting board before taking a long sharp knife and skillfully slicing them into neat rows.

He pulled two indigo-colored plates from the cupboard and used the pasta spoon to load a large helping onto each plate. Then he used a spatula to lift a chicken breast and splay it over the top of the pasta. He grabbed a slice of garlic bread and set it on the side and added a sprinkle of the parmesan. With a mock bow he held the plate out to her.

Brooke took it with a heartfelt thank-you and walked over to the table to set it down. "My God," she said with genuine admiration. "I don't know where you got the ingredients for this, but it looks insanely delicious." She smiled warmly at him and Cole found himself noticing that it was the first real smile she'd given him since he'd found her. He couldn't help returning it with a wide genuine smile of his own.

Brooke felt the air leave her lungs as his face warmed into the sexiest beautiful smile she had ever seen. One cheek dimpled and his dark eyes sparkled with warmth and sex appeal all rolled into one. God help her, was all she could think. Even formidable and moody, he was irresistible to her, but this genuine warmth made her actually feel giddy with butterflies. She forced herself to look away from him.

She walked to the fridge and pulled out a water bottle. She held it up in question and he nodded. She grabbed a second bottle and then without a second thought reached for a beer as well. She walked over and set them both next to his plate. He grinned up at her from his chair. "Thanks."

Brooke stared into those dark eyes feeling trapped and exhilarated at the same time. She tried to tell herself to walk away. Tried to get her feet to move. His eyes darkened as the gold flecks disappeared and they were nearly black now as he watched her. She nodded her head and tried once again to move away. Her feet wouldn't obey and in absolute horror she saw her hand reach out and touch his long hair. It was soft as she ran her fingers lightly threw the waves watching as they curled slightly around her fingertips and brushed the back of her hand. She stared transfixed at her hand as she ran her fingers lightly down his neck following tenderly along the muscled contour of his collarbone and then his shoulder.

He growled something unintelligible and his arm shot out to wrap around her waist and pull her against him.

Fear spiked, and she wanted to pull away but couldn't. Her body seemed uninclined to obey her. She met his gaze again and saw the raw need there. Felt that same need inside herself. She refused it, wanting more than anything to deny that need. He didn't move, only watched her with his dark eyes alive with desire and something else she didn't recognize. She attempted to smile at him as she tried to figure out what that other thing was. She bit her lip instead. That drew his gaze and she felt a surge of heat that started in her belly at the animalistic way he watched her teeth scrape lightly across her lips.

She swallowed hard and watched his gaze travel down to her throat. It felt like he was intently aware of every move she made, so she didn't dare move a muscle. Her hand was on his shoulder now and she was running it slowly back and forth from the downward curve of his shoulder and back up to just behind his earlobe to brush the dark waves there again. His cheekbones were high and prominent and from here she could see that his long aristocratic nose was just ever-so-slightly crooked. That drew the attention of her fingers and she ran one hand lightly down from his dark arched brow and over the slant of his nose. Her finger barely brushed the top of his silky-smooth top lip and suddenly intent on that she ran a very light finger over the slant of his mouth completely enthralled by the perfection there where his top lip drew up toward his nose with sharp points. He opened his mouth and bit her finger lightly, teasingly.

That move surprised her and a hot spike of need shot through her as she jumped back nervously. Cole gave a low throaty laugh. "I think you're trying to kill me," he complained in a hoarse voice as she pulled away. He let her go.

Brooke hurried around the table and sat down in the chair farthest from him. She was relieved he hadn't held on to her. She couldn't allow herself to get carried away with him. It had hurt too much already when she'd left Idaho. She knew she couldn't handle the pain if she cared any more for him. She was beginning to be afraid that she was falling for him and that just couldn't happen.

Cole watched her silently from across the table, his gaze still intensely dark. Since she couldn't think of a single thing to say, she forced a lame smile and took a bite. Her eyes widened, "That is really good," she said. Cole didn't respond but took a bite of his own food and then nodded.

They ate in awkward silence. At least it felt awkward to Brooke who couldn't seem to think of anything she could say that didn't sound fake or way too over-thought. Cole didn't look awkward at all. In fact, he looked quite satisfied with himself. He grinned at her every time she dared to meet his gaze.

He watched her with his intense, knowing eyes as they ate. It felt as though he studied her every move and waited for her to make a wrong move so he could pounce. That intensity made her feel so awkward that for the first time in her life she had a hard time eating the food on her plate. That fact only seemed to please him more as he smiled knowingly at her only half-eaten plate of food. Brooke stubbornly forced bite after bite down.

Plate finally empty she threw a polite smile toward him. "Since you made dinner, I'll clean up," she offered a bit too hopefully as she stood to walk her plate to the sink.

Cole grinned. She was finally where he wanted her and he wasn't about to leave the room and give her time to get all worked up about it. He stood and hauled his plate to the sink. "That's okay, I'm happy to help," he said mildly.

Brooke shot him a sideways pleading glance. "I'm sure you have something to do or catch up on after spending all day at the café," she said kindly.

Cole chuckled. "Careful, Brooke, or I might think you're trying to get rid of me."

She blushed and shook her head. "Of course not. I just figured you might have things you want to get done."

His hard gaze met hers in challenge. "Nope, I came here for you and I intend to spend all the time I can with you."

Her hand trembled slightly as she gave him a quick nod. They washed and dried the dishes with crackling sexual tension in the air. Brooke felt hyperaware of his tall masculine body next to her own. Their fingers brushed as they exchanged dishes and it sent steady tingles of awareness down her spine. She avoided looking at him at all since that seemed to help focus her intention away from him.

When they were finished with the dishes, Brooke quietly announced that she was going to bed.

Cole raised a challenging eyebrow at her announcement. "It's only seven thirty," he told her with a pointed look at the old-fashioned owl clock on the wall.

Brooke shrugged. "I get really tired sometimes now that I'm farther along," she lied. She knew she was being a coward. Hated the fact that she was okay with being a coward. Still, she couldn't let herself get attached to him. She was going to have a baby soon and had to put her focus on that first. She couldn't keep kissing him and not get attached. She was already worried that she was half in love with him. She couldn't give him that last little part of her heart or she wasn't sure she would ever be able to get over it when he got sick of her.

Cole gave her a knowing smile and held her gaze locked with his. "Are you running again, Brooke?"

She felt heat rising to her cheeks and willed it back down. "I'm just tired. Good night, Cole."

He watched her walk across the room. Waited until she was almost out of sight before saying softly, "One of these days you are going realize, running from me doesn't work. I will always find you, Brooke."

She stopped walking and turned back. "I don't even know what that means, Cole," she admitted as angry sparks lit up her blue eyes like lightning. "I'm a socially awkward girl from a religious cult out in the sticks. You are … well, you." Her tone turned shrill with desperation. "I really wish you would stop toying with me. For God's sake, I'm nearly eight months pregnant; you couldn't possibly want me now." Sparks were shooting at him as she declared her final statement.

Cole shrugged. "And I'm just an over-analytical, socially awkward guy from the sticks. I don't see how any of that makes you any less you." He held her gaze and with dead seriousness said slowly and distinctly, "As for the pregnancy, I've discovered that I don't have a problem with it." He shrugged. "If I'm honest, I thought I would have an issue with it, but I got here and was pleasantly surprised to find that I don't. Also, Brooke?"

He waited for her to have the courage to meet his gaze again. "I'm not playing with you," he said softly, and Brooke could see the sincerity in his eyes.

She nodded then and used the last excuse she could think of. "You will be going back home soon and I will still be here dealing with whatever is left from all of this. I don't need another disaster in my life to deal with in the aftermath of your visit."

He didn't smile. Just stared at her with a coolly blank expression and those mysterious dark eyes. "You are coming home with me, so there will be nothing here to deal with and this…." He raised a hand to encompass the space between them. "Is shaping up to be anything but a disaster." His jaw hardened and a stubborn glint in his eye told her it would do no good to argue with him.

She turned on her heel and hurried into her room closing the door solidly behind her. Damn him, she thought in desperate frustration as she went to her closet to get ready for bed. She looked through her pajamas searching for some that fit and weren't the least bit sexy or suggestive. She pulled out a pair of gray satin pajamas that had a lace trimmed top with spaghetti straps and a pair of knee length shorts that had the same lace trim around the bottom. With an irritated huff she dressed and then marched out and into the bathroom where she brushed her teeth. She rinsed her mouth and turned to see him leaning casually against the door frame. She glared at him through her lashes.

He grinned. "I need to brush my teeth too," he justified in a sensible voice.

She marched past him without a word. He heard the bedroom door slam closed and watched the closed door with speculation. He didn't know why she kept trying to run away from him but he intended to find out. A small grin turned up one side of his mouth. He was going to have to get her to come to him because damned if he was going to watch her get all scared of him only to run away again.

When she came to him this time, she was going to be begging and mindless with need so that the fear she'd felt was a distant memory. He smiled the smile of a hungry wolf as he brushed his teeth and then because he knew she was listening he left the door wide open and stripped completely naked before stepping into the steaming hot shower.

At dinner he had realized that she was every bit as attracted to him as he had always been to her. It was a raw animalistic need that drove him now needing to be ever closer to her. He had seen that same raw hunger in her sapphire gaze at dinner tonight and he had gone from soft to rock hard in an instant.

Brooke rolled her head into her pillow and gritted her teeth with a groan as she heard him turn on the shower. It was too loud and suspiciously she rose to tiptoe silently across the floor. She opened the door only the tiniest crack and could see that the bathroom door was definitely opened wide. She closed it quietly and laid her hot cheek against it as she breathed in deeply. Unable to help herself, she opened the door again and widened the crack. She could see the mirror from this angle and the clear plastic shower curtain did little to hide his sleekly muscled physique. She groaned inwardly in self-disgust and followed the curve of his body down to the V between his legs where he had dark curls.

Transfixed she watched as he seemed to lengthen and harden at once. Heat surged and she moved her gaze up to study his lean muscled stomach and then she followed that dark line of hair up to his thickly muscled chest with a light sprinkle of dark hair across the muscle. She felt wet heat between her legs and clamped them together. She followed his shoulders and arms up to his neck and froze. He met her gaze through the steam in the mirror and smiled.

Brooke slammed the door closed and hurried back to her bed. She was hot and uncomfortable and something not unlike an itch deep inside kept her from relaxing. She heard the shower turn off and pictured him toweling crystalline drops of water off all that sleek hard ridged muscle. Her mouth went dry and she realized in frustration that she had forgotten to bring a water bottle to bed in her haste to get away from Cole.

She groaned miserably. The more she thought about the water now, the thirstier she felt. She heard him in the hallway outside her bedroom door. She listened tensely as he walked up and rapped his knuckles lightly against her door. She waited mutely for him to go away.

"Brooke, are you okay? I heard you from the other room. You're not in any pain, are you?" His voice was warm and husky and she shivered.

"I'm fine, I just forgot to get some water," she snapped.

To her relief his footsteps faded but then he returned a minute later. He knocked again. "I grabbed you a bottle. Can I come in?" he asked quietly.

Brooke's heart thundered in her ears, but she gulped and said, "Yes, that's fine." She pulled the black and white floral coverlet to her chin as he walked in. He was wearing a black tank again that conformed to his chest with black boxer briefs. She trained her gaze somewhere over his shoulder as he held out a water bottle that dripped with condensation from the warm air. She let one arm slide from beneath the blanket to grasp it from him. "Thanks," she mumbled and wished he would go away now.

He stood there for a long moment, his face in the shadows. As though he were reading her guilty ashamed mind, in a low sultry voice he said, "It's okay to be curious, Brooke. I'm very curious about your body as well." He didn't press her but turned then to go. "I just wanted you to know that I really liked knowing that you wanted to look at me. In truth I would like to do a lot more than look at you, but I won't push you," he admitted quietly and with unusual sincerity. Then he turned and stalked determinedly out, closing the door behind him.

Brooke gulped water down her dry thirsty throat. She felt like her senses had been attacked and she felt jittery as well as on edge. She tried to quiet her mind and force sleep to come. She kept thinking about his body and she wanted to touch that wondrous body. Wanted to trail her fingertips across that body. Dangerously, she wondered what it would feel like to run her tongue across those hard etched abs. Her throat went dry again and she gulped some more water.

Cole had made it abundantly clear that he still wanted her, pregnant or not. As she lay there in the dark, fear would seep in and then dissipate again as she thought of all the wondrous places she'd like to touch on his body. Then heat would surge. She lay in agonized torture as she tried without success to settle herself down.

It was the realization that she was going to be having a baby and would soon be busy changing diapers and soothing a crying baby and not having time for much else for the next several years that had her reconsidering her choice. Would it really be so wrong to take this one thing for herself? She groaned at her own weakness. It might break her heart once he left, but she suspected that was already going to happen either way.

With sudden clarity that scared the hell out of her, she knew with surprising certainty that she already loved him. Had loved him for a while now. She loved that he was his own man but could also be a thoughtful gentleman. She loved the intensity that he had when facing anything in his life that mattered to him. She groaned again, but this time it was because she knew she was going to give in and it pissed her off.

She was going to let him make love to her and then when he was gone, she would face the excruciating loss and she would get through it. Mind made up now, she slid from under the covers and walked slowly to the door. She opened it and paused to take a deep breath for courage. Then she walked into the lamp-lit living room. He sat there on her couch waiting. She gave him a shaky smile. He watched her and waited patiently for her to speak.

Brooke cleared her throat, "I um…." She hesitated and took another deep breath. Her chin raised ever-so-slightly with pride. "I want to do more to you too," she confessed.

Cole gave her an encouraging smile. She looked so brave and proud in that moment that he felt overwhelming pride in her courage. His cock jerked to attention from just looking at the curvy line of her body. Her hair was flowing down her back except for the wild rebellious ones that sprung forward to circle her face.

She was breathtakingly beautiful and he sat still, waiting for her to move. She met his gaze pleadingly, desperately wanting him to say something, anything. He stayed still unwilling to spook her now. He wasn't sure he could take it if she ran away again. He was genuinely amazed he didn't already have a bad case of blue balls.

Brooke stood in front of him awkwardly. She wasn't sure why he wasn't coming to her. Maybe he had changed his mind? She cleared her throat again and licked her dry lips. "I'm sorry, did you change your mind about this?" she asked nervously.

He shook his head as he held her gaze and then put one hand on the couch next to him in invitation. Her gaze darted down and then back up to his. He saw the fear there in her blue eyes along with the desire. He watched patiently. Slowly she dragged her feet toward him and lowered down to the couch.

He smiled then and held out his arm. One moment she was sitting stiffly with her back straight and the next she had flung herself at him clinging to him with her head on his shoulder while trying to find comfort there in his arms. He wrapped his arm around her waist and pulled her close. She smelled of lilacs and clean air and he breathed her scent in.

She lay on his shoulder for a long while as he held her. She didn't cry or say anything just lay there quietly. After a long while, her fear eased away somewhat and she leaned her head back to look up at him. She gave a sexy little laugh. "This must be so weird for you," she said.

He lifted an eyebrow in question.

Brooke looked away. "I just meant that girls are probably usually throwing themselves at you with much more sophistication."

He shrugged. "I like simple."

She smiled at that and somehow felt oddly at ease. "Me too," she agreed. "I hate it when people run around saying a bunch of stuff they don't mean while hoping everyone will somehow figure out what they really mean on their own. It seems like such a waste of good time."

He laughed in pleasure. His head tilted back and she could see the rise and fall of his sculpted shoulders. She lifted a hand there to trace that wide defined muscle, intrigued by the way it rolled. "You are truly beautiful you know, Cole," she said in honest admiration.

His eyes darkened and she felt his arm tighten instinctively. Fear surged momentarily before he relaxed his hold again. He saw it, felt it, wanted it gone. He met her gaze. "Please kiss me, Brooke." Her eyes widened at that request.

She didn't know how to kiss someone. Panic raised its ugly head, but she fought it off. She knew that he was aware of it by the careful way he gentled his hold and waited patiently. She tried to kiss him but felt overwhelmed and instead she leaned down and kissed his shoulder. The tight muscle there rubbed her lips pleasantly and she took a little exploring nibble.

He tensed but when she would have pulled back to see if he was okay, his free hand cupped the back of her head lightly and held it there. She took that as a sign that he liked it and nibbled her way up his neck. His whiskers rubbed seductively against her own sensitive neck and she gave an excited little moan. She kissed her way up his jaw and then nibbled at the corner of his mouth.

He swore savagely and wrapped his long fingers around the back of her neck and took her mouth hungrily with his own. He kissed her softly at first and then gradually added pressure as his tongue made a fiery foray into her own open lips. She moaned and rubbed her body against him. He started to lose focus, felt her tense in fear, relaxed his hold. She rubbed against him again as her own tongue touched his once quickly and then again as she leaned into him as though trying to absorb him into herself while her tongue rubbed suggestively against his own.

He wanted to lift her to his lap against him but remembered her fear. Feeling like he might die in the process, he settled his arms loosely around her as he let her lead them where she wanted to go. She kissed her way down his shoulder and tried to lift his shirt to kiss beneath. He helped her out by yanking the thing over his head and tossing it. She might have been nervous about that if she hadn't been so fascinated with the lines and grooves she saw there.

She trailed kisses across and then gave a tiny bite at his nipple. He groaned low and stiffened beneath her. That gave her courage and she started scraping her teeth against his skin in gentle little nibbles. She leaned back to look at his shuttered expression. His eyes were completely black now as he watched her. She put her hand on the side of his face, held it there for a long moment before running it down his neck. Her other hand came up to help with her exploration and she ran them both down his chest and across his stomach. His stomach clenched and he shook a little causing her to smile. She was getting hotter as she felt turned on by the way he was reacting to her touch.

She ran her hands daringly low molding a path down the sides of his V-shaped pelvis. She could feel him there hard against her arm and she rubbed it against him briefly as her hands began the long trail back up. His body jerked hard against her and she felt a surge of power as a little thrill ran down her spine.

Because of Richard she had thought of that very masculine part of a man as scary and vicious, but in this moment, she reveled in the knowledge that it could also be something erotic and tender that brought as much joy and pleasure as it could bring pain and shame.

Tentatively she touched a finger to the cotton covered tip. It surged up against her hand and she heard Cole swear under his breath. She pulled back uncertainly. "I'm sorry, does that bother you?" she asked innocently.

Cole tried to smile to reassure her, but it looked more like a grimace. She was driving him fucking mad. For all her fear and nervousness, she was turning out to be quite the bold intuitive lover and he was about to lose his ever-loving mind.

She smiled a little. "I haven't ever done this before, so I'm not sure what men like," she said honestly.

His gaze hardened at her attempt of innocence. "I find that a little hard to believe given that you are quite pregnant," he challenged a little harshly. He regretted it instantly when a look of pain crossed her beautiful face before she could cover it with a smile.

"Oh," she said and seemed at a loss for a moment. "I just meant that this is a lot different than anything I've done before."

He watched her with those damnable dark eyes. "Are you trying to say that you didn't derive pleasure from your other sexual experiences?" he asked gently.

A horrified look crossed her face. "God no. I think it's pretty safe to say that I felt no pleasure."

Her answer both mystified and intrigued him. The devil inside him couldn't help but raise his ugly head. "Not ever?"

She looked at his shoulder. "Nope. To be honest there was just the one time and it wasn't the best experience. I don't really like talking about it. I just meant to point out that if there is anything I do that you don't like, I would rather you tell me."

He lifted her chin to meet his gaze. "I can confidently say there isn't anything that you would like doing to me that I won't enjoy." There was primal joy in his male ego at the thought that she had never been pleasured by another man and he looked ever so forward to making her moan with pleasure. If only he could survive that long.

He reached out and looked at her from under his dark lashes as he ran a gentle hand up and down her arm. "Do you like it when I touch you, Brooke?" he asked, but her little shiver of pleasure had already answered his question.

They took turns exploring each other for a while. After a long needy kiss, he put his fingers in all that glorious hair and held her still as he bit his way gently down her neck. She moaned and instinctively rubbed her pelvis against him. He licked each spot tenderly after scraping his teeth there. She was moaning now and rubbing herself against his cock as she settled herself in his lap. He nearly exploded right then.

He lifted her gently off him and stood holding out a hand to her. "Let's take this to the bed before I end up taking you on your very lumpy couch," he suggested with a devilish grin.

Brooke took his hand without hesitation and stood. He kissed her lightly and wrapped his arm around her waist as he whisked her quickly down the hall. He stopped only long enough to turn the lamp on the bedside table on. He wanted, no needed desperately to see her as they made love.

He turned back to her then and ran a hand lightly down her arm. She was staring nervously at the bed. He smiled gently. "We can go as slow as you want to," he told her reassuringly. She looked at him and then ran her gaze down his body and the nervousness vanished.

It didn't take long for her to beg him for more. She was rubbing against him as she ran her hands along his body exploring every detail. He let her lead and only gave in to his own basest desire when she seemed unclear of what she wanted. She lifted her arms urging him without words to remove her top. His hands brushed the sides of her breasts delicately and she moaned and pushed them into him.

They were aching and heavy as his hands cupped them before he rubbed a thumb slowly across her sensitive nipple. She moaned and threw her head back arching into his hands. He watched in reverent wonder at her wild abandon. Her breasts were enlarged and swollen from the pregnancy. When she reached back and undid her own bra so she could feel his bare hands on her skin he came undone. He surged up under her and took one breast into his hot mouth as his thumb and forefinger worked at the other one circling and squeezing it.

He tasted something hot and sweet and suckled at the nectar in crazed hunger. She screamed and straddled him rubbing herself against his aching manhood. He felt the damp heat as she shoved against him and with a low groan gave in to the fire that licked inside. He sucked and licked and then switched to the other side. He ran hungry hands up and down her sides and finally slid them inside her underwear to gently cup her ass. Her belly was round and surprisingly beautiful and he told her so as her ran gentle hands around the mound. There was a pure little life inside that mound and it awed him what a gift a woman's body truly was as it sheltered and protected that life within.

He lifted her hips and then pulled her down to rub against him again. She bucked and nearly came undone in his arms. She held on to his sides and rolled her hips to rub against him again. He was happy to comply. She had her first orgasm before he even got her pants off. He watched through heavy lids as she threw her head back and a high moan erupted while she held on to him as waves of pleasure washed over and through her. He watched her face, arrogantly pleased that he had given her pleasure.

When she finally opened her eyes, he smiled and then proceeded to take her right back up. He kissed her hard always making sure to give her an escape should she choose it. He tugged her pants down while sliding his hands down her thighs. She leaned into his touch hungry for everything he could give her.

She ran impatient hands down his body tugging at his shorts. He hesitated; he wasn't sure how long he could last once he felt her naked skin against him. She tugged at him again and with a groan he helped her pull them off. His breath caught in his throat as her warm hand slid around to gently cup him. She touched him and moved back to watch her hands as she thoroughly explored his most intimate parts.

He couldn't breathe, couldn't stop the low groan that escaped his lips that were pressed tightly together in concentration. She looked at his face and saw the tension there. She hesitated. Then she rubbed her hand tightly against his shaft. His hips jerked up toward her of their own free will and she smiled as power surged through her again. She rubbed him again and again until his hands came down hard over hers and she stilled. He looked at her through half-closed lids. "Hold on, honey. If you do that anymore, I'm going to come right now."

She laughed in pleasure and reached for him again. He rose to his knees and bent to kiss her deeply holding her hands up gently with one of his own. She leaned into him and reached up to wrap her arms around his neck. He ran his hands down her sides and then over the feminine curve of her hips. He cupped her butt and squeezed with his palms as he pulled her pelvis tight against him. She moaned and he ran one hand around to lay still in the soft red curls at her entrance. She bucked against him and he felt the dampness on his fingers. His tongue darted into her mouth as he placed one finger at the entrance and pushed gently inside her.

She moaned and tried to ride his finger. He groaned in pleasure and dipped it deeper. Then, because he couldn't resist, he pulled back from the kiss just long enough to suck the honeysuckle liquid off his finger. Brooke stared at him in surprise and then tasted her own honeysuckle flavor on his lips as he took her mouth again.

She moaned, needing something from him not knowing what it was. She felt empty and needy somewhere deep inside her core and she tried to rub him against that need but he wasn't touching it. She was confused and then a little angry. She pulled back and waited for him to look at her. "Please" was all she said. Somehow, she knew that he could give her what she was looking for.

Cole lay back then, pulling her with him. With exquisite tenderness he lifted her hips and settled her on top of him. The tip of his shaft pushed gently against her core. Her eyes widened in pleasure and she tried to push down hard on him.

He groaned and held her back working himself ever-so-slowly into her tight body. She was hot and wet as her tight body stretched and slowly opened over him. He would have thought she was a virgin if he wasn't literally staring the evidence in the face because she was so exquisitely tight. She was trying to rock hard against him. Needed to fill that empty void inside herself with him.

He sunk all the way into her and with a shudder of pleasure let go of her. She rode him. Instinctively lowering herself over him and then rocking her hips to pull away only to push over him again. She was breathless now as she rubbed her breasts against his arm. He lifted his hands from her hips and gripped them squeezing as she started a slow easy rhythm. He pushed his hips up in a thrust to meet her surge and she moaned in pleasure. Her body sucked tightly at him as he plunged deep and then pulled back out. He felt her muscles begin to spasm around him and he surged into her speeding up the rhythm.

She met him thrust for thrust as her body exploded into an inferno of heat and need. She ground down on top of him until lights exploded behind her eye lids as pleasure blossomed and then spread in colorful waves through her body. She collapsed and stopped moving for a long moment. She opened her eyes to look down at Cole in wonder. His face was taut with need as he stared up at her. She wanted him to need her the way she needed him. She reveled in the beauty of that strong face and body and started moving slowly on him again.

His jaw went taut and he held himself intentionally still. She wanted to give him what he had given her, but he was holding back now, trying not to move and she knew instinctively that he was trying to hold it off for her. "Please," she begged raggedly and through heavy-lidded eyes he met her gaze and knew what she was asking.

He let out a wild growl as his control snapped. He grasped her hips and thrust himself deep again and again. She screamed in surprise as the waves of pleasure took her over that edge yet again. He groaned low in his throat and with one last hard thrust emptied himself in her. He felt her there with him as the waves of pleasure washed over them. She moved against him the slightest movement and he jerked up as his body emptied into her yet again. They lay tangled together for several long minutes before either had the energy to move again.

CHAPTER 31

Brooke woke up in his arms. He had one arm curled gently over her side with his palm resting gently over her stomach. One of his long legs was casually thrown over her knees. The heat from his hot body seeped into her, keeping her warm despite the chill in the air.

She smiled as she thought of the night before. It had been like a dream. The heavy-lidded passion had been overwhelming and yet so gentle and real. She had never dreamed that sex could be like that. She wondered idly if it was always like that or if it was simply because Cole was just that good. Maybe it was even different for her because she loved him.

She yawned and tried unsuccessfully to move without waking him. Her rear end rubbed against him as she tried to wiggle out and she smiled as she felt his length harden and then push against her. He groaned and reached for her hips to still them. "Stop moving unless you are ready for a repeat of last night," he growled in a low drowsy voice.

Brooke giggled. "Do you actually think that is a threat to me?" she asked as she wiggled suggestively and then turned in his arms to face him.

He opened one eye and scowled at her. That made her laugh and run her hand playfully across his long lean torso stopping just shy of his now rock-hard member. With one sleek move, he pounced, turning her onto her bąck, he straddled her hips as he leaned down for a deep kiss. He waited for the fear to come but was pleased when instead she melted into him and then kissed him back.

He growled as she laughed again and then he kissed his way down her neck, across her breasts, until finally making a large kissing circle around the mound of her belly. "You are so damn beautiful," he told her in a slumberous tone as he licked his tongue across her protruding belly button. "I wasn't sure how it would be with you being so very pregnant, but it is beautiful and it seems so natural with you." He seemed a little surprised at his own words.

Brooke smiled at his darkly intrigued gaze. "It is natural" was all she said as he leaned gently down and proceeded to take her back into that cloud of desire and passion that took her breath away.

They lay in bed together working to calm their breathing as they floated back down. When her phone rang, Brooke lifted a limp arm to grab it off the side table next to the bed. Her hand fell short and she groaned. Cole grinned down at her and easily reached it only to set it squarely in her palm. He rolled onto his back and lay his head on his upward stretched arms as she answered the incoming call.

"Hello, Don." She tried for a wakeful cheery tone.

"Hi, Brooke I just wanted to let you know that I approved the time off that you requested. I found people to fill in for you over the next few weeks," her manager said in a cheerful voice.

Brooke lifted the phone and stared dumbly at it for a moment before placing it back on her ear. "Come again? What are you talking about?"

She could hear the smile in his voice as he responded, "The time off you requested. For the record I think it's a great idea to take a few weeks before the baby is born for yourself. Go do something fun. When Gwen and I had our son, we went on one of those little vacations a couple months before. Best decision of our life since it took another three years before we had time to do anything like that." He laughed at his own story. "Anyhow I think it's great. Just give me a call when you get back in town. Oh, and when you have the little guy, let us know." He hung up before she could respond.

Brooke turned to stare suspiciously at Cole who was maintaining a relaxed, casual look. "What did you do, Cole?" she asked a slight bit piqued.

He grinned. "I thought you might need some time off since we're going on a trip today."

Brooke shook her head with her lips pressed tightly together. "I already told you that I can't, Cole. Even if I didn't need the money, which I do by the way, I'm not sure I'm ready to go back yet."

Cole smiled stubbornly. "I'll give you whatever money you need and I will be with you the whole time, so it will all be okay. Besides that, the whole family will be so excited to see you that it won't matter."

She climbed out of the damp sheets. "My car is having problems right now and I don't trust it on a long trip and I really can't afford a new one right now." Brooke was putting her clothes on as she stomped around the room gathering them. In an angry fit, she threw his shirt and boxer briefs at his stubborn grinning face.

He laughed and caught them out of the air before they hit. "I will take a look at your car when we get back but you'll be riding with me, so you won't need it now anyway."

Brooke shot him a hot glare. "You can't just come in here and boss me around and expect me to follow your unreasonable orders." She put her watch on and glanced at it before turning in dismay to grab her phone. "Damn it and now you made me late. I'm supposed to be meeting Janae for breakfast right now." She had dialed and was waiting for her friend to answer as she finished.

Cole was silently watching her with a carefully blank expression.

Janae answered on the third ring. "Hello, Brooke, I'm kind of surprised you're calling me. I thought your young man might be keeping you otherwise occupied today."

Brooke turned to Cole, a look of angry disbelief on her face as she said in a sharper tone than she intended, "Oh did you now?" She calmed herself with a deep breath knowing that it wasn't fair to take it out on her friend. "And what exactly gave you that idea?" she asked. "Because last I knew we had plans to meet for breakfast today. You know to finalize the birth plan?" She tried not to grit her teeth.

Janae laughed quickly. "Oh, I see, so your young man didn't talk to you about it yet, then. He called me yesterday to let me know you were going out of town with him for a bit. I'm sorry I just assumed you had made up with him." Her friend sounded less sorry and more joyful at that prospect. "He is the father, isn't he, Brooke?"

Brooke stared hard at Cole. He lifted his hands with a wide grin in mock surrender. She just shook her head. He hadn't told Janae that he was the father, had he? Quietly she asked, "Did he tell you that as well?"

"Oh no, hon, that was just my own assumption." Janae laughed. "I'm glad he's whisking you off to do something fun before you have all those endless days and nights without sleep. It'll be good for you."

Brooke's shoulders slumped in defeat. She said goodbye to her friend and turned to sit on the end of the bed. Slowly she met his dark gaze with her blue icy one. "Why don't you just go ahead and tell me who else you talked to before I make a bigger fool of myself," she suggested through gritted teeth.

Cole looked serious and then turned an apologetic look on her. "Look," he said, "I knew you were going to fight going back with me and I needed some leverage so you couldn't say no."

Brooke sighed, having a hard time staying mad at him when he obviously felt bad. Curiously she asked, "Why do you even care if I go back anyway? You hardly know me and I'm not sure what you think is going to happen here."

He met her gaze evenly. "I don't know what will happen either." In a low steady tone, he told her, "What I do know is that you have a nasty little habit of running away whenever you get scared and I didn't spend all of this time searching for you just to leave you here so you can run away again."

She stared at him in disbelief. "Why would I run away from here? I bought a house for God's sake. I'm having a baby in a few weeks, and for the last time, I didn't run because I was scared!" She nearly shouted the last at him.

It didn't faze him. He gave her a small smile. "Why did you run, then?"

That surprised her and she had to stop to think about it. "Because I didn't want to take advantage of Ivan and Jacob," she finally said.

He nodded. "And why did you think that you were taking advantage of them?"

She looked exasperated now. "I didn't *think* I was taking advantage of them, you jerk. I *was* taking advantage."

He raised one eyebrow at her.

She gritted her teeth again. "Oh my God, Cole," she ground out. "I grew up on a farm with my family such as it was. My father just always took care of me and I never really had to do anything to take care of myself. When I left home, I knew I would have to find a way to take care of myself. But before I had a chance to get a job, I ran into your dad who, as you know, brought me home for breakfast and then offered me a job. And a house. And friends. And this whole beautiful life that I was doing very little to earn. All because I worked for him.

"Jacob gave constantly to me. He showed up and helped me find my way through all the drama. Even when he went back to California, he called and texted all the time. I called him whenever I needed to talk through something or needed help with anything and he was there for me without ever once complaining.

"When your mom told me that she wouldn't stand for me taking advantage of her family anymore, I realized she was right. I had been feeling guilty from the start. I knew then that I had to leave and let you all get on with your beautiful life without the burden of me in it." She was nearly pleading with him to understand now.

Cole looked deep into her blue eyes and asked softly, "Did you work for your father?"

Brooke shook her head. "No, I didn't. He just took care of all of us. He was always telling me how hard of a time it was to take care of me and all I did was disobey him."

"Did you do work on the farm, though, Brooke?"

She looked exasperated then wondering if he was daft. "Of course, I did. I tried to do my part. Besides that, it was very boring there and I would have gone completely insane if I didn't find stuff to do."

He smiled and she suddenly got the point he was making. "So, you did work for your father then. All that work you did saved him from paying someone else to do it. So, in reality you were always taking care of yourself. In fact, you probably would have had much more had he actually paid you to work for him. The same goes for my dad. You worked as hard as any of the men, harder than most of them.

"My dad and Jacob not only got a lot from you working for us, but they also care about you. The real reason you left was because you were afraid that people didn't think you were valuable enough to keep around, so you left before they had the opportunity to tell you as much," he told her with a knowing smile.

She stared at him a long moment before finally shrugging. "Okay, maybe that's true, but I also didn't want to take advantage of them because I care about them too."

Cole reached out and tucked a curl behind her ear. "I know. I also know that you are such a giving person that you can't help but give more than you get in every situation." He looked down at her belly and ran a long lean finger across the rounded curve. "You are willing to give everything you can for this child inside you." He smiled warmly. "My family cares about you too. And like it or not you became part of our family in the short time you were there. They all deserve for you to care enough to go back and see them." He felt slightly guilty because he knew it was the only way to get what he wanted and he did it anyway. "At the very least they deserve to know that you are okay."

There were tears in her eyes now and his guilt got heavier. He tucked her under his arm and pulled her close to his side. She turned her face up to his. "I never meant to hurt anyone." She looked at him with honesty written across her lightly freckled face. "The only thing I don't understand is why *you* are going to all of this trouble, Cole. You don't even like me." She sounded sad when she admitted it out loud.

He stared into those shimmering sapphire eyes. "I couldn't just let you run away and get the best of me." He gave her honesty when he knew he should have reassured her. He didn't want to lie. Had never liked when people lied to each other.

She smiled at that. "Of course not." And for some inexplicable reason his admission made her feel like everything was going to be okay. He was stubborn and intelligent and always had to feel like he got the upper hand. She knew his number now too if she ever needed it. Her heart ached because she knew she was nothing more than a conquest to his ego. She leaned her head on his shoulder and closed her eyes soaking in the smell and feel of him for soon these memories would be all she had left. No sane man would want to be with her and another man's child.

They took a long hot shower together before she packed a suitcase for the road. He brought in orange juice and a fresh croissant as she finished folding most of her maternity clothes into neat stacks. She emptied the cup and ate the croissant in three bites. He whistled teasingly and walked out only to return a moment later with two more warm crispy croissants, which she happily inhaled.

He loaded their bags into the trunk of his car while she checked the windows and doors to make sure everything was locked up tight before they left. He shot her a cocky little grin as she walked to his car. "Don't worry about the house. I asked your friend Jill to look after it while we're gone. She assured me that she has a key."

Brooke laughed and rolled her eyes. "Of course, you did" was all she said.

CHAPTER 32

From the trees Richard watched the man throw his luggage into his trunk before he and Brooke left for her work the following morning. With a happy smile he watched the car drive away. That would only make his plan easier since he would only have to take one of them on at a time now that he was leaving. He hummed an angelic hymn pleasantly as he hauled the plastic, rope, and tools to the door of her house. Her going to work today just made everything easier as it gave him hours to prepare. He could be inside and surprise her when she got home. He left his supplies on the front porch humming a little off tune as he hurried around to the back and used a flat screwdriver to break in. He closed the back door carefully behind himself and hurried to haul in his supplies.

An hour later he was ready. He had drawn all the curtains in the house for privacy. He would have to remember to open the ones facing the front of the house later before she came home but for now didn't want nosy neighbors seeing him. He checked out every inch of the house. Memorized the details of the space so he would know it, should it become necessary.

With a happy little grin, he used her restroom and then went in search of some lunch. He found a coffee pot and in disgust threw the entire machine in the garbage can. Coffee was a sign of the wicked after all. He didn't even stop to think of how many cups he drank on a daily basis. After all he'd never bought a coffee pot himself only drank coffee from those who were heathens already.

A quick search of the fridge revealed some leftover chicken and pasta so he re-heated it as anger surged. She had probably made this for that bastard. She was no better than a whore at this point. She had been given to him by God and yet she had cavorted with some man other than himself. He licked his lips as he ate, thinking of all the ways he would teach her that she was his and his alone.

After his meal was over, he walked through the house again still thinking of his glorious plans. Intrigue settled and he walked into the nursery looking at and touching things as he moved about the room. Brooke had obviously put a lot of hard work in this room so sadness and anger warred within him. She could have done this for his child. A tear formed once again and he brushed it away impatiently. The walls were painted a warm shade of yellow with blue and green stripes down the wall that the crib was against.

He ran a hand across the top of the railing of the crib. He stared, almost entranced at the enlarged photo canvas of Brooke. She had hung it there where the baby could see her face from the crib. So thoughtful of her, he mused as he studied her slender face with high proud cheekbones. Enlarged this way, he could see the tiny sprinkle of delicate freckles over her nose. Her brilliant blue eyes stared back at him sparkling with joy and innocence. He ran one finger down her cheek and remembered that night months ago. He had held her and touched her lovingly before he had made her his own in every sense of the word.

He felt the crazed surge of lust against his pants and unzipped them reveling in the joy that was his love for her. There was a small soft blue blanket hanging on the side of the crib and with a laugh he rubbed its softness against himself. His member jerked. How fitting it was that her dirty little deeds with that bastard were bringing *him* joy even now. He stared into that beautiful face and allowed himself the release he had so long been waiting for.

For hours more he wandered the house. Idly looking through all her things. Touching, smelling, and even tasting some as though the scent and taste of her had somehow become attached to the objects. Then he did smell her on the pillows. He breathed it in and rubbed his face into its softness. Another scent filtered through and he turned away in agonized horror. He pulled the blankets and the sheets back. Richard could smell the aftereffects of her sins and whatever hope he'd had that he was wrong about her lost soul washed away to be replaced by only his anger and full conviction in what he had to do.

Five o'clock came and went with no sign of either of them. He watched the clock now sitting there in her kitchen. He had opened the curtains back up and sat there in the afternoon light waiting patiently. Maybe she had taken a later shift. He sighed and picked up his phone. He looked up the number for the café and dialed. When the perky woman answered he politely asked how late Brooke was scheduled to work. With a little laugh the woman helpfully informed him that Brooke was on vacation and wouldn't be back for a while.

He barely managed to click the phone off before he howled in frustration. A sudden image of the way the dark-haired man had held her arm as he helped her into his fancy little sports car flashed in his memory. They had been leaving together and now he was going to have to find them again. He tipped his head back and howled again in frustration before he began gathering his things. He couldn't leave them here in case they beat him back. He didn't want anyone to know his plan until it was too late.

After he loaded everything into the back seat of his truck once again, he reached for his phone. The first call he made was to the private detective who he told what little he knew. Then he hung up and called her brother. "Hello, Isaiah."

Brooke's brother hesitated for only an instant before responding. "Richard, my father isn't very happy with you and wouldn't want me to be talking to you right now. You didn't exactly keep your word to him."

Richard sighed and gave a quick little laugh. "That's why I'm calling you instead," he cajoled. "I was wondering if you or any of your siblings have heard from Brooke."

"Mom mentioned that she called a while back. Did you know she's pregnant?" he asked in a low judging voice.

Richard could barely contain his impatience with the imbecile. "Of course, I know." He forced a smile into his voice. "I've been with her up here in Montana, but she just took off and I can't seem to find her. Just tell the guys that if anyone hears anything they should give me a call."

Isaiah guffawed dramatically on the other end of the line. "And why would we do that?" he challenged with a disrespectful slur.

Richard clenched his jaw and then relaxed it. "Because, jackoff, anyone who does will get a pretty chunk from me."

There was silence for a long moment before Isaiah talked again, but this time he was much more reserved. "Okay, I'll mention it to them. Good luck finding my sister. She can be a real bitch, you know, so watch out. Seriously, though, Richard, I don't even know why you want her back anyway. She has always had a tendency to stray from God's path for her."

Richard didn't respond to that, though he finally understood the full truth of that statement. He clicked off and started his truck. He knew the guy Brooke was with was either one of the Burtons or someone who worked for them since he had seen him around a few times when he'd first found her there. They could be headed anywhere, but he figured he might as well start driving that way until he heard something different.

Jacob was pacing the length of the pool table as he waited for his dad to finish taking his turn. They hadn't heard from Cole since the day before and he wanted more than anything to know where he and Brooke were, but Cole wasn't answering his calls again. He heard his father clear his voice and turned to look at him.

Ivan watched his son as he stopped to look back at him. He sighed and set down the pool stick. Jacob, it seemed was too preoccupied to appreciate the skillful way he had just pocketed the yellow and purple balls both in one hit. "Are you okay, son?" he asked as he reached for his glass of scotch and took a drink.

Jacob stared right through him. "Yeah, I'm good. Just wondering where Brooke is and wanting to wring Cole's neck for not answering my calls."

Ivan hid a smile. "Can you really blame him, Jacob? Since we started this game, you've tried calling him at least four times. Maybe they're busy. You know your brother; he can be a little stubborn, but he'll let you know when he has any prudent information."

Jacob grabbed the beer he'd set down and took a long drink in exasperation. "I know, it just feels like Cole doesn't want to tell me what's going on." He met his father's concerned gaze. "I really miss her, you know?" He lifted one arm and rolled his shoulder back. "I know I said before that she wasn't the one for me, but I just don't know." He looked down at the floor in consternation. "Lately, I just haven't had any interest in other women," he admitted. "I go out with them and they're beautiful and everything that I used to love about them, but there's no spark for me." He met his father's knowing gaze again.

Ivan smiled. "It sounds to me like you're thinking of settling down."

Jacob shook his head. "Not really, I guess it's just that me and Brooke have a deeper connection than I've had with any other friends and we spent a lot of time talking about things that really matter to us and to the world. Now it just seems like everyone I meet is shallow and self-centered. To be honest, I have been wondering if I should ask Brooke to marry me after all." He quickly raised a hand to stop his dad from speaking. "I know we don't have that physical spark, but we're so good for each other in other ways and she is going to have a kid now. That is a lot for anyone to handle and she is still so young. I could help her raise the baby and take care of it."

Ivan couldn't stop the grin this time. "Don't you think Cole might have something to say about that?"

Jacob stopped pacing and looked at his father. "I know that he has a physical thing for her, but you know Cole. He never really takes the time to create anything deeper. He's always too busy with whatever he has going on. This fascination will pass and then Brooke will be on her own trying to handle life by herself again. Maybe it will be different now between us. I do know that I have missed the hell out of her and I'm sure she has as well." He sounded hopeful at that suggestion.

"Maybe" was all Ivan said as he walked around and put a hand on his son's shoulder. Wisely he kept his opinions to himself.

They were still standing there with drinks in hand when Jacob's phone rang. He reached automatically for it and looked down. He stilled and then met Ivan's curious gaze. "It's that same Montana number," he murmured with furrowed brows as he lifted it to his ear. "Hello?"

A wide grin broke over his ruggedly handsome face as Brooke said quietly, "Hello, Bestie."

He threw a wide smile at Ivan and set his beer back down as he casually stepped toward the pool table. "Hello, beautiful."

There was a short pause before Brooke spoke again and he could hear both uncertainty and emotion choking her voice. "My God, I missed you."

Jacob chuckled. "Tell me about it. I was just talking about how much to my dad."

"I'm coming home," she said hesitantly.

Jacob's smile widened. "Thank God. I was wondering how long you were planning to torture yourself before you finally got your head back on straight and realized we all need you as much as you need us."

Brooke swallowed and took a deep breath. "I can't stay long, Jacob. I'm just coming for a visit. I have responsibilities that I have to get back for."

Jacob didn't hesitate. "We'll get it all figured out. When wiil you be here?"

He could hear Cole's low voice in the background as Brooke relayed the question back to him. She came back on. "I guess it will be a couple of days. Cole doesn't want to push too hard."

"Where are you coming from?" he asked, wanting to look at the map.

She sighed. "Northern Montana, but it's a long story that I would rather tell you in person."

He nodded and agreed. "A couple of days, then. I'll see you then."

He hung up the phone and relayed the conversation to Ivan who listened with a smile. He had already heard it all, but Jacob looked like he really needed to talk it through. He smiled as he thought about Brooke. He threw back his scotch in celebration. His daughter was finally coming home.

CHAPTER 33

Brooke's nerves settled in as they passed the Idaho state line. She went quiet and didn't speak for a long time. Cole drove calmly, shifting down a gear as the falling snow began sticking to the blacktop. He slowed down again as the large flakes fluttered past the windshield making it harder to see. He glanced over at Brooke who hadn't spoken for a long while. "You okay?" he asked as he turned on the wipers.

She nodded her head and then realized he couldn't see her. "I'm fine," she mumbled morosely.

He looked at her then. No woman had ever told him they were fine and meant it. In his limited experience, a woman saying she was fine was the first sign that she was anything but. He turned his eyes back to the road. "Is the storm worrying you?" he asked carefully. He'd also learned that women didn't like it when challenged about being fine.

Brooke stared out the window at the flakes flying by. She hadn't really even noticed the storm until he'd mentioned it. She smiled. "No, I hadn't really thought about that. It's just being back in Idaho. I'm not sure that coming with you was the best thing to do," she admitted quietly.

She felt his warm gaze on her before he replied confidently. "It was the only thing to do." His steely tone brooked no argument.

She stared at the falling flakes of white as they floated past in a gust of wind. "I didn't have to give in to you, you know." She needed him to understand that she was her own person and hadn't just given in to him because he'd strong-armed her. "I thought it all through before I made the decision," she told him with a little smile. "Truth is that I have wanted Jacob and your dad involved in the baby's life since I found out I was pregnant. Then I found out it was a boy and he is going to need some good role models." She rubbed a loving hand over her precious mound.

Cole was frowning as she finished. She wasn't sure why he was upset and wasn't sure if she wanted to know. He stared fixedly at the road with his jaw tight. "I'm sure you would have done well either way," was all he said, though she sensed he'd wanted to say more.

She shrugged. "I know that, otherwise I would have come back before. I would have done whatever he needed." She patted her belly and the bug kicked. "Ultimately, I came because I really miss everyone."

He didn't say anything for a long while. He was considering suggesting they stop for another night and let the storm pass. The old classic was great for a lot of reasons but not so great in the snow. He didn't want to take any chances with their safety. Beyond that he wasn't ready to share her with his family yet.

The snow started to slow and he saw the road was looking better, taking away his perfectly good excuse. Still, it might be better for him if they had one more night together before they got back to the farm. The last few nights had been warm and passion filled. It seemed that once he had let himself touch her, he couldn't keep his hands off of her curvy body. Since she hadn't turned him away since that first slap, he figured she must not mind so much. His body tightened in anticipation and he groaned inwardly. He felt like a damn teenager that couldn't focus on anything but sex. She did something to him that he wasn't sure he altogether liked.

He'd had a lot of time to think on the drive back. Since his focus wasn't on finding her the way it had been on the way up here, he found his mind sifting through the recent events. He thought of all the projects he had that he could have done. Over the last several months he had simply put them all on hold while he searched for her. He had never been one to put anything before his work.

Sure, he'd had his fun, gone to parties, and spent time with his family and such, but never just put it all on hold. Something about the way he had been able to put it all out of his focus for her bothered him. Hell, she bothered him. For the life of him he couldn't figure out why he had done it. He didn't need the hassle or headache of trying to help her or make her life better. That was Jacob and his dad's area of expertise. He had never been one to try and help the lost.

Let them spend the time and energy on trying to save her. He had a plan for his life. Had been working steadily on that plan since his fourteenth birthday. Now here was this young woman that had turned everything upside down for him. He glanced over at her perfect profile. It was about the sex. It had to be, because he honestly couldn't imagine what else it could be.

He grinned. He'd had his fair share of sex these past few days so it ought to be out of his system. Problem solved—as soon they got home, he was going to turn her over to Jacob and he was going to go back to his plan. Let Jacob deal with the emotional fallout. Mind settled once again he turned and lifted the lukewarm coffee to his lips.

Brooke turned her attention to the phone in her lap typing rapidly. He watched her for a long while before his curiosity got the best of him. "What are you doing?" he asked, sounding grumpy.

Her eyes shot to his, surprised by his sudden mood shift. "I'm just trying to find a decent hotel room that isn't too overpriced."

"You don't need a hotel, Brooke." He sounded obstinate.

She met his stubborn look with one of her own. "Of course, I do," she insisted. "I wouldn't dream of putting your family out and I'm no longer working for your dad, so I assume he rented out the old house by now."

He groaned. "Can't you just make things easy for once?" he sounded surly.

Brooke gave him a sincerely innocent frown. "I don't know what you're talking about. I'm about as easy as they come."

He laughed rudely. "Oh yeah sure. Easy peasy but not so breezy Brooke."

She didn't like his tone or his attitude and didn't hesitate to let him know it. "What has gotten you in such a bad mood anyway?" She watched his carefully bland face.

He grunted under his breath. She couldn't hear what he said. "Sorry, what was that?" she asked.

Cole met her gaze for just a second before he looked back at the mostly clear road. "Nothing I'm in a perfectly good mood."

She laughed at that. He scowled. She laughed harder. "Okay. Well, I was thinking if I have you drop me off at the hotel room tonight, I'll rent a car tomorrow and drive out to see everyone after."

His hands tightened on the steering wheel in an aggravated grip. "You are not staying at a hotel." His tone was clipped. "No one is living in your place and Jacob would have my throat if I even thought of letting you get a hotel. Besides Mom and Dad have already planned a little dinner party for tonight, so I can't take you into town."

Brooke stared mutely out the window. "Why haven't you rented out the house?" she asked curiously trying to change the subject.

Cole looked sideways at her. She still didn't know the house was hers and he wasn't about to be the one to break that news to her. He shrugged. "It isn't mine to rent. As for Dad, it seems like your place now and I think Dad kept it empty in case you came back."

She looked alarmed at that revelation. "Oh no! That means I owe him even more. I had hoped he would rent it right out and get a little extra money for it now that it's fixed up."

He grinned in helpless disbelief. "Of course, you would go there. Someone tries doing you a solid so you hurry to figure out all the ways you must pay them back. By the way, that old place hadn't been rented out for a year or more before you moved in there, so I'm sure it's not just about you."

"Well, I don't have bedding and all that stuff there anymore, so I'm not sure that would even work," she said quietly.

He gave her another sideways look. "Jacob said everything is good to go, so I guess you're running out of excuses."

Brooke rolled her eyes and sighed heavily. "Fine. I'll just have to figure out how to pay you guys back for that too."

"Good God. It's never easy with you, is it?" He sounded tired and exasperated. He grinned suddenly; he could think of a few choice ways she could pay him back, but he was far too much of a gentleman to suggest them.

Brooke felt a little guilty and she turned and touched his arm. "I'm sorry. I guess I don't sound very grateful, do I? I just always imagined that if I ever came back, it would be with more to offer. I really am grateful. It will save me a lot of money that I really do need for him." She pointed at her belly.

Cole smiled. "If you had any idea what a favor it is to let Jacob and Dad pamper you, I think you would be asking for their thanks. The two of them can't help themselves from wanting to save you like you're some kind of damsel in distress. I think it makes them feel manly or something," he joked, trying to ease the tension from her stance.

Brooke looked at him with a little look of doubt furrowing her brow. "And you, of course, are above such things?" she teased. She wasn't sure she liked the idea of them thinking of her that way.

He only nodded. "Of course. I'm the last guy to try to save anyone." His lips stretched into a sexy little grin. "I guess it takes a little more than my black heart to want to be the hero."

"Uh-huh" was all Brooke said. She thought of how much time he'd spent looking for her. Thought of the many days of searching down leads. She hadn't fooled herself into believing he cared about her. But he had still done it and she suspected after everything he'd said he had wanted to find her for Jacob and his dad. That was still him being a hero; she just wasn't the target of said heroism.

Cole wondered what she was thinking as she smiled to herself but didn't ask. Now that he had made up his mind, he didn't intend to spend much time with her once they got home and it seemed like a bad idea to get any more involved in all of this. Instead, he reached out a hand to scroll for a local radio station. They were getting close enough to home now to be in range of the familiar oldies country radio.

The next hour and a half went by in a blur. Brooke had fallen asleep with her head against the headrest and he reached over and gently touched her shoulder. She didn't wake up right away, so he took advantage since this would be the last time and studied her face for a long minute. Then he leaned across and kissed her—*a goodbye kiss*, he told himself as he tasted her intoxicatingly sweet mouth. She responded by leaning into the kiss as she stirred from sleep. He pulled back then as she stared sleepily up at him. "We're home," he said quietly. He climbed out and walked around to open her door for her. The front door opened and he turned his cool dark eyes to meet the cold angry green ones of his brother.

"Hello, Brooke, Cole," Jacob said as he quickly strode down the stairs and rushed to Brooke's side. He took a long moment to look her up and down. "Damn you look so good, sweetheart. Pregnancy sure does agree with you." He smiled widely and swooped her into his arms for a tight hug. Cole watched them coldly before turning on his heel to walk away.

CHAPTER 34

Ivan walked into the long foyer as they came in. He looked at Brooke with a wide excited grin. "It's good to see you, dear," he said as he stepped toward her. She took two steps and then hesitated, looking uncomfortable. He took the last few steps and wrapped his arms around her in a warm bear hug.

Brooke reacted by holding on to him with her eyes closed. "It's good to see you, sir, uh Ivan," she mumbled as he set her back to get a good look at her.

"You are quite far along now, aren't you?" He smiled and set a gentle hand on her stomach. The baby chose that moment to kick and he laughed in joy. "I don't think I could ever get sick of that," he admitted with a shake of his head as he turned. Brooke saw Anne step into the room and met her steady green gaze with her own uneasy one. She gave her a friendly nod.

Anne stepped forward and to Brooke's surprise gave her a warm hug. "Hello, Brooke, it's so good to have you back here with us." She looked down at Brooke's belly and asked. "How are you feeling?"

Brooke smiled, a little shyly at first. "I'm really good. We both are," she answered with a pat to include her son. Anne was still looking at her expectantly so she stammered on. "I'm not sure the doctor would approve of this visit so close to my due date, but I plan to be back well in time for the delivery, so I'm sure it will all work out fine."

Ivan frowned at that. "You aren't planning to stay, then?"

Brooke shook her head. "Oh no, I really couldn't." She glanced around. "I don't have a job or anything here and I wouldn't put you all out again. In fact, I tried to get a hotel room booked for the next couple days, but Cole wouldn't give me a ride. Maybe one of you would be willing?"

She stopped talking as all three heads shook in unison.

Jacob took her hand and squeezed it. "There is no way I'm letting you stay in a hotel," he declared quickly. "Now, if you're more comfortable with it you can stay at the old house, but I … *we*, would be thrilled if you stayed here at the house with us."

Brooke glanced around and shook her head. "I couldn't stay here. I really don't want to put anyone out."

Anne smiled. "It's settled, then. You can stay at your house but you will be coming over here to have meals with us." She sounded like her mind was set, so Brooke didn't dare argue. She nodded her agreement.

She turned to Ivan and Jacob and after a deep breath stammered. "I'm so sorry for leaving without any notice before. I just felt like I needed to go take care of myself and my baby. I knew you both would try talking me out of it and I cared so much that I wouldn't have wanted to let you down. I'm am sorry, though, if either of you felt that I didn't care about you."

"Oh now, it's just fine, dear. I didn't have any doubt that you did what you thought was best for everyone." His dark eyes met Anne's for a minute before he continued. "I did miss you around here, though. I still haven't been able to find anyone to replace you." He grinned.

Jacob put a friendly arm over her shoulder and tucked her close. "I never doubted our friendship for a minute, Brookie. I did, however wish you would have given me a chance to help you out." He chucked her gently under the chin. "I could have gone with you and helped you get settled or something." He gave her a severe frown.

Brooke smiled and shook her head. "See? That is exactly why I couldn't tell you I was leaving. I knew you would try to jump in and take care of me." In a quietly serious tone, she informed them, "It was something I had to do by myself. I guess I just needed to know that I could do it, you know?"

Ivan nodded in understanding. "I do know what you mean but just so *you* know," he started and put extra emphasis on the you. "You are family and we care about you, so you don't have to do it alone."

Anne nodded. "Exactly," she agreed.

"Brooke, I don't know how you don't understand by now that we love you and it's not a burden because you're an amazing person who gives us so much more than you need to," Jacob explained in a rare serious tone. He waited until she met his warm gaze. "I have missed having you around here more than you can know."

Brooke smiled a little self-consciously at her friends. "Well, thank you all." She met Anne's intelligent green eyes. "I also wanted to apologize to you, Anne. I know that you felt like I might be taking advantage of your family and I want you to know that I love them and I wouldn't ever want to do anything that doesn't work for all of you. If you ever feel like there's anything that way again, please talk to me," she pleaded in a sincere honest voice.

Anne's eyes filled with tears and she stepped forward to take Brooke's hand. "You have nothing to apologize for, Brooke. Those things I said were coming from a place of worry for my family. A mama bear's protective nature I suppose." She smiled at her own weakness. "I have since realized just how much you did for all of us and I think it's high time I thank you."

Brooke stared uncomfortably at the older woman. "Thank me for what?"

Anne gave a little laugh. "I think your response to what I just said proves my point exactly. You worked hard and earned every dollar you were paid. On top of that, Ivan informed me that you always insisted on paying rent and I saw all the repairs you did to the old house." She paused for a breath. "I think we would have paid several thousand dollars to have all that work done. And yet here you are wondering what I have to thank you for." She smiled at the irony.

Brooke felt heat rising to her cheeks and tried to push it back down. "All that stuff was for my pleasure. You guys took me right in and gave me a home and a great job and I just wanted to try to make it worth it for all of you."

Ivan and Anne exchanged a long look. Then Ivan turned and looked around the room. "Speaking of all of us, were is Cole?" he asked.

Brooke shrugged. "He walked away as soon as we got here. He probably has things he needs to do after taking all that time looking for me and twisting my arm to get me here."

Ivan and Anne exchanged worried looks that Brooke couldn't define. Worry seeped in and she stepped closer. "Is everything okay with, Cole?" she asked. "Is there something going on with him that I don't know?"

Anne and Ivan both raised hands to soothe her, but it was Ivan that spoke. "No, at least not that I'm aware of either. He's just been a bit…" He paused to think about what he was saying. "…offish as of late," he finished.

Jacob chuckled. "That's putting it a bit mildly. He's been a grumpy, grouchy, absentee lone wolf ever since you left."

Brooke didn't know what to think of that. She smiled at her friends. "I'm sure he just has a lot on his mind with school and everything he has going on. While this virus hasn't made much difference in the small town I live in, I've heard it's caused a lot of havoc other places around the world. What with schools going online and all the extra work around here, he's probably just stressed out." She wasn't even aware of how much she gave away by standing up for him. All three of them looked at each other and then back at her with smiles.

"I'm sure," Jacob agreed, though his tone suggested anything but.

Heavy footsteps came tearing down the hallway and everyone turned as Ryker burst into the room "Is it true?" he asked excitedly and then came to a quick halt as he saw Brooke standing there. He looked at her face and then stared at her belly for a long while.

It was Brooke who stepped forward. "Hello, Ryker." She smiled and held her arms up for a hug. Ryker flew into them.

"You are here," he exclaimed as he hugged her tightly.

Dominic who had been racing Ryker, ran straight into both of them. Brooke stumbled back a little under the pressure and Cole appeared from nowhere reaching out to steady her with hands on her shoulders.

Ryker laughed as he held on to her so he wouldn't fall over. "What is that jiggly feeling that's tickling my face?" he asked as he stepped back and rubbed his cheek.

Everyone laughed except Cole who just gave a half smile. Brooke leaned down to Ryker's ear to whisper, "That was my baby saying hello."

His eyes grew big. "Is that why you're so fat?" he asked.

Another round of chuckles went through the room. Cole was the one who answered his youngest brother. "It is why she has a round belly, but I'mma do you a favor, little brother. I don't recommend you ever tell any woman that she is fat. For some unknown reason that us men don't really understand, it makes them upset." He winked at Ryker.

Ryker grinned and nodded. He turned back to Brooke. "So, is that why you have such a round belly, Brooke?"

She laughed and nodded as she stepped forward to hug Dom who had been standing awkwardly to the side since he had bumped into them. "Hello, Dom. I have sure missed you." She kissed his cheek.

He turned red and then hugged her back. "I'm sorry I ran into you," he muttered quietly. He sent an accusing look in Ryker's direction. "Ryker started running way before he said we were racing, so I was trying to catch up." He turned to Ryker. "I would have beaten you too if you had played fair."

Ryker just shook his head. "Nope. I said, race ya, right when I started running so it was a fair race, Dom, and I beat ya."

Anne rolled her eyes and the men held back grins.

Anne walked to Cole then. "It's good to have you home, Cole," she said as she wrapped him in a hug. Cole excepted hugs from his family before he made up an excuse about work and left.

Ryker and Dominic plodded Brooke with endless questions in between arguing with each other. Finally, Anne stepped in. "Boys, let's give Brooke some room to breathe. Why don't we all move into the front room where it's more comfortable and I'll go get some drinks. Does anyone want some fresh lemonade?" she asked and the boys raced to answer her first. Brooke offered to help but Anne refused and told her to sit down and rest.

Resting was all she had done since she left her home in Montana, so she wanted to argue. She didn't, however, because she also wanted to visit with Jacob and Ivan.

She told them all about her job and her friends. After a while she explained how she had applied for a loan even though she didn't think she could get it; the bank had surprised her by accepting her application and now she was buying a house. She didn't miss the exchanged look between Anne and Ivan but didn't want to be rude and ask them about it.

Jacob sat next to her with his arm slung over her shoulder and listened to everything she shared with enthusiasm. She told them about the doctor and how special her baby shower had been. Then she smiled proudly and announced that she was having a boy. That started another round of congratulations.

With a hopeful smile, Anne informed her that she would like to throw another little shower for her if she was open to it. Though Brooke hesitated at first, she finally acquiesced because according to Anne you could never have too many baby clothes or diapers. Ivan readily agreed with Anne. When Jacob also chimed in with agreement, she laughed and held up her hands. "Okay, okay, I get it."

The conversation soon turned to dinner and Anne informed her that they had put a roast on and were planning steamed vegetables, salad, and mashed potatoes to go with if that sounded okay. Brooke licked her lips in anticipation and Jacob laughed. They all moved into the kitchen to help prepare the meal. Even Zack finally joined them stepping over to help the boys peel potatoes after saying a polite hello to Brooke.

It was a warm joyous evening that Brooke would always remember. The only sad spot for her was that she missed Cole already and had a sinking feeling that whatever was between them had been officially deemed over. She laughed and joked and asked how things on the farm had been since she'd left. She asked Jacob about school and graduation. They enjoyed a lovely meal as conversation raged and everyone filled up. When the table was cleared Anne pulled out apple pie and ice cream.

Despite Anne sending Zack to find Cole and tell him dinner was ready, he didn't come in. After pie and ice cream, Ivan quietly asked her to go with him to take a plate to Cole. She readily agreed and they heaped a plate with a thick slice of roast and all the sides. Brooke grabbed a second plate and put a slice of pie on it topping it with a scoop of vanilla ice cream.

She followed him carefully across the snow-packed yard to the garage in back. Ivan opened the door and held it for her. She stepped inside and then stopped, looking around in surprise. She didn't know what she had expected, but bumper-to-bumper, old broken-down hunks of metal was not it. "Are all of these yours?"

she asked curiously.

Ivan chuckled. "Not a one. These ladies are all Cole's."

Brooke's brows lifted in surprise and then curiosity. "What does he do with them?" she asked a little stunned.

Cole stepped out from behind a rusty old Cadillac. "He fixes them," he responded with a grin. "This here is Iris."

Ivan handed him a rag first, which Cole used to wipe the majority of grease from his hands. Brooke stared with wide eyes around the garage. "Do they all have names?" she asked.

Ivan laughed. "Cole usually names them all before he buys them. If not, then by the time he brings them home."

Cole dug into the food without comment.

Still a little stunned she asked, "How long have they all been in here?"

Cole swallowed his food and looked around. "Most of these ones I picked up over the last year." He pointed down the row. "Jessica down there I've had a little longer." He gave a casual shrug. "I haven't quite been inspired on what to do with her yet. Most of them come and go within a few months, though."

Brooke nodded and then with avid curiosity asked, "What do you do with them when they're done?"

He looked at Ivan and then finally turned to meet her eyes. "Usually, I sell them. I have given a couple of them to friends, though, and I've also kept a couple, as you know." He forked in a bite of salad.

"So, what is the silvery blue Mustang named?" she asked suddenly, wanting to know. He didn't respond right away so she laughed and added. "Wait, don't tell me. Let me guess, you named her Maria, no Eleanor, no wait, I bet her name is Sophia." She turned with a silly smile and looked back and forth between them.

Ivan grinned. "I suspect her name is Sophia now."

Brooke looked at Cole in confusion. He shrugged and then smiled wide enough for his dimple to appear. "Sophia, it is."

Still confused, Brooke turned to Ivan. "So, what is her name really?"

He grinned. "I think you just named her, dear. Cole here was having a hard time naming her, but it seems that you've done it for him."

Brooke smiled uncertainly. "No, I really wasn't trying to pick for you," she rushed out.

Cole turned that dark steady gaze on her. "It's not that at all. It's just that Sophia seems right somehow. I'm not sure why I didn't think of that myself."

Ivan smiled at the look that passed between them. He gave himself an inward pat on the back. He had been right. There was definitely something going on between them. He cleared his throat and asked Cole, "Does that mean you're going to sell her now?"

Cole shook his head. "No way, I'm still going to keep her."

CHAPTER 35

It took him four days to find her again. He parked his truck on the road just out of sight of the house and walked to stand under a tree on the edge of the property. The private investigator hadn't been of any use this time, but he had come directly here when he got back to Idaho. He hadn't seen any sight of her the first day he was back. The second day he had nearly shouted in his excitement as he saw that familiar sports car. He laughed at his own ability to handle such things when he needed to. He was smarter than any dumb PI, and he decided not to pay the guy for this last work since he hadn't really helped anyway. Besides, within a few days now everything would be well worked out.

He watched the house for hours, but it wasn't until early evening that she finally came out. He stared at her bulky stomach with fresh anger. In the five days since he'd seen her, she had definitely gotten fatter. His lips curled back at the thought of that sick bastard's baby inside her. No matter, he soothed himself, it would all be in the past soon.

She walked over to a dark-colored jeep and the man who had hit him rushed around to open her door and help her inside. Richard squinted and stepped a bit closer. It didn't look like the same man from Montana. He looked similar enough, but he didn't have quite as dark of hair and his body looked a slight bit lankier. Anger burned deep and his heart throbbed. Did she have more than one beau? The possessive way the man half lifted her up into the jeep had him scratching his now long beard.

He had been too busy lately to take the time to shave, so he was getting a bit on the scruffy side. He combed dirty hands through his greasy hair. He really should go take a shower and get himself prepared in case tonight was the night he got his love back for good. First, though, he would follow them for a bit and see where they might be off to.

They drove down the road on the opposite side of where he was parked, so he slowly pulled out onto the road behind them and followed at a distance. Less than a mile away they pulled into a driveway in front of a small red brick house. He drove past without slowing down before circling back to find a place to park his truck. The front of the house was too open but he found a back road that pulled up to the back of the house from behind. There was a row of tall maple trees that were bare from the cold winter months. In front of those were thick green pines that essentially gave him a nice private place to park his truck.

He climbed out and walked into the thicket of trees and bushes. He was wearing dark clothes to blend in and stood watching the house for any sign of occupants.

He watched the house for a couple of hours but all he saw was the man coming to the kitchen for water a couple of times. He thought about that. Found himself wondering if she had been forced to whore herself out just to survive. She had been kicked out on the street, after all, by her father. His heart warmed hopefully. Maybe that was all she had been doing those nasty things for. He smiled a little. It didn't change the fact that her body was carrying another man's child, but it might give him a good enough reason to actually keep her alive.

Regret seeped in. He had wanted to kill her father when he had calmly explained to him that he had kicked Brooke out. Old Man Reynolds had given him a pointed look and told him that she was unclean and that he'd do best to forget about her. Richard had nearly taken the man by his neck when he'd casually mentioned Brooke's younger blonde sister was coming of age soon. He had stopped himself after taking only one threatening step toward the guy. John had given him an amused little grin as though he knew that Richard wanted to beat him senseless.

Instead, Richard had walked away because of Brooke. How would she feel if he had to tell her that he had killed her father when he found her? No, he didn't want that and so he'd left. It had taken him a long while to find any trace of her again. If he had only found her sooner, he could have told her that he would take care of her. She would have been so grateful to him and they could have started their life together then. Guilt soared through him. If it was his fault that she was sleeping with men for money he wouldn't kill her for that.

He would have to punish her, of course, for that was what required of any decent husband and father. But he could allow her to live the rest of her life trying to make it up to him while paying for her mortal sins.

A tiny doubt seeped into his pleasant euphoria as he remembered how she had fought him at both the shop and then once again at the barbecue. It was dark that night and maybe she hadn't been able to see him, though. Love and anger warred inside him. Once he had her he would find out the truth and only then would he know what he should do with her.

Excitement soared and he hurried to his truck. He was going to go to the house he had been renting in the valley since he had first taken the job with her father and take a long hot shower. He wanted to clean up a bit before he came back to talk to her tonight. With a little satisfied grin, he backed up in the snow and drove away.

It took him longer than he planned to be gone since he had also taken the time to make himself some dinner. He hoped it would be the last time he had to cook for himself. Dreamed of Brooke telling him with humble tears that she had been desperate to survive and had been sleeping with men only to earn a living. With pride he likened himself to the story of Jesus and how He had forgiven the harlots. He was, after all, a good God-fearing man. With a refreshed little hop in his step, he drove back to the little house.

He parked and slipped through the trees in the moonlit darkness feeling much better now. He made his way quickly around the house. There was only one light on now and he smiled. A frown creased his brow when he spotted the jeep. Was the man still there? He could take them both he was sure, especially now that he had tools, but it would all be easier on his bride if he waited until the man left.

After twenty minutes in the frosty air passed by, he hiked back to his truck and dug the hat and gloves out of the loaded glove box. He took a minute to start the engine and warm up before securing them on his hands and head. Warm again, he shut off the truck and went back around to where he could see the front windows. The curtains were drawn, but he could see occasional shadows as she moved about her room.

When the man hadn't left at two in the morning, he swore under his breath before telling himself to be patient. He walked stiffly back to his truck and started it. He pulled off his gloves and rubbed his frozen fingers together trying to get circulation flowing again. Richard was willing himself mind over matter to be patient. It really wouldn't matter if it took more days as long as he got it right when he took her.

Cole tossed restlessly in his bed. He couldn't seem to sleep tonight. He had an uneasy feeling that he couldn't seem to get rid of. He thought of Brooke in the cozy house down the road and wanted to go to her. He pulled the pillow over his face and swore into it. The thought of her soft curvy body tied him in knots, but he'd sworn to himself that he wouldn't go. Had already made the choice. With cool determination he resettled the pillow under his head and closed his eyes tightly. He had way too much to do tomorrow to stay awake all night. Within minutes, his breathing deepened and he was out.

The dream came vivid and startling. He saw a truck and some guy hurting Brooke. He woke himself up and laughed inwardly at his own obsession. He was aware his overactive mind was only trying to give him a good reason to go over there. If he gave in this time, he wasn't sure he could ever stay away. He turned onto his side and stared at the maps through the darkness. His job was done, he assured himself. After all, hadn't he gone after her to give his family peace of mind? Well, she was back and they all had peace of mind, so his part was played out. Resolutely he closed his eyes and slept.

CHAPTER 36

Brooke didn't sleep well. Her back ached from all the constant sitting she had been doing. It had been two days since she arrived back at the Burton's and while she had immensely enjoyed her time with friends, she was starting to feel restless. She needed to get back home and get the rest of her things ready for the baby. Anne had planned a little baby shower for the following day and she soothed herself by promising she would go as soon as that was over.

After trying without success to get Brooke to stay in their guest room, Anne had suggested that someone stay at the house with her at all times. She hadn't wanted her to be alone at the house because she was so far along. The house was a long way from the nearest hospital and everyone wanted to make sure she had someone close by in case anything happened. Jacob offered to stay with her and had spent the last night in the extra room.

Brooke had been happily surprised when they first arrived at the house. It felt like even in winter the house opened its loving arms and welcomed her inside.

Much to her surprise the house was warm and free of dust when they entered. The bed, which she had stripped down before she left now sported eight hundred thread count sheets and a down comforter in a warm white tucked duvet. There was a matching white lamp on the side table and a small cedar chest at the foot of the bed that was a new edition. She was happy to see that the paint hadn't peeled and all the rooms still looked fresh and nice.

The flat screen that Jacob had bought for her was still in the same place in front of the long couch. She chided him for not taking it after she left at which he shrugged and told her it had been a gift and he wasn't going to take it back. Brooke had rolled her eyes before heading to the bathroom. If he wanted to give it to the new tenant that was his business.

They watched a couple of movies and visited for a long while before she had finally told him between yawns that she needed to get some sleep. A quick shower and toothbrush finished her off and she was out like a light.

The second night however was proving to be a different story. Her body felt exhausted from the long day she'd had. Breakfast had been a warm affair with the family. Then Anne had begged her to go into town to help do some shopping for the shower. Despite Brooke's refusals and insistence that she didn't need anything fancy they had come home with the back of Anne's SUV loaded to the roof with decorations, food, and supplies.

They unloaded it all with Anne protesting Brooke's help and Brooke reminding her once again that she was still working eight hour shifts at the café and usually hauled more weight than the bags they carried in.

Leaving a huge pile of party supplies in the front room, they moved into the kitchen and put away the hordes of groceries they had also picked up. Since Anne insisted that she wanted to make all the cookies and desserts they would serve for the shower, they spent several more hours cooking. They did as much prep work as they could for the shower before moving on to make a shrimp pasta salad and a large pan of chicken tortilla soup with fresh rolls for dinner.

Dinner had included more visiting and laughs and had then ended with everyone getting into a game where they were spies and trying to signal to their buddies without anyone noticing, while also trying to catch anyone signaling to another person. Hours had passed with laughter and giggles and tea for Brooke while Jacob and Ivan drank a beer. Anne opted for white wine and Cole had long since excused himself. The boys managed to coax hot chocolate out of the deal and everyone had an immensely fun, if a little strange, evening.

When Brooke started yawning, Jacob offered to take her home and they had driven over to the house. For some reason, the hair on the back of her neck had been standing up all afternoon. She knew she was a little worried about getting back to Montana to get things ready, but this kind of irritation was unlike her usually calm self. She couldn't stop shivering, though, she felt warm and toasty. She brushed it off as hormones and after a long visit with Jacob tried to go to bed.

She thought about Cole tonight. Wondered if he would ever touch her again. She missed him, and though she had known she would, she hadn't expected the loneliness to feel quite so much like betrayal. He hadn't made any promises, nor had he ever pretended that what they had was more than a few quick steamy nights in bed together and yet she had foolishly hoped that it might turn into more. Somehow, though unfair, she felt a little betrayed that he hadn't been as drawn to her as she was to him.

After she took a long hot bath and was ready for the night, she went to her room. She tried to sleep but for some strange reason, the house hadn't felt quite as warm and cozy tonight. She burrowed under the heavy quilt and told herself it was because she wanted Cole to be there in her bed keeping her warm. She turned onto her side with a pillow tucked between her legs for comfort, which nearly always helped. Her back throbbed and she adjusted again trying to get the kink out. Her leg went numb and she groaned miserably as she tried to massage the pins and needles out.

Finally, she threw the covers off and walked quietly down the hall to the kitchen. She didn't want to wake Jacob. She got a glass of water in the dark and drank half before setting it down. She stared out the window at the moonlit expanse of snow-covered lawn, that had once been her backyard. Oh, how she had wanted to call this place home. Had wanted to have her child here and teach him the ways of farm life.

Out of the corner of her eye, she saw movement but when she tried to focus on that spot again saw nothing. A chill ran down her spine and she thought of Richard. She shook it off. Surely, he had long since moved on, after all her fighting should have tipped him off that they were over. She had been gone for months now and hadn't seen any sign of him. She smiled at her own paranoia; he would have realized she wasn't worth the effort by now.

She thought of Cole and remembered him telling her how long and hard it was for him to track her down. Richard hadn't really had any real feelings for her just an unhealthy level of lust due to his lack of religiously approved ways to alleviate it. Surely by now he had made some new deal with another unlucky girl's father and was already married to her. She turned and walked away only moments before the headlights of his truck swept the tree line as he turned to drive away.

She ran into Jacob in the hall. He was coming out to check on her. "I heard you up again. Are you feeling okay?" he asked with concern written on his handsome face.

Brooke smiled in the darkness. "Yes, I just can't seem to get comfortable tonight." She rubbed at her lower back.

He reached around her to flip on the light. "Come on in here and I'll rub it for you," he offered as he sat on the couch in his blue short-sleeved pajamas. "I remember Mom getting a lot of backaches with the boys and Dad would always rub it for her before bed."

Brooke sat next to him with a sigh. "See, now this is why I always wanted you to be a part of my baby's life. You're such a great role model."

Jacob looked a little surprised by her comment.

Brooke leaned back against his gentle hands. "I know I'm the one who left, so I have no right to feel bad about missing you. I just didn't want you all to be in my life because you felt obligated or whatever."

Jacob used his fingers to gently knead down her lower back and then back up. "I'll admit I wondered if maybe you didn't want us to be involved enough to have a say," he said in a quiet voice. "I know you've always felt like you were on your own growing up and I thought maybe having all of us close to you worried you because it might influence your decisions." He moved to her shoulders and kneaded them in his fingertips.

"I'm really sorry, Jacob." A tear slipped out and down her cheek. She rubbed it off with a fist and turned to face him. "I'm sorry about leaving everyone, but I'm especially sorry about you."

He nodded. "I get it, I think. I even get not wanting to be a burden, but hell, Brooke, how could you have thought that I felt that way about you?"

Brooke met his earnest and hurt eyes. "I don't know. I think maybe I didn't understand people very well at that point." She smiled. "Since I went to Montana, there have been so many people that have been kind to me and done such nice things for me. I just didn't realize how many people there are in the world that are so kind and good. I realize now that people do nice things for each other and in return they do nice things back. It just took me a long time to see that I mattered too."

Jacob slid an arm around her shoulder and pulled her close. "You run around making the world this bright beautiful place that changes people and then somehow think that you owe them." He tugged her hair. "You have changed some part of me in a deep inexplicable way that I don't even understand yet. I actually see the world differently because of you," he said gently and with a deep sense of love and appreciation.

Brooke smiled wide. "You make it sound like I shit rainbows and unicorns."

Her comment surprised a quick laugh out of him. "Wow," he said, adding a little whistle. "My bestie has gone wild on me. You swear now?" he asked in mock disappointment.

"Oh, come on, Jacob I was never a saint," she declared.

He looked her deadpan in the eyes and said, "You are the closest thing I've ever seen to one."

Brooke laughed so hard tears streamed down her cheeks and Jacob joined her in the sheer joy of it. She wiped at the tears. "I think you had better find a better crowd to hang out with."

Jacob yawned and Brooke guiltily told him she was going to try sleeping again. She stood to walk away and then turned back to meet his eyes. "By the way, Jacob I forgot to tell you thank you for cleaning this place up and getting it ready for me."

A strange look passed over his eyes. "It wasn't me," he admitted. "Though if I had realized how much it would mean to you, I would have done it."

She frowned. "Was it your mom?"

He hesitated to answer. When he did, it was with a sigh. "Cole has been keeping the place up here since you left."

Brooke stared around thoughtfully for a long moment, looking around the room before she turned to go. "Well, thank you anyway for everything you do. You have been a great friend to me." She missed the slightly disappointed look on his face as she had already stepped into the hall. "Good night, I love you."

She slipped into the bed and snuggled under the heavy quilt. Her last thoughts as she fell asleep were of Cole. Though she woke twice in the night due to dreams about him she didn't mind, at least she was finally relaxed enough to rest.

CHAPTER 37

Anne was already going hard at it by the time Jacob and Brooke got to the Burton's home the following morning. She shooed them into the kitchen to eat some breakfast. Reluctantly, Brooke conceded since she was a little hungry and walked stiffly down the hall. Jacob followed closely behind her. "Just so you know I will be taking you back home," he informed her in a pleasant tone.

Brooke looked back at him and smiled. "That's fine," she said. She was too worn out today to argue with him and she did need a ride back to Montana so she couldn't be choosy.

His eyebrows shot up in surprise. "I really thought I was going to have to fight you on this." He almost looked disappointed.

Brooke sighed and walked over to the coffeepot. She had rarely allowed herself coffee since finding out she was pregnant, but this morning, she decided firmly, was going to be one of those times. She stirred in a scoop of sugar and a little cream. She leaned back against the counter and closed her eyes as she took a sip. Eyes still closed she murmured, "You are more than welcome to come for a little visit."

Jacob turned to give her an irritated look. "I plan to stay for a while, Brooke."

She was already shaking her head as she took another luxurious sip of her hot coffee. "I don't have a guest bed, so whatever time you spend will be on the couch and I really can't say it's comfortable."

"Should you be drinking that?" Cole asked from across the room and Brooke spun to look at his ruggedly handsome face. He looked as though he hadn't used a razor since they'd gotten back and the dark growth accented his already ruggedly handsome good-looks making him look as sexy as ever.

He had thrown her off guard because she hadn't seen him there. "I can drink coffee if I want to," she stated grumpily as her chin jutted out in defiance.

He met her hot gaze with a steady one. "I thought coffee wasn't good for the baby." He walked toward her as though he might take it away.

Brooke lifted the cup and chugged her threatened coffee. "The doctor said it was fine to have an occasional cup," she said as she gulped. "I really haven't drunk much of it, but I need it today." Her voice was soft and pleading now.

One side of Cole's mouth turned up. "Rough night?"

Brooke nodded. "A little. It took me a while to sleep and then I kept waking up all night."

He stepped up and put his hands on her shoulders. He turned her for better access as he massaged his strong fingers gently into the muscles at the base of her neck. Unable to stop herself she leaned into him and moaned as her eyes closed in pleasure.

"Does this help?" he asked quietly next to her ear.

Brooke felt the brush of his warm breath on her neck and shivered. God, she missed his hands on her. In sudden horror she opened her eyes to meet Jacob's curious stare. She threw him a casual smile.

Cole forced himself to step back and take his hands off her. He was already kicking himself for giving in to the urge to put his hands on her at all. He had been going crazy watching her but not being able to touch her. He had already been spending most of his time away in the garage, but if this got any worse, he'd have to resort to sleeping out there just to avoid her.

He turned a challenging look at Jacob, who was looking between him and Brooke with a knowing smile. He gave a polite tip of his head to both of them before turning to walk out.

Jacob turned to Brooke and watched her for a long moment. "So, what is going on with you and Cole?" he asked in a friendly voice.

Brooke shrugged. "Nothing really."

Jacob snorted. "Sure. Well, I'm gonna say that I have never seen him act the way he has been lately and now I am wondering just how much of that is due to you."

Brooke looked at him in silent misery. "I wouldn't worry too much about it. He doesn't even like me very much." She gave a shaky little laugh. "I think he would actually be quite happy if I could cease to exist."

Jacob walked over and stood next to her. "That's just Cole. He was born that way. For as long as I can remember it has always felt like he thinks he has to do life alone." He reached out and squeezed her shoulder. "Do you want him to like you, Brooke?" he asked seriously.

She shook her head hard and then nodded, finally she said, "I don't know. It's a lot simpler if he doesn't like me."

Jacob chuckled. "Amen to that sentiment. He is one of the most complicated people I know." He handed her a plate as he began loading pancakes, bacon, and eggs onto another. Brooke loaded her own and they walked to the table in companionable silence.

"Don't look so depressed, you'll always have me," Jacob joked a while later when Brooke seemed quieter than usual.

She pasted on a bright smile. "Good, because that is all I need."

After they ate and cleaned the kitchen, Brooke went in search of Anne. She found her in the long front room. Brooke stared in awe around the room. There were curly silver and blue decorations hanging from the ceiling. There were balloons in the corners announcing a baby boy. There was a long table Anne had set up for gifts and Brooke saw with a little uncomfortable twinge of guilt that there were already several gifts on it. To one end of the room was another long table that was set up for refreshments. A stack of blue and silver plastic plates, cups and bowls were lined up on one end. She smiled as Anne looked up. "This is too much, Anne," she exclaimed.

Anne shook her head. "On the contrary. If you think this is a lot, you should have seen the one Ivan's mom threw for us when we had Jacob." She smiled warmly at Brooke. "How are you guys feeling today?"

Brooke smiled as she looked around the room. "I feel pretty good." It was even mostly true. The coffee was starting to kick in so the heavy fatigue she had woken up with was starting to clear a little.

Anne laughed lightly. "I don't know that any woman ever feels good at thirty-eight weeks, but you do seem to handle it well."

Brooke smiled and bit back a yawn. "Most of the pregnancy has been fine. It just seems like the last few weeks, it's hitting me a little harder." With another glance around she asked, "What can I do to help?"

Anne looked thoughtful as she scanned the room. "I think we're pretty much ready in here. If you really want to help, we can go start the food."

Brooke nodded. "Sounds good. Just tell me what to do."

They walked together down the wide hall. They made cute little chocolate cupcakes with sprinkles and tiny diapers, bottles, and baby rattle toppers. They cut a huge tray of assorted fruits and another of fresh vegetables and a thick ranch dipping sauce. While Anne baked cookies and lemon squares, Brooke made little sandwiches on small croissant rolls. When there were three huge trays of sandwiches, she slid them into the fridge and started on a cracker and cheese tray. Brooke had no idea how they would eat all of the food.

Anne had invited a few close friends and some of the women Brooke had gotten to know when she had worked for the Burtons. With all the food ready for the party, Anne and Brooke sat together to eat a late lunch. Anne pulled out a pitcher of freshly made iced green tea and offered a cold glass to Brooke who took it gratefully and sipped. It was icy cold and tangy with a hint of lemon and honey.

Anne sat watching with a small smile as Brooke inhaled yet a third sandwich. "Do you have a birthing plan all figured out, then?" she asked to make conversation after a drink of her own tea.

Brooke smiled and nodded. "I do. There is a really nice birthing clinic just outside the city that I was able to get on with. They have these nice little birthing suites that feel cozy and private. I don't even have to cover most of it since the doctor helped me get signed up with a nonprofit organization that helps young single women cover medical bills due to birthing."

Anne smiled at that. "That's good. I admit I was a little worried that you might not get the help you needed with everything. But then, if I'm honest, I underestimated you in nearly every way."

Brooke met those knowing green eyes. "It's okay, I'm used to people underestimating me. It seems like my whole life everyone has always thought that I'm less than capable. That was a big part of why I needed to leave and show that I could do it on my own."

A sad smile crossed Anne's lips. "I think that is the saddest part. I treated you the way that everyone else did when I had the perfect chance to see that you were so much more." She reached out and covered Brooke's hand with her own. "I see now the deep strength and courage that the rest of my family saw from the start. I am so glad you've come to spend this time with us. I know things haven't always been the easiest between us, but I'd like to change that. You are always welcome here for as long as you like."

Brooke smiled. "Thank you."

"I know you have everything all figured out but if you do have a mind to stay then we do have a birthing suite at the clinic. Just the one suite but out here in the country it is rare that we have a birth that goes fast enough that we can't make it to the hospital. It's mostly used for emergencies, but it's nice enough." She met Brooke's eyes. "I know you probably don't want to hear my two cents, but I wouldn't be able to forgive myself if I didn't at least offer. I have noticed how close you are with Jacob and if this feels like home to you, I want you to be here."

Brooke smiled at her mention of Jacob. "While I really do appreciate the offer, I have a house back in Montana and I have to keep making payments. My job there pays me surprisingly well." She held the older woman's gaze. "I hope you know that me and Jacob are just friends, ma'am."

Anne looked horrified for a moment and then half stood. "Oh, heavens no, I will not abide being called, ma'am. Call me Anne and let's not ever revisit that," she commanded as she sat back down.

Brooke laughed out loud. "I hear you."

When Anne reached out to take her hand again, Brooke felt uncomfortable. The older woman met her nervous look with a steady one of her own. "I know we talked a little before about this Brooke and I hate to bring it back up." She hesitated a long moment. "Are you sure you don't want to let the father know? Maybe he could help out?"

Brooke jerked back involuntarily pulling her hand from Anne's to clasp them both tightly in her own. "I get that, but I don't want to. I understand why you might ask and I can appreciate that you care, but I have made up my mind about this," Brooke said quickly.

Anne watched her intently. "Is he from around these parts?" she pressed on.

Brooke shook her head. "He was from Utah, but he knew my family. He wouldn't want anything to do with me now," she rushed out, praying that what she said was true.

Anne gave her a comforting smile. "I understand. I just feel like women should know that it might make things easier to have the extra money and support."

Brooke stared down at her hands, "Well, thank you again, but I am more than capable and happy to do this on my own." Her hands cupped her belly protectively. She relaxed into the chair and watched as her belly moved with her son's strong kicks. So relaxed was she that she was completely taken aback by Anne's next question.

"Did you know the man that attacked you after the barbecue?"

Brooke froze and then her gaze swung to meet those knowing green eyes. She forced air into her lungs and forced a casual shrug. "It was so dark I really couldn't see much that night. It was hard to see anything so I really couldn't know," she replied.

Anne smiled. "I guess I was thinking maybe it was something more personal since there haven't been any reports of anything similar happening since then. They never caught that horrible man and I had wondered if maybe it was something more personal with you."

Brooke shrugged again. "It could have been. Like I said, it was dark and it's hard to say who it could have been."

She met the older woman's sharp look. She forced herself to breathe calmly in and out. Anne finally didn't hate her and the last thing she could have wanted was to give her another reason to. She couldn't stand the thought of them all knowing the stunts she had pulled while trying to get out of marrying Richard. There was no telling what any of them would think of her then.

CHAPTER 38

Cole finished the long grueling process of going through the engine and was putting it back into the car when Jacob came in. He looked up and raised an eyebrow in question as Jacob walked over to stand next to the car. When Jacob didn't immediately say anything, Cole nodded. "Jacob."

Jacob walked around the car looking it over for a bit. "Nice," he said. He walked back around to where Cole had one arm shoulder deep under the hood, ratcheting a bolt into place. The cherry picker was next to the car, though it had already been unhooked from the engine. "Did you just finish the engine?" he asked to make conversation.

Cole nodded. "Yeah, I had to pull it to do a complete overhaul. I want her to run smoothly when I'm done with her, and that's the only way I can guarantee it." Cole ran a grease-stained hand over the front fender as he said it.

Jacob grinned, his brother had always had an uncanny knack of giving new life to all things mechanical or electrical. "I don't know how you do it," he confessed. "Spending so many hours working on broken things to make them work again. I don't think I could do it."

With a casual shrug Cole answered, "It helps me think."

Jacob waited for him to add more but Cole worked silently. "I do get wanting the time and space to think," he finally said.

Cole turned to give him a small grin as he turned to angle his arm down to reach another bolt. "So, what's up?" he asked. Jacob rarely made his way out here and only ever if he had something important to talk about.

Jacob walked around the car again then stopped next to Cole. "Can we talk?"

Cole turned and gave his brother a toothy grin. "I thought that's what we were doing."

Jacob smiled wryly. "Right. I've just been thinking about a lot lately and I need to talk it out with someone."

Cole pulled his arm out and bent down digging through a pile of tools at his feet. He palmed a wrench and tossed it to Jacob. "Fine, but we work while we talk." He pointed to the other side of the engine. "I got them all started over there, but they need tightened down."

Jacob set the wrench down long enough to take off his jacket and roll up the sleeves of his denim button down. He grabbed the wrench again and walked around to see what needed tightened. "So, I've been thinking a lot about everything with Brooke," he started.

Cole turned and looked at him as his gaze narrowed. "Okay, what about her?"

"I don't like watching her go through it all alone. I don't know who the father is and every time I ask her, she doesn't want to talk about it," Jacob complained. "I don't want to pressure her, but I wonder if I should."

Cole turned his arm again. "Then don't. If she wanted to talk about it, don't you think that she would?" He fashioned an unaffected expression.

Jacob laughed softly. "That's easy for you to say."

Cole turned to look at him sharply. "What the hell is that supposed to mean?"

It was Jacob's turn to shrug. "Brooke keeps telling me how much you really don't like her. I guess I just think that it's easy for you to be a little blasé about it all." Jacob watched Cole's face waiting for any sign of what his brother was feeling.

Cole shrugged. "I don't have any problem with her. I want things to work out well for her as much as the next guy."

Jacob dropped the wrench on his toe. He swore and got down to get under the car to get it. He stood again and started on the next bolt as he said under his breath, "Or so you would like everyone to believe anyway."

Cole's gaze narrowed again. "We can't all be saints, Jacob. I think you and Dad pretty much have that part covered."

Jacob fought a surge of anger. He knew Cole well enough to know that he was trying to get a rise out of him. "I guess you won't mind if I ask her to marry me, then? I'd like to adopt the baby to raise as my own."

Cole's jaw tightened and his eyes flashed. "Why would you do that? According to both of you, you're only close friends."

Jacob grinned, knowing he had him, "She's beautiful and spunky and full of life. I could do a lot worse. In fact, right now I can't imagine anyone I'd rather spend my life with than her. Besides all that, we have kissed," he stated with a noncommittal shrug.

Cole's eyes went black and he stood deadly still. "Keep your grimy hands off her," he threatened in a soft drawl.

Jacob laughed out right. "That's what I thought," he said. "Good to know you do like her."

Cole gave his brother an unaffected good-natured grin. He relaxed his stance and met his brother's laughing eyes. "Do whatever you want, Jacob. I'll back you up if that's really what you want. I don't have any claim on her."

Jacob sighed. "You can pretend all day long that you don't have feelings for her. You have even managed to convince her that you don't even like her.

You can keep coming out here and pushing her away. But at the end of the day, we both know it was you that put aside everything to find her. And you know what? I didn't even realize until last night just how much you've been doing to take care of her. By the way, she really appreciated that you took care of the old house while she was gone and it struck me as odd that you had somehow known how much it would mean to her. You keep pretending like you're unaffected by all of this, but I know the truth." Jacob turned midspeech and tossed the wrench down on the pile of tools. He started to walk away but turned back. "Oh and, Cole?" He waited until Cole turned to face him. "If you don't do something soon, I am going to marry her and take care of her. God knows she needs it more than she will ever admit." He turned on his heel and walked out, pausing only long enough to grab his jacket.

Cole stood staring after him for a long while before going back to work. When he almost had the car back together, he glanced down at his watch. His mother had let him know when the shower started in case he wanted to go. Anne told him it might mean a lot to Brooke for all of them to show up, but he had stubbornly decided not to go. Cole was already in over his head with her and wasn't willing to risk his infuriating lack of control when it came to Brooke.

He cursed under his breath and threw the wrench at the concrete floor, watching as it bounced a few times before skidding to a halt by the overhead door. He picked up another wrench and then threw it too. None of this was part of his damn plan. He hadn't even planned to have kids until his late thirties and yet here he was pining after a young pregnant redheaded vixen.

He hadn't known if he ever wanted to get married. He knew that was what his family wanted for him, but he just hadn't had that normal connection with women that made him want to spend his life with someone and try to make things work.

He thought about Jacob marrying her and kicked a white-walled tire nearby. It wasn't, however, until he thought about Jacob quietly saying he'd kissed her that he realized he was beaten.

He gathered his tools and was just washing his hands when Ivan came walking in. Cole glowered at him. "What do you want?"

Ivan took a step back and held up a hand. "Whoa, I come in peace," he joked.

Cole plastered grease paste all over his hands and arms scrubbing viciously. "Sorry, if you came in here to give me a lecture as well; you can stop. Jacob beat you to it."

Ivan looked curious then. "Jacob came in here preaching about something?" he asked carefully.

Cole gave a chilly little laugh. "He did" was all he offered.

Ivan searched his son's expression. "Are you okay, son? Forgive me for saying so, but you seem a little burned out of shape as of late."

Cole gave him a dark laugh. "I'm great. Just fine. Did Jacob come and tell you his big plan as well?"

Ivan shook his head not sure what his son was going on about. "I don't think so. I did talk to him briefly about the baby shower and Brooke, but I spent the day at my office handling some urgent paperwork."

In a hard voice Cole stated, "He says he's going to ask Brooke to marry him and adopt her baby."

Ivan raised an eyebrow at that. "Well, that's news to me. I thought they were just friends." He hid a grin at how that news had obviously upset Cole.

Cole laughed darkly again. "They are. Unless you count the kisses that they shared."

Ivan did grin then as he recalled Jacob informing him that there were no sparks between the two of them because he had kissed her. "Well, I'm sure that Jacob means well, son. He loves that girl and he really could do a lot worse." He met Cole's hot glare. "Does the idea of that bother you?"

Cole shrugged. "A little. The problem is that I don't see myself as the type to settle down, so I can't really offer her anything. Brooke has been through hell and anyone who has spent much time around her can see the pain she has suffered, but I just don't think I could ever be of much help."

Ivan nodded in understanding. "She has. And she does deserve happiness. I agree with Jacob about that. I don't know that everyone can see her pain, though. She tends to hide it pretty well." Ivan held the dark gaze of his very stubborn son. "Are you thinking you wish you could offer her something instead of Jacob?" he asked seriously.

Cole shook his head looking horrified. "God no. I'm not a romantic like Jacob. It's just that Jacob said if I don't do something, he will."

Ivan chuckled. Jacob was probably back at the house by now having a good laugh about it. Very rarely had any of them been able to ruffle Cole's very slick, smooth feathers and the fact that this had gotten to him spoke volumes. He turned serious as he saw Cole's jaw tighten angrily. He sighed. "I wouldn't do anything you don't want to do, Cole. Let Jacob do what he will and see where it all lands," he advised gently.

Cole turned and rinsed his hands in the small shop sink. "That's just it, I'm not sure I can just stand by and watch Brooke choose something that isn't about love."

Ivan raised one eyebrow. "I do think that Brooke and Jacob love each other," he stated pleasantly.

"Oh, I don't doubt that. Hell, we have all had to sit there and watch as they're friendship got so hunky-dory. It's just that she is so young and she is already going to give up the world for the baby. I'm not sure I can't sit by and watch her give up on love for the baby's sake." He turned and grabbed a clean rag to dry off his hands and arms. "Maybe there is something I can do or offer that will be a solution but leaves her open to love when she's ready."

Ivan watched his son in silence. He had wondered if there was something between Cole and Brooke but until now hadn't known just how much. He smiled. His son was smitten. He tilted his head slightly wondering just *how* smitten Cole was. There was one way to find out. He looked into his son's eyes and asked, "And the baby?"

Cole looked unfazed. "What about the baby? I have no problem with the baby."

Ivan grinned. "I see. On that note I'm going to go into this party your mother has planned. Are you coming?"

Cole stared at his feet. "Maybe in a bit" was all he would concede.

CHAPTER 39

Brooke smiled as Jacob came in to ask if he could help with anything. His hair was damp and he had on a blue and green square patterned button down with tan slacks. The brown leather loafers added a relaxed vibe. "You look nice," she told him.

He grinned and bowed slightly. "Why thank you, my lady."

Anne smiled at his mock seriousness. "I think we're all set up now. Jacob, you can help me haul all the food trays from the fridge while Brooke goes over to get ready."

"I'm at your service, my lady," he bowed with a wink and a grin at Brooke. He reached in his pocket and pulled out the keys to the jeep and tossed them to her.

She caught them out of the air. It only took a couple of minutes to drive down to the old place. It was the first time she had come home alone since she had left and she took a long moment to stare at the cozy house before she ran in. She took a quick shower and looked through the clothes she had brought with her. Unsure what to wear, she finally opted for a dark blue knee-length dress with white polka dots. It was too cold out to go barelegged so she pulled on a pair of long hip boots and a black matching dressy coat.

She heard a car approaching the house and went to the window to look outside. There wasn't anyone in sight and her brows furrowed in confusion. Maybe she was just hearing things. She shook her head and went into the bathroom to try to work out her curls. After several minutes of trying to tame them, she finally sighed and did a loose braid down her back. She quickly applied makeup and a dash of perfume before she slipped into the coat and went back out to the jeep. She slid into the black leather seat as a chill ran down her spine. She glanced around the yard feeling like there was something out of place, though try as she might she couldn't see anything wrong. She slid her seat belt into place with a click and started the engine. After another quick glance around, she backed out of the drive and pulled onto the road. A shiver ran down her spine as she sped back to the Burtons.

There were a few people already at the house when she walked in. With a wide smile, Brooke said hello to Isabel and Luis. They both pulled her in for a hug and asked if she was going to stay. Sadly, she shook her head and informed them she had to get back home soon but she would definitely come visit again. One of Anne's good friends came in and she called Brooke over to meet her. Jacob came to her side and stood with her as she said hello to some she remembered and others she hadn't met yet. The room was soon full and everyone stood visiting with cold drinks and plates of refreshments in hand. After everyone had arrived and the gift table was overflowing Anne announced that a game was starting for anyone who wanted to participate.

All of the women and most of the men joined in a timed game where pens and papers were passed out and they had one minute to put as many little boy names as they could going through the alphabet. The minute went by quickly and everyone laughingly shared the names they had gotten. Jacob won, having completed all of them and even had an extra name on a couple of the letters. His prize was an oversized baby bottle filled with fancy chocolates. With a laugh he set it on the gift table declaring it would now be a gift for Brooke.

Next, they played a diaper game where the diapers had been filled with different chocolate bars smashed and the goal was to properly identify which was which. In a surprising turn Luis won and was forced to deal with the teasing about his legendary sweet tooth.

Brooke had hoped that Cole would come but when the shower was halfway done and he hadn't shown up she resigned herself to the reality that she might not see him again before heading back to Montana. She excused herself from a conversation with Ivan and some of the men to slip out to the restroom. She splashed some cool water on her cheeks and breathed in the quiet before she walked back to the party.

There was soft music playing in the background as she slipped back into the room. Feeling self-conscious she looked around for Jacob. She didn't see him anywhere and fought the urge to sneak out and hide. Before she had a chance, she felt a warm hand on her shoulder and felt heat seeping into her cool skin. She turned and looked up to meet Cole's dark eyes. "Hello," she said, sounding a little breathless.

He was wearing a black button down with blue, purple, and silver stripes running down it. His sleeves were rolled up nearly to his elbows and his collar was still damp from his hair. He was wearing dark jeans that tapered slightly down to his black leather loafers. He took her breath away.

He didn't smile just held her gaze. "Looking for someone?" he asked with an ironic eyebrow.

She swallowed. "I was just looking around for Jacob," she admitted.

"Why do you need him?" His eyes were black now.

She shrugged. "I just wanted to hang out with him."

He grinned coldly down at her. "Are you sure you're not looking for him so you can kiss him again?" His smile didn't falter, though his tone was hard and cold.

Brooke stepped back with a confused smile. "Excuse me? I don't even know what you're talking about."

He reached for her arm and wrapped strong fingers around her wrist pulling her out and then walked with a fast pace down the hall. She nearly tripped while trying to keep up and he slowed down slightly and put a hand at the small of her back. Within moments they were standing in the game room with a long wooden bar on one end. There was a pool table in the center on one end and she pulled away from him. She turned and looked up at him in alarm.

His gaze was hard and unrelenting as he stared coldly down at her. He stepped forward and she backed up. A tiny sliver of fear inched its way through her and the smile she had forced wobbled. He stalked her until he had her backed into the pool table. She tried to turn and run but his arm shot out blocking her path. Her voice shook as she stared up at his angry face. "Cole, what is going on?"

He smiled then, though it didn't reach his eyes. His black eyes held hers in challenge. "Were you looking for Jacob so you could kiss him again, Brooke?" His tone was soft but ever-so lethal.

Still confused Brooke met his dark venomous stare with courage. "I just felt uncomfortable with all the people that came to the party…," she trailed off as a disbelieving smile curved one side of that strong elegant mouth. She mumbled, "I thought it was just going to be a few close friends of the family, but there are so many people out there and they all brought fancy gifts and they don't even know me," she tried to explain. The fear that curled its way down her back to settle in her toes had her breathing hard.

He ignored her explanation. "Did you really think I wouldn't find out that you kissed Jacob?" he asked then as his lips curled in distaste. He pressed his hot body against hers.

She cried out a little in distress as terror seeped in to muddle her thinking. He stilled and stared down suddenly. She looked absolutely terrified of him. Anger seeped through him hot and heavy, but he calmed it. He stepped back slightly not giving her room to leave but enough to give her breathing room. "Why are you so afraid of me, Brooke?" he asked suddenly, changing the subject from Jacob.

She looked at a point somewhere near his shoulder. "You are really mad and I don't know what you are going to do to me," she admitted in a strained voice.

He stared silently down at her as he willed her to meet his gaze. She finally took a deep breath and her gaze slid up to his. He lifted a hand to tuck a curl behind her ear. Then he took her chin holding her head up so she couldn't look away. "I am very angry, Brooke. In fact, I am furious, but I would never hurt you." He held her gaze, forced her to see the honesty in his own. "Do you believe me?" he needed to hear her say it. Couldn't stand the way she had looked at him as though he might beat her on the spot.

She finally shrugged. "I guess so."

He squeezed gently and rubbed his thumb across her lips. "I have a fierce temper and as it turns out a bit of a jealous streak when it comes to you, but I have never, would never hurt anyone who doesn't deserve it. I can't stand it when you look at me like that." He sounded tortured, the anger completely gone now.

"I'm not really scared of you, Cole," she admitted in a whisper. "I think my mind just kind of takes over and reacts. It feels like my brain freezes and I can't do anything about it. I think I know deep down that you wouldn't ever hurt me."

He stared long and hard as though searching for the truth in her eyes. "I'm the one who should be sorry. This is the second time I've scared you like this." He rubbed a tired hand through his hair. "I swore after that first time that I wouldn't touch you again. But then I realized you were pregnant and not so innocent as I'd thought and then I couldn't deny myself a kiss, which eventually became so much more." He gave a self-mocking grin. "Then this morning Jacob told me that he had been kissing you, which didn't bother me too much until I saw you in that dress." He ran a finger down the shoulder following the V-neck to its point between her cleavage. "You look so sexy and I just kept imagining Jacob's hands all over you and my temper got the best of me."

Her shoulders shook a little and his gaze swung suspiciously to her face. *Was she laughing?* He stared as she tried unsuccessfully to hold back her laughter but the smile widened and her shoulders shook with it. He stared at her in intrigue. Finally, she said in a laughing voice. "I actually forgot there was a kiss. Back shortly after

I came here, Jacob and I kissed." She grinned up at him.

He frowned. "Just once?" he asked in a controlled voice.

She nodded and her eyes sparkled with amusement. "Oh yes. One kiss was all it took to realize there were absolutely no sparks between us. To be honest I think Jacob was more disappointed in the lack of spark than I was."

Cole thought about Jacob and a grim smile warmed his face. He was going to kill him. His brother had obviously been trying to get under his skin and he should have seen it. He leaned close rubbing her lips again with his thumb. He couldn't stop now. He could feel her velvety smooth skin under his rough hand and her curvy body still slid against his length. He looked into her now-shuttered gaze. "I'm going to kiss you now, Brooke," he warned in a low voice.

She met his kiss. Lifted her head to give him better access. Even arched into him as he coaxed her lips open and he slid his tongue in to rub against her own. Heat soared then to settle low in her belly. He stepped back and looked down at her with victory on his face. "No chance of there not being any sparks here," he said in satisfaction.

Brooke laughed and the warm light tinkling sound had him leaning down to take her mouth in another long deep kiss. It had only been a few days and yet it felt like forever since he had allowed himself to drink her in. She arched against him and he groaned as he lifted her easily to sit on the edge of the pool table. She slid her arms up around his neck and pulled him closer. She nearly fell over when he suddenly stepped back and away from her. Feeling bereft without his hot body, she reached out for him.

He turned his head toward the door. "Hello, Jacob," he said coolly.

Jacob chuckled. "So, this is where you are, Bestie. I've been looking all over for you." He gave Cole a very pointed look. "I thought you weren't coming."

Brooke looked at Jacob and couldn't stop the slight blush that crept up her neck. She hadn't even heard him come in. Had been so involved in Cole and their kiss that she wasn't sure she would have ever noticed him there. "I'm sorry, I'll be right there," she stammered as she tried to slide off the table. Cole reached out to steady her as she slid to the floor.

Jacob grinned. "By all means take your time…." He paused for effect. "Although come to think of it, if you wait too long, Mom or one of your many guests might come in here looking for you."

Cole gave his brother a dark look. "You'd best wipe that smug look off your face or I'll do it for you." He turned and walked past Jacob and out of the room.

Jacob held out his arm for Brooke to take. "He doesn't like you, huh?" he teased near her ear.

Brooke punched his arm and grinned when he grunted. "He doesn't. Just because he kisses me sometimes doesn't mean he likes me," she denied. "In fact, he does everything he can to avoid me most of the time."

"Maybe he avoids you because he likes you more than he's comfortable with," he said gently. "And as for the kissing, if I was a betting man, I'd guess that you've done a whole lot more than kissing. I'm beginning to think that Cole more than likes you." Even he sounded surprised by that admission. He didn't miss the hopeful look that crossed Brooke's face before she could hide it. He smiled. "Let's get back, shall we?"

She nodded and they walked arm in arm back to the front room.

There was another game that Anne had prepared for the men. This one involved several dolls and diapers and a bunch of rough handed men racing to do the best diaper change while five older women with children judged the winner. With a grunt of satisfaction Cole raised his hands first. His baby was snugged nice and tidy in the miniature diaper and properly swaddled. After all the men finished, the judges talked among each other for a quick minute before declaring Cole the winner.

Jacob groaned in mock distress and Cole turned and gave her a playful wink before stating matter-of-factly. "I guess I'm just good with my hands." The whole room roared with laughter as Anne presented his prize, which turned out to be a diaper shaped glass jar of condoms. On the side was a written sticky note. "Diapers or condoms, decisions, decisions."

Cole grinned in good nature as he handed it off for the guests to read.

With games done, Brooke sat in the front of the room to open all the gifts. There were onesies and sleepers and blankets and toys and by the time Brooke had opened the last gift she looked around the room with overwhelmed appreciation and announced. "Well, since I won't have to buy a single thing for this kid his whole life, I will have to send you all a thank-you gift." Laughter and smiles followed her comment and people soon turned away to visit again.

Soon after gifts were opened people began saying their goodbyes and leaving. Jacob and all the brothers hauled all the gifts out to his jeep. When they couldn't fit anymore in there, Cole pulled his truck around and they loaded the remainder in the back. The sky was clear tonight with no sign of snow, so he just left it parked outside.

Though Brooke wanted to get all the stuff back to the old house and sort through it, she insisted first on helping with the cleanup. One girl that Brooke had been introduced to as Alicia by Jacob, who'd informed Brooke he'd known all his life, hung around for a while after the shower.

It was obvious that she was into Jacob as she hung around hopefully. After several minutes of visiting with her Brooke had pulled Jacob aside and talked him into asking her out. He'd balked a little at first but finally given in at Brooke's insistence that Alicia was definitely into him. Brooke rode with Jacob and Cole followed in his truck as they hauled everything over to the old house. It wasn't until they had everything piled inside the front room that she finally noticed two huge un-wrapped boxes. Perplexed she stared at them and then turned to Jacob. "Where did these come from?" she asked curiously.

Jacob shrugged. "I'm not sure. I'm not the one that loaded those ones up."

Cole stepped through the door with the last of the packages then. He saw Brooke standing with a hand on the box. She looked at him questioningly. "Do you know where these came from Cole?" she asked.

He looked at them and nodded. "They're from me. I hope you like them okay. I noticed you didn't have them yet in Montana."

She was so touched that tears formed in her eyes and she turned away to hide them. "This is all too much," she said quietly as she tore the wrapping off. Inside one box was a very sturdy black and blue car seat and stroller set. She smiled at Cole. "It's perfect, but way too much. This was one of the few things I still planned to pick up." She turned and ripped open the other box. It was a baby swing that had a brightly patterned jungle theme, padded seat. She turned and met his gaze. "This is way too much Cole. At least let me pay you for some of it."

He shrugged. "It's only a gift and I seem to have ended up with an extra hundred dollars from Montana anyway, so in a way you already have."

She smiled. "I didn't think you would notice an extra bill."

"I always know how much cash I have in my wallet, sweetheart," he drawled.

CHAPTER 40

He watched from a distance as the three of them hauled in the gifts and packages. He laughed at their stupidity. Would they ever discover that she was servicing both of them? he wondered in amusement. Or maybe they already knew and just didn't care. She really did deserve a real man like himself. Someone who wouldn't be okay with her dallying about with others.

He retreated slightly as the guy from Montana came out and climbed into the old blue truck. Within a minute he had started the engine and drove off. Richard watched as the tail lights disappeared into the darkness. Then he turned back to the house. And then there were two, he thought and couldn't resist the chirp of laughter at his own cleverness.

He reached around his back to wrap cold fingers around the butt of the nine-millimeter handgun he had bought in Montana. He watched as Brooke moved into view and looked out into the darkness through the window. Though he doubted she could she him through the darkness, he stumbled back quickly into the trees. He smiled and let go of the gun as she reached out and pulled the drapes closed. He watched their shadows as they sat down together on the couch.

Anger seared him; he was out here while she was in there and about to do horrible dirty things with another man. He reached for the gun again. He could just go in there now and kill the bastard. Then he would have her to himself once more. He took two steps forward before his brain caught up with his anger. And then what? He would be running from the law and that just wouldn't do. Patience was key here. He backed into the trees again breathing hard.

The smart play here was to wait until she was alone and then take her. She had left before and no one seemed to care. Her family definitely wasn't going to come after him. She had outgrown any use she was to them at this point. He would be patient and then he would sweep in and take her away to their home in the mountains. He could even have her write a little goodbye note so that no one was the wiser. Then they would slip away and he could finally have the time he needed to interrogate her.

He had long since given up his previous dreams of a future with her having his children and serving him in all the ways he needed. But if the whoring really was about money and survival then he might eventually be able to forgive her, granting that she took proper care of him in bed. He grinned at all the things she would want to do to make it up to him.

There was the matter of the baby though. That thought made him frown but it was easy enough to take care of. He thought of the two men whom it seemed she took turns servicing and wondered which one of them was the father. For that matter the father could have been someone else altogether, though he quickly stopped that thought as he was already having difficulty keeping his temper in check. He wasn't sure he wouldn't go inside guns blazing if he found out there was another man involved.

He watched as she leaned in close to the man. He turned away. He couldn't watch her touch the man this way. He made his way quickly around to the back of the lot where he had parked his truck. He would go home and get some food and take a quick shower and then come back. With any luck she would be alone by then.

Cole stalked endlessly across his room. He wanted her with an intensity that he really didn't want to think too much about. He had wanted to tell Jacob he was going to stay with her. Had in fact wanted to tell his brother to get lost. The fact that it would have given his brother far too much satisfaction kept him from doing it. Jacob was already acting like he knew something that Cole didn't and he wasn't about to add fuel to that fire.

Brooke had been so beautiful today. Her red hair had been hanging in a loose curly braid with tendrils slipping out around her face. Her curvy body was sheathed in a blue dress that hugged every curve and those sexy boots had left only a sliver of naked legs which had only made him want to see more. He'd been imagining Jacob kissing her and touching her body the way he had and his pulse jumped. He'd gone full hulk on her and had once again managed to terrify her.

He closed his eyes in agonized frustration as he remembered her terrified face when she was pinned between him and the pool table. He swore now, as he realized that once again, he had made her afraid of him. It was how she responded when he had backed off that had him so hot and bothered tonight though. After he had assured her that he wouldn't hurt her she had been warm and willing in his arms. He was actually a little grateful to Jacob for interfering then because he might have taken her right there on the pool table and anyone could have walked in on that including one of the younger boys.

Cole wanted to go to her now but knew he wouldn't. Jacob was over there and that complicated everything. He could still smell her perfume on his collar and stalked purposefully to the en-suite bathroom. It looked like for tonight all he was getting was a cold shower. His lips twisted in self-derision. He turned on the cold water then started the jets and moved under the icy spray. The cold shower did wonders and he headed promptly to bed.

Brooke sipped on her warm tea as she sat with Jacob on the couch. They had been sitting together for a long while in relative silence. She turned and looked at him as he stared silently into his beer. Impulsively she reached out and covered the hand that held the beer with her own. "What is going on with you, Jacob?" she asked quietly.

He glanced up to meet her watchful gaze. "I'm afraid you're going to try running off back to Montana," he said slowly.

Brooke smiled. "I'm glad you brought that up because I have been meaning to tell you that I'm going back in the morning." He looked like he was going to disagree so she held up her hands. "I know you were planning to drive me but I arranged for a rental in town that I can drop off in the city when I get there. I don't want you to put your life on hold to take me and you have that date tomorrow night."

Jacob looked incredulous now. "Fuck that date. I am not letting you drive four hundred miles through the mountains in the middle of winter while you're eight months along, alone, Brooke. Besides it's not a date but more of a casual dinner. If I need to cancel it, I will, but you aren't going alone." He studied her face looking serious. "I wish you would just consider staying."

Brooke smiled to soften her words. "I have a job, a house, and quite honestly my life is there now, Jacob. I can't just throw all of that away."

He groaned in frustration. "I don't like the idea of you being there alone, having a baby, and then trying to take care of him all on your own."

"I do have friends there too, you know," she chided gently with a sideways smile. "I won't be alone, and we will come back and visit when we can." She reached out and squeezed his hand. "For that matter you can come visit me too if you ever want to."

Jacob sighed. "No offense but that plan sounds lame and lonely."

Brooke laughed warmly at his disgruntled frown. "I will miss you, but it can't be nearly as bad as before. At least we'll be able to talk on the phone."

"We could just get married and I could adopt the baby," he said quickly. She was looking at him in surprise so he quickly forged ahead. "Just hear me out. I could move up there with you and we could raise him together. I do love you Brooke and my life hasn't been the same since I met you."

Brooke laughed a little. "I appreciate the offer, Jacob, but I love you too much for that. Since you seem to have forgotten that very interesting kiss we shared let me remind you that there was no response on either end. You are going to meet some pretty girl one of these days and you aren't going to be able to stop yourself from falling in love with her. When that happens, I won't be the inconvenient wife stopping you from having the love story you deserve. I will be your best friend, cheering you on and kicking you in gear to go after her. Besides all that, you have a life here and a decent plan."

He shrugged. "I don't care about any of that now. I can take the Montana bar and practice there instead. We could even just live together so I can help you with everything as friends."

Brooke shook her head adamantly, "No way buddy, the whole reason you're going to law school is so that you can help out your dad and all the farmers here in the valley. I am not going to let you throw away your life for me."

Jacob grinned. "It wouldn't be only for you. I need my best friend around."

Brooke smiled and lay on his shoulder. "It will all work out, you'll see."

"At least wait until I can drive you up there," he pleaded.

Brooke nodded her head and said quietly, "If you promise to go on your date tomorrow night, I will stay until the following morning so you can drive me."

There was a long silent pause before he finally agreed. "Deal." He tilted her chin up then and forced her eyes to his. "I just want to know one thing." He paused. "How much of this is about Cole?"

She stared at him in surprise. "How much of what?"

He grinned. "The fact that you won't even consider us together?"

She looked away for a moment before saying quietly. "I won't lie and say there's nothing between us because I respect you too much, Jacob. However, I am not a fool and we both know that Cole doesn't want to be tied down to anything or anyone. I don't even think he likes the fact that he's attracted to me." She laughed sadly at the last.

Jacob smiled and said, "I think he might like you more than a little."

Brooke shook her head. She couldn't afford to think that way. She was already desperately in love with Cole. Had been soaking up everything she'd learned about him since she had come back. Everything she learned only made her want him more which was a big problem. With a long sigh she said, "I don't agree. He hasn't said anything that leads me to believe he is or would ever be interested in a relationship."

"He did search for you," he pointed out with a challenging look.

"We both know that he did that for all of you and just because he is a good person," Brooke responded. She missed his raised eyebrow at her last comment.

He sounded amused as he said, "I believe that is the first time I have ever heard anyone call him a good person."

Brooke hit his shoulder lightly. "Be nice."

She lay on his shoulder for a few more minutes before finally saying good night.

She thought of Cole as she brushed her teeth and hair. She thought of him as she undressed and got ready for bed. She thought of his warm strong hands on her body and that now familiar flush of warm heat started in her belly. She groaned. She would spend tomorrow here and then she would leave the next morning. She didn't even know if she would see him again before she left. A hopeless feeling flooded her and tears gathered in her eyes.

She had known all along that whatever she had with him was purely physical. She shouldn't want more than that now but couldn't help it. Tears streamed silently down her cheeks. In silent torture she imagined the long months of loneliness ahead and with a shudder buried her face in one of the soft pillows that Cole had thought to put here for her. He was so thoughtful and considerate and yet he wanted people to think he was cold and detached.

She let the pain come. Better to face it all now as she was going to need all her strength in the months to come. She cried until she felt empty and then she turned onto her side and tucked a pillow between her knees and held it close as she closed her eyes. She could still hear the shower running from Jacob when she finally slept.

A while later she woke suddenly and stiffened at the warm hard body that was aligned with her own. She stifled a scream as she heard Cole whisper, "It's just me."

She turned to meet his black eyes in the darkness. "Why are you here?" she asked dumbly.

He grinned and his white teeth shone. "I couldn't stop thinking about you," he said it simply, honestly.

Brooke stared at him. "Where is Jacob?" she asked, suddenly embarrassed.

Cole chuckled low. "He was snoring when I passed the bedroom door. He never even heard me come in."

"What are you doing here, Cole?" she asked again.

He shrugged then ran his fingers lightly down her shoulder and arm only to trail softly back up to stop just short of touching the rounded mound of her very full breast. "I couldn't stop thinking about you and all the things I wanted to do to you," he said simply. Then he waited patiently for her to arch into his hand. He drew a little circle there just below that beckoning slope. She moaned and pushed into his hand and he obliged her. He bent over her to lightly whisper in detail the things he wanted to do to her. She moaned breathlessly as his thumb rubbed lightly across her puckered nipple.

Cole spent the next hour doing exactly as he'd promised. He lay next to her sleeping body for several minutes as she curled up against him. His last thought before he fell asleep was that he should really get up and leave before Jacob or his parents realized he had spent the night with her.

CHAPTER 41

Brooke awoke feeling relaxed. She moaned and stretched as memories of last night flooded in. She rolled over quickly, looking for Cole. He wasn't there and her brows knitted in consternation. Had it been a dream? She blushed at the vivid details of her imagination. Then she noticed the indent in the pillow where his head had been. Relief washed through her. He had probably gotten up early to avoid Jacob. She moved over to lay her head where he had been, smelling the faint clean scent of him. She gave herself one lingering minute and then she pulled herself out of bed and headed to the shower. She could hear Jacob banging around in the kitchen as she climbed under the hot spray letting it seep into her joints and ease any soreness from the night before.

Once she was done dressing, she made her way sleepily out to find out what Jacob was doing. She could smell fresh coffee and her mouth watered. "Where did you find coffee, Jacob?" she asked as she rounded the corner into the kitchen. Jacob looked up from the table where he sat with a steaming mug.

Cole stood by the stove and turned when she entered. "He got it from me," he told her casually. He stirred at the pot on the stove. "Want some?" he asked.

Brooke nodded in surprise and joy. He grinned as he poured a mug and then stirred in a little sugar and a dash of cream. He held it out and motioned her over to the table. She walked over and sat next to Jacob. Not knowing what Cole was thinking, she took a sip of coffee and threw questioning look at Jacob.

He shrugged. "Don't look at me. When I woke up, he was already here working at breakfast."

She turned to meet Cole's grinning wink. "I see" was her only response.

Cole loaded three plates with omelets, toast, and a small dish of grits. Brooke stood quickly and hurried to help him haul them to the table. "Don't worry about Mom and Dad. I told them I was bringing breakfast over to ya'll," he informed her as though that might be her biggest concern.

She smiled and nodded, not sure what else to say.

Jacob on the other hand had no such issue. He grinned knowingly at Cole. "So, what inspired this impromptu breakfast of yours, oh brother of mine?" He turned and smiled at Brooke who'd just taken a large tentative bite of grits. It burned her tongue and she sputtered and took a large gulp of coffee that burned all the way down. With a loud curse she jumped up and hurried to the sink for cold water. Cole beat her there and handed her a glass as she rushed over. She gulped it down but the damage was already done. Her taste buds felt numb and tingled slightly.

She smiled in good humor, "Sorry, I just burned my mouth a bit." No one needed the explanation but she made it anyway.

Jacob smiled and then turned to Cole. "So? What brings you over here so bright and early? Did you miss your big bro?"

Cole snorted. "Sure, whatever makes your chest hair grow."

Brooke smothered her laughter at his joke. She looked at Jacob and then Cole under her dark lashes. It appeared that she might be filling the role of peacemaker today. She smiled at Cole. "I, for one, am glad you came, Cole," she said warmly.

Jacob laughed. "Of course, you are. And why exactly is that?" he pressed.

Brooke gave him an annoyed look. "I happen to like Cole," she defended. "In fact, I quite happen to like your whole damn stubborn family," she added for emphasis.

"Right, right. And none of this would happen to have anything to do with whatever energy is constantly pinging between the two of you?" he mocked with a grin.

Both Cole and Brooke turned clear innocent looks toward him simultaneously. Jacob laughed and held up his hands. "Fine, I'll leave it alone, but you two are going to have to talk about it at some point."

"What is there to talk about?" they both said in unison and Jacob laughed.

After breakfast Cole excused himself and left as Brooke began sorting through the pile of gifts. She looked at the list Anne had made for her of all the gifts people had given her. She talked Jacob into helping her as she wrote little notes of appreciation in the thank-you cards she had picked up. He addressed envelopes and attached stamps as she wrote.

When that was done, she walked out and put them in the mailbox making sure the flag was up before walking back to the house. The hair on the back of her neck stood up as she crossed the snow-packed lawn. She paused for a long moment to look around. She saw no one and nothing seemed out of place so she picked up her pace and hurried back inside.

Once the thank-you cards were finished, she began sorting the baby items by age and variety. She needed to condense everything so they would be able to fit it all in the jeep. She found a couple of large boxes downstairs and loaded the clothing and blankets into one. Then she loaded bottles, toys, diapers, and all the other baby paraphernalia into the second box. She turned to Jacob with a doubtful expression. "Do you thing we're going to be able to fit all of this into the jeep?"

He nodded absentmindedly and went back to his laptop where he had spent the last little while working. Lunch came and went as she did her laundry. She wanted to be ready to go first thing in the morning and so she packed up anything she wouldn't need before leaving.

Jacob was still working on his laptop when she finished cleaning the kitchen. When everything was shiny again, she walked over to where he sat and smiled at him, "Hey, I just wanted to let you know I'm going out for a walk."

He looked a little unfocused. "Sure, I'll come catch up in a few minutes."

Brooke pulled tall furry boots on and a long thick coat before adding a cap and some gloves. It hadn't been too cold earlier when she'd gone out to the mailbox, but the wind could kick in fast and add an unbearable chill to the air.

She stepped out onto the gravel road and looked to her left and then to her right debating which way to turn. Wanting to be close to Cole, she found herself walking the direction toward the Burton estate. She had only walked a quarter of a mile when she started feeling uneasy. She thought about turning back but told herself not to be a wimp. She wouldn't be able to get fresh walks in for a while after she had the baby since it was so cold in Montana and she wanted to soak it up now. She pushed on. Twice she thought she heard someone behind her but when she slowed and turned to look back there was no one there. The nerves settled in and she shivered reaching for the phone in her pocket.

It wasn't there and in a moment of panic she realized she had left it on the table when she'd put her gloves on. She heard something behind her and turned but no one was there. She squinted, back several yards away she thought she could see something dark just beyond a large snow drift. Her skin prickled with nervousness. She couldn't get herself to go back to check it out. Instead, she pressed on at a faster clip now. She could see the trees ahead that marked the long driveway to the house. She could even see a little of the house itself where it stood behind the trees. She heard that steady thumping sound behind her again. The sound of boots crunching against icy snow. She didn't dare look back. It would be Jacob coming to catch her she tried to reassure herself as she picked up her feet and ran.

She turned up the driveway and ran toward the house as fast as she could go. She looked at the house and then the garage a little indecisively. With a quick gait she ran toward the garage and grabbed at the doorknob. Her icy fingers slipped and her hand flew back off. She glanced behind herself as her fingers slid around the knob once again. Over near the trees stood someone or something. It looked like a large man and icy fear gnawed its way down her spine. She watched, rooted to the spot as he moved along the tree line weaving quickly in and out of the dark trees moving ever closer to her. She yanked on the door praying that she hadn't just made the biggest mistake yet and ran into the lit interior.

Relief surged through her as she saw the figure bent by the hood of the car. She ran toward him as the door banged shut behind her and Cole straightened up looking toward the door in curiosity. He barely realized who she was before she barreled into his arms clutching at him in wide-eyed fear. Good God, she looked terrified. Her skin was so pale that the shimmer of freckles across her nose stood out. He was greasy but she was clutching at him anyway so he wrapped his dirty arms around her and held on.

In a low quiet voice that was meant to be soothing he asked, "What in God's name is going on?"

She trembled and took gulping breaths as though she'd been running. He moved back just enough to lift her chin. "Brooke, breathe, baby. Were you running?" he asked in disbelief as he gave her belly a pointed look.

She gulped. "I'm so sorry," and tears welled up in her eyes. "It's probably all just my imagination," she murmured.

He shook her gently. "*What* is probably your imagination? Talk to me, honey." He ran a soothing hand up and down her back.

"I think," she gulped again. "I think someone was following me."

His gut clenched and his mind jumped immediately to that gray truck in Montana. He lifted her chin and met her upturned gaze. "Who would be following you, Brooke? And where is Jacob?"

She stared at her boots. "He's at the old house. I decided to go for a walk and I thought I heard someone following me, but then I looked and no one was there. Then I realized I didn't have my phone and I couldn't call anyone, but I thought I saw a dark shadow in the snow and I didn't dare go back, so I ran here. I don't know why, but when I got to the driveway, I thought you might be out here, so I came here instead of to the house. I saw him in the trees, though, Cole. He was trying to stay out of sight, but I could see him moving around the trees."

Cole looked toward the door in alarm. "Just now?" he asked already moving toward the door, adrenaline surging. "Stay behind me, but I gotta go out there. I need to make sure everyone is okay."

She nodded and let go of him. They walked out and he ran his gaze around to scan the yard. Nothing looked out of place. She searched the tree line, fear evident in her face. Their eyes met and he asked, "Where did you see him?"

She pointed to the trees at the edge of the road. "He was walking toward me through the trees." She turned and looked all around.

Cole reached for her hand. "Let's get you inside so you can warm up and I'll get my dad. Together we'll go out and see if anyone is around."

She nodded and turned, nearly running back to the house. "Be careful," she said in a very serious whisper.

Ivan was in the kitchen and Cole quickly told him what they needed and he and Cole locked all the doors before going out together. Anne came in to sit with her and Zack came in moments later saying, "I told them to come in here, Mom."

Anne nodded and turned to Brooke. "I don't know what is going on, but I'd feel better if we are all in here together."

Brooke shivered and nodded. Anne stood and insisted on making her some hot tea. As she sipped, she retold them about her walk. The more she talked about it, though, the sillier she felt. By the time Ivan and Cole came in through the front door, she had convinced herself it was all just her overactive imagination hyped up on hormones.

Ivan smiled at her. "Look who we found," he said as Jacob followed them in.

Brooke stood up and walked over to them. "Was anyone else out there?" she asked shortly.

The men looked at each other and then back at her. "No, sorry. We didn't see any sign of anyone." Ivan looked concerned. "We did see some tracks by the trees, but there were a lot of them and they could have been from anyone."

Brooke met his gaze and then stared at the floor. "I'm so sorry to worry you all. I probably just imagined it."

Anne watched her closely. "Is there any chance it was Jacob you heard?" she asked. "It appears he did follow you after all."

She shook her head quickly but then nodded. "Maybe."

Jacob walked over to hug her shoulders. "I lost track of time and when I remembered you had gone out, I followed. When I didn't see you, I jogged it over here. I ran into Cole and Dad out by the trees looking around. I didn't see anyone," he added helpfully.

Brooke burst into tears. "I'm so sorry I worried you all," she murmured as she wiped desperately at her eyes.

Ivan enveloped her in a bear hug. "Don't be sorry, dear. We just care about you and we're glad you're safe."

Cole watched her with those uncanny dark eyes. "You seemed pretty certain there was someone following you," he stated quietly refusing to believe that nothing had happened. "Why would Jacob be skulking around in the trees anyway?"

Jacob looked at Cole. "I wasn't skulking in the trees until I saw you guys there."

Brooke shook her head. "I probably just imagined it all. I've been a little jumpy lately and I think my imagination just got the best of me."

Anne nodded. "Fluctuating hormones can have a lot of different effects on women. Plus, with that whole incident here after the fourth who could blame you for being a little jumpy?" She soothed as she, too, walked over to give Brooke a warm hug.

"Well, I'm sorry about it." Brooke looked around the room. "What can I do to make it up to you all?" she asked glumly.

Cole was still staring at her, so she avoided looking at him and focused instead on the others. Ivan grinned. "Well, Jacob told me that you plan to leave in the morning so maybe we could all have dinner and spend some time together as a family before you go back."

Brooke nodded and forced a smile. "Sounds like fun," she said lightly with fake enthusiasm. They all made their way into the kitchen again. Brooke was halfway across the room before she turned back suddenly. "I almost forgot. Jacob, you have that date tonight so you better go get ready."

Jacob shook his head. "I'll just cancel it. I don't want to leave you with all this." He pulled his phone out.

Brooke glared and opened her mouth to argue, but Anne beat her to it. "Jacob Burton, you'll do no such thing. That poor girl has been trying to get your attention for years now and you finally agreed to go out with her. You are not going to cancel when we are all perfectly capable of being here for Brooke. Go get dressed and then go and have fun."

Cole sent a mocking smile at Jacob. Jacob's hand dropped back to his side with his phone. "Yes, ma'am," he said as he walked over and gave Brooke a quick squeeze before telling her to call if she needed anything. She reminded him that she didn't have her phone but that she would borrow one if she needed. He reluctantly left.

Everyone helped whip up some spaghetti with meat sauce, garlic bread and a fresh garden salad. They all ate as Anne forced small talk to ease the awkward silence.

Everyone looked surprised when Cole stood., "What game do y'all want to play?" he began clearing the table as he asked.

Everyone stared at him for a minute before Ivan finally suggested monopoly. Everyone else groaned and a debate began about the rules. Brooke was so grateful for the normalcy that she looked at Cole and mouthed a heartfelt thank-you when he met her eyes. His eyes twinkled but he only gave her a quick nod.

It was early when Brooke finally begged off for the night. She wanted to get home and get some sleep before the long drive tomorrow. Cole offered to drive her since Jacob was gone and she readily agreed. Anne gave Cole a long look and then told him to hurry back and they would keep him in the game. He insisted they didn't need to wait, but his mother wasn't taking no for an answer. Finally, feeling a little exasperated he nodded as Brooke hugged everyone and told them goodbye.

They drove in silence to the house. He put the jeep in park when they pulled up and turned to her. "Are you going to be okay?" he asked softly.

She nodded quickly, a little too quickly in his mind. "I'll just go in and get some sleep." She hesitated before opening the door. "You don't happen to have a bat in there do you?" she asked, her voice trembling a little.

His brow shot up and he chuckled. "You really are shaken up, aren't you?" He climbed out and came around to open her door. He lifted her from the truck and slid her softly down his body. "What am I going to do with you?" he asked in a truly confounded voice.

She smiled up at him. "I don't think there is much that you haven't already done." Her heart ached and she wanted to say, *"keep me,"* but instead she held her tongue.

He kissed her softly then and held her for a long moment before releasing her. "After you get back north, don't be a stranger, Brooke."

She nodded and took one hesitant step toward the house. She was so reluctant that Cole walked ahead of her. "Let's just make sure the house is secure and that no one is here before I go." He said it in a matter-of-fact voice and Brooke smiled in relief. The door was still locked and no one was inside.

Brooke smiled up at him a little embarrassed. "I'm sorry for all of this. I'm sure there was nothing to it."

He nodded and looked down at her lips. He wanted to kiss her, but that would lead to more and his mother had been crystal clear that they were waiting for him. He met her blue eyes and smiled. "I better get back before Mom starts calling." He tipped his dark head toward her once more and walked out the door. She quickly locked it behind him and turned back to the bedroom. She had felt chilled all evening and a nice warm bath was just the thing to warm her up.

She took a long soak and then got out. She put on a cozy pair of flannel pajama bottoms and a matching tank top. She climbed into bed and was just starting to relax when she suddenly remembered that she had left her phone on the table. She climbed back out of the bed and padded down the hallway turning on lights as she went. She stared at the table in puzzlement. Her phone wasn't there. Jacob must have taken it but forgotten to give it to her. She yawned and turned out the light.

There was a soft playful rap on the front door and she smiled. Cole had come back after all. She hurried over to unlock the door as she turned on the porch light. She was smiling as the door swung open. Her face froze as Richard stepped forward with a gun in his hand. She didn't move and he raised it to her head. "Hello, darlin'" he said, his voice lusty. "Well, aren't you going to invite me in?"

She shook her head no even as she stepped back when he advanced. Her mind was screaming, *no, no, no*, as she slumped to the floor in a dead faint.

CHAPTER 42

Brooke opened her eyes in confusion. She saw Richard standing next to the chair she was sitting on and her memory came flooding back. She stood abruptly, "What are you doing here?" she asked groggily.

He chuckled and it came out with a hint of a high-pitched cackle. "It's okay, my darlin' I'm here to save you now." He held the gun pointed at the floor and watched her through his cold blue eyes.

She tried to step away, but he raised the gun and she froze. "I am here because I want to be Richard. Do you think I would ever go back with you after what you did to me?"

His eyes bulged slightly. "What I did to you?" he spewed. "What about what you did to me? Teasing me all that time so I would be desperate to have you. Costing me thousands upon thousands of dollars for all that damage so you could what? Make me want you more." He reached out a hand to squeeze her breast. She swung her arm up to stop him. Hit his arm so hard it went swinging. He swore and punched her with his other fist. Brooke didn't see the fist until it was too late and the hit landed solidly on her abdomen. The air swooshed out of her lungs with a loud groan. She went wild jumping at him and trying to grab the gun.

He pulled back the gun hand in time but she clawed at his face. He swore and backhanded her across her cheek. She flew back from the blow and would have fallen to the floor if he hadn't already gripped her hand. Her shoulder twisted at an odd angle and she heard a loud pop just before pain surged through her arm. She cried out once before she bit her tongue. She wouldn't, no couldn't give him the satisfaction of knowing he had hurt her. She remembered his crazed lust as she had been afraid before and vowed she would not let him rape her again. She tried to hold her stomach as terror for her baby's safety threatened to overwhelm her. He pinned her arms to her sides as he pulled her back up against his groin. She felt the hard point there and knew he was excited by all of this. Her mind screamed but her lips never opened.

She relaxed suddenly and it threw him off guard. As soon as she felt the tiniest give against her arm she yanked forward and brought a fist back hard toward his balls. He let go of her and screamed in pain as he reached a hand to cup the offended member. "I think you broke me, you bitch." He seethed through his teeth.

She was already running away from him. She looked frantically at the door and then instead ran toward the hall. In this cold weather she would be just as likely to die from the cold while hiding from him, as if he found her and killed her himself. She had to get to the bedroom and get a coat and boots before going outside.

A shot rang out and she froze as the bullet bit into the painted sheet rock next to her head. He laughed and grabbed her arm. "Next one goes through your head," he promised as he trained the gun on her forehead. He reached for her good arm and yanked her toward him. The gun pressed against her scalp and he smiled down at her with his putrid breath seeping out to rasp offensively at her nose. "That's a good girl. I just want to talk to you awhile darlin'. Let's sit for a moment and talk," he rasped out again as he shoved her down on the couch.

Her shoulder throbbed and she bit her tongue hard to stop her cry of pain. She stared up at him afraid for hers and her baby's life but refused to let him see that. "What could we possibly have to talk about, Richard?" she asked with a voice full of disdain.

He smiled gently now. "We had a good thing once, Brooke darlin'. Remember? We had all those plans to be married and live together and have a family." His voice was a little shrill now. "I was doing everything I could to get your father to give us the go-ahead, but you kept sabotaging things. I only did what I did to punish you because you really do need to know who is boss." He gave her a crazed smile as though he thought she'd understand.

A tear slipped down her cheek. She knew her life was in his hands at this moment and she licked her dry lips. The metallic taste of copper filled her mouth and she wiped at the blood on her lip with her good arm. "I'm sorry things didn't work out with us, Richard," she said softly. Maybe she could talk her way out of this. She thought of Jacob and Ivan and even Cole and wondered why she hadn't said something sooner to them about him. She hadn't wanted the shame of them knowing all she'd done and now she was probably going to die tonight. A fresh surge of pain squeezed at her heart at the realization that her little bug would also die. A renewed sense of survival took over and calmly she asked. "What is it that you want here?"

His blue eyes darted to hers suddenly as disbelief stretched his eyebrows up. "Why you of course. I want a family and a life with you darlin.' That is all I have ever wanted."

She stared numbly at him. He sounded as though he had some maniacal fairy tale in his head of how their life would be. She licked her lip again. "You mean like a fairy tale?" she forced a gentle tone now. She could see a light at the end of this very long tunnel of death. If only she could convince him that they had a chance maybe she could get safe long enough to call Jacob or the police somehow.

He shook his head. "No not like a fairy tales! It would be a godly union that could be celebrated in holiness."

She stared blankly at him.

Richard rubbed a hand down her thigh then and though she tried to stay still she couldn't keep herself from jerking away from his soft touch. "I understand that you have been whoring yourself out to men to survive. I will take care of you now. I will even forgive you eventually for that," he said in what she could only assume was meant to be a reassuring voice.

She stared at him in confusion. He wasn't making any sense until she realized he must have been watching her for a very long time and had assumed any man who came to see her was there for sex. She almost laughed at that notion but didn't as she didn't want to anger him. The thought of herself sleeping with men for money nearly gagged her and she knew most of that feeling was due to him and what he had done to her.

He took her silence as some level of agreement. "I mean we'll have to take care of that." To her horror he pointed the gun at her belly. "Because that would have no godly place in our holy matrimony, but we could still work it all out."

Brooke was scooting away from him now, unable to hide her terror any longer. She would *not* let him kill her baby and keep her alive. In that moment she suddenly knew she would do whatever she had to to keep her child alive and safe.

He grabbed for her arm, but she had already gotten far enough away to stand and make a run for it. He pounced on her tackling her from behind. She fell hard and felt a sickening lurch in her belly as she rolled trying to protect the life there. He straddled her and pinned her arms again. She fought to get away but his whisper made her go limp. "Please don't make me kill you darlin'. I do love you but if you keep insisting on not allowing me to lead you, the way a man is meant to I will have to blow those pretty little brains out."

He started to slide off of her with the gun trained on her head as he stared into her bright blue eyes. "That's it. Stay calm now." He reached out a hand to pull her up like a gentleman.

She scooted away pulling up her arm up and pushed herself to sit up with her back against the wall. Brooke watched as he got down on his knees and leaned toward her. "Don't you see that all we have to do is get rid of the baby and everything will be all right?"

Watching his every move, her mind twisted and turned trying to find any way out of this. She tried to stand but her shoulder screamed in pain, and somewhere in her lower chest pain shot out nearly making her scream. She had to think, had to formulate a plan in which both she and the baby survived. She thought of Jacob and prayed that his date would end soon and he would come home. Then she imagined Richard shooting him as he walked through the door and her prayer changed to hoping his date lasted all night.

Richard edged closer, looking down at her with a happy grin. "I looked up all the ways to get rid of a baby that is semi-safe for the survival of the mother," he shared with enthusiasm. "I have a plan, but you just have to trust me."

Brooke tried to spit but her mouth and throat were dry from the heavy exertion of breathing through the pain. "I will not do anything to kill this child, Richard. I would rather die." In one swift motion she stood and lurched into the hall. He grabbed at her ankle but missed. She ran three steps before he caught her. She stopped instantly as he reached around and shoved the tip of the gun into her stomach. "You can either help me or not darlin' but either way I am going to rid you of this abomination," he said coldly and without feeling.

Brooke stood very still. Clarity dawned as the fog of fear lifted and she knew that this was her one and only chance to save her baby and herself. She took a deep breath and turned slowly to lean into him, she rubbed against him suggestively and smiled. "Okay," she said softly into his lips and his eyes shuttered slightly in response. His hold on the gun loosened as she rubbed her breasts against his chest. His eyes closed and he gritted his teeth in ecstasy.

Now! her mind screamed and she brought her arm up and slammed his gun hand against the wall in the same moment that she brought her knee up hard into his groin. The gun clattered to the floor and went off as it bounced back behind him.

He dropped to his knees screaming in agony. She turned toward the door a few steps away, tried to run, stumbled as his hand closed around her ankle. His elbow came down hard into her belly and she felt a sickening gurgle as pain threatened strobes of light and then darkness behind her eyelids. His fists hit her then, again and again as she fought off the darkness that was threatening to take over. She twisted and tried to escape those fists. One missed her stomach as she tried to curl up and her jaw popped back hard as stars shone again. His relentless blows lit all over her body as she twisted and scooted in a dying attempt to protect the mound of her stomach. She heard him cry out, "I will rid your body of that bastard's child if it kills us both."

She tried to process what he was saying, but her mind was dark. She felt something sticky oozing between her legs as his words sunk in. As the darkness took her mind, she whispered the one thing that might save both of their lives: "The baby is yours, Richard."

Even as everything was turning black, she forced her lips to say the words over and over, willing him to hear and hoping it would somehow matter. Then the pain faded and the darkness took her.

CHAPTER 43

After dropping Brooke off Cole drove home deep in thought. Something was nagging at him about all of this. He kept rolling it over and over in his head as though it was on repeat because something didn't add up.

He strode into the house and walked toward the kitchen. He could hear the laughter of his family before he stepped through the door. He stopped walking and started once more at the beginning. He thought first of meeting Brooke and trying to kiss her. Her fear then, her fear in Montana. That gray truck that kept nagging at him. The feeling like something was always off. He thought of the terror on her face tonight as she had run into his arms. *"Someone is following me,"* she had said. She had been running scared the whole time he had known her. The attack on the fourth. Her baby. Everything slid into place with terrifying clarity. He looked at the kitchen table, where his family had been staring at him in curiosity since he had stepped through the door and stopped.

He looked at his mom and dad. "Fuck. It has been the same bastard all this time."

Anne looked stunned. "Language, Cole," she began with a quick glance at the younger boys but then she looked at him and her mouth closed with a snap. His eyes narrowed as his skin paled.

"Mom, come with me now. Get your medical bag." He turned on his heel and strode out.

Anne stared after him and then quickly stood. She hurried to the cabinet where she kept an emergency medical kit and slid it out. From the other room, she heard Cole yell, "Hurry up Mom, now!"

She hurried out as she heard his car roar to life. He was already turning it around when she walked out. He stopped just long enough for her to slide in and close her door before he skidded out of the driveway fishtailing onto the road.

Anne held on to the dash in fear. "Slow down, Cole and tell me what's going on," she said through fear-clenched teeth.

He didn't look at her but kept his eyes on the road as he did eighty on the snow-packed gravel. "I hope to God nothing is going on, but if my guess is right, please God let me get there in time."

Anne stared at him in frustration as she quickly clicked her seat belt into place. Not that it did any good as a minute later, he swerved to a screeching halt in front of the old farmhouse. He was opening the door even as he yanked the gearshift to neutral. "Stay here until I come for you," he ordered as he slid out.

A loud bang sounded then and Anne watched in surreal horror as her son ran to the door. It slammed against the wall as he threw it open and barreled inside. What was that bang she wondered, thinking it had almost sounded like a gunshot. With the image of her son running into a gunfight in mind she quickly undid her own buckle and grabbed for her medical bag.

The first thing Cole saw was a large splotch of blood on the wall. He strode quickly that direction. As he got close, he saw a gun spinning on the hardwood floor. He reached for it without thinking. Then he saw her. She was laying slumped on the floor half curled into the fetal position. There was blood on her swollen face and she looked dead. Fury seized him and he raised the gun to the back of the head of the man who was busy pounding his fists into her. Cole heard a hoarse gurgling sound and saw her lips moving but couldn't hear what she was saying. His finger itched on the trigger. He took a deep breath. "Get off her or I will pull this trigger and blow your brains out," he said, his voice hard and stony.

The man stopped before he even got the words out. He didn't turn, though but only bent down to lean close to her face as she went still. "What did you say darlin'? Did you say the baby is ours?" He gently kissed her pale bruised cheeks.

Cole resisted the urge to pull the trigger then and there. His finger tightened and he heard his mother walk up behind him. "I won't say it again, man. Move away from her."

It was as though Richard never even heard him. He was touching her all over now. Tenderly whispering words of love as he tugged at her clothes as though to make love to her.

Cole didn't have a great shot now without taking a chance on hitting Brooke. He swore low and vicious. He should have taken the shot when he had it. Without a moment's hesitation he lowered the gun and shot the bastard in the ass.

That got his attention and he reared up screaming in pain. He turned and lunged at Cole who lifted the gun to aim it directly at his head.

His mother's hand on his arm was the only thing that stopped him from pulling the trigger. He lowered the gun and handed it back to his mother. Then he lunged forward and punched the guy in the nose. He grabbed him by his shoulders and threw him down the hallway away from Brooke.

Her body was limp and a large puddle of blood oozed out around her legs. Numbly he stumbled forward and then turned to his mom. "You have to save her," he said simply and hurried around to gently lift her head and rub a hand gently across her pale bruised cheek. Blood oozed between her legs and he scooted around trying to hold the oozing red inside of her.

Anne stood rooted to the spot staring down at the broken bloody bruised mess that was Brooke. She looked at the gun in her hand and suddenly moved forward. She handed the gun to Cole. "Take this."

He took it but set it on the floor beside them as terror shook him to the core. He felt for a pulse. He didn't know he was holding his breath until he felt a tiny beat and the air shoved out of his lungs in a relieved sigh. "She's still alive, Mom, what can I do?"

Anne was already cutting away her pajamas. "Hold her and help me turn her Cole," she said in a strong matter-of-fact tone as she cut at the fabric. "I need to see where the bleeding is coming from." After turning her onto her back Cole moved back toward her head numbly. "Cole, call 9-1-1 now. We need an ambulance and we need the police to come for him." She pointed a thumb over her shoulder.

He nodded and made the call quickly as his mother worked quickly and efficiently on Brooke. Suddenly Brooke groaned and her eyes opened to look at him. The terror cleared and she tried to get up.

"Cole, hold her down I need her to stay still." Anne's firm but gentle voice had her leaning up to try to see who was talking. Her eyes widened in fear and she reached for the gun with her left hand. She pulled it up and Anne's eyes widened in surprise as she pulled the trigger. She kept pulling the trigger long after the gun was empty.

Richard crumpled behind Anne and the knife he was clutching clattered to the floor. The remaining shots hit the wall where Richard had been standing sending tiny puffs of dust out. Anne turned then and looked at the man who had almost stabbed her and then bent down to do whatever she could for Brooke.

Brooke collapsed again as the darkness once again overcame her.

Cole was still on the phone and he informed his mother that the ambulance was fifteen minutes out. Anne looked up at him with tears in her eyes. "I was able to slow the bleeding from the bullet wound, but she is hemorrhaging and I don't have what I need to stop that. She won't make it that long, Cole."

He wouldn't lose her or the baby. His jaw hardened and he stood then bent down and lifted her easily into his arms. "Then we will have to meet the ambulance halfway," he stated tersely. "I'll drive and you will do whatever it takes to keep her and the baby alive," he stated simply.

Anne wasn't confident in either one surviving but she wasn't going to tell him that. She gave a quick nod and gathered her tools and shoved them in her bag as she hurried out behind him. The man on the floor lifted a hand. "You can't take my wife and my baby. They belong to me," he tried to get up but slumped back on the floor.

Cole turned back for one moment. "Is that what you think, you fool? Both Brooke and that baby are mine."

Anne raised an eyebrow at that but didn't say anything, only followed her son out to the car. It was still running and Anne quickly leaned the front seat forward and climbed into the back. "Lay her here, Cole. Try to elevate her hips to help staunch the hemorrhaging."

He gently laid her head down and lifted her hips onto his mother's lap. Then he slid in and drove as fast as he dared. 911 was still on the phone and he told them what he was driving and to have the ambulance prepared for a pregnant woman that was hemorrhaging. At his mother's order he also told them about her condition as he sped down the highway.

Off in the distance, he saw flashing lights, and when they were getting close, he informed the operator that he could see the ambulance and he was pulling off the road. He had just lifted Brooke from the car as the ambulance skidded to a stop. He hung up the phone and walked quickly to meet the woman as she jumped from the front of the ambulance. They loaded her onto a stretcher as Anne talked steadily, telling them what to do. When they had her loaded into the back she climbed up. "I'm a doctor and I am coming with you because I might be able to help." The EMT nodded as she worked to start an IV.

Cole jumped in and closed the door behind him. "I'm the father," he said tersely and got another quick nod.

He had never been so terrified in his life as he was sitting there helplessly watching the life and blood seep out of Brooke. He had been running from the truth. How pathetically ironic it was that it meant her dying in front of him to realize he had feelings for her and that baby.

His phone rang and he looked numbly down at his father's face. In a voice devoid of emotion, he answered and promptly explained where they were. In a steady voice he asked Ivan to go to the old house and make sure the police had gotten the guy before he came to the hospital. Ivan agreed in a voice husky with emotion.

"Take care of her, Cole." Ivan murmured as he hung up already walking to his truck. He hollered for the boys to come quickly as he threw a thick coat on and opened the door. By the time he turned the truck around all three of them had coats and climbed quickly into the cold cab.

He sped down to the old house and jumped out telling the boys to stay put inside. There were a couple of the sheriff's vehicles with flashing lights parked in front and he skirted them as he walked hurriedly into the open door.

The sheriff was talking to a deputy and stopped when he walked in. He hurried over to Ivan to quickly inform him that there was no one in the house when they got there. The gun was gone as well but there was blood smeared all over the hall floor and some more in the front room. They had followed a bloody trail outside in the back where they had found truck tracks but the guy was in the wind.

Ivan thanked the sheriff and drove away. He looked at his boys. "Brooke has been injured and is going to the hospital and I need to get down there. Would you boys rather go to a friend's house or do you want to come with me?" he asked quietly. They all wanted to go with so he pulled onto the highway and drove toward town and the nearest hospital.

With a prayer in his heart and one foot on the accelerator he said, "Please God just let her live and we will make sure she knows how loved she is for the rest of her life."

Cole watched as his mother and the EMTs worked frantically on Brooke trying to get the bleeding slowed. It seemed like whenever they finally handled one issue another one started. The EMT managed to get a heartbeat for the baby, but it was erratic and accelerated. Brooke's blood pressure was getting too low. When the wheezing started from her blue lips he reached for her hand and held it with his head bent as tears slid down his whisker studded jaw. "Brooke baby, you have to come back to me." His heartbroken plea made Anne tear up. How she hadn't noticed before now was beyond her but it was painfully obvious that her very untouchable son was in love with Brooke Reynolds.

She squeezed his shoulder. "We are doing everything we can for her," she soothed.

His shoulders slumped and he laid his head down on her limp hand. "You have to save them both because if you only save her, she will never be the same again." His voice was raw with emotion.

They arrived at the hospital and the waiting staff loaded her onto a gurney. They rushed her down the long hall and told him that he couldn't come. Anne held on to him as he collapsed against the wall and then slid down to sit on the floor. Blood covered his hands and torso and he looked up and realized Anne was also covered in it. He launched to his feet suddenly, "It's too much blood," he said numbly.

Anne took his hand. "Come on let's go get cleaned up, Cole. They will do everything they can. She should have been dead already. The fact that she survived this long is because she is a fighter. She will keep fighting."

He just stared at the blood. "It's too much blood," he repeated. He let her lead him down the hall to a bathroom so they could wash up. A nurse brought them some clean T-shirts and she changed her own and then ordered him to do the same thing. The nurse took the garments they wore telling them that they were evidence in a situation like this. Cole didn't argue just wiped the blood from his chest and slid the gray T-shirt on top. He followed Anne silently to the waiting room that the hospital staff directed them to.

He sank heavily into a chair next to Anne. Ivan came in then with Zack, Dom, and Ryker in tow. He held two hot cups of coffee and offered them each one. He sat next to his son and reached out to put a hand on Cole's shoulder. "Tell me exactly what happened, son."

Cole looked up at him blankly for a moment and then a cold amused smile twisted his lips. "I'm pretty sure I just got her killed is what happened," he responded bitterly.

CHAPTER 44

Jacob got to the hospital shortly before the surgeon came out to give the family an update. The doctor quickly informed them that both Brooke and the baby were stable but still had a long way to go. They had already performed a C-section and the baby was struggling so they were going to fly him to Salt Lake City to the children's hospital there where the best fetal doctors there could work their wonders with him.

Cole breathed a sigh. At least they were still alive. He stood and informed the surgeon that he would be accompanying his fiancée and baby to Salt Lake. The surgeon shook his head and insisted that it simply wasn't possible.

Cole picked up his phone and called the airport. There were no flights out tonight so he asked for the name of some of the private companies. Twenty minutes and several thousand dollars later he was climbing into an Uber headed for the airport. His parents tried to stop him but he told them he would keep them updated until they got everything settled and drove down themselves.

The pilot met him by the private hanger. Cole thanked him for being willing to fly him out tonight. He quickly explained that his wife and son were being life flighted and he needed to be there with them.

The forty-five-minute flight gave him just enough time to work out a plan and within minutes of landing he was climbing into a rental car. By the time he made it to the hospital Brooke had been rushed into surgery again. He called primary children's and they informed him that the baby was doing a little better.

With nothing left to do but stand around and wait for Brooke to come out of surgery he drove down and was immediately taken to the ICU where the baby was in a small cooling bed. A nurse came and asked him if he was the father. He assured her that he was and she promptly brought in paperwork for him to fill out. He didn't even hesitate to write all of his information under the correct place for the father. He filled in what he knew of Brooke's information and called Maude for her social security number and the rest. He returned the completed paperwork to the nurses' station.

Quietly he walked into the small room. Beeping noises felt like hammers on a drum and he cringed. An open incubator with tubes strung through it, sat in the center of the room. There was a wooden rocking chair off to one side and a constant beep beeping of the monitors as they tracked his vitals. Cole walked over to stand next to him. His hand shook as he reached out to touch his tiny hand. He had a thick swath of reddish-brown hair and his handsome little face already looked like his mother. A tear slid down his cheek as that tiny hand curled around his finger. He bent down. "Hey, little guy, I know this has all been a terribly rude introduction into this big bright world." He ran his other hand lightly over his tiny cheek.

A nurse walked in then and softly instructed him not to touch him too much. He was on a cooling blanket that was designed to keep his temperature down to help the swelling in his brain. Cole nodded but couldn't bring himself to let go of that little hand. "Is he going to be okay?" he asked the nurse, who gave him a smile.

She walked over close to him and said softly, "He is doing a lot better now. The doctor will be in soon to talk to you. She pointed to the name tag that was calling him Baby Reynolds at the end of the little plastic bed. "Do you have a name for him? I'd sure like to put something other than baby on his bed."

Cole looked down at him and replied, "Let me think about it for a while."

The nurse nodded and smiled before walking back out.

Cole stared down at his little round face outlined in that bright hair and slumped down into the rocker. He still didn't know if his mother was going to live. He squared his shoulders and stood. He reached a gentle hand down to lightly touch his little bare feet. It was astounding how small he was. Cole thought he would probably fit into his palms. "You are a little survivor like your mom." He clucked his tongue lightly. Tears filled his eyes as that tiny hand curled around his finger once again. "No matter what happens to your mama, I will be here for you, son," Cole vowed and ran a thumb through that soft, soft hair.

He turned and walked to the edge of the room so he wouldn't disturb the baby. He called the hospital where Brooke was. He was curtly informed that Brooke was still in surgery and they would notify him as soon as she was out. He thanked the woman in a husky voice and went back to stand by the baby. He watched that tiny chest pushing out and pulling in as he breathed. Smiling down he asked softly, "What is your name, little guy?"

The baby only responded by continuing to breathe so he sighed and sat lowering his head to rest in his hands. He closed his eyes and the image of Brooke laying there in all that blood haunted him so he opened them again. He should have killed the guy when he had the chance. Of course, Brooke had tried to and the sheriff had said if he was injured that badly he probably wouldn't make it very far anyway but still he wanted to know the bastard was behind bars or dead so he couldn't hurt anyone else. Unable to sit still he stood, and walked out to pace the hallway. Every few minutes he went back in to check and make sure the baby was okay and still sleeping soundly.

He was looking down at him and smiling when the doctor came in. He motioned Cole over away from the baby and said quietly, "I have him lightly sedated for now. I understand he sustained a lot of pressure before delivery and he had some swelling in his brain. I have him on medication that should help with that and the cooling bed will help keep his tiny brain from overheating. I plan to keep him that way until the swelling goes down. We won't know if he will have any lasting brain functionality until the swelling is completely gone and we wean him off the sedatives but he is showing good signs. The best thing we can do for him now is keep it quiet and calm in here."

Cole nodded. "Thank you, Doc. How soon will we know any more?"

The doctor looked thoughtfully at the bed. "I planned on doing a full exam in about an hour. I'd like to give him several hours on the cooling before we even think of warming him up. The good news is that all his other organs are in good health and he is breathing on his own."

Cole gave a ghost of a smile.

"Look I don't know all the details but it sounds like you and your family have been through quite an ordeal tonight. He is lucky to be alive if the rumors are true.

He is a fighter and doing well. Why don't you go to a hotel and get some rest and I will have the nurse call you as soon as we have any more information."

Cole shook his head. "I'll be fine, but thank you. His mother wouldn't want me to leave him alone. I will tip my head back and doze in here though."

After glancing quickly over the charts, the doctor nodded and left. Cole walked over and stood silently staring down at his son. He smiled suddenly. "Hello, little Jamison Cole Burton." He walked out to the nurses' station and told the nurse his name. She handed him paperwork to fill out and he did it feeling a tiny burst of happy energy for the first time tonight. He walked to the small waiting room nearby and pulled out his phone to quickly update his family on the baby's condition. His father texted him right back that they were just getting into town now and they were going to settle the boys in a hotel before coming over.

Jacob texted to let him know that he was just getting to the hospital where they had Brooke in surgery.

Brows scrunched in thought, he walked back out to the nurses' station to ask how soon they might get baby Jamison moved to the same hospital as his mother. The nurse told him she would ask the doctor about it. With nothing else to do Cole walked in to sit next to Jamison's bed again. He thought a little guiltily of Brooke and how he had essentially named her baby, but god dammit, he didn't care. He loved them both and he was going to do whatever he had to do to take care of them.

His phone vibrated in his pocket and he jumped up and pulled it out as he quietly opened the glass sliding door to step into the hall. "Hello," he said crisply.

"Mr. Burton?"

"Yes, what is it?" he sounded a little impatient and so he forced a calming breath.

"This is Dr. Benton over here at University Hospital. I just came out of surgery with your fiancée."

Cole held his breath. "How is she?"

"Sir, she came through surgery okay. There was a lot of damage, though and we had to do several different surgeries while we were in there. When they did the C-section in Idaho they had to detach and clear out the placenta as it was torn to shreds. Her bleeding was under control when she came here to us, but she had a broken rib that punctured her lung on the right side. We were able to repair the lung and her shoulder was dislocated and the muscle there was torn pretty bad. We have a great surgeon here who was able to repair it to give her the best chances at full mobility when it is all healed. The bullet wound was to her lower abdomen and we were able to extract the bullet in one piece. We also had to remove her appendix as it was nicked by the bullet."

Cole sucked in air. "Is she going to live, Doc?"

The other end was quiet for a moment. "She has a good chance, sir. The next few hours will be critical. I understand the baby survived?"

Cole's voice thickened. "He did, I'm here with him now. When can we see Brooke?"

"She will be in transition for the next hour or so as we get her moved to the ICU but after that you should be able to visit." He was silent for a moment. "I just wanted to say, sir, that the fact that they are both still alive is a real miracle. In these kinds of cases, we usually see the loss of one or both of the patients. I understand that you and your mom were there with her and got her to the ambulance as soon as possible. If you hadn't done that, there's a pretty good chance they would both be dead. Be grateful."

"I hear you," Cole murmured. "My mom is a doctor and she was the one working nonstop to save them not me."

Dr. Benton sighed. "In situations like these, every steady hand makes a difference, but it sounds like your mother deserves a big thank you as well."

They said goodbye and Cole quickly clicked off the call. He walked back into the baby's room just as the nurse put his name tag on the bed. He smiled and thanked her. Then he placed a finger against Jamison's cheek. Tears filled his eyes as he leaned down and whispered, "Good news, little Jamison. Your mama is doing a little better and hopefully you'll be able to see her soon. Now, I know it's just been you two for a while, but Daddy is here now, and I'm going to make good and sure you're both okay."

The nurse smiled and slipped silently out of the room. It was things like this that made her job worth all the rest of the heartache. A father that obviously loved his son and fiancée was such a beautiful thing.

Cole never heard her leave but when he realized he was alone again he sat in the chair and leaned his head back. He rubbed his tired eyes and then closed them for just a minute. He woke up with a start when Anne put a gentle hand on his shoulder. He stood and she wrapped her arms tightly around him.

He smiled tiredly at Ivan over her head and then whispered quietly, "Would you guys like to meet my son, Jamison?" he beamed with pride as he told them softly. "We can't touch him too much as they are keeping him cooled so his brain won't overheat while the swelling goes down but it's okay to hold his hand a little."

Ivan grinned as he saw the name tag. He pointed it out to Anne, whose brow lifted. She turned to Cole suddenly. "There is no way you knew Brooke long enough to be the father, right?" She sounded a little worried and uncertain.

Cole met her questioning green eyes with his steady dark ones. "I didn't, but I am his father and I will be marrying Brooke as soon as she is well enough."

Anne stared at her younger son in consternation. "I had no idea how strongly you felt about her."

Cole gave a half grin that made him look tired. "Neither did I, but when I realized what was going on with that bastard, I have never been so afraid in my life. I thought she was dead when I first saw her lying there like that and I almost killed that guy." He paused, and in a soft but sure voice said, "It turns out that how I feel about her is pretty strong."

Ivan smiled and leaned down over Jamison. "Hello, little guy. I'm your grandpa Ivan." He set a hand on his hair softly for a moment before moving back. He turned to Cole. "Jamison Cole Burton, I like it, son. It is a strong name."

Cole looked at his shoes. "I hope Brooke likes it because it's on the paperwork now."

Ivan chuckled softly and Anne leaned down to smile at the baby. "I like it but for now, Grandma is going to call you Jamie. Is that okay with you?" she whispered as she touched first his little hand and then his tiny foot. She stepped back after a long while and turned to Cole. "How is Brooke then?"

Cole motioned for them to step out into the hall. He quickly explained what the surgeon had told him. He looked back and forth between his parents. "I have been wanting to rush back over there, but I couldn't leave him alone here. Brooke wouldn't want that." He motioned toward his son's room.

Anne gave him an understanding nod. "You go now. Your father and I will stay here and watch over him for you.

Cole hugged them both. "Thank you. I wonder if you ought to take turns getting some rest while I'm gone."

Ivan nodded. "Our hotel isn't far from here. We did book rooms for you and Jacob as well in case you want to get some rest." He reached into his pocket and handed Cole two room cards. "Give one of these to Jacob so you guys can get some rest when you get a chance."

Cole nodded and thanked them again before he turned and walked quickly down the hall. The elevator was already on this floor so he quickly got on and pressed the ground floor. The elevator opened and he walked quickly out and crossed the street to the parking lot where his rental was. He slid in and started the engine. There was a McDonald's just up the street and he pulled in and ordered two large coffees. This late at night the cafeteria was closed and he couldn't handle coffee from a machine right now.

He sipped at it as he made his way across town to the hospital where Brooke lay fighting for her life. He looked out the window at the stars in the sky and for the first time in his life prayed, please God let her be okay. I know I haven't always been the best man I could be, but if you did see fit to send her to me. Give her the strength to live and I will love and cherish them both and give them a place to call home.

CHAPTER 45

Jacob was sleeping with his head against the wall in the darkened waiting room when Cole arrived. He set the extra coffee on a table by him and left him there while he walked to the nurses' station nearby. A young man sat behind the desk and looked up when Cole walked in. "Excuse me but I wondered if you could tell me if Brooke Reynolds is settled and ready for visitors?" he asked.

The young man with Nurse Ryan on his name tag smiled. "Are you family?"

Cole nodded. "I'm her fiancé."

Nurse Ryan looked down at the computer and typed quickly. "Let me see here. Okay, it looks like she just got settled in the ICU. The doctor did put a note that it was okay for you to go in and see her," he added. He wrote her unit number down on a pad of paper and then tore off a sheet to hand to Cole. "We also have a waiting room close by there if it's easier for you and your family."

Cole thanked him before walking down the hall in the direction the nurse had pointed. He saw a sign for the ICU and followed it. Two wide doors stood at the entrance and were locked. There was a button to ring for help and he did so, quickly explaining why he was there. The doors buzzed and unlocked and he made his way inside. There was a desk just through the doors and a couple of nurses looked up expectantly as he walked up. "You said Brooke Reynolds, right?" one asked.

He nodded. "I have her unit number right here." He held up the paper with the number scribbled on it.

"That's fine, then, sir. Go ahead and go back. Just be quiet, please. We try to keep it quiet in here after nine."

"No problem," he murmured as he started away. He walked down the line of glass fronted units until he came to hers. There was a sticker on a wooden plaque next to the door that had Brooke's name on it. He hesitated, took a long deep breath and then with a shaky hand slid the door open and stepped inside. His stomach clenched hard. She lay in a hospital bed with the back leaned slightly up. Her face was nearly white except for bruising and her eyes had dark circles around them. Even before he got close, he could see the huge welted bruise on her jaw. An IV ran from just above her wrist to under her gown. She had an oxygen tube pressed and taped under her nose. He moved over and reached hesitantly for her hand. "My God, he really got you good," he whispered in agony.

Brooke didn't move but just lay there. She was still in an induced coma he knew, and yet somehow, he had expected her to jump up and laugh as she brightened the room with her cheery personality. The constant beeping of the monitors in the background gave the whole thing an eerie feel. He bent and gently kissed her forehead.

Then he saw her hands. There were small cuts and bruises all over them. Her fingernails were rough, some of them broken and torn. He closed his eyes and the image of her fighting for her life flashed. His heart was in his throat as he kissed each of her fingers one at a time. He stopped when he got to her middle finger. The nail was pulled clear back and nearly detached from her finger. He lowered his head to her hand in agony, "Oh God, baby, you fought so hard. I need you to come back to me." A tear fell onto her hand and he brushed it gently off.

"I don't know why I didn't see it before now. Honestly, I don't understand how I missed this." He groaned in misery. "I should have told you long ago." He looked down at her broken body. "I love you so damn much. I think I might have loved you that first day when you came to us and handled yourself so well right after leaving your childhood home. I knew that you were a survivor when I came over to see you. You looked so beautiful then, with your bright hair and your long prudish skirt all tied up in rebellion. I could see your stubborn spunkiness then and I think I may have fell for you right then and there."

"You were so afraid when I kissed you and I hated myself for wanting to touch that bright light that was you. I tried to stay away, I really did, but you were always there somehow in the background tempting me to take a taste."

"When you left us, I felt angry and bereft. I didn't want to face those feelings so I focused instead on looking for you." He lifted his hands tiredly to his face and rubbed at his eyes. "I should have known he was after you, should have put it together sooner." He groaned again quietly. "I should have been able to stop this from happening to you. I wish you would have told me about him. I would never have left you alone."

Cole walked around and scooted a chair close to the bed where he could sit and hold her hand. "I'm going to marry you, Brooke, just as soon as you get better so you need to come back to me. Come back to me and our son. Oh baby, he is so perfect. You did such a great job with him you know. He is a little fighter just like you. The doctor said he shouldn't even be alive but you fought so hard to protect him and he fought hard to stay here with you. He has bright red hair just like you." He smiled through the tears in his eyes.

He couldn't even remember the last time he had cried and yet now he couldn't seem to stop the tears from flowing. "I know you want to meet him, but you have to rest and let the doctors take care of you so that you can come home with us." He closed his eyes then leaning his head back against the seat.

Suddenly they snapped open, "God, I almost forgot. I named him for you. His name is Jamison Cole Burton. I know it's a little presumptuous of me, but I don't ever want him to question that I'm his father. I know we'll have to tell him the truth one day, but even then, I want him to know that he is more mine than he ever was that bastard's."

He heard the door slide open and looked up as a nurse came in to check her stats. "You must be the fiancé," she said quietly and smiled. "So far so good."

He nodded but didn't say anything.

"She is quite the little fighter." She grinned as she wrote on a pad. "A bullet wound, a C-section, a wrecked shoulder, busted ribs and a punctured lung and still she fought to live through it all."

He nodded seriously. "She also saved my mother's life," he added softly.

The nurse raised an eyebrow at that bit of news. "What happened?" she asked curiously.

Cole blew out a breath. "She was laying on the floor bleeding out after barely surviving a horrifying fight with the crazy bastard who is obsessed with her. Me and my mom were doing what we could to stop the bleeding while she was passed out. She wakes up and suddenly reaches for the gun that I set on the floor next to her—with her left hand, mind you—and starts shooting." One side of his mouth curled up slightly. "I never even saw the guy or the knife until he was crumpling to the ground after two shots to the shoulder. He was ready to stab my mother for helping the woman he had just beat to hell." He shuddered at the memory. "She is forever my hero."

The nurse grinned. "You and me both. It looks like she is in good hands so I will go out and leave you to it." She looked at the fatigue on his face. "I'm not going to tell you to go home because I can already see that you won't listen but at least try to rest in the chair when you can." She walked over and pulled a pillow from a cupboard and handed it to him. "She has a long road ahead of her and she is going to need all the help she can get." She turned on her heel and left.

Cole sat heavily in the chair and took Brooke's hand in his own again. In the morning he would have to find some clippers and try to fix her nails. He leaned his head back and closed his eyes for a moment.

He didn't know how long he was asleep but he woke to machines screaming loudly in the room. Two doctors and a nurse came running in and started frantically working with Brooke. Voice hoarse with worry he asked several times what was going on but nobody heard him. He stood with his thumbs in his pockets watching as they shouted orders around the room. One doctor started chest compressions, and a minute later, they wheeled her out of the room. He tried to follow but a nurse held on to him and told him he couldn't go. He stood frozen in fear staring after them.

One doctor called to a nurse nearby. "Call upstairs and let them know we have to get her back into surgery." Cole leaned against the wall, gulping in deep breaths. A nurse hurried over to show him to the waiting room promising to come get him as soon as she had an update. He slumped down onto a soft couch and let his head fall helplessly into his hands as hopeless tears fell unchecked to the softly carpeted floor.

A hand on his shoulder had him looking up dazedly. Jacob stood there looking pale now. He moved to sit next to Cole. "What's going on? I was informed that Brooke was settled into the ICU and that I could come see her. But when I got up here her room was empty and no one seems to know what is happening."

Cole's eyes looked desolate as he met Jacobs green ones. "They had to rush her back into surgery. Oh God Jacob, I don't know how much more she can handle."

Jacob searched his expression lengthily, "She'll be all right, bro. It's Brooke here. She is a fighter and she loves that baby. She won't leave us."

Cole hoped he was right. He ran hands through his hair and hung onto Jacob's words. "They wouldn't tell me what was going on but I heard something about a clot."

They had a doctor for a mother and both knew how serious that could be. They sat in silence for a long while before Jacob finally said. "You know what? I don't ever remember you crying even when you were a kid. You must really love her."

Cole didn't argue for once, just looked him in the eye and nodded. "I have been so stupid about this. I should have told her a long time ago. Hell, I should have realized it a long time ago."

Jacob grinned. "Well, no one can blame you. After all, you are that guy who has basically done life as though you are bullet proof and don't need anyone else. It can't be easy for you to realize that you want to be vulnerable with and emotionally attached to someone else."

Cole laughed coldly. "Easier than you might believe. Especially in the face of possibly losing her."

Jacob held out the coffee. "Thanks for this by the way. I assumed it was your way of letting me know you had stopped by." He bumped Cole on the shoulder. "You should have woke me up, bro."

Cole shrugged. "It was something I had to do on my own."

"Uh-huh" was all Jacob said.

Cole looked over at him then. "Okay, okay I get it. There are people that care about me and I should let them in."

Jacob grinned and clapped mockingly, "Now you are starting to get it. Keep going while you're on a roll."

Cole chuckled low. "I know you are just trying to distract me but thanks anyway. It means a lot that you're here." He reached for his phone. "I need to call mom and see how Jamie is doing."

Jacob reached out a hand to still Cole's before he had a chance to dial. "I just talked to her Cole she said the doctor just checked in and said he is doing really well. So well in fact that in a couple of hours they might even begin to warm him up and bring his sedation down."

Cole lifted the phone again but Jacob swiped it from his hand. "Don't worry, dude, the doctor is going to let us know when, so that you can rush over and be there for it."

Cole sighed. "Good then."

Jacob walked over and grabbed a pillow from a stand in the corner and tossed it to his brother. "Get some sleep, superman. I will sit here and stand guard over the city and wake you as soon as you are needed." When Cole made no move to do so he groaned in frustration. "I promise I will wake you up if anything changes Cole. I will even pester mom and dad every few minutes for you." Grateful, Cole finally agreed and leaned his exhausted head back and slept.

He dreamed of Brooke and Jamie. In sleep his mind found peace in the only way it knew how, by conjuring dreams of Brooke and their son healthy and happy in the sunshine.

CHAPTER 46

Richard stumbled to the door on the old trailer house. He knocked hard once. Isaiah opened the door and then upon seeing Richard glanced behind himself before quickly stepping outside. "What are you doing here brother Richard?" he asked. Then he raised eyebrows as he looked him up and down. "Holy crap, what happened to you?"

Richard gritted his teeth against the jarring pain. "I need your help."

Isaiah chuckled. "It looks to me like you need a hospital."

Richard's eyes narrowed. "You're going to help me, now."

Isaiah raised his eyebrows. "And why would I do that?"

Richard thought about pulling the gun on him but didn't want to spook him. "Because this is all courtesy of your bitch of a sister and you are the one who helped me find her. If you don't help me, I will tell everyone how you took money from me for information. Let's see how your father likes that," he threatened.

Isaiah chortled. "You can't exactly say that we didn't all warn you what a rebellious little thing she is." At Richard's threatening look he held up his hands. "Fine but I can't do it here. We need to go somewhere else before my father sees you here."

Richard turned slightly toward his truck that was parked just behind him. "I have a place but I need you to drive. I managed to slow the bleeding some but it hurts like a son of a bitch." He tossed a set of keys to Isaiah.

Isaiah opened the truck door for him and gave him a shoulder to lean on as he boosted him up. Richard yelped and swore as his shoulder wounds were twisted leaving a trail of fiery pain coursing through him. After helping him inside Isaiah hurried around the truck and climbed in. "Where is your place anyway? I haven't ever seen it."

Richard gave him instructions through gritted teeth.

Isaiah glanced over at him in surprise, "That's only a few miles from here."

Richard nodded.

They pulled up in front of the house and Isaiah hurried around to help Richard inside. Once inside Richard lowered slowly into a kitchen chair. "I have an emergency medical bag right over there," he said and tipped his head toward the bar.

Isaiah grabbed the kit. "Okay but what do you want me to do man?"

Richard yanked the buttons of his plaid shirt open and worked it off of his shoulder. A huge gauze bandage was stuffed inside and he started slowly pulling it off. "She shot me twice. One of them went right through but the other one is still in there and I need you to dig it out."

Isaiah's eyebrows shot up. "I don't think that's a good idea man."

Richard narrowed his eyes angrily. "Just man the fuck up and dig it out. Then clean the wounds good so they'll heal."

Isaiah looked uncertain. "So where is this spicy sister of mine anyway? Last I heard you were still out looking for her."

Anger lit his eyes, but he said only. "She is here in the valley staying with some friends. Apparently, she wasn't exactly thrilled to see me after all these months." He looked pointedly down at his shoulder and then his leg. "I think I also might have one near my ass but I don't know if that one is still in there or not."

Isaiah cringed. "I don't think I'm okay with this, man. Why don't I just take you to the hospital and we can get a real professional to help you out."

Richard shook his head. "No can do. I need you to do this ASAP, so I can get back to business. The hospital takes way too long and they ask too many questions."

Isaiah slowly opened the pack and started looking through it. He pulled out some gloves and a small silver pair of latching pliers. There were several suture packs there and he pulled a few of those out. Next, he grabbed a few packs of gauze and medical tape. Then he stared at Richard's shoulder as blood oozed out. His face went pale. "I'm not sure if I can do this," he muttered under his breath feeling sick.

Richard's left arm twisted behind his back and suddenly he was looking down the barrel of a shiny black handgun. "Quit yapping and get it done," he said coldly.

Isaiah went another shade paler. "You don't have to use that, bro. I will do my best to help you," he whined.

Richard turned the gun and set it on the table laying his hand over it for quick access. "Then hurry it up."

Nodding, Isaiah stepped close to study the wound. He looked at the jagged holes and could see how the upper shot had gone clear through and was also oozing blood on the back. He remembered disinfectant and walked over to search the bag. A bottle of alcohol in hand he hurried back to Richard's side. He quickly dumped a little over the tools and then some on Richard's shoulder. Richard swore vehemently as white-hot pain followed the trail of alcohol.

Isaiah started with the lower shoulder wound, prodding the layers of flesh open to try and locate the bullet. He gagged for a minute before the anger in Richard's eyes turned the sickness to fear. He couldn't see much with the blood all around but he felt something hard against his fingertip and reached for the pliers. He heard the slightest plunking sound as the tip of the pliers touched the bullet deep inside the flesh.

He had to work at it for several long minutes before he finally got a good grip on it and pulled it slowly out. Blood gushed and he gagged again as he reached for a large square of the gauze and ripped it open. He pressed it against the wound to slow the bleeding then used his teeth to rip strips of the tape to secure it.

"You are going to have to close it up with stitches," Richard told him through his clenched jaw.

Isaiah looked appalled. "I don't know how to do stitches man."

"I don't think you fucking know how to dig out bullets either, but you figured it out," Richard pointed out gratingly.

Isaiah ripped open one of the suture packs. He started pushing it in through the flesh, the needle made a faint popping sound as it finally exited the flesh and he gagged. This time he turned and hurried over to the sink. His stomach emptied, he returned. He poured more alcohol around the wound and forced his mind away somewhere else as he slowly sowed the three holes closed. The stitches looked sloppy and uneven but the wounds were hardly bleeding anymore so he figured that was a good sign.

Richard stood then and unbuckled his pants. Isaiah groaned in complaint. "I really don't want to see this man."

Richard just continued to undress yanking down his briefs as he leaned over onto the bar.

"Get it done and you don't have to see it anymore." Richard commanded hoarsely. "By the way did I tell you that Brooke and I are having a baby?" He sounded proud.

Isaiah chuckled. "That figures." He moved closer to dump half of what remained of the alcohol over Richard's ass cheek. Blood seeped out as Richard jerked up against the pain. Because he was a little pissed at the guy for making him do this, he was rougher than he needed to be while digging out the second bullet. He poured alcohol directly into the wound and grinned as Richard screamed and his ass bobbed up and down in uncontrollable pain.

He kept his tone solemn as he said. "Now, I just need to stitch this one up." He looked at the wound uncertainly as he pushed the curved needle through the skin. "Are you sure you don't want to go to a doctor? What if the bullet's hit something vital?" he asked.

Richard chuckled hoarsely. "If they'd hit something like that, I would already be dead."

Isaiah shrugged. "It's your life, man. It's up to you." He finished the rugged stitching and put a large Band-Aid over the top of them. "There you go, man, you're all fixed up. You can just call me doc," he joked. And then because he was finally starting to enjoy himself, he reached out and slapped Richard's other butt cheek. "Dr. Isaiah got you all fixed up."

Richard came up so fast he nearly knocked Isaiah down. "Don't ever touch me like that again," he said in a deadly tone.

Isaiah chuckled. "You got it, boss." He stared at Richard thoughtfully as he watched him pull his pants back up with a series of grunts and moans. "You know what? I think I deserve some real compensation for all I did for you here today."

Richard turned his empty blue eyes to look at him. "You do deserve something a little extra, I think," he said softly as he lifted the gun suddenly to Isaiah's head and pulled the trigger twice. Richard smiled feeling gratified as Isaiah's body folded to the ground. There was a wide spray of blood and brains on the wall behind where he had been standing.

After being made a fool of earlier with Brooke and her friends, it felt excitingly good to be in control again. Besides, Isaiah had known too much about him already and now that the sheriff was after him he needed to be doubly cautious. He slowly dragged the body to a back room before getting out the mop and bucket to meticulously scrub all the blood from the square patterned vinyl floor. He reached for a towel and scrubbed down the wall with bleach. He would have to bury the body soon but he could give it a day without it stinking too much. Come to think of it, if he put the body in the garage, it would freeze so it wouldn't stink. He pulled a coat painfully over his shoulder and dragged him out.

Feeling a little better about himself now he grabbed a cold bottle of water and stretched out on the couch. He would rest now and then tomorrow night he would take care of the body. He would give himself a chance to heal and get back into shape before he went after Brooke and his baby again.

CHAPTER 47

Ivan sat with Jamie whom the nurses had just returned to his room. The doctor had ordered some tests run and they had wheeled away his clear plastic bed. Ivan walked down to the cafeteria for a hot cup of coffee, and when he got back, they were wheeling his bed back in. He stood there next to the bed watching over his grandson. Even without Cole's feelings for Brooke, he would have inserted himself as Grandpa. The fact that Cole was obviously smitten and had called Jamie his son had only made it easier.

Jamie whimpered a little and Ivan reached for his hand. As those tiny fingers curled around his finger he settled again. "My very first grandson," he murmured with awe. "I can't wait to see you awake and alert," he spoke gently.

The doctor walked in and Ivan turned to face him. Unlike the other times he'd come in before, Dr. Ivers smiled widely. "I guess Dad is still over with this guy's mama, huh?" he asked in a cheerful voice.

Ivan nodded. "Yes. He said he'll rush right back over here as soon as there's any change."

"Good. Well, let's get him over here, then, because there has definitely been a change." Ivan looked up nervously, but the doctor grinned. "After looking at all the test results, it looks like this little fighter is doing quite well." Dr. Ivers continued. "The swelling is almost completely gone and everything else is within healthy parameters." He put a hand on Ivan's shoulder. "After a long hard struggle the past couple of days, I am going to warm him up and wean him from the sedatives to see how he does."

Ivan smiled then. "Well, now that is great news." He pulled out his phone excitedly. "I will just go and call Cole now. He will want to be here for this, I'm sure."

Dr. Ivers nodded. "I will have a nurse call as well but I'm sure he would love to hear the news from you first."

Cole answered on the third ring sounding tired. "Tell me everything is okay there?" he said in a gravelly voice.

Ivan couldn't stop grinning. "You need to come down here if you want to be here when your son wakes up. The doctor just came in and told me he is going to warm little Jamie up and stop the sedatives."

A smile broke out on Cole's grim face. He stood quickly and turned to Jacob. "I gotta go see Jamie but keep me updated on Brooke, okay?"

Jacob nodded the affirmative and Cole hurried out. He stopped by the coffee shop on the first floor and gulped coffee like it was the only thing keeping him alive. He was already in the car driving when the nurse called and gave him all the details.

By the time he got to Jamie's hospital the nurse had more paperwork for him to sign in order to start the procedures. Paperwork complete, he walked quickly to his son's room. Ivan gave him a cheerful hug. "I'm glad you're here," he said as they both walked to the side of Jamie's bed.

After a half hour with no news, Cole rubbed wearily at his eyes. "Do you know when the doc is coming to do this?" he asked as he reached for Jamie's tiny hand.

Ivan shook his head. "He talked like it would be soon but I don't know much else."

Just then Dr. Ivers entered the room with a nurse right behind him. "Hello, Dad," he said as he nodded at Cole. "You made it. How is his mother doing?"

Cole turned and forced a hopeful smile. "She made it through surgery again. She is still critical though. She threw a blood clot yesterday and they had to rush her into emergency surgery to remove it. She pulled through but now it's just a waiting game."

Dr. Ivers nodded. "We will all pray for her." He walked around the bed and started pushing buttons as he ordered the nurse to get supplies. In a calm explanatory way he said, "We haven't given him anymore sedatives since before his last tests so he should start coming out of it in the next little while. I'm going to have nurse Black here change his nutrients out. If he does well, I'd like to get him eating on his own as soon as we can. If all goes well, we can remove his IV as well." He and the nurse worked together as they changed the settings on the bed a few degrees at a time while carefully monitoring his stats.

"If all goes well, is there any way we could get him moved over to the same hospital as his mom?" Cole asked. "It would sure be a lot easier if I could go back and forth at the same hospital instead of driving across town."

The doctor smiled in understanding. "Well, we will have to see how it goes first, but if Jamie does as well as it seems, we won't need to worry about that."

Cole raised an eyebrow in concern. "What are you saying doc?"

The doctor exchanged a smile with the nurse before meeting his gaze. "Well, first things first. Let's see how he does. But if he does well you might be able to take him home as early as this afternoon. I'll need to make sure there isn't any lasting damage from the swelling and we want to make sure he is eating okay without the feeding tube. If all that goes well, then I will discharge him today. I'll want you to watch him closely, and if anything changes you would need to bring him back here but we'll worry about that if it happens."

Cole smiled and nodded. "That sounds like a plan."

Every few minutes they raised the temperature a little more. As Cole leaned down and set a hand gently on Jamie's head, he could already feel the difference. His skin felt slightly less cold to the touch. Jamie stirred a little with a small kick of his feet. Cole grinned. "Hey there, tough guy," he murmured. "I can't wait for you to wake up and meet all of us."

The doctor grinned at that. "I love when these stories have a happy ending. But I want you to be prepared that there could possibly be lasting damage from the initial swelling. I hope it doesn't come down to that but it's best to prepare yourself in case."

Cole felt confident now as he watched Jamie wiggle his arm, "Every odd has been against both his and Brooke's survival and health. At this point I am going to be positive about whatever I can be. I'll deal with the rest when and if I have to." He raised tortured eyes to meet his father's brown ones. "A few days ago, I was sure I had lost them both."

The nurse smiled. "I think positivity is great."

The doctor adjusted the temperature one last time. "That should be it on the warming up. I have to go check on another patient but I will be back shortly to check on him." He motioned to the nurse. "Nurse Black will be in and out to keep a close eye on him in the meantime. You can just wait and if he wakes up come out and get a nurse." He smiled and nodded as he turned and left the room.

Nurse Black checked his vitals and recorded them on her pad once more before leaving. She promised to be back in ten and left.

Cole caught himself holding his breath as he watched Jamie slowly come back to life. His chest rose and fell steadily as he breathed. He stirred a little from time to time and Cole held his breath all over again.

Ivan gently squeezed the baby's hand and said, "I'd better go call your mom and let her know what is going on. She will want to come down here."

Cole nodded. "Okay, would you also shoot Jacob a text? I don't want him to worry."

With a quick nod of agreement Ivan stepped out.

Cole waited what felt like an eternity. He didn't dare leave Jamie's side so afraid was he that something would happen and they wouldn't catch it fast enough. So, he stood tall and silent watching his breathing and praying for him to wake up. The nurse came in again and removed his IV. "Doc said to remove this now so he will get hungry faster. It will encourage him to take the bottle when we try to feed him." She left after putting a tiny blue band aid where the IV had been.

Still Cole waited. His father came and waited with him awhile again before walking out when his phone rang. Jamie gave a little murmur of a cry and still Cole held his breath. He put a hand on his warming tummy and he stilled again. It was when Cole turned to look at his watch for what felt like the hundredth time that Jamie finally let out an ear-piercing wail.

Cole let his breath out as tears of relief filled his eyes. A young nurse hurried in. "Oh, good he's awake," she said as she quickly checked his vitals. All the while he squirmed and hollered his face turning crimson. "He's looking very alert and good," she said and grinned at Cole.

As soon as she stepped back, he reached down. He couldn't handle listening to his terrified little cry any longer. He lifted him possessively, careful not to snag the oxygen hose near his nose. He cooed softly and held Jamie up against his chest as calmness settled over him. He had been constantly afraid that he would lose them both for the past couple of days and something about holding that miniature version of Brooke there against his heart soothed him as nothing else could have. Tears fell unnoticed as he kissed the soft tufts of hair. "There, there, baby. It's all going to be okay. Daddy is here to take care of you now."

The nurse smiled and brushed a tear of her own away as she slipped quietly out to get the doctor.

Cole settled him into the crook of his arm and grinned down as those little eyes looked up at him curiously. "I'm so glad you're here and finally awake."

Ivan walked in then with Anne right behind him. They both rushed over to coo happily at their grandson. Cole noticed the large diaper bag that Anne had over her shoulder and thanked her for thinking to stop and get what they would need if they got to take Jamie with them today.

The doctor didn't make it back for another hour and by then the nurse had told them it was okay to sit and hold Jamie. They took turns cuddling him. When the doctor came in, he smiled at the happy picture. He asked to take Jamison and then listened to his lungs and heart. With a little nod he turned and grabbed a light to shine in his eyes. Jamie gave an unhappy squeal at that which only made the doctor chuckle. "He is sounding good and strong," he commented. He checked the baby's ears and took his temperature then did a series of other tests before turning back to say. "So far so good."

Cole stood next to Jamie. "He is getting kind of fussy now, do you thing I should try feeding him yet?" he asked with a concerned frown.

The doctor nodded. "I will have a nurse come in with a bottle. He is doing really well but I still want to monitor him for a couple more hours before I let him go. The nurse will go over a feeding schedule for the next few days as well." He turned and left.

Cole lifted Jamie again and turned to his mom. "He feels a little cool to the touch. I don't suppose you brought any clothes that are small enough, did you?"

Anne smiled. "Of course, I did. He is so tiny; I didn't think anything but preemies would fit him." She dug around in the bag and pulled out a tiny blue sleeper with bright green stripes down one side. She handed it to Cole who laid him gently on his bed and then carefully tucked his legs inside before lifting him to wrap it around his back and snap it closed on the front. He had just settled Jamie back on his arm when the nurse came in with the bottle. Jamie sucked at his own tiny fist.

She handed it to Cole. "Here, Dad do you want to do the honors?"

He grinned. "Of course." Though it had been a while since he had given a bottle to a baby and only his youngest two brothers. he remembered something about rubbing the nipple on the roof of his mouth to stimulate sucking. When Jamie didn't immediately latch on, he did that for a few strokes until his tiny little mouth closed over the nipple and sucked at it. A little milk bubbled out the side of his mouth and he whimpered as he lost hold of the nipple. Cole readjusted the bottle and waited patiently until he started sucking again. Jamie nearly emptied the bottle and the nurse watched with a smile.

"You did great for a first-time dad." She bent over Jamie and tickled his chin. "And you little guy did great for a first feeding. The doctor is going to be thrilled." She took the nearly empty bottle out to have it cleaned.

Jamie squirmed and Anne reminded Cole that he needed to be burped as she handed him a small strip of fabric to lay over his shoulder under the baby's head.

By early evening Cole had signed all discharge paperwork. He hummed a little nursery rhyme under his breath as he gently strapped Jamie into the small car seat the hospital provided them before gently tucking a blanket around his legs. Anne produced a cozy little car seat cover from the depths of the diaper bag to help keep the chill out of the car seat and they put it on together while Ivan went out ahead to warm up Cole's rental.

The sun was just about to set as they made their way out of the hospital with little Jamie in tow. Anne insisted on riding with Cole in case Jamie cried on the way. She really hadn't needed to though as he had just eaten good and now settled in for a long nap.

They got to the waiting room where Jacob was, shortly before the doctor came in with an update on Brooke. She was once again stable he informed them and they would be able go in and see her soon. He motioned Cole off to one side as Jacob got acquainted with Jamie.

Cole followed the doctor with a frown. "What is it?" he asked with concern.

In a low tone the doctor informed him, "She is stable right now but her milk has come in and we are going to have to do something about it soon or she is going to get mastitis."

Cole looked uncertain. He didn't know what Brooke had planned as far as nursing. He met the doctor's eyes and asked, "What are our options?"

Smiling, he said, "If she's planning to nurse, I usually recommend she be pumped until she is able to handle it herself. We do have a medication that helps to dry it up sooner if she either doesn't choose to nurse or is physically unable to. Do you know what her plan was?"

Cole made a split-second decision that he was confident Brooke would want. "She definitely wanted to nurse him so if there is anything we can do to make that possible."

The doctor nodded. "I will have a nurse head in there right away."

Cole remembered how shy Brooke had been when she had first left home. He reached out a hand to grab the doctor's shoulder. "Hey, Doc?"

The doctor turned back to look at Cole in question.

Cole took a quick unsteady breath. "Brooke has been through a lot of trauma in her life. Would it be okay if I was the one who did it?"

The doctor raised an eyebrow in surprise. "Do you know how to?" he asked quietly.

Cole shook his head, "No, but I'm a quick learner and I'm sure a nurse could give me some pointers. I just think it would be a lot easier for her in the long run if I do it instead." The doctor nodded consent and Cole followed him to the nurses' station.

CHAPTER 48

Brooke fought the fog in her head for what felt like an eternity. She heard several different voices talking and though she knew she recognized some of them couldn't formulate a clear memory of who they actually were. It seemed as though people talked nonstop to her. She tried to listen, tried even to respond to those voices but no matter how hard she fought the heavy fog she couldn't quite reach them.

Hours faded into days until she had no clear idea how long she had been floating in the empty expanse of nothingness. She heard the constant beep beeping around her that wouldn't stop but she couldn't tell if she was just hearing her own heartbeat. She heard a baby cry as though from a distant and heard that constant beeping spike. Something about that little cry made her fight through the fog harder. The fog closed in again and she forgot what she was searching for. She felt something tugging gently at her breasts and then that baby cried again. Rushing she flew forward on light feet through the heavy fog toward that heartwarming sound. Everything went black again.

She breathed evenly as she came to again. Brooke stared up at the white ceiling through the haze of fog. The voices around her hushed and she tried to turn her head but the fog threatened to overwhelm her again so she held it ever so still. Her vision was blurry around the edges so she blinked hard and then opened her lids again. It was a little clearer now. She heard a man's voice saying her name and tried to turn her head. Her head spun. Dizzy again she closed her eyes trying to still the spinning world. The gentle whimper of a baby was what pulled her out of it. Her eyes flew open and this time she lifted her head to look around.

Jacob stood on one side of the bed and in detached awareness she realized he was holding her hand. That little whimper came again and her eyes moved achingly around the room. In the corner she saw Cole and even through the confusion her heart sped up. She gasped as she saw the tiny bundle laid there against his shoulder. His dark hair brushed that round red splotch as he bent and spoke softly to the bundle. She tried to talk but it came out as a gurgle. She tried to look at Jacob again but her head hurt and she fell back exhausted. That tiny whimper came again and with a painful surge she lifted her head, trying to once again identify that sound. The bundle on Cole's shoulder wiggled and she watched in fascination as a tiny booted foot peeked out of the blanket.

Her memory surged suddenly and she gasped in horror as she remembered laying on the floor with all that wet stickiness around her and looking up at Anne and Cole knowing it was the last time she would see them. She closed her eyes as terror surged and she watched Richard rise up behind Anne with a knife in his hand. She knew without a doubt that he meant to slit her throat. She gasped out in fear at the memory. "Anne…." She tried to sit up to ask.

"Oh my God, Brooke are you awake?" It was Cole's deep baritone that brought her back again as she watched him through heavy lids as he rushed over to the bed. "Thank God, baby. I was starting to think you weren't ever going to wake up."

Jacob was grinning. "I told you she was still with us bro," he said.

Brooke furrowed her brow in confusion. She tried to speak but her voice only creaked. Cole reached for a cup of water on a table by the bed. He held it out. "Jacob, give her some water. Her throat is probably dry," he commanded forcefully.

Jacob took the cup and held the straw to Brooke's lips. She tried to gulp big swallows but gagged. Jacob pulled it back again. "Just take little sips Brookie," he said as he put the straw next to her lips again. She took a little sip. Her mouth was so dry it felt like a sponge. Not a single drop made it to her throat until she had taken several sips.

Finally feeling a little less dry she licked her lips. "What happened?" she asked hoarsely. She turned to Cole. "How long have I been out?"

Those dark eyes met hers and he gave her a proud little smile. He hesitated, not knowing if he should wait for the doctor to come in before telling her the details. Finally, he just said, "Too long. The doctor should be in soon to check on you. Do you need anything?" he asked in concern.

She shook her head and then had to close her eyes to fight the fog again. A sudden realization hit and her hand flew to her flattened stomach and her eyes flew open as she tried to sit up. "Is my baby okay?" she gasped in terror.

Cole stepped forward and held up the bundle turning it now so that she could see a tiny face peeking out of the blanket. "He is fine and strong." He moved to her side and lay the tiny kicking bundle next to her face. "Mama meet little Jamie."

Tears of relief fell from the corners of her eyes as her gaze locked on that beautiful rosy cheeked baby with a shock of bright red hair on his head. She lay her cheek against his and closed her eyes against the tears. "Mommy is so glad you're okay." She adjusted her shoulder to lift a hand and ran it over his head and body in wonder. She looked up at Cole and he met her gaze, held it there, "I don't even remember having him," she said with fear in her voice.

He reached out and put his hand on her shoulder. "You were out when they did the C-section. How much do you remember?"

She ignored his question as her eyes narrowed suddenly. "Wait did you say little Jamie?"

He grinned and put his thumbs in his pockets. "Yes. Jamison is his name now," he said simply. He held her gaze and waited for her explosive reaction.

Brooke stared at him for a long moment and then said it quietly as though trying it out. She turned and looked down at him. "Jamison," she said softly as she smiled down at him. He let out a little whimper and cuddled against her.

Cole suddenly looked hesitant. He hadn't expected her to take it in stride. "Jamison Cole Burton to be exact," he said quietly, sounding slightly uncertain.

Brooke looked up at him in surprise. "I don't understand."

There was a rustling sound near the door and Brooke raised her head a little as three hospital personnel rushed in. "Good, you really are awake," said a dark-haired man with glasses as he stepped forward and began checking her vitals. "I'm Dr. Goodwin, Brooke. How are you feeling?"

She blinked and met his blue eyes. "I'm okay, I guess," she answered.

He pulled out a flashlight and flicked it on. "I'm just going to check your pupil response, try not to blink," he explained as he shone the light into her eyes quickly before turning it away again. "Good," he said simply as he dropped it back into his white coat pocket. "Follow my fingers," he instructed in a friendly tone.

Brooke watched as his fingers moved from side to side and then back again. She stayed silent as he scribbled on a pad of paper and turned to give the other two instructions. He turned back only a moment later and met her curious stare. "Do you know where you are Brooke?" he asked gently.

She shook her head, "I'm guessing a hospital but I have no clue which one." She looked down at her fingers that were lightly running up and down the baby's arm. "I don't remember much to be honest."

The doctor's brow furrowed. "Do you remember getting injured?" he asked.

Brooke nodded and fought through the surge of fear that teased at the back of her mind. "I do remember that part, just not much after."

The doctor nodded and smiled. "That is perfectly normal. You were likely unconscious through most of it which is why you don't remember."

Brooke stared hard at her hands. In a small pained whisper she asked, "Is he dead?"

The doctor looked confused but Cole leaned in and squeezed her arm in understanding, "He got away, baby. I don't think he is dead but the police haven't been able to find him and are saying he could have gone off somewhere and died alone."

Brooke attempted a brave smile.

He squeezed her hand. "I won't let him near either of you ever again," he promised in a lethal baritone voice.

She shivered as she looked into his hard unyielding eyes. Those entrancing gold sparks were evident as he made the statement. She sighed, "I'm not asking because I'm afraid, Cole." She took a deep breath as though searching for the words. "I just needed to know if I killed him," she tried to explain.

Jacob moved forward and leaned down next to her. "I don't think you did, which is a shame if you ask me. If you did, it was one hundred percent self-defense and you are not going to feel guilty or worry about it, do you hear me?" His voice was slightly hoarse. "My God, you have been through too much already."

A hard look from the doctor had Jacob moving back and away from her as Dr. Goodwin smiled. "You will have a chance to catch up on everything soon. Right now, though, I have a few questions for you." He waited until Brooke nodded her head in agreement before continuing. "Do you know what day it is?"

Brooke shook her head. "Is it December tenth? That is the last date I remember."

"It is the twenty second of December. The tenth was the day that you were first brought here." The doctor informed her easily. He looked at her for a minute and then at Jamie. "I see that you met your son already."

Brooke beamed a proud smile at him. "He is so perfect," she said softly as she turned her head and kissed his cheek. "I thought he might not have made it," she admitted honestly and her eyes filled with tears once again.

Dr. Goodwin smiled. "He is strong and healthy and a fighter." He paused and Brooke looked up at him before he said quietly, "You both are." He turned to Cole and Jacob. "So far everything looks good. You are welcome to stay for a bit and fill her in on all the details but if she gets tired at all let her rest."

Cole and Jacob both nodded and then Cole stepped forward and shook his hand, "Thank you doc." He moved back over next to the bed by Brooke and Jamie.

The nurses trailed out after the doctor and Brooke turned to look at Jacob. "So, talk to me. Tell me everything."

Jacob shrugged and looked at her and then at Cole. "Cole is probably the one who should talk since he was there and involved in it all."

Brooke turned to stare up uncertainly at him. "I'm actually a little surprised you are here Cole."

He didn't respond, just watched her calmly.

Jacob chuckled loudly. "Of course, he is here."

Cole threw a dirty look over his shoulder at Jacob. "Lay off man," he said and turned back to Brooke. Jamie let out a little cry then and he reached down to lift him carefully from Brooke's side. "There, there little man, did you wake up?" he cooed low as his lifted Jamie and gently rocked him against his strong shoulder.

Brooke stared at them in reluctant confusion.

Jacob leaned down to tickle Jamie's neck. The baby turned his head to try sucking on his finger and he chuckled.

"You are hungry again aren't you little guy?" Cole murmured and glanced at his watch.

That was Jacob's cue and he turned and walked out saying over his shoulder, "I'll just go call mom and dad now and tell them she's awake."

Brooke stared transfixed as Cole walked over to her with his bundle. "What do you say mama? Do you feel like feeding him?" he asked as he gave her a half grin. Brooke's cheeks grew warm. She had always intended on nursing but she had imagined she would have the time to get it all figured out in private. He leaned down toward her. "It's okay, hon, he's actually getting pretty good at it now," he murmured as though he were reading her mind.

Her gaze flew to his. "You mean with a bottle, right?" she asked, suddenly feeling unsure of herself.

Cole grinned and shook his head. "Nope, I mean he's getting pretty good at nursing." When Brooke just stared at him in horror, he chuckled. "It's not like it's anything I haven't seen before," he said in a soothing tone.

Brooke gasped. "That just makes it worse, you idiot." She fought the ridiculous smile.

He met her gaze and held it. "I know this is all a bit of a shock to you. I will give you all the time you need to adjust but right now Jamie is hungry and it is time for him to eat." He spoke gently. "When you wouldn't wake up, I asked the doctors if I could help him nurse." He looked apologetic. "You weren't awake to give me your opinion but I just thought you would want to create as much of a bond with him as you could even though you were out of it."

That pulling at her breasts from her dreams popped into her mind and she opened her mouth. "Oh, I think I remember it!" she exclaimed softly. Her breasts did feel heavy and a tingling burning sensation was sliding through them now. She lifted a hand to massage at it. "Ouch, why do I hurt?"

Cole grinned. "You might want to get used to that. Your body is on a steady schedule with Jamie now, so I'm guessing it's your milk letting down."

Her gaze narrowed on him. "Why do you know so much about this?"

He shrugged. "I've had a lot of time here waiting so I may have read a few books about it." He leaned down then and kissed her forehead. "I'm so glad you came back to us. You really had me worried there for a while." Jamie screeched in protest and with a little pat Cole lowered him to the bed by her side. "I can help you with it," he offered in a quiet tone.

Brooke fought the embarrassment. She really did want to hold her baby again and it sounded amazing to get some of that stinging pressure off. She groaned, "I don't see as I have a choice, I can't do it alone and you are the only one here."

Cole smiled but shook his head. "If you really don't want to, I can go get a nurse or a bottle.

Brooke was already shaking her head in denial. "No, it's okay."

He nodded and turned Jamie to lay across her chest. He watched as she fumbled to open her hospital gown to access her breasts. She finally got herself freed and leaned up a little to give Jamie better access. He rolled his head back and forth slobbering all over her while trying to get her nipple into his little mouth.

Without a moment's thought, Cole reached down and lifted her breast and held it so that her nipple brushed against the baby's lips. He latched right on and went to town.

Brooke stared in wonder as he opened his eyes and stared up at her while he suckled away at her breast. His eyes were blue now and warmth surged through her. "I'm so glad you're here and safe, Jamie. Mama loves you so much."

Cole watched his son feeding at her breast and in a whisper said, "The two of you are the most beautiful sight in the world."

Brooke looked up in surprise. She had almost forgotten he was there, she'd been so taken with Jamie. "What did you say?" she asked, uncertain if she had heard him correctly.

He met and held her sapphire gaze. "You two are the most beautiful thing I've ever seen," he repeated in a much steadier voice.

Brooke smiled and looked down. "He is really beautiful, isn't he?" It was more of a statement than a question. She watched Jamie eat in silence for a few minutes before looking back up at him. "So, who picked the name out?" she asked, wanting to know all about it.

She watched as he tucked his thumbs in his pockets uncomfortably before he answered, "I did."

She laughed aloud at that. "Of course, you did. I should have known you would be the one that decided he should have your name."

He didn't smile, just watched her. "I need you to know that I did it because I fully intend on being his father and I want him to know that he is connected to me. When he hears about his biological father, I want him to have every reason to know that I am his real dad."

Brooke's eyebrow's shot up. "Why on earth would you want to be his father, Cole? You don't even like me that much."

Cole held his feelings in check. "While I'll admit that I may not have liked the fact that I couldn't resist you, Brooke. I do however, like you very much." He paused to let his words sink in. Then in a voice raw with emotion said. "I am, in fact, very much in love with you, Brooke Reynolds."

Her stunned, naked gaze brought an amused smile to those perfectly sexy lips of his. She honestly didn't know how to respond to him.

CHAPTER 49

Cole spent two hours filling Brooke in on everything that had happened in the two weeks since Richard had come after her. At one point he turned an intense look on her and asked coldly, "I know he's the biological father of Jamie but who is he to you?"

She hesitated a long while before finally telling him the truth about everything. She told him about her father and her family. She told him about the engagement and everything she had done to try to stall it. He had smiled proudly as she recounted her many schemes in detail.

He looked at her with a warmth that she hadn't seen before and said quietly, "Remind me to never get on your bad side, babe."

That made Brooke laugh. Then she turned somber again as she told him about that cold night nearly a year ago now when he had raped her. She stared at her hands as she recounted it in a tiny voice devoid of the pain that surged inside when she remembered it. He stood near her and clasped a hand over hers in support. When she finally had the courage to look up at him, she had to suck in a breath. His jaw was tight and his eyes blazed with anger, which somehow took her by surprise.

He noticed her concern immediately and said gruffly, "Don't worry, I'm calm. I just wish I had known sooner so I could have done things differently." He squeezed her hand and forced an easygoing smile. "I suspected as much, but thank you for telling me the truth," he said quietly.

Brooke breathed in life and said, "I don't think I have said this yet, but thank you for saving my life, Cole. We wouldn't have survived if you hadn't come."

A look of fear crossed his face before he hid it. "I have never been so terrified in my life as I was when I put it all together and was trying to get to you. Then I saw you there bleeding all over the place and I thought you were dead. I would have shot him in the back of the head if Mom hadn't stopped me."

Brooke shivered. "I'm really glad you didn't. For a long moment earlier, I was sure I had killed him and it didn't feel good to me."

Cole looked away. "I'm not sure I would regret it," he admitted softly.

Brooke shrugged. "Now the police can find him and deal with it. Thank you for coming to my rescue. I owe everything to you and Anne." She gazed down sleepily at her son laying on the bed next to her.

Jacob walked in then. "Good, everyone's still awake." He walked to the opposite side of the bed and grasped her hand in his. "Mom and Dad are on their way and bringing all of the boys."

Brooke adjusted uncomfortably. "They don't need to do that. I'm sure I'll be getting out of here soon."

Jacob grinned. "I hope so, but in the meantime, we have all been crazy worried about you. Besides we're all slightly addicted to spending time with Jamie and since Cole won't let him or you out of his sight, that usually means we have to come here to see him." He threw a disbelieving glare at his younger brother. "Thank God, he at least talked the doctors into getting you transported back to an Idaho hospital. We were all going a bit stir crazy in that hotel."

One side of Cole's mouth turned up in a grin. "I was fine," he assured Brooke as though to dispute Jacob's accusation. "It simply became clear to me that if we didn't get back home, Jacob or Dad was going to end up taking someone's head off." He grinned at Jacob's raised eyebrows. "I took pity on the hospital staff."

Jacob guffawed at that remark. "Me and Dad were the least of the problem. What was it that one nurse started calling you? Oh yeah, that's right, that 'handsome demon dude.'"

Cole grinned. "Now, I think you're just passing the buck."

Brooke looked back and forth between them unable to tell if they were serious and who was telling the truth. She cut in like the peacemaker she was. "Well, I, for one, am glad I'm back in Idaho. I'm already not looking forward to the drive home and it would be excruciating if it was the four-hour drive from Salt Lake."

Jamie stirred and opened his eyes and all three of the adults immediately turned their attention to play with him and talk to him. He gooed happily at his audience. At one point Jacob picked him up to hold him in the air and his face turned red as he squawked loudly. He didn't stop until he was snuggled happily back at Brooke's side. That pleased her an inordinate amount.

Just to bug Jacob, Cole picked him up and held him high in the air. "That's my guy JC," he said as he twirled slowly around once.

Brooke laughed and Jacob groaned as the baby gave his brother a happy grin. Leaning down next to her ear, he said in a disgruntled tone, "Now, Cole just has one more reason to think he's better than the rest of us. Thanks a lot, Bestie."

Brooke grinned at him and turned to smile happily at her laughing baby and the man who had told her he loved her. She wasn't really sure if she believed him yet, but she felt a warm glow near her heart every time she thought about it anyway. He hadn't seemed to expect her to say anything in return and she hadn't. Had simply stared at him for a long while before switching Jamie to her other side to nurse.

Jamie started squirming again and Cole patted his diaper. He turned and reached for the gray and green diaper bag. "You need a diaper, young man." He glanced over at Jacob in jest. "Weren't you talking about wanting to connect with him, bro?" he asked with a grin.

Jacob held up his hands and backed away.

Brooke watched quietly as Cole laid him gently at the end of the bed and deftly changed his diaper. She met Jacob's knowing gaze and he grinned. Turning back to Cole she asked a bit curiously, "Have you been the one changing all his diapers?"

Cole was silent, but Jacob piped in helpfully, "Cole here has been mighty territorial about the both of you with everything," he informed her in a cheery voice.

The doctor came in again and checked on her. After asking a lot of questions, he informed them that he wanted to keep her one more night for observation before releasing her. Cole readily agreed. It wasn't worth taking any chances of complications.

Brooke groaned, "I just want to go home and be in a normal bed."

The doctor smiled and assured her that she would be able to go soon.

Jamie got hungry again and Brooke was trying to feed him when the rest of the family showed up. The boys were unusually quiet as they filed in. They each came and gave her a hug and told her they were glad she was okay now. She finished feeding Jamie, and Cole swooped in immediately to burp him. Ivan kissed her cheek and then raised an eyebrow. "I can see that you are still feeling a bit possessive, son. Now give me my grandson. I can burp him just fine."

Cole grumbled but handed the baby over. He turned and immediately came back to her side. "Here you go, drink some water, Brooke. You need to drink lots of liquid for nursing."

"What sounds good is ice cream and real food," she grumbled, but she drank the cup empty and thanked him.

Anne crowded through the men to stand next to her. "How are you feeling, dear?" she asked quietly as she bent to hug Brooke's shoulders.

Brooke smiled. "Stir crazy, but I feel good. I really want to leave the hospital, though."

Anne nodded. "I know it can be hard, but it's only one more night. You have a long road ahead of you with the physical therapy but the time will go quickly. I understand all the stitches are healed up from surgeries but your shoulder was damaged pretty badly and your muscle tissue around the incisions can often take longer to get back to normal. You're going to need a good physical therapist and lots of patience," she warned with a cheerful smile. "We're all here to help, though, so don't hesitate to lean on us."

Brooke smiled and nodded. "I'm not in much pain," she admitted to the older woman.

Anne smiled. "Pain meds. It could all kick in later when they stop the pain meds."

Jacob announced that he was going out for a bit and asked if any of the boys wanted to go with him. Zack jumped up from the chair he had just sat on. "I'll come."

They left as Ryker talked to Jamie and tried to take him from his father. The next hour was loud and chaotic and to Brooke absolutely wonderful. It seemed like every time she looked around for Jamie someone else had him and was playing with him. Cole noticed her watching and finally walked over to his mom who was busy playing with the baby's feet. "I think Brooke wants to hold him now," he told her quietly. "She hasn't had much time with him yet."

Anne smiled in understanding and handed him to Cole who promptly took him over to sit next to Brooke. "Here you go, Mama," he said gently as he settled Jamie on the side with her good shoulder.

Brooke smiled in gratitude up at Cole before turning back to her son. "Thank you, Cole," she murmured as she bent to kiss his tiny cheek. She rubbed a finger under his chin. "My goodness, Jamison, you look like you grew a little just in the past hour." She reached for his hand and watched mesmerized as he curled his fingers around one of her own and grinned up at her with pride. Her brows furrowed, was it her imagination or was he already starting to mirror Cole's own attitude and actions? She stared in wonder as he blinked up at her and gurgled happily.

She smelled the delicious scent of food before Jacob entered the room. Her eyes widened in wonder as he walked in with a huge brown bag. He winked at her and handed her a large Styrofoam cup with a lid on it. He bowed low and grinned. "A milkshake for the lady."

Brooke slipped the red straw into her mouth and slurped happily. She closed her eyes in wonder. She felt Cole lean down and opened her eyes. He was leaning in next to her ear and murmured. "I forgot just how sexy you are when you are hungry," he whispered and then gave her a quick kiss on the cheek.

She blushed but wasn't about to stop drinking the heavenly thing. She felt the beginning of an ice cream headache and tried to pace herself. Jacob pulled a burger out and handed it to her and she gratefully relinquished the shake to Cole who was just brave enough to take a drink of it himself. She gave him a hands-off glare, but he only grinned and took another slurp. She stared in wonder at the juicy cheeseburger and then went in for the kill with gusto.

She was aware of Jacob handing burgers around the room but didn't actually see it as her main focus was on that juicy thick burger. Anne turned to her with a carton of fries. "This is probably the last thing you should be eating but here you go anyway, fries to go with your burger." She paused to look down at Brooke who licked some ketchup off her fingers.

The burger was completely gone and Brooke reached for the tub of fries with a happy smile. "Yes, please," she said as she stuffed three into her mouth.

Anne stared at the frail-looking woman lying in front of her. "Did you eat that whole burger already?" she asked in surprise.

Brooke was too happy to be offended. "I was starving; by the way, thank you, Jacob."

Anne just shook her head feeling mystified as Brooke reached for the shake from Cole who held it just out of her reach while grinning at her. He bent close to her and said softly, "It'll cost you a kiss."

Brooke grumbled and then reached up and grasped his head to pull him in and planted a fry flavored kiss on his lips.

The room went quiet for a moment but then Brooke looked around the room and said simply. "Well, I really need that shake."

Everyone laughed then. The doctor came in. He gave a horrified look at the carton of fries on Brooke's lap. "You may not want to eat solids yet and especially not junk food," he said as he reached to remove the carton.

Brooke beat him to it and with wide eyes shoved a couple of fries in before he could try to wrestle it out of her hands.

He stared in disbelief as she crammed a couple more in. He scratched his head uncertainly. "Well, I guess you could try a few and if it doesn't make you too sick it's probably okay for you to have a few." He looked around at the half-eaten burgers. "As long as it's just the fries. I wouldn't recommend a burger yet."

Brooke swallowed the fries in her mouth and nodded. "For sure. Just some fries for now."

He relaxed when she agreed but then tensed again as disbelieving looks passed around the crowded room. He held up his hands, "I'm sorry guys but she hasn't had solids in a couple of weeks and its best to start her off with light foods." Everyone gave him strange big smiles and he relaxed again. "Okay, well now that that's settled, let's look you over and see how you're doing."

Brooke smiled pleasantly as she sucked on the milkshake again. She waited patiently for him to continue as she loaded more fries in. He stood staring at her as she moved back and forth between the shake and the fries. It was a little awkward for her to hold the shake and get fries at once but she had learned her lesson with letting Cole hold the shake before. She would use her two end fingers to grab some fries from the carton which was now tucked in her elbow while she held the shake with her thumb and forefinger. She watched the doctor curiously as he stared at her in silence. Finally, he shook his head.

Jacob stepped in to fill the awkward silence. "Would you like a burger doc? I brought plenty."

The doctor turned to stare at him in surprise. He watched as Brooke managed to shimmy a couple more fries in her mouth and then his shoulders dropped in defeat. He sighed and smiled. "Why not."

Jacob handed him a foil wrapped burger and went back to eating his own. Conversation buzzed through the room around burgers and fries. Cole managed to sneakily get the milkshake from her hand when she wasn't paying enough attention. He took a long drag and smiled knowingly as it registered on her face. She reached for him and it but he smiled and stepped back to take another long sip. Her lip curled into a sexy little pout that had his pulse racing and his mouth burning to kiss it right off her lips. He was fighting that very urge when Ryker hurried over to swipe the drink and hand it to back to Brooke. "Cole, can't you see that Brooke really wants that? She is an invalid so we have to take care of her and keep her satisfied," he instructed solemnly as he squared his shoulders and puffed out his chest.

Cole chuckled. "I shudder inside when I think of all we might have to do to keep her satisfied." He turned a naughty little wink at her.

She didn't even bother to blush only plugged that bloody red straw back in and took another long slurp. His groin tightened and his gaze narrowed as he stared at a tiny drop that clung to her bottom lip. She licked it off and he nearly groaned aloud. God that woman would be the death of him. He forced himself to turn away and faced knowing grins from both Jacob and Ivan. He gave them a cold unaffected frown before popping the last of his own burger into his mouth.

Through the din of voices, he heard Anne talking to the doctor, and he immediately moved over to hear what they were discussing. He heard therapy and possibly another shoulder surgery as he sidled up to his mother but didn't hear the details. He would pester Anne later but for now he frowned at Dr. Goodwin. "How is she doing, Doc?"

Dr. Goodwin smiled. "She is doing excellent. Her labs came back with no abnormalities. Her iron and blood count are up, which is good. I'd just like to keep an eye on everything now that she is awake for a bit. She will need to get right on the physical therapy but other than that we just have to wait and see how she does."

Cole relaxed and walked back over to Brooke. He leaned down and smiled at her. "Did you hear that sweetie? It looks like we really might be going home tomorrow." He reached for the milkshake and was surprised when she let it go without a fight. He grinned dumbly a moment later as he realized it was empty.

He looked down at the empty fry tub in her elbow and couldn't resist leaning to kiss her ear. "That's my girl," he said low and quiet against her neck.

She shivered but wouldn't meet his gaze. He chuckled low. "Chicken," he taunted.

With a stubborn tilt of her chin, she fixed her gaze on the doctor and tried to read his lips as he spoke quietly to Anne.

A nurse came in and was immediately offered a burger which she graciously accepted.

Cole watched in silence as first Jamie and then finally Brooke passed out, falling asleep despite the noise. He bent and adjusted her blanket to keep her warm and then carefully lifted Jamie from her side to rest in the crook of his elbow. He leaned down and pressed his forehead to hers for a long moment. "Rest and know that I am watching over you and tomorrow I will take you home." He didn't see the smiles that went around the room at his back.

Anne leaned into Ivan and whispered. "Look at him. I never dreamed I would ever see him so happy."

Ivan simply bent his head and kissed his wife in agreement.

CHAPTER 50

Cole insisted on following Brooke as the nurse pushed her in the wheelchair toward the hospital exit. He was pushing Jamie in a stroller as they walked. Every time the wheelchair came to a stop Brooke would try to stand up and walk but the male nurse would grab her shoulders and shove her back down gently spouting off some line about hospital policy. Brooke swore up a storm becoming very creative with her opinions of exactly how stupid that policy was. Wasn't she going to walk as soon as she was home anyway? She kept asking.

The nurse was grinning at first and giving noncommittal un-huhs, but by the time they actually walked through the sliding front doors, he was grumpy. He held the chair as Brooke stood and walked to the car that Jacob pulled to the curb. As she walked away the nurse met Cole's eyes and chuckled. "God, she is stubborn, Good luck man you're going to need it." He tipped his head to Cole before turning to wheel the chair back inside.

Cole grinned and looked down at Jamie. "Did you hear that, son? Mama is pretty stubborn and headstrong, so us guys gotta stick together."

He walked around the car and lifted the car seat from the stroller and slid it inside and listened for the click that indicated it had locked in place. He quickly folded the stroller and hollered thanks to Jacob who'd opened the back gate automatically so Cole could load it inside the SUV. He strolled around the bright red car and slid into the back seat behind Brooke.

"All aboard." Jacob joked as he made a train honking sound. Jamie gurgled in response. Cole reached a hand forward to squeeze Brooke's shoulder. "You doing okay Brooke?"

Brooke let out a long dramatic sigh. "I would be just fine if those damn hospital people would let me have real food," she grumbled. She turned a bright smile on Jacob. "Thanks so much for the burger yesterday. You really are a true friend."

Jacob smiled right back at her. "I know you, Brookie. I knew you wouldn't survive hospital food for long."

Cole was glowering from the back seat at their obvious comfort with each other. Here he was all in and fully committed but Brooke didn't seem to get that. Ever since he had proclaimed his love to her, she hadn't said much about it. She definitely hadn't said she loved him back though instinctively he knew that she did. Last night she had planted that kiss on him without any hesitation but something about it all felt off somehow.

He watched as Brooke reached out a hand and set it on Jacob's arm for a brief squeeze. "I don't think I told you yet but thanks so much for everything you've done for me through all of this."

Cole's scowl darkened and he forced his gaze out the side window. He took a calming gulp of air and turned his attention to Jamie. Jamie who was easy to please. Tugging on his little fingers softly he said in his best baby-talking voice, "Hey there, little guy, how are we doing?" Jamie turned his head and smiled up at him. Cole tugged on the bright yellow giraffe with bright splotches of colors up and down its body. The neck extended out as he pulled and the giraffe started to sing a nursery rhyme. Jamie went cross eyed as he tried to focus on the giraffe and Cole grinned.

Feeling eyes on him he turned and met Brooke's brilliant blue eyes. She had been watching him play with her son and looked away when their gazes collided. She still wasn't sure what was happening with them. She had wanted more than anything for him to love her for all these months. But when he had told her just that she hadn't really believed him.

She knew he was worried about them because he was a good person. She just wasn't sure if that was all there was to it. The one thing she did know was that she needed to get out of Idaho before she couldn't leave. Her heart was on a one-way track toward absolute devastation when he moved on and realized he didn't want them after all.

In a split second she made her decision. She would take a couple days to rest and heal and then she was going back to Montana while she still had at least a small piece of her heart to take with her.

They were already twenty minutes into the drive before her eyebrows scrunched up and she asked, "Who's car is this?" She had never seen the red car before. At first, she had assumed it was a rental but now wondered why they would have rented this car when they were so close to home.

Jacob adjusted the rearview mirror and looked at Cole with a grin. He didn't say anything for a long while as he waited for his brother to respond. When Cole remained stubbornly quiet, he turned and met Brooke's curious gaze for a quick glance. "I believe it's yours," he said in an overly cheerful voice.

Brooke shook her head. "No, it's not. My car is still in Montana."

Cole met Jacob's glance in the rear view. He wasn't ready for the battle that was coming but there didn't seem any way to avoid it. He sighed and said shortly, "I picked it up for you and Jamie a couple of days ago."

Brooke blinked and then suddenly relaxed. "Oh, thank you for getting me a rental. I know I mentioned it before all of this, but I thought you would have forgotten that in light of how busy the last couple of weeks have been."

Jacob chuckled. "Yeah thanks, for picking up this rental for Brooke to head back to Montana, bro," he mocked.

Cole shot him a cold look that had Jacob's smile faltering but only a little. He reached a hand out and touched Brooke's shoulder in an attempt to comfort as he told her the truth. "It's not a rental. I picked it up from the dealership."

Brooke frowned and then her eyes sparked angrily, "I can't afford this car. You shouldn't have done that."

Cole gave her a subdued grin as she glared hotly at him. "I don't need you to pay me back hon. Just consider it an early Christmas present."

A look of disbelief flashed over her face and then annoyance. "I can't except this as a gift Cole."

He nodded and his jaw tightened stubbornly, "You can and you will. Even if I could take it back at this point the salesman there wouldn't let me out of my end of the deal."

She stared at him. "What deal?" she asked suspiciously.

Cole grinned. "I may have told him I had an old caddy that I'm currently rebuilding, when I realized he was a major classic car fan. He gave me a really great deal and I agreed to give him my current project for cost."

Brooke stared hard and then she glared again. "That only makes this worse. On top of this ride, which I'm sure is about as much as I make in a year, I will also owe you for your time and effort on the car." She raised agitated fingers to brush the curl that kept falling into her eyes behind her ear.

Jacob surprised Cole by coming to his brother's rescue. "Now, Brooke honey, Cole just wants to do something nice for you guys. Besides haven't you heard that he is loaded?" he joked.

Brooke didn't smile but at least quit giving Cole the stink eye. With a loud humph she sat back in her seat. "We aren't done discussing this," she threatened in soft determination.

He nodded as Jacob took an exit off the freeway. With a grin Jacob asked, "Is anyone hungry?" When Brooke smiled happily, he winked at Cole and added, "I know this great café that has awesome sandwiches and salads."

A couple minutes later they pulled into a parking lot of an old white brick building that had painted black trim and shutters. There was a flashing open sign in the window and even as they parked Brooke could smell a smoker and the scent of freshly roasted meat. She licked her lips in anticipation. Cole jumped out and opened her door for her before going around to lift Jamie's seat from the cradle.

Car seat slung across his arm he walked swiftly back around to hold out his other arm for Brooke to hold onto to steady her trembling legs. She latched on gratefully and Jacob asked for a booth as they made their way inside. The cheerful, short, and plump dark-haired waitress took their drink orders before walking into the back. Cole slid the car seat into the booth and checked that it was secure before turning back to Brooke. He motioned to the bench next to the car seat. "Why don't you sit there Brooke so you don't have to slide. The doc said you'll still be sore for a couple weeks." He waited for Jacob to slide in and then joined him across from Brooke and Jamie. Brooke groaned as she adjusted to a more comfortable position. Cole raised an eyebrow. "Do we need to skip this and hurry straight home?" he asked with concern.

Brooke shook her head adamantly, "No way, I'm just working out all the kinks." Her shoulder throbbed and her stomach jolted as pain soared from her center out but she was starving and nothing was going to keep her from a decent meal now.

Cole accepted her excuse but only because she had been complaining about being hungry since last night. He smiled at the waitress as she came with their drinks and the girl blushed. Brooke glared at him which was completely uncalled for since he was only trying to be friendly. Then she turned and smiled up at the waitress herself as she ordered a double BLT with a large serving of fries and an extra side salad. Jacob ordered a turkey melt and Cole went for the philly cheese steak and a salad.

When their order came out a few minutes later Brooke stared in wide eyed wonder as she watched that stacked platter of food heading their way. She looked at that plate the way he felt whenever he saw her. Like she wanted to gobble it all up and then lick her fingers off after the fact.

It was sexual torture watching her inhale that sandwich but he stared anyway as she plopped the last bite into her mouth before reaching for a napkin. The memory of her licking at him that way tugged at his jeans and he had to adjust his position on the bench. In self-preservation he finally forced his gaze to his own food and ate. He saw her hand coming for his plate and quickly pulled it back before she could get it. His amused gaze slid up to her disappointed one. He grinned. "How about I buy you a piece of pie?" he suggested in compromise.

She smiled in sheer pleasure at his suggestion. She shrugged. "Sure, but only if you add a scoop of ice cream."

Both he and Jacob chuckled as he raised a hand slightly to signal the waitress over. He ordered three pieces of pie and ice cream and then went back to his sandwich.

It was Brooke's turn to stare now. With irony he thought, the only difference was that she was jealous of him having a sandwich where he had been jealous of her sandwich having her. He took great pleasure in licking his fingers off as she watched.

By the time their meal was done Brooke had eaten most of the three servings of pie and ice cream and Jamie was hungry again. She sat in the back seat of the warmed-up car and fed him. When she was done Cole came and took him around to strap him so she didn't have to move to buckle him into his seat. She leaned back exhausted. As the final buckle clicked into place Cole murmured, "That seat tilts back if you need it, Brooke."

She looked around until she found a series of adjustment buttons. Content now she tilted the seat back and closed her eyes as Jacob pulled out of the lot and headed back to the freeway.

CHAPTER 51

With an exasperated sigh Brooke plopped back on the bed as Cole quickly walked out of the room. He disappeared from sight only to return a moment later rocking Jamie to soothe him. He walked directly to her and held her son out to her.

With a grumpy glare at him she reached for Jamie and pulled her pajama top open to feed him. Once he had latched on and suckled noisily at her breast she turned to Cole. "I can go get him sometimes Cole. You don't always have to do it." She gave him a very pointed look. "You are exhausted. You have been up every night with him and then up early again to take care of me. You need to give yourself a chance to rest."

He met her worried gaze steadily, "I'm fine. I sleep as much as you do. And for the record I will keep getting him for his nightly feedings until the doc actually clears you to lift his weight from the crib."

Brooke's eyes filled with tears but she fought them off. "I don't know why you keep doing all of this stuff for me," she said quietly. "I honestly don't see how you are getting anything out of all this."

Cole sunk down and slid his mostly naked body to sit next to her and lifted her chin. "You do know why; you just don't want to face it."

Brooke tried to look away. Cole had been phenomenally amazing in the past two weeks since she had come home from the hospital. When they first got to the old house Brooke had soon seen that the spare room had been completely furnished as a nursery and all the clothing and items had been washed and organized for Jamie. Jacob assured her that Cole had done it so she could stay while she recovered.

When she called her friends in Montana to let them know she might be a bit longer they reassured her that Cole had already filled them all in, and everything was being taken care of. They told her to focus on getting better. When she called her boss to let him know she'd had the baby and didn't know yet when or if she could come back, he'd chuckled and congratulated her before informing her that Cole had already filled him in, and that her job was there any time she wanted it back but to take whatever time she needed in the meantime.

She checked her account at the bank to pay her mortgage and was informed that it had been handled for the next three months. Finally, when she'd called the hospital to arrange a time to go over a payment schedule for all their services, they'd happily informed her the large bill had been handled. When she asked Cole about it, he told her that Ivan had refused to let him handle it and had paid it before he could arrange it.

The last two weeks had been hard on them both as they adjusted to a baby waking all night long and the constant trips to town for her physical therapy. The only time Cole left them alone was when Jacob or Anne and Ivan came over and spent a few hours visiting each day. They all insisted on taking care of her and Jamie until Cole returned.

After the first week she finally got the nerve to ask Jacob where Cole would go when he left. Jacob smiled and admitted that he was over at the garage working on that car he owed the salesman at the dealership. When Cole got back that day, she tartly informed him that she would pay him back for everything he was doing somehow. Looking tired and a bit frustrated, he turned to face her and said quietly, "I don't want your money, Brooke. Money doesn't and has never meant much to me."

She had looked perplexed then and asked, "What can I do, then, to repay you?"

He'd sighed and came over to kiss Jamie's head. "I don't want repaid, Brooke. I want you. I love both of you."

Brooke hadn't known what to say to that so she had snapped her mouth closed and then said simply, "Well, thank you, I'm not sure how we would have gotten through these past few days without you."

She thought she had seen disappointment then, but when she'd studied his face, he smiled and nodded before taking Jamie out to play with him for a while.

The next few days flew by much like the week before with one big difference. She was getting very hot and bothered now at having him and his sexy body lying in bed next to hers every night. She dreamed of him, and then she would awaken to find herself curled up to a very turned-on Cole. He never tried anything and that made her even more frustrated. He would sometimes wake up and ask if she needed anything before turning onto his back and going back to sleep. Sometimes she spent hours staring at his lean naked form before she would finally get so exhausted, she would sleep again.

Two days ago, Jacob had come to see them and Cole disappeared, telling her only that he would be back in a bit. She visited with her friend for a long while and then Jacob suggested a movie. They ended up watching two movies and she was starting to worry when Cole finally came in through the back. She heard him in the kitchen washing up before he came in and sat by them.

When she looked up, he seemed more relaxed than she had seen him since the attack. She'd smiled and asked, "How are you doing?"

He'd grinned and replied, "I'm really good."

Jacob groaned and said, "You look like the cat that just got the cream, bro. What's up?"

Cole smiled. "I just gave the keys to that salesman from the dealership." When Brooke looked hesitant, he added, "Easiest ten grand I ever made."

Brooke looked aghast. "He gave you ten grand for that?"

Cole shook his head. "No, he gave me ten grand off the price of your SUV for the labor on the Caddy. He paid cash for the total of the invoices from my cost to buy and repair it. And I just want to say that I got the better deal. That ten grand was a third of the cost of the SUV."

Brooke stared at the television miserably. When she finally drummed up the courage to look at him, she asked. "How am I ever going to pay you back that much?"

He looked frustrated then. "For God's sake, Brooke, I thought we already settled this. I don't want your money."

Brooke looked at him and then Jacob before bursting out in her own frustration. "Then what in the hell do you want, huh?"

Jacob stood then and smiled a little. When he walked to the door, Brooke glared at him. He raised his hands, "I'm sorry, Brookie, but you are on your own with this one. Even I know what he wants and I don't claim to be the smartest guy in the room." He added for emphasis, "And he didn't tell me either."

Brooke's heart thundered in her chest as she turned back to Cole who watched her with mild interest to see what she would say. Her mouth opened and closed twice, but she said nothing.

Cole grinned. "That's what I thought. Chicken."

She just humphed and stood to go to the bathroom. When she returned, Cole was standing in the kitchen making dinner while talking to Jamie who was busy chattering right back in his garbled baby talk. She helped Cole finish the meal and was grateful when they sat again. She tired a lot easier now than before and it frustrated her. Every day she felt a little better and that helped.

They ate in mutual silence and then she sat in the rocking chair in the nursery and fed Jamie as Cole hauled laundry down the stairs and started the washer. He returned and sat on the floor leaning his strong back against the crib to face her. When she finally met his eyes he said quietly, "This is something I need to do. I need to take care of both of you. I don't know how to explain it, but I need it and it would mean a lot to me if you could accept it."

Tears had filled her eyes then, and she'd nodded. "I'll try."

That night she hadn't been able to sleep much at all, so aware was she of that long lean body next to her own. She could feel the heat from his skin even without contact but wanted to feel that heat seep right into her own cold body. She slid her leg against him and sighed as heat enveloped her side. He woke up and asked if she was okay to which she quickly said she was. He squeezed her hand and turned over to go back to sleep.

She knew he was bothered by the closeness as well. Could see the desire there in his eyes as he watched her feed Jamie. At times throughout the day, she would catch him watching her, and his eyes would be so dark, they were nearly black with desire and yet he wouldn't touch her.

Brooke was frustrated and confused by how much she missed him touching her. Her core ached with heavy longing and a need to hold him close. The problem she knew, was that she couldn't get attached to him. At any point he could decide that he didn't want them anymore and walk away and she would be devastated. The longer she stayed here in this valley the more she was going to hurt when she left.

She also had Jamie to consider as she didn't want him to get so attached that he was sad and traumatized when Cole was no longer in their lives. She always came to the same conclusion. She needed to get back to Montana as soon as possible.

By the end of the third week, she was feeling much better. Her shoulder hurt only minimally and her ribs had healed nicely. Even her stitches were only bright pink scars at this point. She woke up Saturday morning with a heavy sense of dread. It had been five weeks since that awful night with Richard.

As soon as she opened her eyes, she knew that she had to go soon. She rolled over in the bed and stretched out languorously before sitting up. Cole wasn't in the bed with her, but that wasn't unusual as he had selflessly insisted on her sleeping as long as she could to recover. She heard a happy little baby gurgle coming from the kitchen and quickly pulled on some soft stretch denim skinny jeans and purple, lace bodice V-neck T-shirt and brushed her fingers through her hair before pulling it back into a quick ponytail. She didn't worry about makeup, only splashed cool refreshing water on her cheeks before hurrying into the kitchen.

She stopped just inside the door and watched as Cole lifted Jamie into the air and wiggled him which made Jamie gurgle and giggle in delight. Somewhere near the vicinity of her heart an ache burned hot and searing and she couldn't stop the tear that fell down one cheek. "What am I ever going to do about this?" she muttered softly.

Cole turned and looked at her. "Oh look, Jamie, Mama woke up. Why don't we go say good morning to our favorite lady, huh little guy?" He settled Jamie on his arm and walked over to her. "I'm sorry, I didn't hear you before, what did you say?" he asked as he held Jamie toward her for a kiss.

Brooke shook her head, "Nothing. I was just talking to myself."

Cole's gaze had narrowed in on that single tear on her cheek. Concerned he leaned toward her. "Are you okay?" he asked quietly.

Brooke nodded and kissed Jamie softly as she took him from Cole. She ignored Cole. "Good morning, you handsome guy," she said as she buried her face in his neck. He smelled like fresh coconut and she raised her head to meet Cole's worried gaze. "He smells so good, did you already bathe him this morning?"

Cole nodded and patted Jamie on the back. "Yeah, us guys took a refreshing shower first thing." He grinned at her. "He also had a bit of a blowout with his diaper so it was just easier."

"Thank you, Cole, but I'm feeling a lot better now and you don't have to spend all your time taking care of us, you know. You have a life and you really should be getting back to it," Brooke told him.

Cole shrugged. "I have still been working on the things I need to do. I'm not going to leave you to cope with everything on your own."

Brooke looked up and her core ached again as she said suddenly. "I think it's time for me and Jamie to go back to Montana."

He met her gaze and nodded. "I figured you would be coming to me with this soon. Me and Jacob have discussed it, and if you are determined to head back, we are ready to pick up and go with you."

Surprise widened her eyes. "Why on earth would you do that? You guys need to get on with your lives."

Cole's lips turned up in a sardonic grin. "I won't be getting on with anything, my dear. You and Jamie have become the most important part of my life." He paused for a long moment as she looked away. "I have been looking at some job opportunities in Montana and I have a couple of pretty great offers on the table. If you are simply happier there, then we can go, but I am going with you."

Brooke cursed loudly and then covered her mouth as she stared down at Jamie. "What about school and your work here and your dad?" she asked with a narrowed gaze.

He didn't blink as he looked at her. "I graduated a few weeks ago. I have several job opportunities with tech companies around the country, but I intend to stay near you and Jamie. I can go to Montana or I can stay here if that is what you want. Or if there is somewhere else you want to go, I'm willing to do that too." He lifted a hand and tucked a loose curl behind her ear before saying casually. "I'm pretty open, Brooke, so whatever you want, I will do."

Brooke raised her eyebrows in disbelief. "Why won't you just make this easy on us and let me go?" she asked, lifting her chin stubbornly, her blue eyes flashing fire.

Cole met her gaze and she watched as he looked at her lips for a quick moment before raising them to her eyes again. She licked her lips to moisten them. He smiled, then, "I love you Brooke." He said it in a tenderly aching voice. "I love you and I love Jamie and I am not going to walk away from you ever."

Brooke stared at him in horror. This was the worst possible thing that could happen to her right now. She was already needing space from him before she started to depend on having him around loving her. She simply could not survive it if she went all in with him, and then he decided she wasn't enough after all. It would kill her.

She stared at her feet for a long moment before finally meeting his gaze again. "Look, I understand that you think you love me, Cole, and I do believe you care for us, but let's face it. You could quite literally have any woman in the world that you wanted. Everywhere we go women flirt with you and try to get a piece of the devilishly handsome tough guy that they see in you. I can't compete with that. Honestly, I don't even want to try. Please just let me go away and leave me alone," she pleaded. Her eyes filled with tears and she looked away.

Cole looked offended, but he leaned down close to her. "I love *you*, Brooke Reynolds. Every last frustrating part of you makes me crazy and drives me mad, but it also makes me want you more, which makes no sense. I am a patient man and I can wait a little longer, but I'm not God. At some point I may give in and try to take you again before you've made up your mind about this. It isn't fair for you to blame me for the flirting or whatever else women choose to do. I haven't even seen another woman since I met you. And, yes, I mean dating or otherwise," he said heavily as she opened her mouth to argue.

He lifted his hand to stop her. "Just listen for a minute because I need to say this. I haven't even been able to see straight since I walked up to this house and saw you there with your shirt and skirt all tied up in knots and showing off that gorgeous body of yours. I actually did tried to go out a few times, but I couldn't stop picturing you and I decided going out with women while I was thinking of you was far ruder than canceling the dates and so I did."

She looked unsure, so he continued. "When I saw that fear on your face that first time I kissed you, it nearly killed me. I swore after that I wouldn't touch you again and believe me, I tried to stay away." His tone was honest and his voice was hoarse as he told her. "I thought it was because you were a virgin and that I had nearly taken advantage of you. But when I realized you were pregnant, my first impulse was jealousy because some other man had gotten to touch you and I hadn't. Then I was pissed off for holding myself back so hard when you obviously weren't so innocent after all."

He brushed a strong lean hand across his face, "I know that sounds crude especially now that I know that you were innocent and even worse, raped, but that was how I felt. And then when I knew you were gone, I was angry with you for running away, because we hadn't even had a chance to see where this could go. I was sure that when I finally found you, I was going to be pissed off and angry and give you a piece of my mind. But then I saw you with that beautiful mound and you were so soft all I wanted to do was protect you and be with you. I think I knew then how I felt, but I hid from it for a long while."

He took a ragged breath. "When I put everything together and realized someone was following you that night and I remembered this truck I kept seeing outside the house in Montana, and the attack on you after the barbecue, I was terrified. And I drove like a madman to your house just hoping you would still be alive and I would get there before that bastard hurt you again.

"I felt like I died that night when I didn't know whether or not you would make it. But then there was Jamie and he needed me to be there with him whether or not you survived and I realized that I had loved you both all along." He reached for her chin and tilted it up gently. "I love you," he said slowly, distinctly. "There is no goddamn way I am letting you or my son go to Montana on your own with Richard still out there somewhere." His hard tone left no room for argument.

Brooke argued anyway. "That's just it, Cole. He isn't your son."

Cole's eyes narrowed dangerously. "He is in every way that matters."

Brooke looked away in shame. "I'm sorry, I shouldn't have said that."

He sighed next to her. "If you truly don't want me in your life, Brooke, I will let you go. I will follow you to Montana and work there and get my own place, but I still want to be able to see Jamie and I want around the clock protection for both of you if I'm not there with you." He looked dejected then. "My only condition is that you have to look me in the eye and tell me that you don't want me in your life." He looked away as though gathering courage and then said, "If you can do that, then I will give you my word to leave you alone."

Brooke stared bleakly at her shoes. "I don't want you to give up some big amazing life because of us," she admitted as she slowly raised her gaze to his.

Cole grinned, feeling like he had already won. "I have every intention of living an amazing life. That plan will happen with you and Jamie by my side."

Brooke's bottom lip trembled, "Do you really think these feelings can last?" she asked nervously.

Cole lowered his head to hers and took her mouth in a hungry kiss. When they were both breathless and desperate for more, he raised his head and grinned down at her. "Yep, I'm pretty sure it'll last," he assured in a low raspy voice.

Brooke laughed breathlessly. "I was starting to wonder if you were ever going to kiss me again."

Cole leaned in for another long earth-shattering kiss. "You drive me fucking mad," he groaned.

Brooke pulled back and looked up at him with a wide happy smile. "Oh, and Cole?" she waited until he met her gaze. "I love you too."

He responded by lifting Jamie from her arms and laying him gently on a blanket that was spread on the front room carpet and then taking her into his arms. When they both came up for air a few minutes later Cole turned to look down at his son.

"Are you ready for a nap, Jamie?" he asked hoarsely.

Brooke laughed a little desperately.

CHAPTER 52

Two weeks went by in what Brooke could only describe as heavenly bliss. With a lot of training and effort on hers and Cole's part, Jamie finally started sleeping through the night. Cole took advantage of the free nights by loving her with the potent intensity of a savage and then holding her gently through the night only to wake her again in the morning with more kisses and loving.

Now that she was feeling better, she insisted that he should take more time to work and he took her up on it. They would eat their breakfast together, and then he would help clean up before he headed off to his garage for the day. When Brooke started missing him, she would load up Jamie into his car seat and go over to the shop where Cole was in the process of rehabbing an old Chevrolet. She would watch him and listen as he talked to Jamie as though the baby understood rocket science, going into great detail of how the engine worked. Often, after a while, she would kiss him goodbye and then stop by the Burton house to visit with Jacob, Anne, or Ivan. Jamie loved seeing everyone and it got her out of the house. She was starting to feel fidgety from hanging around the house all day and was anxious to get back to work. Cole suggested she talk to Ivan about working for him, but Brooke felt like it would be taking advantage of him so she refused.

She didn't mention Richard to anyone, but she was nervous whenever she and Jamie were alone at the house. Her gut told her with deadly certainty that if Richard was alive, he would come for her and Jamie. She had told him the baby was his as a last desperate attempt to keep herself and her baby alive. With his level of obsession with her before he'd known the baby was his, she felt like he would certainly come back for them now that he knew.

Cole had installed a security system with cameras so he could check on her from his phone at any time. He had given her a panic button to wear around her neck that notified his phone and the police if she ever had a reason to push it. She was also hypersensitive of keeping a phone on her person at all times and never let it out of reach no matter what she was doing. She called the police every day to see if they had any more information and she knew that Cole called as well since one of the deputies had commented grumpily on how many times people were calling about Richard's case.

Mostly, though, she missed having a productive life. She needed a job so she could build security for Jamie and know she could continue to take care of him. Cole had been generous and kind, but she couldn't keep letting him take care of everything. She just wasn't wired that way.

It was a cold morning in January and a storm was brewing in the air blowing snowflakes in swirls around the banks when it all finally came out. She had fallen back asleep after Cole spent thirty minutes thoroughly loving her that morning. When she woke up, she heard Cole in the kitchen and hurried in to help him. He already had a stack of pancakes and was frying eggs and bacon by the time she dressed and joined him.

"I'm sorry, I fell back to sleep, I guess," she murmured as she reached into one of the oak cabinets for plates and glasses to set the table.

Cole grinned, looking proud of himself. "Yes, you did. I think I am wearing you out." He winked suggestively.

Brooke smiled but couldn't muster a laugh. "I guess," she conceded quietly.

Cole went on alert as he watched her usually happy face with concern. "What is it?" he asked as he loaded a heap of eggs and bacon on a plate and grabbed the stack of pancakes, before meeting her at the table with the food. Since she'd had Jamie and was nursing, she was eating even more and she was still looking a little frail from the weeks in the hospital.

She shook her head slightly, "I don't know. Nothing, I guess," she replied for lack of knowing what to say.

Cole walked over to her and pulled her against his chest. "Don't do that, Brooke," he said quietly as he bent and kissed her forehead.

Brooke looked at him in surprise. "Do what?" she asked a little offended at his quietly harsh tone.

His eyes held her own as he watched her unblinking. "Don't push me away. I feel like we have finally been starting to get somewhere and I don't want you to distance yourself from me again." He searched her face intently as he said it.

Brooke teared up and looked away. "I'm not meaning to push you away, Cole. I'm just going a little stir crazy," she admitted as he wiped a tear off her cheek with his gentle thumb.

"All of the books I've read about birth say that it's normal to feel that way after a while."

She looked at his shoulder. "Okay, I guess that's probably it, then," she said slowly as she turned away.

Cole grasped her shoulders as she turned away and pulled her back. "Hold on, I'm sorry. I don't know how you feel, and I shouldn't assume that I know what you're feeling. Why don't you explain it to me," he suggested as he tugged on her shoulders pulling her back to lean against his solid frame.

As she turned back to face him, she smiled a little. He was far too perceptive and she wasn't sure she liked it. With a little shrug she said, "I don't know how I feel. I think that is the problem. When I'm clear how I feel, then I can focus on putting it out of my mind but until then, it's just all this worry floating around driving me crazy and not working isn't helping. I have expenses, you know, and my savings account is getting low."

Anger flashed in his dark eyes, "If you needed money, why didn't you just ask me, Brooke?"

Brooke stared at him dumbfounded. "Are you serious?" she asked, feeling a bit piqued herself. When he only nodded tersely, she lifted her chin. "Just because we are in a relationship, Cole, doesn't mean I automatically expect you to take care of me. I still want to be able to hold my own financially."

His gaze was steady now as he met her flashing sapphire gaze. "I get that, but this is a tough situation for anyone and I told you that I don't care about the money. I just want to know that you're taken care of. I love you for God's sake," he finished, sounding gruffer than he'd intended.

Brooke stared at him stubbornly. "That doesn't mean that I'm going to take advantage of you and expect you to take care of us," she reiterated.

Cole gulped in a frustrated breath and stepped back as he ran his fingers through his hair. Eyes shooting those gold sparks, he grit out, "What is it going to take for you to realize we are in all of this together now, Brooke?"

Brooke teared up then, and her words spilled over. "I don't know, okay?" She sucked in a deep calming breath. "Growing up, I had very little and what little I did ask for, I got belittled for. My father used to always tell me how much I cost him." She held up a hand to stop him from speaking when he opened his mouth. "I know it doesn't make sense. I worked hard my entire life for him for very little. I know that now, but I still find myself feeling like I'm not worth much to people."

The anger was gone now as he reached for her hand and squeezed it as he pulled her close again. "I'm sorry, baby; I know it's hard for you. I just get so tired of fighting with you to take care of you when that is the most important thing to me." He bent and kissed her softly. "I just want us to be together and take care of each other in everything."

Brooke sighed and leaned into him, pressing her forehead against his. "I hear you, I do," she promised softly.

She could feel the rise and fall of his chest against her breasts as he breathed and warmth flooded her. He stared down at her for a long quiet moment and then whispered softly, "Marry me, Brooke."

Her heart skipped a beat, but she didn't realize she was holding her breath until it swooshed out loudly.

Cole watched her intently, waiting for her to respond. When the moment stretched out long and she didn't say anything, he swallowed the lump in his throat. "Please, Brooke, marry me and let me spend the rest of forever showing you just how much you mean to me. I love you and I feel like I can't breathe when I think of being without you and Jamie. I'm constantly worried that you're going to run away again and leave me alone." He knew he was begging at this point and though he couldn't ever remember lowering himself this way, he found in surprise that he really didn't mind. Raggedly he finished, "I'm not sure I could even live without you now, please say yes. Be mine."

Brooke stood frozen, still staring at him. In all the time she had known him, she would have never guessed he had this level of emotional honesty in his bones. As his words sank in fully, tears welled once again and she leaned into him. "My God, Cole, how could I refuse you after that? I've known for a long time that you were the only one for me, but I never dreamed that you could feel the same. If you are really serious, then my answer is yes."

He lowered his head to take her lips in a tender kiss, but before she closed her eyes she saw the glimmer of tears in his. Joy surged through her like a dose of adrenaline and she laughed suddenly. Cole stared at her and then grinned as she laughed until her eyes watered. When she was finally settled a little, he chucked her under the chin. "I have a sinking feeling that you might just be the death of me yet, my dear," he grumbled cheerfully and she burst into laughter again.

That night he asked his family over for dinner with them and he and Brooke shared their news over steaks, potato wedges, and grilled vegetables.

Ivan grasped Cole's hand and pulled him in roughly for a bear hug at the news. Anne cried and then rose from her chair to hug all three of them joyfully.

Jacob pounded Cole on the back, "It's about time, bro," he teased as he turned and pulled Brooke in for a tight hug.

Ivan grabbed her next and pulled her in for a hug and then to kiss her cheek as he said happily. "Now I can officially call you my daughter," he grinned and winked at Anne. "I told you she was a good one, dear," he said a bit too smugly.

Anne rolled her eyes and smiled. "And so you did."

Cole opened champagne, and for the first time in her life, Brooke sipped at the bubbly liquid happily, though she couldn't drink much due to nursing.

They spent the evening planning future events and celebrating the good news. They were discussing wedding options and plans when Brooke suddenly turned serious. She turned to look at Cole and with a frown said, "There is one big problem, though."

Cole raised an eyebrow at her look of concern. "What's that?" he asked.

Brooke looked at Jacob pointedly, "I assume you were planning to have Jacob as your best man, but that just isn't possible as he is my best friend and will be acting as my bridesman."

Cole stared for a second before leaning his head back in a deep laugh. He looked at Jacob and then back at Brooke. "It's okay I'm sure you can find someone else," he assured her in a cocky male tone. He grinned. "What about your friend Jill?"

"What about all your other friends?" she challenged without missing a beat.

Ivan was grinning at Anne when Jacob piped in. "Don't worry, you two. I will be the tie breaking vote. He winked at Brooke and grinned at his brother, then said. "You can both spend the next few months trying to win my favor by plying me with gifts, and then I'll decide."

Cole paled slightly and looked worried. "Next few months? I think not, Jacob. I figured we would be getting married sometime this week."

Anne, Ivan, and Jacob burst into laughter simultaneously as Cole and Brooke stared at them stupefied. Then Brooke smiled at Cole. "I like Cole's idea…," she began.

Laughter drowned out anything else she may have said.

CHAPTER 53

"We could just elope," Brooke suggested to Cole two days later as she stared at the gorgeous diamond engagement ring on her finger.

Cole grinned. "Now you're talking, though I'm not sure my mom would ever forgive me." He bent and finished zipping up Jamie's cute little denim patterned sleeper. He lifted his son and gave him a kiss on the forehead. "What do you think, little guy? Would Grandma forgive us if we didn't have a big fancy wedding?"

Jamie gooed happily and tried to suck on Cole's hand. He touched his son's cheek and then handed him to Brooke. "I think he's hungry, babe," he said as Brooke tickled Jamie's chin.

Brooke walked over and plunked down into the rocking chair. As she fed her son she looked up at Cole. "It's just that your mom said that it would take at least six months to plan a decent wedding. Am I supposed to stay here that long? Or do I go back to Montana while we plan it? Also, I just realized we have never even talked about your post-graduation plans. I know what Jacob has planned, but you have never even mentioned what you wanted to do after graduation."

Cole's thumbs slid into his pockets the way she had noticed they did when he was feeling unsure of how she would react. He met her blue gaze and gave her a little smile. "Well, before all of this," he said, waving a hand at her and Jamie, "I had planned to go to work right away for one of the most prestigious tech companies in Seattle. They offered me a position about a year ago and I told them I would give them a call when I was finished with university." He shrugged and leaned against the wall casually watching as Jamie suckled at her breast. "Since then, I've realized that you and Jamie are the most important thing in my life and I can get a job anywhere." He smiled. "My end game was never to work for someone else anyway. I always figured I'd work for someone for a couple of years to get a little more experience in the field and then start my own company." He looked at the window in thought.

Brooke watched his face and asked intently, "What would your company do?"

Cole turned his gaze to her. "Don't laugh, but I have an idea about how to possibly create a free energy generator. I would have to take on some other jobs as well of course, to help pay the bills while the research and trial runs are being handled. I don't know how much you know about power, but all the farmers around here pay a huge chunk of their profits every year to power pumps and pivots, not to mention their shops and cellars. If I get this generator to work, it would be something people would only have to invest in once. After the initial cost, they would essentially have free power."

Since she was staring at him wide-eyed, he expanded, "In areas of the world where power isn't established, people could use my generator to get water where they couldn't before. It would be similar to putting in solar but a much higher output so storage wouldn't be necessary to have the needed power."

Brooke looked at him in wonder. "My God, Cole, do you really think you could do that?" she asked in awe.

He nodded and grinned. "I know I could with enough time and resources. That was why I wanted to work for someone else first, you know. Make a bunch of money and make contacts that I can also use when I start my own company." He walked over to sit on the floor close by her feet. "I can open my own company from anywhere, though and I think I could get my foot in the door with about any tech company. Which means I'm happy to go anywhere that you want to be," he asserted quietly.

Brooke frowned. "But there must be a reason you were considering going to Seattle instead of somewhere else, right?"

Cole shrugged. "The company there offered me a job with a huge salary and they have a ton of resources that could eventually land me right where I need to be. I have thought a lot about this, though, and I realize now that I can do it from anywhere. I only want you to be happy."

Brooke stared into the distance for a long while before she said uncertainly. "What if I don't fit into your world at all, Cole?"

He stood and walked around the rocker and leaned down to place his hands on her shoulders. When she looked up at him, he kissed her and then replied calmly, "You do and will. If you don't fit or don't like it, I'll change or fix whatever doesn't work. I want you with me wherever I go, and if that doesn't work, I will go with you wherever you want to go."

Brooke smiled up at him. "I want that too." She was thoughtful for a moment then said, "It's strange to think that less than a year ago I was looking for a job and a way to survive and now there is all of this." She rolled her hand around to encompass the room and Cole. "Somehow it all just feels so natural and like it's meant to be. Not that long ago I thought my only option in life was to marry some prick of a man to have his children and live under his rules. Isn't it truly amazing the kind of life we can actually create when we want to?" she asked, her face lit up with excitement.

Cole chuckled. "I have always been able to see that potential in front of me but I can imagine how tough it can be coming from your situation." His eyes twinkled as he bent close and said low by her neck, "One more thing I love about you. You have quite literally had a lifetime full of challenges that most of us will never have to face and yet here you are in awe and wonder because you have had the courage to keep moving and creating this beautiful existence." His dark eyes held hers as he asked quietly, "Have you ever considered being angry at or blaming a baby that happened because someone raped you?"

Brooke's eyes widened and she glanced down at Jamie. "Good God, no. Why would I blame him? He didn't do anything except exist and he is so precious." She met Cole's gaze again. "I wouldn't change it either," she added as her chin jutted out slightly. "As horrible as it was, I would go through it again if that is what I had to do to have him."

Cole nodded. "Exactly my point, and I agree. I hate that you had to go through all that pain and yet if it hadn't been for all that would you have ever come here?" He lowered his head and took her mouth in a passionate kiss. When he lifted his head, she was gasping for air. "You are my soul mate, Brooke. I feel it in a way that I don't feel things very often. I know it in my head as well. That is why I know that we will be good together and create a wonderful life together."

Brooke smiled through her kiss swollen lips. "I have the house in Montana and I have friends there, but I don't feel held to that place. If I can find a job, I would be proud to go to Seattle with you. I don't care where I am. I just wish they would find Richard so we could all stop worrying about it."

Cole turned serious. "I swear the police aren't even doing anything to actively find him. Every time I call, I get the same old response. They are still looking and don't have any leads."

"That's what they tell me too." Brooke agreed. Her eyes lit up then and she said, "What if we don't have to keep waiting?"

Cole walked around the chair to face her. "What are you talking about?"

She smiled a little nervously. "What if he has been watching and waiting for a chance to come at us again but you or someone else is always around so he hasn't had a chance. I could go back to Montana alone with Jamie and we could have the police watching the house so when he tries to come at us, they can arrest him."

Cole's gaze narrowed. "We are not using you and Jamie as bait."

Brooke lifted a hand to him, "We wouldn't really be alone, Cole. You could go ahead of us and hide out in the house so that when we get there, you'll be there with us, but Richard would think we are alone."

He thought long and hard about it. There were rumors circulating around the valley that one of the Reynolds brothers had gone missing and he hadn't mentioned it to her because he didn't want to worry her. But given that it was the same brother who had known she was still in the valley, he'd assumed Isaiah had also told Richard she was here to begin with. He worried that Isaiah was helping Richard now as well.

Finally, he gave her a small smile. "Let me think about it for a bit?" he asked softly.

Brooke nodded and smiled. "Sure, but I really think it could work. If he's still out there, I think he would try coming for us if he knows we're alone."

Cole went back to work for a while, but he dropped Brooke off with Jacob on his way. With Richard fresh on his mind, he didn't want to leave her alone even for a second. He rolled her suggestion over and over in his mind playing out every scenario as he worked.

Brooke enjoyed a long visit with Jacob who was working on a project for his final semester of law school. Anne came in to sit next to her on the couch and reached for Jamie. "Well, hello there, I'm so glad you guys came to visit," she said as she tickled a little laugh from his now double chin. "And how is your mama doing?" she asked as she looked up at Brooke.

Brooke smiled. "Amazing," she said as she met the older woman's green eyes. Brooke turned curious then. "Hey, have you guys heard Cole's plan for the generator he wants to build?" When both Anne and Jacob gave her blank looks, she rushed on. "I guess he has this plan to build a free powered generator that can be used anywhere, even where they don't have electricity ran yet."

Jacob looked at Anne and then back at Brooke. "This is the first I am hearing about it."

Anne nodded. "Me too, although I imagine he has been planning it for some time." She smiled. "He isn't exactly the most likely to share his inner thoughts and ideas with anyone."

Brooke laughed in agreement. "I asked him about it and he told me a little, but I suspect he wouldn't have ever said much about it if I didn't dig."

"I think you just might be my favorite new daughter," Anne joked. "I will now be finding more out about Cole than I've been able to since he was born."

Jacob groaned, "Oh no, he already causes enough trouble as it is and he usually keeps to himself. God help us all if we all have to endure the depths of that deep well of a mind of his. We all know it's turning nonstop, but I think it would drive me insane to live in all that complex confusion."

Both Brooke and Anne laughed before the conversation turned to the wedding. Anne looked at her sideways, "So what do you guys have in mind for the wedding dear?"

Brooke paused with one of Jamie's baby crackers halfway to her lips. "Oh, I don't know. We just both agreed that we want it really simple and as soon as possible." Just for fun she held a straight face and added seriously, "We have been talking about good places to elope to."

Anne was so horrified that even Jacob laughed before he said, "Even Cole is smart enough to know that would be suicide."

Anne relaxed a little. "He'd better know that. I have been waiting your whole lives for this day and he won't be cheating me out of it."

Brooke laughed and then with chagrin said, "And here I thought weddings were all about the couple getting married and what they wanted."

Anne continued unperturbed. "We have a lot of family and they would be very unhappy if they didn't get invited to the wedding. Are you thinking summer or winter wedding?"

Brooke's eyes twinkled mischievously as she said, "Which would get us married sooner?"

Anne threw up her hands, "You're wedding should be special and something to remember for the rest of your life."

Brooke glanced helplessly at Jacob. When he just lifted his brows but said nothing she turned back to Anne with a sigh. "I don't know all that much about weddings as I have never been to one outside of the religion I'm from, and believe me, a date at the courthouse beats that. I do trust you, though, and I wondered if you would want to just plan something simple for us. Invite only those who are close to the family and do it as soon as possible."

Anne's face lit up. "Are you sure? I wouldn't want to take over."

"I'm sure." Brooke hid a smile. "I have my hands full with this little guy, and Cole won't hardly leave my side, but I'm fairly confident I will love anything you do."

Rubbing her hands together Anne smiled. "It's settled, then. I will see when I can plan it and if I have any questions, you will be the first one I ask." Excited, she stood and handed Jamie back to Brooke. "I had better start talking to people to see how soon we could all get together." She hurried out of the room.

Jacob raised an eyebrow. "Are you sure you want to do that?" he asked, looking worried. "She is bound to get a little carried away."

Brooke shrugged. "If we can't go to the courthouse and it won't work to elope, she might as well be happy." With those blue eyes twinkling, she added, "Besides I think I'm finally starting to understand her. If I give her a challenge the wedding is far more likely to be sometime in this century."

Jacob laughed. "Smart. By the way I really like seeing you this happy."

Brooke frowned at him. "When are you going to find your soul mate, Bestie?"

He looked glum. "I'm not even sure I want one. I really don't much like the dating game lately," he admitted.

Thoughtfully Brooke stared at Jamie. "Come to think of it, me and Cole have never even gone on an official date."

Jacob laughed, "I wouldn't expect much from Cole in that department or you might be disappointed.

Brooke only smiled as she thought about how thoughtful her lover was and all the meals he had cooked for her, not to mention the hot steamy nights. A little breathlessly she said, "I think I'll survive."

CHAPTER 54

It was an icy cold day when Brooke drove to Montana. Every few minutes she would see a swirl of snowflakes along the side of the freeway as the miles flew by. She made good time while Jamie slept, though every couple of hours found her stopped at fueling stations taking the time to take care of him for a while, before getting back on the road. The farther north she got, the icier the roads were and she found herself thanking Cole under her breath for the added safety of the all-wheel drive car.

As she drove through the city, she felt nervous. She suddenly wished that Cole had come with her. They had gotten into a huge fight the day before when she told him she was going back to Montana with or without him. She had talked to the local police and they assured her it was a good plan. She would go up to her house there and they would have unidentified officers watching the place closely for any sign of Richard.

Brooke felt bad to go against Cole and she understood how scared he was for her to be putting herself in danger like this. She just couldn't stand waiting for them to find a lead on Richard any longer. Her and Cole had argued back and forth about it for two days before she finally just told him she was going with or without his blessing.

Two days before the sheriff had called her and told her that her older brother, Isaiah had gone missing. At first, they thought he had just taken off, but then her older sister Renae had admitted that she saw him talking to Richard late at night and that seemed to be the last time anyone had heard from him. Though she didn't know exactly how she felt about Isaiah as he had bullied her even as a child, she didn't want anything bad to happen to him.

The sheriff had finally tracked down the address to a house that Richard had rented from a local farmer and gone there looking for him. There wasn't any sign of him there and he had long since moved on but the dogs had sniffed out blood. Forensics found only a few spots on the wall but the whole area had been bleached so they really didn't know what had happened only that Isaiah had bled there. They had been able to match the blood to Isaiah from the sample her father had given them and Brooke had a sinking feeling of dread.

Nervously she watched her mirror as she drove. She kept feeling like any minute she would look and his gray pickup would be right there behind her. Her heart thundered but she saw nothing on the long drive.

Everything felt a little surreal as she pulled into her own driveway. She hadn't told her friends she was coming. Didn't want to take a chance of putting them in danger. The house looked dark and empty as she parked out front in the driveway. She looked down the street at a black SUV she hadn't seen before and fear spiked again as she saw a man sitting in the front seat. She stared for a long moment, but then he tipped his head and waved at her. With a sigh of relief. she recognized the signal the police had given her to identify themselves. She pulled a hat off the passenger seat and pulled it down over her ears. Even through the dark she could see that icicles hung from her roof signaling the freezing temperature.

She thought of Cole and tears flooded her eyes. She hadn't liked leaving him that way but what else could she do? No matter how hard she had talked he just stubbornly disagreed with her. She had actually wondered if she should have left the engagement ring behind. What if they never got past this? Her heart ached and through her tears she slid into her thick coat and climbed out. She stepped up to the back door of the car and opened it to quickly pull the cover down over Jamie's car seat to keep him warm. With a little click she pulled the latch loose that released the seat from its cradle and reached for the bags on the floor under his seat. She didn't want to leave him in the house alone and come back so she had to carry both him and both bags in at once. Her shoulder throbbed a little as she settled the weight of the straps over it. It was a surprisingly good reminder of why she was here doing this and she squared her shoulders against the cold.

Cole had been true to his word. The driveway and walkway to the front door had been shoveled and salted recently. He'd told her he had worked it all out to be taken care of while she was gone and she made a mental note to thank him if they ever spoke again. She made her way quickly up the steps and set down the bags as she reached into her pocket for the key to unlock the front door. It clanked a little from the cold but then slid open with a click. Grateful she opened it and picked up the bags as she stepped inside.

She reached a hand out for the light switch and turned it on. Then she turned on the porch light. Best that she have as much light on the outside as possible to ensure the police would actually see Richard should he come calling.

"Here we are Jamie, this is the house that I thought I was going to bring you home to, you know," she said quietly and more to herself than the sleeping baby. She closed the door and carefully locked it before she dropped the heavy bags to the floor. She reached down and opened the seat cover so Jamie could breathe easily and then turned to the fireplace. The house was just a bit chilled and she had always loved using the fireplace. It would warm it up and make it feel cozy again she hoped. She remembered Cole sitting on the couch only half dressed the last time she had been here and a sad smile stretched her cold lips.

She soon had a pile of logs burning nicely and moved over to unstrap Jamie carefully from his seat. She had already put him in pajamas at her last stop in case he slept through the night and so she carried him into the little nursery. She looked around in surprise at the carefully organized room. Everything was clean and tidy unlike she had left it when she went with Cole.

He must have talked the girls into coming over to get everything organized for her as well. She glanced up to the window and shivered. Richard could be watching them right now. She quickly laid Jamie into the padded crib and hurried over to close the blinds and pull the curtain closed. Feeling a little jumpy she walked through the house closing all of the window coverings for privacy. Richard would know she was here if he had been following her anyway but somehow knowing he couldn't see her gave her some small level of comfort.

She set the diaper bag inside the nursery and then tossed the luggage just inside her bedroom. It was the only room she hadn't closed the blinds on yet and she noticed with relief they were already closed. Her stomach growled and she walked to the kitchen to see if she could find any food. She stepped back in surprise as she opened the fridge which had been nicely stacked full of food. Everything from eggs, steaks and hamburger patties to fresh fruits and vegetables stared back at her in organized splendor. Brow furrowed in concern she thought about Cole. Had he done this as well? Or was this the doing of the police to keep her safely inside?

With a little shrug she turned and opened a cupboard where she had normally kept food and found it also fully stocked. She reached for a bag of potato chips. Whomever had put them there would have to wait until later to be thanked. She pulled some grapes from the fridge along with a cold cola. This would do nicely for a late-night snack. She walked to the table intent on her food and sat as the memory of her and Cole sitting here together flashed again.

She quickly downed the snacks and then put the leftovers away. She was exhausted from the long drive and she wanted to get some sleep while Jamie was still sleeping well. She took a quick peek in on him to make sure he was okay and then left the door open so she could hear him if he cried. She made a quick stop in the bathroom to brush her teeth and hair before she walked tiredly to her room.

She nearly tripped on the bag she'd tossed on the floor but managed to right herself just in time. She bent to pick it up and straightened back up to move it off to the side. She heard the movement of air and froze. Ears perked she reached for the light switch and her phone in her pocket at the same time. She had her finger on the dial button even as the fixture above flooded the room with light.

He stepped up behind her and wrapped her in a gentle hug. "I thought you would never get here," he said softly into her ear.

Brooke whirled and punched his arm. "You bastard! You scared the hell out of me. I didn't know you were here," she nearly shouted as her heartbeat thundered in her ears. Tears of relief filled her eyes, "I thought you were him," she mumbled as she wrapped her arms around herself protectively.

Cole wrapped his arms around her shoulders. "I'm sorry baby I really wasn't trying to scare you. I couldn't risk leaving this room and alerting anyone that I was here. I had to wait for you to go through your normal routine so it would look like you were alone."

Brooke pulled back and stared up at him suspiciously, "I thought you were mad at me." Her face lit up then and she punched his arm again. "That was all for his benefit, wasn't it?" she asked but didn't wait for an answer. "Wait, did you think he was watching us or something."

Cole grinned. "I really missed you Brooke," he tried to change the subject and leaned down to kiss her.

She sidestepped the kiss. "Oh no you don't," she warned in a hiss. "I just spent the last three days wondering if we were ever going to be okay again and feeling all alone in this." She glared up at him darkly.

He stepped toward her. "I know and I am sorry. I just felt like in order for this to work he needed to see us fighting a lot before you took off so it would look like you left because we weren't working out. It needed to be believable," he said quietly.

Brooke's eyes narrowed suddenly, "That whole dramatic goodbye was about him seeing it?"

Cole nodded and had the decency to look at least a little sheepish.

"But you said horrible things to me. You said if I didn't value Jamie or myself then neither would you."

He nodded and then lifted his hands, "I couldn't very well kiss you and wish you good luck. I'd have made out all over you and he would have known that we weren't really fighting."

Brooke glared, "But I was really fighting."

Cole couldn't stop his grin, "I know. That's what sold it. But if it makes you feel any better, I purposely said things that I knew would piss you off." When Brooke just stared at him grumpily, he continued. "Like when I told you that I was the boss and any fiancée of mine would do what I asked if she really cared."

Brooke's eyes shot sparks in memory. "That is such a pigheaded misogynistic thing to say."

He nodded. "It really is." He was fighting the grin that was attempting to take over his face.

It took her a moment to realize he had agreed with her and her mouth snapped shut before she continued. "God, you are exasperating," she said as a smile spread across her lips.

Cole looked at her with those dark intense eyes. "I agree," he said as he stepped toward her with promise in those black depths. Brooke backed up a step for each that he advanced until she felt herself pinned against the wall. With a little sigh she lifted her head as his lips came down hard and promising on her own. He was hoarse when he pulled back a long moment later to say, "God, I missed you."

Brooke only murmured in agreement as she wrapped her arms around his neck and pulled him back down for another breathtaking kiss. He groaned and lifted her. She wrapped her legs around his waist as he took the few strides to the bed and laid her down gently. He sat beside her and let her come to him for the next kiss. She didn't hesitate which made his heart swell in joy as he remembered those first few kisses and her fear of him.

She had finally realized she could trust him and it pleased him very much. In return, he removed her clothes slowly while kissing every bare inch before finally lifting her naked hips to straddle his face as he took a gentle nibble. She squirmed with the pleasure of his tongue rasping gently against her core and he took his sweet time showing her exactly how pleased he was with her trust.

He woke the following morning to Brooke sliding her naked body against him erotically. With a low growl he reached for her roaming hands and trapped them above her head as he rolled on top of her to straddle her thighs while he kissed his way up her stomach through the valley between those gorgeous breasts and up her neck before taking those soft lips in a biting kiss. She moaned and squirmed under him and he smiled in pleasure.

He enjoyed every minute that it took to make her beg. Then he parted her legs with a little pressure of his fingers against her inner thigh. She opened like a flower for him and he looked down at her in wonder as he slid into her welcoming heat. With a growl he leaned down and whispered into her ear. "Thank you for bringing such wonder and joy into my life."

She moaned and lifted her hips to meet his thrusts. She screamed as the orgasm racked her body with shudders and he took her mouth with his own to quiet it.

He didn't allow himself release until his deep thrusts brought her to the peak once again. With a shudder she convulsed around him and with a low growl he went up up up and over that sparkling void with her. They floated in euphoria, tangled together in the sheets for several minutes.

When her stomach growled loudly, he chuckled and rolled over to lay on his back. "Okay, Okay I get it. I'll go get breakfast started."

Brooke smiled across at him but didn't budge. She lifted a finger to his lips and whimpered, "One more minute. Just one more minute."

His hand laid gently on her flattened stomach as his fingers lightly brushed the scar there. His fingers moved up to the small scar near her lung and then to the rounded rough one low in her abdomen near her hips. In a solemn voice he said. "I look at these and I remember how close each one came to taking you from me. I hope you know that I want things with this bastard handled as much or more than you do. I don't ever want anything like this to happen again." He turned and lifted her chin, meeting those enigmatic blue eyes and held them. "I would never let a silly little disagreement come between us like that. I need you to understand that." He held her gaze watching her reaction.

Brooke met his gaze and nodded. "I get it now. I don't know how I even fell for it."

One side of his mouth turned up in a grin, "I do." When she stared at him, waiting curiously for him to expand, he said, "You don't understand how important you are to all of us, but especially to me." He looked a little unsure as though he searched for the words to use. "I always felt just a little out of touch with everyone around me. I knew I was a little different than everyone else and it didn't really bother me because I didn't know what I was missing but then you came along. Your joy and willingness to trust and connect with people even with everything you had been through, amazed me. Then I kissed you and I began to feel things I had never felt before. Even with my family it opened me up to so much more that I hadn't felt before. Honest to God, I think you saved my life from being empty of love and what really matters. There isn't any way to really thank you but I want to be your home if you'll let me."

His earnestness brought tears to her eyes and she reached for his hand and kissed his fingers. "That is by far the best thing you could ever be for me. Thank you for showing me that I am worthy of love."

Jamie gave an upset wail and she grinned and rolled up and off the bed. "That's my cue."

Cole was right behind her as she threw on his shirt from the previous night and hurried in to lift him from his bed where he was exercising his lungs. The wailing stopped as soon as she held him close. Cole came in and kissed both Jamie and Brooke before saying warmly. "I'll get some breakfast going." With a little kiss on the top of her head he turned and strode out.

Brooke laid Jamie down on the diaper pad and tickled under his chin before reaching down to unzip his blue sleeper. "Good morning baby, how are you feeling this morning?" With a happy little smile, she listened to Jamie gurgle with joy as she changed his diaper. She slipped on a pair of knit denim-colored britches and a little yellow shirt with a blue pickup on the front that actually looked a little like

Cole's truck. She had just lifted him to place a kiss on his chin when she heard Cole walk in behind her.

With a wide smile she turned. "Well, that didn't take long," she said in reference to breakfast.

The gun that was trained on her head made her freeze and suck in a terrified breath. Eyes wide with fear, she met Richard's unfeeling blue ones. His face twisted into a terrifying smile. "So, you were waiting for me, then?"

CHAPTER 55

Brooke's hands shook as she pulled Jamie close to her chest protectively. She started to turn sideways in an attempt to protect her son but Richard waved the barrel of the gun as he stepped closer. "Don't move," he commanded as he stared in some kind of obsessed wonder at the baby boy in her arms. "Come over here and bring my son to me, my love."

Brooke shook her head, her mind spinning. She had left her cell phone in her bedroom. Having Cole with her had made her relax too much. She swore inwardly and reached for the panic button that lay against her neckline. It was missing and with dawning horror she remembered Cole lifting it over her head so they wouldn't accidentally push it while making love.

Her eyes filled with helpless tears as Richard stepped toward her lifting his empty hand toward Jamie. She backed up a step but then found herself backed against the diaper stand. She considered screaming but then thought of Cole running in and Richard shooting him. She swallowed and looked around the room frantically for any sort of weapon that could somehow miraculously offset the shiny black metal gun pointed at her head. Desperate, she tried to smile. "Please put down the gun, Richard. I don't want you to hurt Jamie."

Richard looked between her and Jamie. "I'm not sure that is a suitable name for my son, but we can talk about that later." He stared for a long moment at the tufts of red hair on the baby's head. "He looks like you," he commented cheerfully.

Brooke nodded. "He does."

Her fingers latched on to the baby monitor behind her and she fumbled to turn on the switch. She couldn't remember where the receiver was or if she had put new batteries in it yet but it was something.

He reached behind her then and pulled it from her shaking hand. "What's this now?" He asked, looking a little bored. "What were you planning to do with this?" he asked without much concern as he tossed it into the corner.

Brooke wasn't sure if he knew Cole was in the house yet or not. She couldn't do anything to give it away just in case. Fear surged as she realized she couldn't hear him in the kitchen now. Had Richard already shot him? She shook her head, no she hadn't heard a gunshot so he hadn't shot him. She gulped air into her burning lungs and then smiled through her teeth. "What is your plan here, Richard?" she asked softly, hoping to throw him off his guard.

He smiled happily. "I have had a lot of time to realize that you have definitively dishonored me and my name." He motioned the gun toward Jamie then before retraining it on her head. "My son is still pure and innocent, though, so I will be taking both of you with me." He touched her shoulder with his free hand and she fought the urge to shake him off. "I will give you a chance to repent, you know, and if you do it to my satisfaction, I may let you live. I need someone to care for our son anyway until he is old enough to take care of himself." He shrugged as though it didn't matter to him either way.

Brooke stared at him in horror. "I will never do the things you want me to do,

Richard, so you may as well just leave me now."

He looked a little sad. "I was afraid of that." He turned slightly and motioned toward the door. "Walk now. I have a place all set up for us not too far away."

When Brooke didn't move, he cocked the hammer and pushed the cold metal against her forehead. "Move or the only memory our son will have of you is your warm blood splattering his clean face and clothes."

Brooke stepped forward and then hesitated thinking rapidly. "I need to get his things first," she stammered as she pointed to Jamie's diaper bag.

Richard only nodded once and she hurried to grab the diaper bag and started shoving things into it with her free hand. He watched her silently, his eyes cold, "Hurry it up now, we need to get out of here before more of your so-called friends come looking for you."

Brooke looked around the room helplessly searching for anything that she could use to protect her son from this psycho. Helpless tears filled her eyes as she found nothing. It couldn't end this way, not after everything Jamie had survived. He simply couldn't end up being raised by this horrific monster. She would find a way she vowed.

Richard chuckled behind her. "If you are stalling, you needn't bother. Your boyfriend or whatever you call him is already dead."

Brooke turned to stare at him in dawning horror, but he only smiled.

"It was a nice little bonus. I had no idea he was here with you, but when I saw him coming, I hit him over the head and knocked him out and then shot him in the head."

Brooke gasped for air as panic and pain warred at the thought of Cole lying bleeding out on the floor. She stared up at him. "I didn't hear a gunshot," she denied.

Richard tapped a finger lightly against the end of the gun, "I had the foresight to bring a silencer, my dear."

Brooke stared at the round end piece that she hadn't noticed before and racked her memory for any sound that would have signaled the popping sound of a shot through a silencer. Nothing came but tears ran helplessly down her cheeks. She would kill him for this she resolved with a cold seeping anger that swept through her making her shiver with the force of it.

She stepped into the hall with Richard right behind her. She looked down the hall and stared at a large bloody spot on the hardwood floor in front of her. Cole stepped into the hallway then a silver gun in his hand aimed at Richard who grabbed quickly for her and wrapped his arm around her waist and pulled her against him as a shield. The cold metal against her temple sent another shiver through her.

Blood dripped steadily from the side of Cole's head and she tried to get away from Richard and get to him. Richard grunted and swore. "Hold still or I will shoot you now and take my chances with Burton here afterward," he threatened in a deadly tone.

Brooke stopped fighting as Cole smiled at her and winked. "I am going to give you one chance to let go and walk away. You have three seconds to make up your mind or you're a dead man." Cole's voice sounded almost relaxed as he met Richard's beady eyes.

Richard laughed, "Just try it and I will blow her brains all over the place."

Cole didn't move, didn't smile, only watched Richard with those dark unblinking eyes. He counted to three and then pulled the trigger.

Brooke stumbled back as she felt Richard's hand loosen and his body jerked behind her. Warm wet liquid splattered across her face and ran down her neck. In shock she started to turn to look behind her at Richard but Cole launched forward and pulled her into his arms. "Don't look honey, you don't want to see that," he murmured gently as he kissed her hair and leaned down to check that Jamie was okay. He was crying after the loud bang of the gunshot and Cole shushed him softly. "It's okay, little guy, everything is going to be okay now."

He met Brooke's glazed-over eyes and held up his phone as he said softly, "The police are coming."

No sooner had he told her that then they heard the front door bang against the wall as it was forced open and officers ran inside.

Brooke reached up for Cole's head, "My God, he shot you in the head." She tried to turn his head to get a better look at the wound.

Cole grunted as pain engulfed him as she touched the area near the long gash. "Don't worry, baby, I'm okay. He was a terrible shot, it's only a graze." He pulled her hand from his face.

Brooke didn't look like she believed him, but he held her hand tightly in his own so she couldn't touch it again.

As the officers rushed into the hall, Brooke watched Cole step away from her with his gun held out and pointed down. One officer took it from him and another stepped past her to check Richard for a pulse. She wanted to turn to look but couldn't get herself to do it. With a sudden gasp she bent over Jamie who also had tiny splotches of blood on his clothes. "I'm sorry, baby. It's all going to be okay," she cooed softly. She lifted him and cuddled him against her cleanest shoulder.

As though from a tunnel she heard the officer radio for an ambulance and then for the sheriff to come. She focused on settling Jamie and then let Cole lead her into the front room as he wrapped one arm around her shoulders. "Come on, baby, let's give them some space to work," he said quietly as he pushed her gently down onto the couch.

Brooke resisted. "I'll get the couch all bloody, Cole."

He smiled gently, "We'll get a new one. You are in shock and you need to sit." He walked swiftly into the kitchen before returning with a glass of water. "Drink this. You are going to need it because the police are going to want to get your statement."

She just rocked Jamie back and forth for a long moment feeling numb. Feeling soothed he finally stopped wailing and she settled back and reached for the water. What she wanted to do was climb into the hot steaming shower. She took a couple of sips and then met Cole's eyes. "Can I at least wash up first?" she asked quietly.

Cole reached for her hand. "I'm sorry baby, I think they are going to want to take pictures first for evidence."

Brooke's eyes widened. "Evidence of what?"

His dark eyes were steady as he held her gaze. "Evidence that it was a clean shoot and not murder."

She stared dumbly at him. "You saved both of our lives, Cole. How could they even dare to believe anything else?"

He shrugged. He could see the officer standing just to the side of the couch but knew Brooke hadn't seen him. He gave her a reassuring smile. "It's all just protocol," he told her gently as he turned to meet the middle-aged officer's eyes. "What's next, sir?" he asked coolly.

The officer stepped forward and Brooke turned in surprise as he started to speak. "This all looks pretty straight forward but we need to collect all of the evidence just to make sure and so we have a record of everything." He met Brooke's worried eyes. "Your boyfriend is right Ms. Reynolds we are going to need to take photos and then we will need your clothing once you remove it. Let's go ahead and get started and then you are welcome to take a shower and get in clean clothes before we interview you."

The wailing of the ambulance interrupted him and he rushed to the door to greet the EMT's as they hurried in with a stretcher. They rushed past her and Cole to disappear down the hall. More police officers rushed in and soon they came through with Richard on the stretcher. One of the EMT's was holding pressure against Richard's head wound as she said loudly, "We still have a pulse and we are going to rush him to the hospital now."

Brooke stared numbly as they rushed past her and through the front door. Cole sat next to her and squeezed her icy hand before threading his fingers through her own. He leaned toward her and said softly, "It'll all be okay. I will make sure of it."

She attempted a smile but her lips wobbled and so she firmed them into a straight line.

Another officer walked in then and by the way he started ordering everyone around, Brooke assumed that he was the sheriff. After talking quietly on the side of the room with the first two officers that had come in, he came over to them. Cole stood and held out a hand for a handshake but the sheriff only looked at it before saying quietly, "They need to check your hand for gunshot residue before you shake anyone's hand. You understand, it's just a precaution."

Cole nodded and the sheriff motioned a crime scene officer over to swab at Cole's hand. She quickly bagged the swab and smiled at Cole before nodding at the sheriff and walking off.

As Cole sat back down, the sheriff lowered onto his haunches and held her blue gaze. "Are you and your baby doing okay, ma'am?"

Brooke nodded jerkily and looked down at Jamie. "Yes, we're fine." She looked back up at him. "I'd like to take a shower and clean up," she said it so softly that he barely heard her. He nodded and stood up motioning a female officer to them. Officer Priscilla Rand hurried over to the sheriff and smiled gently at Brooke.

"Take some pictures of them quickly and then escort them into the bathroom and collect their clothing as it's removed." The sheriff instructed in a quiet undertone.

Officer Rand nodded and turned back to Brooke. "Come along, then, ma'am. Let's get you all cleaned up."

She waited patiently for Brooke to stand and then steady her shaking knees.

Cole reached out a hand. "Can I come with to help steady her?"

The officer shook her head. "I'm sorry, sir, but that isn't possible. I will take good care of her and get her back to you soon." She smiled to erase the sting of the truth.

Cole nodded once and then sat back down heavily. He watched as techs walked around photographing and taking samples of anything they saw as relevant. He saw them take several photos of Brooke and Jamie from different angles and then watched in silence as the woman cop ushered her down the hall and past the puddles of smeared blood to the bathroom.

The sheriff sat down next to him and asked calmly, "So you are the one that took the shot? Is that correct?"

Cole met the man's direct gaze and nodded.

"Okay, then, walk me through what lead to the shooting."

Cole stared off into the distance as he recalled the morning. In a serious tone he asked, "Should I have a lawyer here before I talk to you?"

The sheriff raised an eyebrow. "Do you need a lawyer present, son?"

Cole met his gaze unwaveringly. "I didn't think so, but with the way this is all going, I'm starting to wonder."

The sheriff grinned, then. "If you would like to have an attorney present, that is your right. However, you are not under arrest here at this time, unless there is something you would like to share that would lead to your arrest?"

Cole chuckled quietly. "Nice try. I don't have anything to hide here. This just all feels a little surreal and somewhat dramatic."

The sheriff nodded. "I understand that it can all be a bit much after this kind of trauma. Have you had anyone look at that head wound yet?"

Cole had two fingers against the wound pressing to stop the bleeding. He shook his head. "They offered, but I'm fine. It's just a graze."

Gaze narrowed, the sheriff asked, "A graze from a bullet?"

"Yes, sir."

"Let me get someone to come look at it before we get into it." He stood and walked out the front door and returned shortly with a medic. "Clean up and check his wound so we can start interviewing him."

Cole stood but then realized he towered over the shortish young man and sat back down as he removed his fingers.

The medic dabbed some wet gauze at the cut and it burned with a vengeance. Cole bit his cheek and held still. "This is going to need several stitches but because it's on your face you should probably go into the hospital to have it done by a plastic surgeon. It helps with the scarring."

Cole shook his head. "I'm not leaving here without Brooke and Jamie. Can't you just throw some stitches in it so it will quit bleeding?"

The medic hesitated before saying, "I can do some stitches, but I would really recommend you go in, sir."

Cole gave him a charming grin. "Recommendation noted. Now, will you throw some stitches in for me?"

With a disapproving smile the man reached for a suture kit. While he worked, Cole worried about Brooke and wondered with concern how she was doing. This had all taken a huge toll on her and Jamie.

CHAPTER 56

Brooke gathered clean clothes for herself and Jamie shakily. Officer Rand kept up a steady line of small talk in an effort to relax her. It wasn't working but Brooke didn't tell the officer that. Instead, she kept moving as she cradled Jamie protectively. The blood on her arms and face had long since dried so she wasn't worried about smearing it as she stacked a clean quilt on the pile of clothing. With a sigh she lifted the stack of clothing and made her way ahead of the officer to the bathroom.

Once inside, she laid Jamie on the soft rug as she removed his clothes, folded them, and then handed them to the detective who bagged them. Once Jamie was down to his diaper she stood and awkwardly began lifting the hem of Cole's shirt over her head. Officer Rand turned her back as Brooke finished undressing and handed the folded clothing to her. "That's all of it," she said quietly and Officer Rand thanked her and then quickly left her in the privacy of her own bathroom.

She reached for the hot water valve and turned it on. Without thinking she turned on the shower but then looked down at Jamie before turning the shower back off and plugging the bath tub. She wasn't sure exactly how she was going to get all the blood off while holding her baby but she would have to figure it out. She tested the water to make sure it wasn't too hot and then washed as much of the blood off as she could with a washcloth at the sink. Then she lifted Jamie and stepped into the water.

It wasn't as hot as she would have preferred, but she was still grateful for what little warmth it offered as she slid down to sit. She lay Jamie against her chest and he turned his head to suck at her. It jarred her back to the present in a way that nothing else could have. It was midmorning and she hadn't even fed him yet. She settled him against her curved arm and reached for a clean washcloth.

As he ate, she wet the cloth and washed his pudgy little body. He didn't have much blood on him but just to be safe she washed every inch anyway.

She started as she heard a knock at the door. She sat up higher and pulled the shower curtain partly closed. "Who is it?" she called.

Cole opened the door with officer Rand right behind him. "Brooke, honey I can take Jamie while you shower. We aren't supposed to talk to each other until they take our statements but I managed to convince the sheriff that it would be much easier for you if I came to get Jamie."

Brooke lifted the now satisfied baby and stood. "He is all clean and fed," she murmured softly as she pulled the curtain back to hand Jamie out.

Cole squeezed her hand before he lifted Jamie away. "Are you going to be okay baby?"

Brooke nodded and looked away, "I will be a whole lot better once I shower."

He nodded. "Take as long as you need. The sheriff can wait."

She closed the curtain as he turned and reached for the fluffy green frog towel that she had set on the counter for Jamie. She heard the soft click as the door closed behind him and reached to turn on the shower head. As hot water sprayed out, she stepped into the stream and let it run over her sticky hair and cheeks. She quickly pulled the plug as she watched the standing water in the tub turn red as bloody water ran from her hair and face.

Finally, alone now she leaned against the white tiles and allowed her shoulders to sag as shudders shook her body and the tears finally poured out. Everything that had happened over the past months had been stressful and overwhelming. It all seemed to culminate into this one hour this morning when she had thought both she and Jamie were going to die.

There was that painful fear that Richard was right and Cole was dead. She had never been so horrified or relieved at the same time as she was when Cole had stepped out with that silver gun. The blood dripping from his face had her worried that he was seriously injured and yet he had stood alive and that had been a huge relief.

Cole's face in mind she rushed through the rest of her shower in a hurry to get out and make sure his injuries were being taken care of.

She pulled on clean underwear first and then a V-neck T-shirt and a pair of soft, gray knit leggings. She looked in the mirror and saw the dark circles under her eyes and her pale freckled face. With a sigh she shrugged, it would have to be okay. She turned and opened the door to walk carefully past all the blood back to the front room.

She found Cole in the kitchen making a pot of coffee. He smiled as she walked in, "Feel any better?" he asked.

Brooke nodded and eyed the coffee pot. "I could use a cup of that though."

With a grin he reached for a mug and poured it almost full leaving only enough room for a little cream and sugar. Jamie sucked happily at his fingers as he was cuddled against Cole's muscled arm. She nodded her thanks and turned to add cream and sugar. Behind her she heard him say, "This is the third pot of coffee. These officers sure love their coffee in this icy weather."

Brooke forced a small smile and sank gratefully into a chair. Someone had opened the curtains and she stared out at the evergreen trees around the edge of the property. She heard someone else walk in and turned to meet the sheriff's thoughtful gaze. He walked over to her and held out his hand. "I didn't get a chance to introduce myself before," he said with a small smile.

Brooke reached automatically for his hand and shook it firmly, "Brooke Reynolds, sir."

He nodded. "I'm the sheriff here. The name's Brick Colton. Do you feel like talking ma'am?"

Brooke took a few quick sips of hot coffee and then set it down as she nodded. "We might as well get it over with."

The sheriff gave an officer a pointed look and he rushed in to ask Cole to come with him.

Brooke watched suspiciously as they left the room together. So, Cole was right, then. They didn't want them talking to each other or in the same room while they gave their statements. That seemed odd since they had both been through the exact same thing, but whatever. She turned back and met Sheriff Colton's blue gaze. "What is it you need to know?" she asked firmly.

The sheriff smiled in an attempt to disarm her. She didn't bite, only kept her gaze steady on his. He finally cleared his throat and pulled out a notebook as he sat across from her at the small table. "So, the man who was shot was your ex-fiancé then?"

Brooke nodded. "In a manner of speaking, I suppose he was." The sheriff raised an eyebrow at her cryptic response so she continued. "He was promised my hand in marriage by my father when I was sixteen."

That got a surprised and confused look from him. "I understand that you are now engaged to this Cole Burton?" He hesitated for a moment. "Is this also an arrangement by your parents?"

Brooke laughed then. "God no." With a smile of sympathy, she filled him in. She told him about leaving home and everything that had happened since then. She finished by describing in detail every moment of the morning including their lovemaking before Jamie had awakened. When she was done, she lifted her coffee to her lips again for a long sip.

He scratched his head thoughtfully as she finished. A wide grin broke across his handsome face as he said a bit reluctantly, "That is quite a story. I'm assuming if I call the sheriff in Idaho, he can confirm it?"

Brooke nodded and kept sipping the now lukewarm coffee.

He set his notepad down then and said quietly, "If all this is true, then you have been through quite the ordeal. I don't want to make things any harder than I have to, Miss Reynolds. I just have one more compelling question."

Brooke looked at him curiously then. "What is that, Sheriff?"

He held her gaze and watched intently as he said, "Who is the actual father of your son?"

That took Brooke by surprise and she could see that he knew it. She hesitated, "Why does that matter?"

Still watching her closely he said softly, "Because if Richard Jessup is the father, then that would give Mr. Burton a couple of very powerful motives to kill him."

Brooke didn't blink but just stared at him. A small frown knit her eyebrows as she asked, "What did Cole tell you?"

Sheriff Colton raised an eyebrow but answered, "He said he is the father by any and all means and offered to produce the birth certificate as evidence."

Brooke smiled. "I think you have your answer then, sir."

He held her gaze for a long moment with a thoughtful expression. "Don't get me wrong, miss. I want this all to work out in the best way possible for y'all, but I need to get the facts straight here." When Brooke didn't offer anything more, he said quietly, "If I find out something differently about all this, it could lead to the arrest of your fiancé, do you understand?"

Brooke gave him a knowing smile. "Opposed to what? You arresting him right now because I've confirmed his motive for you, sir? Thanks anyway, but I'll stick to the truth and reiterate that Cole is Jamie's father in every way that applies here."

The sheriff nodded. "Suit yourself. I am aware that my department was warned that there could potentially be danger to you and we were asked to watch out for you as a courtesy from someone high up in the Idaho police department, but if I find out there is more than meets the eye here, I won't hesitate to arrest and open a case against you and/or your fiancé."

Brooke smiled coldly, "I would expect no less."

CHAPTER 57

Cole had given his statement three times before he finally told the sheriff that if he needed any more information he could speak to his lawyer. Sheriff Colten only chuckled and told him they were done.

Since the crime scene unit was still taking photos and bagging evidence, he took Brooke and Jamie to lunch. Everyone at the café was thrilled to finally meet Jamie and their lunch turned into a three-hour affair as Brooke visited and showed him off to all her friends and coworkers.

She had dark circles under her eyes and looked exhausted, though Jill was the only one who noticed besides Cole. When she asked Brooke how she was feeling, Brooke explained briefly about Richard and what had happened.

"Oh my God, girl you need to be home somewhere resting," Jill exclaimed when she finished.

Brooke ran a tired hand over her eyes. "If only. My house is crawling with police and I don't know if I could rest there anyway."

Cole stood then, lifted Jamie and began strapping him in his car seat. He smiled at Brooke and then gave a friendly smile to Jill. "I think I am going to take her to a nice hotel so she can rest."

Jill agreed cheerfully and the women hugged warmly as they left. Together they walked to the car in silence. As Cole slid the car seat into the holster it clicked. He reached for his phone and dialed Janae's number. She answered with a happy hello. He quickly explained the situation and asked her if she had any rooms open that he could bring Brooke to.

As he slid in and started the car, he thanked her and hung up. Brooke had leaned her head back against the headrest and had her eyes closed. He reached for her hand and squeezed it gently. "Are you going to be okay?" he asked, sounding worried once again.

She opened her eyes and looked over at him. "I am good. I just feel tired and guilty."

One brow raised. "What do you feel guilty about?" he asked quietly as he backed out of the parking spot and pulled out onto the road. He turned left and headed for Janae's motel.

Brooke closed her eyes again, "Did you know that I didn't even ask if he is still alive or okay?"

Cole smiled. "Neither did I."

"I almost don't want to know," she admitted quietly. "If he lives, I just don't want to deal with everything that means. And if he's dead, then there is everything you will have to go through having been the one to pull the trigger." She lifted her head and met his dark eyes.

He looked at the road but didn't say anything.

Brooke continued, "I haven't had a chance to thank you, Cole."

His gaze snapped back to her and she caught a quick glimpse of guilt before he wiped the emotion from his face.

She took a breath. "I thought he had killed you and I thought me and worse yet, Jamie were either going to die or be held captive by that sick bastard and I am so grateful that you were there. You saved us once again." Her voice was raw with unspoken emotion.

Cole cleared his throat. "It wasn't even a hard choice, you know."

Brooke nodded through the tears. "I know, I think I finally get that you do love us and that you really want to be with us for good. I love you, Cole."

He grinned widely. "I can't wait to marry you and make it all official so I can quit worrying that I'm going to screw this all up and lose you."

Brooke laughed. "If it were up to me, we would just sneak off to the courthouse and get it done with, but I'm not sure your family would forgive me."

He thought about that and then agreed with a smile. "No, they wouldn't. And, Brooke?" he waited for her to look at him, then he said, "I don't care what the sheriff does or thinks, but I would do the same thing over and over every time if it means keeping you and Jamison safe."

Tears filled her eyes as she smiled at him. "I think that is partly why I feel guilty. I'm glad you shot him but I kind of wish I had been the one to do it."

That admission startled a low laugh from Cole. He turned and winked. "Tell you what, if he manages to survive this time, I'll let you pull the trigger."

An amused smile twisted one side of her mouth as she replied, "I'm not the best shot. I hit him twice before and he still managed to drive away."

Cole grinned. "Don't forget I also shot him in the ass before, so we're each two for two." He turned serious then, "I bought that gun when we came home from the hospital and I have spent time everyday practicing just in case I had to be that good. I would never have shot him with you in front of him that way if I wasn't sure I could hit my target." He sounded as though he was trying to soothe her and that just made her laugh.

"That's funny because until this moment I never even questioned that. When I saw you step out with the gun pointed at him, I just knew that you were going to shoot him and I wasn't afraid anymore," she stated with a small look of wonder on her face. "What are we going to do, Cole? Sheriff Colton seems determined to prove that this whole thing was more than you protecting our lives. What if he keeps pushing?"

He shrugged. "I'd give him 'til tomorrow to call and apologize for all of that."

He sounded so sure that Brooke stared suspiciously at him. "What makes you say that?"

He looked at the road as he said quietly, "I called 9-1-1 and had them on the line listening the entire time. Plus, I put in three hidden cameras, one of which has a full view of the hall and I sent the footage to his office already. Add all that to what the sheriff in Idaho tells him and he will come back apologizing for the shit he gave us after a traumatizing event we'd just survived." He sounded so confident that she couldn't help feeling better about it all.

When they pulled into the Inn she looked up in surprise and then laughed. "I didn't even pay attention to where we were going."

Janae came hurrying out with a key jangling in her hand. Brooke hurried out and around to give her friend a hug. Janae stepped back for a good look at her and frowned. "You poor thing, you look like you have about had it. Now where is this young man that I need to meet?" she asked, changing the subject mid speech.

Cole had already covered Jamie's seat and pulled it out. He met them at the front of the SUV. "Hello, Janae." He nodded politely.

Janae smiled. "Hello to you too. I have the key right here." She dangled the key in the air. "Come on, I'll walk you in."

She unlocked the sturdy solid oak door and opened it for them. Cole stepped into a chic old-fashioned room with wooden floors and sturdy wood furniture that looked as though it had stepped from the early eighteen hundreds. It was a spacious room with a huge king size log bed and a fire place. As Janae closed the door and turned on the bright overhead lights Cole reached down to pull the cover from Jamie's seat. He didn't even get a chance to pull him out as Janae nearly shoved him aside in her haste to get to him herself.

"There you are honey, I have been waiting way too long to meet you," she cooed as she expertly undid his buckles and lifted him out. Jamie gurgled happily at her as she lifted him high and turned. She sent a pointed little glare at Brooke. "Your mama waited way too long to bring you back to see me, Jamie."

Brooke rolled her eyes and smiled. "I know I should have come sooner. I have been a little busy."

Janae grinned at that. "I know you have." She walked over to sit in a large leather comfortable chair next to the fireplace. "Now what's this your young man was telling me about this Richard fellow?" She looked directly at Brooke.

Brooke sank into the chair opposite Janae and sighed loudly. "I told you what happened in Idaho already. I guess he just waited until he was healed and then came after us again."

Janae turned her stern gaze on Cole. "You shot him again?"

Cole nodded. "Yes, ma'am."

Janae didn't smile but held his gaze. "Did you do it for good this time?"

He shrugged his shoulders. "I shot him in the head, but when the ambulance came, they hauled him off with a pulse."

"Some people have nine lives," she muttered as she kissed Jamie's neck. Then she looked up at Brooke. "Although some of those people are well deserving of those nine lives."

Brooke grinned knowing she was referring to her own troubles.

They spent an hour visiting and then Brooke took Jamie to feed him and Cole walked out to bring a bag from the car that she hadn't even seen him put in it. He set the bag at the foot of the bed and then walked around her chair to rub her shoulders and then lean down for a kiss on her neck. She leaned into him and sighed with pleasure.

The evening was peaceful. Cole ordered pizza and they ate the whole pie before he insisted she go to bed early and get some rest.

It was barely eight o'clock when she awoke to a loud rap on the door. She jumped out of the bed hoping to get to the door before it woke Cole. Sheriff Colton stood just outside. He tipped his hat as she squinted up at him in the early morning light. "Miss."

She nodded. "Sheriff Colton, what can I do for you?"

He smiled though it looked a little tight. "I was just hoping to feel you in on the case and where we're at with it."

Brooke smiled politely. "If you don't mind heading to the lobby, I'll just get dressed and meet you there. I'm sure there's fresh coffee there while you wait and I won't be but a moment."

He nodded and turned away. She closed the door against the bright sunlight and turned to see Cole watching her with a knowing grin. They dressed quickly and she brushed through her hair and added a touch of makeup while Cole bathed Jamie. They walked hand in hand with Jamie wrapped snugly in a thick blanket across the lot to the lobby.

The sheriff was seated on a floral upholstered lounge chair with a steaming mug of coffee when they entered. Cole nodded politely and then walked over to sit on a narrow love seat across from him. Brooke hesitated, Janae was behind the counter and she walked over to say good morning to her. She tried to calm her nerves as she hugged her friend and asked for some coffee for Cole.

Janae smiled. "You just go right over there, dear. I will bring coffee and a breakfast tray right over for you two."

Brooke thanked her and then forced her legs to take her to sit next to Cole. Jamie squirmed when he saw her and so she reached automatically for him. She patted his back and kissed him as she met the sheriff's blue eyes. "We're here, sir, what was it you needed to tell us?" she asked a little forcefully.

Sheriff Colton cleared his throat and said quickly, "We got the camera footage you sent and went over it all. That along with the 911 call seems to make it pretty clear that this was a case of self-defense."

"Well, of course it was!" Janae said with feeling as she stepped up and set a large tray on the table between the chair and couch. "Why would you think it was anything else?" she demanded with a withering glare.

The sheriff looked a little frustrated but didn't reply to her. Only continued to address Brooke and Cole. "The cameras clearly showed the man hitting Mr. Burton on the back of his head with a gun and knocking him out. He then aimed the gun at Mr. Burton's head and fired. You are quite lucky, Mr. Burton, that you're alive and well." He looked at Cole before continuing. "I also followed up with the Idaho department and they confirmed everything you both told both me and my officers."

Cole met his gaze and nodded. "I knew they would."

"Anyway, I wanted you both to be the first to know that I am declaring it self-defense and closing the case."

Brooke breathed a sigh of relief and then with obvious reluctance asked, "Sheriff, is Richard still alive?"

He met her eyes and smiled gently. "I'm sorry to have to tell you, but he died in surgery."

She looked away and out the window. "That is too bad. I'm sure his family will be disappointed."

He nodded. "I also wanted to apologize for the direct way that I treated you both after you had just survived an attack."

She met Cole's eyes and smiled. "I understand that you had a job to do, sir."

They thanked the sheriff and then he said his goodbyes as they ate fresh croissants and scones. Cole laid his arm on the back of the couch and she leaned back into it. Janae joined them with her own cup of hot coffee and they played with Jamie and visited.

An hour later as they loaded their things up from the inn, Cole sat on the bed and pulled her down next to him. He turned his head and watched her for a long while deep in thought. Finally, he asked softly, "Does this town and this place really mean a lot to you, Brooke?"

She was taken aback but responded quickly, "Not really, it's just where I happened to come when I needed to create a safe place for me and Jamie. My friends here matter to me but not necessarily this town."

He nodded, then he tipped her head up and as he lowered his mouth toward her own, he whispered softly, "Can I please just take you home, then?"

Brooke smiled and nodded her consent as his kiss took her breath away.

CHAPTER 58

They arrived back at the old house after ten that night and after settling Jamie into his crib and unpacking, they fell exhausted into the bed. Brooke had nightmares about Richard raising Jamie in his demented way after killing her. She woke soaked in sweat twice before finally sliding out of the bed and quietly going into the bathroom to take a long hot soak in the claw foot tub.

Cole came to check on her once before going back to bed himself. She fell asleep with her head on the gentle curve of the back of the tub and dreamed that Richard stood above her watching her with those emotionless blue depths. When he reached down and shoved her head under the water she kicked and screamed fighting for her life. Her lungs only filled with water and she began choking. She sat straight up with a start and sucked air into her lungs with a gasp. Angry she slapped the water once and then again. It splashed up the sides, but she didn't care.

With a cry of pain, she hit the water and then the side of the tub over and over again as tears fell unchecked from her eyes. She felt Cole come in but couldn't see through the steady stream of tears.

He laid a hand on her shoulder and then as sobs shook her, he climbed into the tub behind her wrapping his arms around to hold her as she sobbed uncontrollably. He murmured softly against her hair but she couldn't decipher the words. He kissed the top of her hair and then her ear saying softly, "I'm here with you. I won't leave you, okay?" Though the words made no sense to Brooke she leaned into him a little and took the comfort he offered. He tucked her hair behind her ears and bent to kiss the tears under her eyes. "It's okay to let it all out baby."

She took a sobbing breath and said in a raw voice. "I don't know why I couldn't sleep. I can't stop thinking about him and what could have happened. It's silly you know to think of it all now that he is really gone. Now that it's really all over, I just can't stop wondering about what could have gone wrong."

Cole rubbed his hands gently up and down her arms. "I know sweetheart, you have been through so much and persevered. God you are so amazing baby," he said in wonder as she tilted her head back against him and she looked up at him.

Tears shimmered against her long lashes and his stomach knotted. He would never get used to this feeling he thought as he gazed into her sapphire eyes. The feeling that he wasn't alone anymore and that he would always have someone on his side forever more. With a helpless sigh she lifted her lips to his whispering softly, "I don't know what I ever did to deserve you Cole but thank you."

The kiss was hot and long and full of unbridled passion. When he finally pulled back to smile down at her he said softly, "I think you, Brooke Reynolds were born for me."

They managed to sleep for a couple more hours before Jamie woke up. When his wails began, Cole rose quickly to get him. He brought their son into their room and laid him on the bed next to his mother. He watched, magnetized as Brooke opened her shirt and fed him. He had never had so little idea of how his life would go and yet he had never felt as happy as he did now. He kissed Brooke and then the top of Jamie's head and went out to make some breakfast.

After breakfast they bathed Jamie together and then tidied up the house. They were sitting on the couch with his arm looped around her shoulder when she finally said with reluctance, "I guess you should probably go back to work sometime." She looked up and gave him a small smile. "For that matter I should really start looking for a job now that I know I'm not going back to live in Montana."

Cole shook his head and pulled her tightly against his side. "For today I just want to stay close and see that you are both okay and happy."

A warm smile broke across her lips and she kissed the hand that lay on her shoulder. "That sounds amazing."

They were still sitting together watching as Jamie squirmed around on the pad on the floor where they had laid him when a sharp knock sounded on the door.

Cole groaned, "Probably Jacob coming to check on you after everything that has happened."

Brooke grinned and stood to open it. Cole stood behind her watching as Jacob's devilish grin greeted her.

"Hello, Bestie, I come bearing gifts."

Brooke's brows lifted in curiosity as she saw the long black bags thrown over his shoulder. He pushed in and past her nodding at Cole. "What is that?" Brooke asked as she closed the door behind them.

Jacob winked, "While you guys have been off playing Scooby Doo, we have all been here doing the heavy lifting."

Cole watched unperturbed but Brooke stared in confusion. "Heavy lifting with what?" she asked.

Jacob grinned and looked at Cole. "I have one here for you as well but you are to report at once to mom at the house."

Cole raised an eyebrow in question as Jacob tossed a long black zippered bag to him. He caught it easily and his suspicions were confirmed as he unzipped it just enough to see the black and white tux inside. He grinned and twirled Brooke around for a quick kiss. "I guess I shouldn't keep her waiting then," he said under his breath as he turned and strode to the door. He glanced back at Brooke's wide eyed gaze. "It'll be okay Brooke. You are in good hands," he said with jovial excitement.

Brooke turned back to Jacob as the door clicked behind Cole. "What in God's name is going on Jacob?" she asked grumpily.

He set down the bags and lifted her by her waist to twirl her around the room. Then he let her back on her feet as he said with dramatic effect, "Why you are getting married today, my lady." He bowed down at the waist and grinned at her astonished face.

Moments later Maude came flouncing in with a bag on her arm. "I hear the bride might want some help getting ready," she announced as she guided Brooke by her shoulders to sit on a chair. She unzipped the bag and began unloading makeup and products as though it was Mary Poppins suit case. Brooke sat stunned as the older woman chatted happily and nonstop while she carefully applied makeup and then began working with Brooke's hair. After a couple of hours of being pampered, Brooke sighed as Maude called Jacob in to check it out.

He came bounding in with a fussy Jamie in one arm. He stilled as his eyes met

Brooke's, "My God you are beautiful. My brother is one lucky dude." He turned and grinned at Maude. "You do have a way Maude," he said as he turned regretfully to Brooke. "Unfortunately, this guy is hungry. Would you rather me just make him a bottle?"

Brooke looked at Maude who shrugged and then said quietly, "It's fine, Jacob. I will just feed him now."

When no one disagreed with her she moved to the couch and fed Jamie. As he ate, she hollered at Jacob, "What time is this thing supposed to be anyway?"

She heard both Jacob and Maude laugh though neither one replied to her. When Jacob came into the room a half hour later, he was dressed in a black tux with a black bow tie. She wiggled her eyebrows and whistled softly, "You look nice."

He winked. "I'm hoping this is okay for my bridesman walk of shame?"

She laughed as she stood, "Of course it is. But what about Cole? Does he have someone to stand up with him?"

Jacob grinned and took another little bow. "I have it all figured out and I will be there for both of you."

She smiled as Jacob walked to the door when a light knock sounded there. Maude hurried into the room without her bag. "Oh, that should be the other bridesmaids, I think."

Brooke stood in surprise and hurried to stand behind Jacob as he opened the door. Both Jill and Janae stood on her front porch smiling. She rushed out to hug them both and exclaimed, "How is all of this even possible?"

"Jacob is the one who has been making all the arrangements. All we had to do was get on the plane." Janae offered.

"Well come in," she demanded as she stepped back inside. She was so happy she nearly forgot to make introductions. She stopped just inside to turn back, "Oh I'm so sorry I totally forgot, Jacob and Maude this is Janae and Jill. Jill and Janae, Maude and Jacob."

Jill smiled warmly at Maude and leaned forward for a quick hug. "It's so nice to meet you." She turned to Jacob and the smile froze on her lips at his mocking green eyes. She knew on the spot that she would not like him. He was one of those overly confident egotistical men that expected women to fall at his feet. She lifted her chin and nodded politely. "Jacob."

He raised one eyebrow in question, with a joking smile he asked, "Don't I get a hug as well?" When she just stared at him with obvious dislike he shrugged nonchalantly. "No problem, I just thought since we are both standing for Brooke we may as well be friends too."

She gave him a chilly smile. "Of course. Friends it is." She held out a hand to give his a quick shake and then turned back to the others.

Janae hurried to hug Jacob and said, "I am so glad I finally get to meet you. I have heard so much from our Brooke here."

After the introductions were over, Jacob and Jill fought over taking Jamie from Brooke. Too happy to care Brooke set him on the floor between them and walked off so they could figure it out. Maude was doing Janae's makeup when she entered the kitchen and she smiled and sat down next to her. "I'm so happy that you are all here. I hated to leave so soon but I just didn't want to stay in that house another night."

Both Maude and Janae gave her sympathetic looks and Janae said, "I understand dear. I admit I was a little worried that this wedding would be called off after the last few days."

Brooke gave a little laugh. "It might have been if either Cole or myself knew anything about it."

That brought a smile to both of their faces. Jill walked in carrying Jamie on her hip and smiling. Brooke looked up and raised a hand to pat his back. "I guess you won then," she said with a little smile.

Jill smiled brightly, "Of course, you think I can't handle that farm boy?"

All three women stared at her in astonishment. She shrugged as though she wasn't sure what the big deal was. Jacob came walking in then with more black bags. He stopped when the three women stared at him and then Jill. "Ladies," he nodded. "Am I interrupting?"

Brooke broke out in a choked laugh, "Nope. Not at all."

He raised his eyebrows at them and then smiled warmly. "I have all of your dresses here," he offered for lack of anything else to say.

That got both Maude and Janae's attention. Maude moved over to him, "You bought me a dress too?" When he nodded, she smiled up at him. "How on earth did you know what size to get."

Jacob smiled. "It's a gift."

Jill snorted at that and shifted Jamie to her other hip. "I'll just bet it is."

Everyone looked curiously at her outburst but she quickly turned her attention back to Jamie. The older women oohed and aahed over their gowns, but Jill ignored Jacob. Finally, he walked over to her with a smile. "I have yours here too."

She met those green eyes set in that devilishly handsome face and shrugged. "Okay."

He watched her curiously for a long moment and then asked, "Have I done something to offend you, Jill?"

His candor took her by surprise and she met his eyes. "Nope" was all he got.

With a small shrug, he laid the bag across the back of the chair and reached for Jamie. "If you want to get dressed, then I will keep an eye on Jamie."

She nodded mutely and finally relinquished the baby to him. Brooke smiled and came closer, "What dress did he get for you Jill?" she asked curiously.

Jill expected some strappy little dress that was revealing. Instead, she unzipped the bag to reveal a long silver gown that draped gracefully across one shoulder and then down to hug the curves of the wearer's hips. It was tasteful and chic and with reluctant admiration she said, "I have to admit it's gorgeous."

All the women agreed and Jacob smiled. "You ladies had better hurry; our ride will be here soon." With that announcement he walked into the nursery with the tiny bag that carried Jamie's miniature tux. He changed his diaper and then slid the tiny black pants on his nephew.

Brooke wanted to see the dress that Jacob had picked out for her but was also nervous. She was still a little uncomfortable at being the center of attention and though she didn't know what the Burtons had planned was sure it would be beautiful.

Once all three of the other women were dressed and ready, she asked Jill to help her with her gown. All the women crowded into her room to see the dress and help her with it. She stared in wonder at the frothy, see-through fabric that covered the bodice and arms. The neckline and back curved low inside with a wisp of soft cover. It had a wide sapphire colored band that wrapped around the high waist line just under her breasts and laced down the back to hang gracefully against the brilliant white embroidered skirt. The train was long but light, made mostly of the see-through fabric from the upper bodice.

She sighed when Jacob walked in with a case in hand that held a diamond and pearl hair piece that glowed in the soft light of the room. "Something old and something borrowed," he said as he handed it to Maude who slid it into her shimmering red hair.

Brooke stared in wonder in the mirror at the beautiful woman with her hair done up in front and then curling down her back. Tears filled her eyes as she twirled around once. "You guys made me beautiful. Thank you," she said as she hugged each of them.

There was a horn outside and Jacob grinned. "Perfect timing, our ride is here."

They all walked together to the front door and the women laughed joyfully at the long SUV limousine that was parked in the driveway. They slid in one by one and then suddenly she noticed Jamie's tux. She reached for Jacob's hand and squeezed, "Thank you for everything Jacob. This is all so beautiful. I love his cute little outfit."

He grinned down at her. "What else would I do for my bestie? I gotta be honest though, mom really helped me out with a lot of it," he admitted with a grin.

"It is all so perfect and I feel so lucky to have you all." Brooke said as she smiled around the limo at all of her very best friends.

CHAPTER 59

They pulled up to a small, white-brick church and the driver opened the door. Brooke noticed another limo was already parked on the side in front of theirs and turned to Jacob. "Who is that?"

Jacob grinned. "I sent one to pick up the rest of the wedding party at our house." He held Jamie toward her for a quick kiss. "Kiss, Mama, buddy and then you're going with Auntie Janae for a while."

Brooke kissed him and thanked Janae as she kissed her cheek and told her she would be inside. Both Maude and Janae walked arm in arm into the church.

She stared at those huge curved wooden doors nervously. The parking lot was full of cars and trucks and she wondered nervously if all those cars belonged to people inside. Hesitantly she turned to Jacob. "Are you sure we can't just go to the courthouse?"

He chuckled and took her arm as he ushered her and Jill toward those doors. "Are you getting cold feet?" He stopped and met her shining blue eyes.

Brooke stared at him for a long moment.

He raised an eyebrow and then grinned. "I wouldn't blame you if you changed your mind Brookie, Cole can be a real pain in the ass." He looked at the church and laughed softly under his breath. "However, with the amount of work Mom put into this whole thing, there will be a wedding today or heads will roll, so if you don't want to marry Cole, then I am happy to stand in."

Jill rolled her eyes. "Of course, you would be an asshole about this."

Both Brooke and Jacob turned in surprise to stare at her, but she only shrugged. Brooke pulled away from Jacob and stepped closer to her. "Are you doing okay, Jill? Ever since you got here you haven't been very happy."

Jill cast an overt look at Jacob before meeting Brooke's worried gaze. "I'm fine," she finally said and waved her hand as though to wave it away.

Brooke stopped walking and took her hand. "Look, Jill, you and Jacob are my best friends in the world and I need you both to be here with me, but I don't want you to be unhappy, so if there's something you need, please just let me know now."

A guilty expression crossed her friend's face before she pasted on a happy smile. "I am so happy for you and Cole. You guys are the perfect couple and I am so thrilled to be here on this day. Please put all of this out of your mind and focus on your happy day." When Brooke still looked uncertainly at her, she lifted her hand with a perfect blue and white striped manicure and crossed her fingers. "I swear I will behave for the rest of the day."

Brooke laughed and hugged her lightly. "Good, because I am about to turn and run already and I don't think I'll have the courage to walk into that church without you both by my side." She turned and caught Jacob staring at Jill with a confused expression before he wiped it away with a wide smile and stepped up to take her other arm.

Together they walked into the church. Just inside was a long wide hallway with another set of large doors at the end and a variety of smaller doors along each side. The room was lined with long strings of white and indigo flowers and white lights twinkled softly all around them. She saw Anne and Ivan standing near the double doors and smiled as Jacob urged them closer.

Jacob introduced his parents to Jill, who to both of their surprise was warm and gave them each a hug. Anne quickly explained the lineup telling Jacob and Jill that they would be walking together in front of Brooke down the aisle. When Jacob uncharacteristically hesitated to take Jill's arm, Anne rolled her eyes. "Like this, son," she said as she lifted his arm and slid Jill's hand through the crook of it.

Brooke stared nervously at the doors. "Are there a lot of people in there?" she asked quietly to Ivan who held her nervous gaze and smiled warmly.

"Not too many. Just our close family and friends."

Brooke remembered a huge yard full of "close family and friends" and gulped in air. She turned to Anne and asked worriedly, "Am I supposed to walk by my-self?"

Jacob stepped over at the same time that Ivan took her arm. "I would be honored to walk you down the aisle and give you away, Brooke. I have always seen you as a daughter but only if you're comfortable with that."

She turned and gave him a tight hug as tears swelled and she blinked rapidly to get rid of them. "I would love that."

After being clear that they all knew their roles, Anne hurried forward to open one of the wide doors just enough to slip inside and disappear from sight.

Ivan took her hands and squeezed before holding one arm out for her to take. She slipped her arm gratefully through his and then smiled at Jacob and nodded. Holding Jill's arm with his own, he stepped forward toward the wide doors.

Ivan stayed several yards behind and then began to move very slowly as well. When Jacob and Jill neared the double doors, two young men swung them open and piano music swelled into the hallway. Brooke felt as though her stomach was in her feet and hesitated.

Jacob and Jill flowed gracefully down the aisle as people smiled and nodded greetings at them. Ivan lifted his other arm to squeeze her hand and smiled down at her white face. "It's now or never, Brooke," he said gently as they stepped up to the open doors. Everyone rose and butterflies soared through her stomach. She met Ivan's warm brown eyes and nodded nervously and took one step onto the bright blue rolled carpet down the center of the aisle. She saw what she assumed was a preacher standing near white pillars wrapped in beautiful flowers and more twinkling lights ahead as she took another hesitant step.

At that moment, she saw Cole. He stood alone on one side of a pillar wearing a white and black tuxedo. His hair had been trimmed a little and curled only slightly over his collar now. His ruggedly chiseled face was unsmiling. She blinked as she realized those dark eyes were on her. One side of his chiseled mouth turned up as she met those nearly black eyes. Suddenly feeling anxious, she hurried forward, pulling Ivan at a quick gait as his own smile dawned when he registered where she was looking.

People smiled and nodded as she walked past but all she saw was Cole. Jacob had moved to stand slightly behind him and Jill across the aisle from him. The closer she got, the wider his smile became until they stepped up and Ivan lifted her hand to place it gently inside Cole's warm rough one.

Tears of joy filled her eyes and she blinked but held his gaze. Someone spoke nearby but she didn't hear what they said. The only thing that mattered was that she wasn't alone anymore. She had this strong beautiful man and Jamie as well the rest of her loving group of friends that had somehow become family.

She vaguely remembered murmuring something but didn't know what. All she was aware of was the beautiful promise of a home and life with Cole, her lover, her friend, and her hero. He had saved her life both literally and figuratively more than once. With a strong voice, she promised to love and cherish and honor him. He cocked his head down at her as he promised the same. Her heart swelled and she watched entranced, as he curled his long fingers behind her neck and tilted her head up as his lips came down on hers in a deep kiss of promise.

She heard the cheering only when they came up for air. She blushed a deep shade of red as Cole reluctantly released her and put an arm around her shoulders turning them both to face the waiting crowd. Everyone cheered and with his hand on her waist, the crowded room felt more manageable as they spent the next hour being hugged, kissed, and congratulated by what must have been two hundred guests.

Janae brought Jamie to them and Cole held him and introduced their son to all those who hadn't met him yet. Happy faces and cheers followed as they sliced a gorgeous rather huge triple-layer cake with tiny blue and silver flowers placed artfully around the base and top. There were several toasts, but she was so engrossed in Cole and Jamie that she barely even heard them.

Cole leaned close and nibbled her ear and said, "I don't know about you, but I think I'm ready to get out of here."

She looked up at him with wide eyes and said, "I don't think everything is over yet. Do you think people would mind?"

He grinned devilishly. "The only reason I came today was because I absolutely had to be married to you, my love. I do believe that already happened, so as far as I'm concerned, I got what I came for."

She laughed softly and had to agree. They slipped out as the floor was being cleared and music started playing. She held Jamie on her hip as they stepped through one door and into the wide hall.

Jacob must have seen them leaving as he rushed out behind them. "I knew you two wouldn't last through the whole ordeal, but Mom said we should insist." He grinned at them and then reached for Jamie. "You should know that everyone has it all worked out for you to take off for a few days."

Brooke looked worriedly at Jacob and reached for Jamie.

Jacob stepped back. "Without Jamie. You two are definitely in need of some alone time. Go ahead, Janae is sticking around for a few days at the house and we will all be here to take good care of him."

Brooke opened her mouth to argue, but Jacob held up a hand to stop her. "Everything you need is in the second limo. We made sure of it. I will go back in there and handle everything else. Now go, before the crowd or Mom notices you're gone and comes after you."

Cole nodded. "Thanks, Jacob, I owe you a few." He reached for her hand and pulled Brooke under his arm to walk her out the door. She glanced back at Jamie several times before Cole said softly, "Don't worry, Brooke, he'll be so spoiled that we'll probably have to retrain him when we get back."

She gave him a small smile and then laughed as the limo driver opened the door for them to slide inside. He took her into his arms for a deep kiss as the car pulled away from the curb.

He came up for air just long enough to say, "I will just have to keep you extremely busy for the next few days so you won't have time to worry."

She couldn't argue with that logic. She pulled his head back to her own and bit hungrily at his lower lip. "I think I can handle that," she whispered and then her tongue darted out to explore the brushing sweetness of his kiss.

EPILOGUE

Brooke stared out at the lake from the blanket she sat on. The sky was starting to turn pink at the edges with the warmth of the setting sun and then clear blue across the horizon in a rare cloudless day.

Seattle had been hectic and busy since they had first arrived here four years ago. She remembered it had been raining and cold as she and Cole pulled into town with Jamie in their new SUV. The kind of day that had seemed to say, *this is what you will be living with for your long stay,* she'd thought happily.

She didn't mind the rain. Actually, she quite liked it. But after four years of constantly feeling like plans had to be made around it, she had learned to appreciate these rare clear and sunshiny days. She felt stirring near her thigh and turned to smile down at the gorgeous ten-month-old girl who was trying to sit up.

"Well, hello, sweetie. Did you have a nice nap?" she asked softly as she lent a hand and then pulled her against her chest for a light hug. The toddler stumbled slightly before righting herself and then planted a wet kiss on Brooke's mouth with a happy giggle.

Brooke wiped slobbers from her mouth and grinned down at her daughter. She had dark, nearly black curly hair and deep blue eyes. Wearing a cute little purple jacket with butterflies on the front and blue jeans, her blue eyes shone brightly back at Brooke.

Suddenly frowning, the toddler's lips started to tremble and her eyes filled with tears. She turned and looked around wildly. "Da-da," she cried out as she remembered she had been playing with Cole and Jamie before finally nodding off to sleep. When she tried to toddle off the blanket, Brooke reached for her.

"Shoes first, baby. Daddy is close by with Jamie, I promise. Let's get your shoes on and we can walk to find them." She reached for a pair of pink and purple unicorn tennies and slid them onto her daughter's sock-covered feet.

In the distance she heard laughter and turned to watch as Jamie came bounding around the corner of the pathway with Cole not far behind chasing after him. He squealed in delight as Cole touched his shoulder to tag him and then he ran over to Brooke. His longish red hair curled around his face as he ran over to hug her. "I beat Daddy," he proclaimed loudly as threw his arms around Brooke's neck.

She acknowledged him with a kiss on his cheek and looked up at a grinning Cole. "What have you two been up to?" she asked as she shielded her eyes from the light over the horizon and then looked out over the lake.

Jamie turned and smiled up at Cole with a conspirator's look. "First we played ball and then Daddy took me around the lake to see some ducks." He grinned proudly at Brooke. "Daddy says I'm getting so good at catching the ball, Mama."

Brooke touched his curls. "I'm sure you are, baby." He was growing up so fast and her heart ached as she remembered when he was a small baby himself.

Jamie's face turned fierce. "I'm not a baby anymore, Mama. Only Georgie is a baby now, remember?" He turned and gave Georgia a hug as she grinned and rubbed the tears from her eyes. She looked up at Jamie and repeated, "Bay-bay."

Cole sat down next to her and leaned over to kiss her softly. "How are my girls doing?" he asked in a low relaxed tone.

Georgia Anne Burton threw herself at her father with a gurgle of joy. "Da-da," she wiggled onto his lap and gave him a slobbery kiss. He kissed her back and then lowered her back to the blanket as he wiped his mouth with the back of his hand.

Brooke smiled knowingly and then turned back to Jamie as he asked, "Did you know my name is Jamison Cole Burton, Mama?"

Brooke laughed under her breath. "I did."

Jamie looked thoughtful and then said in a strong voice. "I think I'm old enough for everyone to start calling me Cole like Daddy." He looked worriedly at her. "Don't you think, Mama?"

Brooke forced a serious face and met his blue eyes. "Well, I'm not sure," she said as though deep in thought. "I mean that might be a little confusing if we have two Coles."

She fought a grin as Cole made a face at her over their son's head. Jamie's eyebrows scrunched up as he thought about it. "Yeah, I guess it might be a little hard for Grandma and Grandpa and everyone to tell the difference."

Brooke reached out and squeezed his shoulder. "How about we start calling you Jamison since you are so grown up now. That is a nice grown-up name."

A happy smile broke over his face and he nodded happily. Then he frowned again and looked up at his mom. "But you have to remember, Mama. You always forget and call me a baby."

Cole chuckled under his breath and bent to tickle Georgia's cheek. She giggled and everyone smiled as Brooke touched Jamie's hair and said softly, "Okay, Jamison, I will do my best to remember."

He nodded solemnly and turned again to play with Georgie. Brooke watched as her two children played happily together and smiled. She turned to Cole and in a serious tone asked, "Have I told you lately how happy you make me?"

He grinned and wiggled closer to take her hand. "It's all part of my plan." He winked and she laughed softly.

She kissed his fingers as they entwined with hers. "Oh, I almost forgot. What was the news that you wanted to tell me earlier? I got so busy with the picnic and the kids I forgot to ask."

His dark eyes captured hers and held it in that sensuous way that he had. He kissed her once on the lips and then leaned back and murmured, "I'm taking you home."

Brooke pulled back and stared up at him in surprise. "What do you mean, Cole?" she asked breathlessly.

Though Seattle had been very good to them and she had enjoyed seeing the sights and everything the beautiful city had to offer, she missed the countryside and her friends as well as their family.

One side of his mouth turned up in a rugged grin as he replied, "I sold all of my shares in the company yesterday. I think it's time to go home and take the kids back to our roots. I want them to be able to run and play in the fields and learn how to work on the farm and go to school at home."

Brooke smiled but then asked hesitantly, "Are you sure that's what you want, Cole?"

He looked at her and then at their children playing nearby. "It's all I want. You are all exactly what I want and I don't want them growing up without knowing where they come from."

Brooke nodded. "Okay but what about your work, Cole?"

He looked across the lake. "These past few years have been great for my career, and I've learned a lot, but I'm ready to start my own company and only take on projects that really matter to me."

As hope dawned bright in her heart, Brooke smiled. "I could help out wherever I'm needed as well."

Cole chuckled. "I'm sure Dad would be more than happy to put you to work. He has spent the last few months telling me what a shame it is for your degree in agriculture and business to go to waste." He met those shining sapphire eyes then, before he leaned down to say, "Have I told you how proud I am of you, by the way?"

Brooke laughed. "Only every morning for the past four years."

He turned serious and said, "Well, I am. You have constantly amazed me in our life together. The way you've just taken everything bad that has happened and turned it into something beautiful. I don't think I will ever stop being amazed by how strong and courageous you are."

Brooke's smile wobbled a little bit and her lips trembled at all of the memories She took a deep breath and looked into his eyes. "It's all for you and them," sh said simply.

He smiled in understanding. "And that is exactly why I love you so much."

The End

He looked at her and then at their children playing nearby. "It's all I want. You are all exactly what I want and I don't want them growing up without knowing where they come from."

Brooke nodded. "Okay but what about your work, Cole?"

He looked across the lake. "These past few years have been great for my career, and I've learned a lot, but I'm ready to start my own company and only take on projects that really matter to me."

As hope dawned bright in her heart, Brooke smiled. "I could help out wherever I'm needed as well."

Cole chuckled. "I'm sure Dad would be more than happy to put you to work. He has spent the last few months telling me what a shame it is for your degree in agriculture and business to go to waste." He met those shining sapphire eyes then, before he leaned down to say, "Have I told you how proud I am of you, by the way?"

Brooke laughed. "Only every morning for the past four years."

He turned serious and said, "Well, I am. You have constantly amazed me in our life together. The way you've just taken everything bad that has happened and turned it into something beautiful. I don't think I will ever stop being amazed by how strong and courageous you are."

Brooke's smile wobbled a little bit and her lips trembled at all of the memories. She took a deep breath and looked into his eyes. "It's all for you and them," she said simply.

He smiled in understanding. "And that is exactly why I love you so much."

The End